'Sofka Zinovieff's second novel embraces ambiguity. It delves deep into the discussions surrounding consent and abuse of power. She has written a contemporary *Lolita* in which the rules of engagement have changed ... The main players are richly drawn, the strange, sad bond that still exists between them convincingly realised' *Observer*

'Superb ... Zinovieff twists the reader's sympathy to and fro ... A finely nuanced study of the way different people make subjective sense of the past, and a reminder that the novel (like the analyst's couch) is a great space for thinking about the unthinkable' *Sunday Times*

'A disturbing, well-structured, nuanced story that provides no simple answers – an important addition to an urgent, current conversation' *Financial Times*

'Zinovieff writes with the necessary sensitivity, inhabiting her characters so convincingly that the conclusion is all the more chilling' Kate Saunders, *The Times*

'Beautifully written and genuinely shocking; it's as if Nabokov had given Lolita eyes and a very clear voice' Andrew Marr, *New Statesman*, Books of the Year

'The perfect book club pick for the #MeToo moment ... Thought-provoking and relevant' *Washington Post*

'Zinovieff's dark and disturbing novel delicately probes the lines between abuse and consent in this atmospheric, intelligent and ambiguous story' *i paper*, The 30 best books to take on holiday

'Involving, beautifully written, and subtle ... There are terribly difficult questions here, dealt with sensitively and intelligently' *Spectator*

'The ultimate taboo brought to life in a way that's thrillingly disturbing and evocative. I couldn't leave it' Mary Portas

'I am reading *Putney* by Sofka Zinovieff, about a love affair between a man and a child and its repercussions decades later' Susie Boyt, *Independent*

'I read this greedily over the course of a day. On obsession, abuse and atonement via three memory threads with complex and provocative consequences. A powerful – and timely – examination of desire and permission, innocence versus experience' Laura Bailey, *Vogue*

'Unputdownable: a modern classic' *The Lady*, Book of the Week

'I read this novel with huge enjoyment ... It is a terrific novel and I look forward to reading it many more times' *Oldie*

'This is a really important book. I loved it. Thought-provoking, emotionally complex, and tackling the topic of the day – the blurred area between consent and abuse' Esther Freud

'I read it at one go, unable to put it down, until 2am ... It's remarkable, a brilliant novel, jolting and shocking and right' Michèle Roberts

'This book is truly memorable and thought-provoking; throughout, Zinovieff sustains wonderfully perplexing and complex ambiguities. It's a great story and a riveting read. I'll remember the characters forever' Louis de Bernières

'You will be seduced, regret that seduction, swap sides, feel complicit, question yourself and the characters, the book, our current world, the multiple stories, yet never feel manipulated in a cheap trick kind of way. Cannot recommend this book enough' Fiona Melrose

'It is really something. She treats the tricky subject with admirable dispassion, tells a good story, and of course writes well. Ralph, Daphne and Jane are all convincing characters – all too familiar to someone of my generation; and the portrayal of the liberated Bohemians of the 1970s is superb' Piers Paul Read

'An intelligent, subtle novel which explores the fallout of sexual abuse all wrapped up in an engrossing piece of storytelling ... Both thought-provoking and absorbing. I take my hat off to its author for tackling such a tricky subject with compassion and intelligence' A Life in Books

'This highly acclaimed book does not disappoint – what starts off as a seemingly sun-kissed romance in the 1970s morphs into a tricky, thought-provoking read that questions the boundaries between love, consent and child abuse ... This brilliant novel is not a comfortable read but it is an important one, particularly in the age of #MeToo' *MINE* Magazine

'Zinovieff's triptych is too nuanced for hashtags, yet perfectly tuned to #MeToo' Vulture

SOFKA ZINOVIEFF was born in London. She studied social anthropology at Cambridge, then lived in Greece and Moscow. She is the acclaimed author of three works of non-fiction, *Eurydice Street: A Place in Athens, Red Princess: A Revolutionary Life* and *The Mad Boy, Lord Berners, My Grandmother and Me, A New York Times* Editors' Choice 2015, and one previous novel, *The House on Paradise Street*. Her writing has appeared in publications including the *Daily Telegraph*, *Financial Times*, *Times Literary Supplement*, *Spectator* and *Independent*. She divides her time between Athens and England.

sofkazinovieff.com

PUTNEY

SOFKA ZINOVIEFF

BLOOMSBURY PUBLISHING

LONDON · OXFORD · NEW YORK · NEW DELHI · SYDNEY

BLOOMSBURY PUBLISHING
Bloomsbury Publishing Plc
50 Bedford Square, London, WC1B 3DP, UK

BLOOMSBURY, BLOOMSBURY PUBLISHING and the Diana logo are trademarks
of Bloomsbury Publishing Plc

First published in Great Britain 2018
This edition published 2019

A catalogue record for this book is available from the British Library.

ISBN: PB: 978-1-4088-9574-0; EBOOK: 978-1-4088-9577-1

2 4 6 8 10 9 7 5 3 1

Typeset by Integra Software Services Pvt. Ltd.
Printed and bound in Great Britain by CPI Group (UK) Ltd, Croydon CR0 4YY

To find out more about our authors and books visit www.bloomsbury.com
and sign up for our newsletters

To Anna and Lara

Man is not free to avoid doing what gives him greater pleasure than any other action.

Stendhal, *Love*

RALPH

The moment he passed through the hospital's revolving door, his mind turned to Daphne. On previous visits, he'd consciously conjured the memories as a way of combatting fear. Now it was like being one of Pavlov's experimental dogs and he pictured her as soon as he smelled the iodine disinfectant and warm rubber, well before he got to the odours of suffering humanity in the lift and started to sweat. Flitting animal movements; narrowed, knowing eyes; dark, tangled hair; dirty bare feet. A boyish girl who ran and tumbled, an adventuring escape artist, a creature on the cusp. The images soothed him. They made him feel alive. The risky element was part of the pleasure.

This was only his fourth session, but he was confident he could manage it by himself. He had strongly encouraged Nina to visit her ancient mother in Greece, playing down the number of treatments. She didn't even know that he'd stopped the hormone medication in favour of the poisonous chemicals. Better alone. Less fuss. More chance of it all disappearing from view. He knew how to bring familiarity and, with luck, intimacy to a new location. It was satisfying to establish a routine. Even if he was only staying one day in a hotel he unpacked all his clothes, laid his old silk dressing gown on the bed and learned the name of the receptionist.

He carried an aged, leather holdall containing a down pillow, a cashmere wrap, earphones for music, a bottle of tonic water and a packet of salted crackers. There was also a battered copy of *Selected Poems of Thomas Hardy*. He probably wouldn't read them, but he would place the book on the bedside table as a declaration: I am a civilised man. It was a message as much for himself as anyone else.

He spotted Annette at the nurses' station across the large, open-plan space of the chemotherapy department. The cancer unit was all swathes of clear glass, making light and transparency the response to the hidden knots growing in the darkness of bowel or brain. It was not yet nine, but there were already people settling into colourful reclining chairs or lying in beds, hooked up to drips, murmuring quietly to companions and carers. Sunshine streamed in from high windows creating bright shapes on the floor.

Annette was his favourite nurse and he was making sure that he became her favourite patient. Drawing up to the desk, he smiled and fished out a beribboned packet of chocolate almonds from his bag, presenting it with mock gallantry. 'To the best nurse in London.' He gave a small bow as if about to take her hand and ask for the next dance. Annette giggled indulgently. He hoped it was unusual to find someone who remained so suave when about to go into battle with a pipeline of Docetaxel. 'Thank you, Ralph. And you're not a bad patient.' She patted his arm with a plump, dark hand and there was a waft of biscuits and Nescafé, mingled with sweet oil from her tightly braided hair. He liked the hints of the Caribbean that came through in her speech, even though she had already explained she was born in London.

'You're looking good today, Ralph. You know, you seem so young. Are you really coming up to seventy?' Papers, lists, dates, certificates, doctors' reports. Nowhere to hide once you're in a system.

'Not quite. Still over a year before I throw that party.' There were already celebratory concerts planned for his seventieth, including a grand event at the Barbican. None of the organisers had heard about his failing health. He knew he looked good, though for how much longer was a question as hard to ignore as the anticipatory nausea now seeping through his stomach. All the same, he still boasted a full head of hair, even if it was not the rich brown of his youth. And his trouser size had not increased since he was a student – no running to fat for him. The crumpled linen jacket gave the impression of an Englishman abroad, while the faded jeans and plimsolls hinted at an attachment not only to youth, but to the garb of his own youth.

Prodded, jabbed, tubed. 'OK, Ralph, just relax now. I'll come and check on you in thirty minutes.' Here we go.

John Dowland through the earphones today. Eyes closed to the melancholy soprano accompanied by a lute. 'Flow, My Tears'. Then 'Come Away, Come Sweet Love'. He was already somewhere else. Back. Not to his childhood home in Worcestershire, nor his student travels to India, but to a garden by the river: Putney. He pulled the cashmere shawl over him, drawing the moth-eaten, mouse-coloured soft-ness across his nose and mouth. It had been his mother's and, despite its long life and many travels with him, it none-theless seemed to carry something of her smell. Hidden from view, he held on to his cock through his trousers.

Limp as a dead fish, he thought. This is what it has come to – a piece of soft flesh, baby-wrinkled and pitiful, unable to do anything but pass a pathetic flow of piss.

It was hard not to contemplate death, but he countered it by listing his successes to himself. At least I've lived my life, he thought. My music is appreciated. There have been television appearances, magazine interviews, university lectures, and trips where I was feted, applauded. Some silly fucker who didn't understand the music had written a biography, and there were even three PhD theses. And, he thought, I've loved.

He was twenty-seven when he met her. It seemed so young now – a boy, practically. Only a few years since he'd left the choking conventions and daunting expectations of his parents' home near Worcester. He had returned from travels in Greece, Turkey and Bulgaria, where he had been recording musicians and storytellers in remote mountain villages. The people he had stayed with were often suspicious or laughed at his foreignness, but they plied him with absurdly generous hospitality. He sat for days on filthy buses, lugging a rucksack into which he could hardly fit a change of clothes after he had crammed in the cumbersome tape recorder and reels of tape. Sleeping in barns and on floors, he ate endless bean soup and hard, goaty cheese with dry bread, filled notebooks and sent back the recordings by registered post when he found a place with a post office. Ending up in Piraeus, he caught crabs from a woman he picked up in a nightclub and was issued with some foul ointments by a local doctor. His intention had been to seek out dives where musicians came together to play *rembetika* music, and though he couldn't understand the words, he found people to translate and appreciated the dual

4

inheritance of pain and humour in these gut-wrenching Greek blues.

London seemed absurdly twee on his return. Cool, damp, muted. He felt burnt and dusty and as out of place as he had in the Balkans. Although he had met Edmund Greenslay several times, he had never been to his house before and didn't know his wife or children. Edmund was older – in his late thirties – but his charismatic energy was boyish. The two men were planning to collaborate on a musical project, so when Ralph arrived at the house in Putney, it was with his battered rucksack packed with the tape recorder and tapes. He walked from his cramped attic flat in Earls Court through a soggy, English version of a summer afternoon. The sky appeared to have a hangover: headache and queasiness held in place by a stained eider-down of clouds. In those days there had always been too much to drink or smoke the night before.

Edmund opened the front door and spread his arms somewhat theatrically to embrace 'the weary traveller'. He was dressed in a long, striped robe that accentuated his etiolated frame and made him look as though he'd walked off with a costume from *Lawrence of Arabia*. A marvellous scent enveloped him – like a new leather bag filled with green herbs.

'Welcome, dear boy; welcome, my dear.' Edmund repeated phrases as if there was doubt the first time around, though the second, unnecessary version often faded away. He looked like a darling of 1970s London bohemia but he used the old-fashioned, almost camp expressions of his pre-war childhood and his voice warbled slightly. 'Come in, come in.' He ushered Ralph ceremoniously into the house, which was painted jazzy colours like arsenic green and acid tangerine. Edmund helped relieve him of the knapsack and put his delicate white hands on his guest's shoulders as if to take a better look.

'Now, you must tell me everything. Chanting monks, flute-playing shepherd boys? Did you find those old women with the improvised mourning songs? And the food? The seductions? There were some of those, I hope? Were you chased from village to village by irate fathers waving blunderbusses and swearing vengeance?' Edmund laughed, but his face was so sensitive it quivered like a deer's, watchful and quick.

As the men talked in the hallway, a slender, dark-haired child ran down the stairs. It was hard to tell if it was a boy or a girl. A sprite.

'Daphne! Hey, Daphne, come and say hello.'

Her eyes flickered past her father towards Ralph, lips opened as if to say something, and then she thought better of it. She was dressed in ripped shorts and a striped T-shirt and wore no shoes. Ralph took in the grubby feet, the burnished skin that must have recently seen more than English sunshine, the muscular limbs and unbrushed, almost black hair. Teasing, moving like mercury, she knew how to disappear before you could get a grip. She laughed, skipped and slithered past them, through the front door that was still ajar and out along the garden path to the road. Without turning, she flicked one of her hands as if dismissing both men.

His intestines juddered. Then, bewilderingly and somewhat shockingly, the beginning of a hard-on. He squatted down to the floor and opened up the backpack to gain time and distract Edmund, who was gazing after his daughter and laughing.

'Daphne's a free spirit. As you can see.'

Ralph smiled, trying to disguise his turmoil.

'I'm glad we can give her and her brother that,' Edmund continued. 'We were so battened down with restrictions. When I was growing up there was nothing but rules and barriers. It's unnecessary. Children find their own way. And it's important to let them.'

'How old is she?' Ralph stood up again.

'Nine. You know, I think that might be the perfect age. A child at the height of her powers. Unafraid to be herself. A nonconformist without knowing it. It's a splendid thing to witness.'

Ralph had never been attracted to children, or at least not since school. He had not ogled young girls or prowled in parks. This was something different from anything he'd known. Beautiful and pure and powerful. The beginnings of love.

Before he had gathered his wits entirely, a striking woman approached. He knew Edmund's wife was Greek; he'd said she was a lawyer who gave up her job with a City firm to try and save Greece. 'You know, these dreaded colonels? The dictators?' But Ralph had pictured someone sturdy and hard-nosed, not an adult version of the spirit-child just encountered. She, too, was agile and brown-skinned, with long, dark hair and discerning eyes that challenged him as if she understood his thoughts. You couldn't say she was short, as her sinewy proportions were perfect, but next to her husband, with his long-boned, Anglo-Saxon extremities, she looked like another species.

'How do you do.' She held out a hand formally, and then, more affectionately, grasped Ralph's with the other, clasping it between her warm, dry palms. 'Ed told me about the young composer — your travels, the tape recordings … fascinating.' Her voice was low and, though her

English was excellent, a faint accent with richly rolling Rs betrayed her origins.

'Ellie, meet my friend, Ralph Boyd. Ralph, this is Ellie, my wife,' said Edmund, looking down with beneficence. 'Eleftheria, to give her the full dues of her Orthodox baptism. Or Liberty, as I sometimes call her.' He placed a tender hand on Ellie's arm and she patted it.

'I've just met your daughter.'

Ellie merely smiled and said, 'Come and meet our friends.' He followed her down a staircase, past walls plastered with photographs, postcards and newspaper clippings in an open-ended collage. They entered a spacious, bright yellow room where maybe a dozen people sat at a refectory table or sprawled in armchairs. The scene spoke of unhurried pleasures: bottles of red wine, coffee cups, ashtrays, orange peel, the remains of a circle of Brie in its balsawood box. Open French doors looked out through a mass of overgrown honeysuckle towards the river.

Ralph was introduced to four or five Greeks belonging to a political protest group, whose names he immediately forgot, and he sat down at the table next to an American woman called Meg. She gave off a potent waft of patchouli each time she fluffed up her mass of hennaed hair and talked about dreams and astrology – Ralph's least favourite topics. He became mildly interested when she let drop that she was not wearing any underwear, something that scrutiny of her long, diaphanous skirt confirmed when she got up to go. As she left she gave Ralph her number, which he put in one of the side pockets of his army-surplus trousers.

In later years, when Ralph discussed the early '70s with contemporaries, he identified it as a flash of light exploding in the drab, post-war darkness. We all believed in taking pleasure where we found it. And why not? We were war babies, children of rationing and the frumpy 1950s. Eating a banana was a highlight of my childhood, for God's sake. We respected men in uniform. We believed the authorities. And then there was this wonderful blast that rearranged all the pieces into a new pattern. It wasn't that we left our parents' generation behind – that's nothing new. All the clichés of sex, drugs and rock 'n' roll are not the point at all. No, we saw the world from a different perspective and were trying to make it into something better, freer and more honest.

He hadn't eaten lunch and Ellie made him up a plate of food – some sort of Greek lamb affair and his first taste of ratatouille, then glamorously unfamiliar in England with its defiant use of garlic, olive oil and audacious aubergines. Ralph had travelled but he was still an innocent in many ways. The Greeks lapsed more and more into their own language, furiously smoking, gesturing and shouting – apparently about the fascist junta which was strangling and torturing their country. They didn't seem to notice when Edmund took Ralph off to his study – an appealing attic room overlooking the front garden and Barnabas Road. There were so many books they had been doubled up on the bookshelves, and the floor was stacked with towers of manuscripts and hardbacks as though it was a game to see how high they could be piled. His desk was a trestle table, also littered with books and papers, which threatened the prime position of a typewriter, and a chaise longue draped with rugs stood against one wall. The windows were almost at the level of the nearby bridge, and each time a Tube train passed there was an impressive roar, the room juddered and a tin of pencils on the desk rattled with sympathetic vibrations.

When still in his twenties, Edmund had written a successful novel, *Oedipus Blues*, and had become quite well-known. 'It's all wine-dark sea and bouzouki riffs,' he had said dismissively. 'A potboiler really, that helped put food on the table.' In fact, it was obvious that Edmund was proud of his idea that turned Laius and Jocasta into a bouzouki player and a singer in the poverty-stricken, twentieth-century port of Piraeus. A film had quickly followed the book and Ralph managed to see it at an afternoon screening in Soho. It included sailors, druggy musicians, thugs and prostitutes and, as Edmund liked to point out, was made a couple of years before *Never on Sunday* with Melina Mercouri. Laius and Jocasta abandon their deformed baby Oedipus in a ruined temple behind the shipyards where he is found by a holidaying English couple who take him home. Eddy (as he is named) returns to Greece as a young man, crashes into his natural father with his motorbike and ends up living with his mother. Ralph found the film rather melodramatic, but loved the book.

'You know, I was inspired by real events,' said Ed. 'I witnessed an old man's death in Piraeus. And that was the reason I met my wife.' How suitable that Ed's life should unfurl like a myth, thought Ralph, and he made an appreciative noise to encourage the storyteller.

'I'd been travelling in Greece, mostly around the islands, sleeping rough, writing poetry, falling into the hands of sirens and enchantresses. You know the sort of thing. On that day, I'd returned to Piraeus. It was early evening and I was tramping around the port, searching for a bus to the centre. Then there was the most almighty commotion and dreadful crashing noise behind me. A motorbike had run over an old man. Ghastly. I tried to do something, though it was quickly apparent that he was beyond help. Blood all over the road. The rider was a young man. He was all right, though naturally very shocked. Then up walked this exquisite young woman – suntanned limbs, dark hair, white summer frock. A vision. And she started speaking to me in perfect English!'

'So a *coup de foudre*?' said Ralph.

'Exactly! A bolt from the blue, Attic skies. I knew immediately that this was *her*. After the ambulance arrived we went for a drink. It turned out that her father was a Greek diplomat. She and her sisters had been brought up in London as well as Paris and Cairo, and she was studying law at the LSE. We stayed up all night, going from one dive to another – all near the port and full of the sort of people I put into the book. By morning I'd asked her to marry me!'

'Did she say yes?'

'Well, it took slightly longer for that,' he chuckled. 'But I knew she was the woman for me. And she agreed to see me again the next evening. So that was all right.'

'What about the book? Did you write it straight away?'

'Yes, it poured out in a few months. Marvellous feeling. Wish I still wrote like that. And then I got married to Eleftheria Manessi.'

Oedipus Blues made enough money for him and Ellie to buy a house, he said. After the film came out, he became not only 'a little bit famous', but had the financial security to live as a writer and part-time academic. Now he was creating a theatrical version and had asked Ralph to write the music. 'Not an opera or a musical,' he said, 'but a play with musicians and music at its heart. The contemporary, street version of a myth.'

Ralph played some tapes of songs he'd recorded in remote mountain villages in Epirus, and for several hours the two men discussed their project: how to bring out the ancient myth and traditions of oral storytelling in a modern setting, how to give a Greek feel to songs which would be sung in English. Edmund produced a battered, blue toffee tin containing Rizla papers and a small bag of grass. He rolled a joint and, spreading out on the chaise longue, took a few deep drags and passed it to Ralph, who had made himself comfortable on the floor.

'Sometimes I come up to work and stay here all day, dreaming.' Both men laughed, Edmund's high whinny sounding like a skittish horse.

It wasn't until he was about to leave that Ralph saw Daphne again. He followed Ed, noting his lopsided lollop on the stairs and the slight limp when he walked – the legacy of childhood polio. The Greek guests had departed, and down in the kitchen Ellie was writing in a lined exercise book while the girl lay sprawled on the sofa reading a comic. Ellie said something in Greek to her daughter that sounded like a question. Her voice was low but had enough authority to make the girl get up and walk over.

'Hello.' She looked at him without fear, as if assessing him, and he felt almost shy.

'Hello, I'm Ralph.' He extended a hand and she took it with a mocking expression as though they were pantomime actors. Her hand was small but strong and suntanned, with bitten fingernails, and it seemed the most beautiful thing he had ever held. Perhaps there was a beat too long in which he kept her palm against his, but the grass was still affecting his judgement. Edmund giggled like a naughty boy and said, 'Daphne, why don't you introduce Ralph to Hugo? I think they'd get on.'

'OK.' The child twisted on her bare feet and darted out of the kitchen. 'Come on.' She did not even check whether he was following her up the stairs.

She entered a room that gave on to the back garden and the river. He took in large, abstract paintings on the walls and noticed a sizeable metal cage in the corner. Before he could see what was inside, Daphne opened the door and approached with a small monkey clinging to her arms.

'He's a capuchin.' She bounced down on to a brown corduroy sofa and Ralph sat next to her, realising he was being assessed for his reactions and smiling like an imbecile. Hugo was less than a foot high, with a dandelion aureole of blond fur around his head, a long tail curling around his young mistress's arm and a grimly enquiring expression. He was the sort of creature you'd see dressed in silly clothes and held by an organ-grinder in a Victorian photograph. In the absence of protocol on introductions to small primates, Ralph playfully made as if to shake hands and, to his surprise, the monkey reached out his scratchy black one in return, cackled wickedly and rapidly retracted it. Ralph emitted a small, involuntary gasp; being stoned wasn't helping a situation that was already like a hallucination.

'Don't be scared!' There was something teasing in her voice, her eyes glinting at having detected a weak spot. 'Hugo's just a baby – he's only a year old.'

'Where did you get him?'

'My grandmother got him in Argentina when he was a newborn, but she's ill so he's come to us.'

'Aha,' he nodded stupidly.

'She may even die,' added Daphne. 'And then we'd keep Hugo. Though you know, in ancient Egypt they used to bury your pet monkey with you. They pulled out their brains through their nostrils with a long hook and stuffed special herbs inside, then wrapped them up in bandages.' Her eyes flickered to Ralph's to gauge his reaction, while she stroked the animal's doll-sized cranium. Hugo bared his teeth and closed his eyes as if smiling. There was tenderness between the two and Ralph was mesmerised as the girl fingered him. Without saying anything, Daphne jumped up and the last he saw of her was as she disappeared around the door, taking the monkey with her.

He was overwhelmed by this girl. But it was certainly not something sleazy or sinister. I didn't want to *do* something to her, he thought. She inspired me. I felt like a child next to her. I felt free. But I was also as captive as the lowest slave with an Egyptian high priestess. She couldn't have known what I was feeling but I wanted to lie down before her and let her walk on me.

* * *

It was hard to keep away. He went back a couple of days later bearing gifts. Having found an Egyptian scarab in an antique shop, he strung the turquoise beetle on a leather bootlace to make a necklace. Placing it in a miniature, metal cash-box with a gold stripe, he then wrapped that in brown paper and tied it with string. En route to Barnabas Road, he stopped at the patisserie opposite Putney Bridge station and bought an extravagant number of chocolate eclairs. His visit was planned so that school would be finished but it wouldn't yet be time for supper or baths or the routines he remembered from his own childhood. He soon learned that strict timetables and daily rituals were not a characteristic of the Greenslay household.

In his fantasy, it was Daphne who opened the door to an empty house and invited him in for tea, and he felt a mild spasm of annoyance when a lanky teenage boy responded to his knocking.

'Oh, hello,' Ralph said, taking in a family resemblance to the girl whom he'd hoped for, though the youth's features had none of the delicacy of Daphne's.

'Hello.' The boy looked out from under a curtain of long hair and didn't sound curious. Another youth (this one spotty and spectacled) was waiting behind him.

'I'm Ralph Boyd. Are your parents in?'

'Um, I don't think so. Hang on.' Then he shouted back into the house, 'Daffers! Is Ed here?'

A disembodied voice replied, 'No, he'll be back later,' and Daphne appeared.

She recognised Ralph and he smiled. 'Hello, Daphne.'

'Hello, Ralph.' She replied in exactly the same tones he had used, as if mocking him rather than meaning it. Dressed in cut-off jeans and a green top, she was carrying the monkey in her arms like a baby and it displayed its teeth to Ralph, emitting little menacing sounds that seemed to mean, 'Don't come closer!'

'I brought some cakes for tea. May I come in?'

'Um, we're just heading upstairs.' The teenage boys scurried off, triumphant at leaving Daphne in the lurch with a visitor.

'Your brother?' Ralph asked as they walked down to the kitchen and he placed the cake box on the table.

'Yes, Theo.' She grimaced as though the name explained the problem.

'He's fourteen,' she continued. 'And that was his friend Liam. They're weird. They don't have any other friends. They're obsessed with electrical things. They spend hours making radios and walkie-talkies and stuff. They've got goggles to see in the dark. Everything goes green.'

Ralph opened the box, revealing eight eclairs that now looked undeniably phallic. 'Have you had tea? Would you like one?'

'We could have a picnic. I'll take you to the tree house, if you like.' This sounded too good to believe. If she had said she'd take him to the inner sanctum of the cult of Daphne, it could not have tempted him more.

She went upstairs to put the malevolent monkey in its cage and he heard it squealing madly as the door was locked. Then Daphne gathered up a few things in a basket – a bottle of Ribena, some tin mugs – and handed Ralph a tray with a plateful of eclairs and a jug of water. Tangles of dusty leaves brushed against them as they walked out of the kitchen door.

'This way.' She led him along the garden path. Or up the garden path, or any path she cares to choose, he thought. Certainly, it was the path of no return. On one side of the overgrown garden stood a large plane tree and as they drew closer he saw that high up in its foliage was a wooden structure lodged in the branches – one or two were actually growing through its walls and out through the roof. Daphne put down her basket and deftly picked up an aluminium ladder that lay in the grass and fixed it up against the entrance platform. 'I'll go up first and then you can pass me the picnic.' She scampered barefoot up the ladder, as agile as a monkey, but with the graceful confidence of a feline. After handing her the provisions, he followed her up into the tree.

I'd move in right away and make it home, he thought. I'd escape the world and keep sentinel below Daphne's bedroom window as the tide came pushing its way up the river and then pulling out again towards the sea. The river ran past the end of the garden and he could smell its sweet, rotted-vegetable odour of mud, with a hint of the grass-edged, rural tributaries that had meandered into the powerful waterway.

Daphne opened the door on its rusty hinges and as he followed her inside he took in the small space. Two glazed windows with red gingham curtains gave a Wendy-house atmosphere and the floor was covered with a rag rug and scattered with cushions. A couple of blankets and a sleeping bag hinted at overnight stays. One wall was hung with an embroidered Indian tablecloth and, on another, a small, tin-framed mirror decorated with flowers and a Greek word. He spelled out the letters ΚΑΛΗΜΕΡΑ. 'It means good morning,' the child explained. The faint smell of damp wood was offset by a day-after-the-party aroma of incense – a packet of sandalwood joss sticks lay in the corner, along with candles, matches, an empty wine bottle, a packet of tarot cards and a few children's books and comics.

'Oh *Beano*! I love Dennis the Menace and Gnasher, don't you?' He hoped he didn't sound ingratiating, remembering grown-ups who tried to be pally when he was young.

'Yeah.' She didn't pay much attention to his questions, busying herself instead with the drinks. She poured measures of Ribena, purple as poison, into the enamel mugs and filled them with water. 'Here.' They both drank deeply and Daphne wiped her mouth with the back of her hand, leaving a smear of mauve across one cheek. He felt a welling tenderness at the sight of her lips, stained as though she'd been blackberrying. There was a short silence, not quite awkwardness, but as if the girl suddenly wondered what she was doing up a tree with a man she barely knew.

They ate two eclairs each. Daphne systematically made her way through them without hurry but with concentration, delicately gripping the edges so her fingers didn't touch the chocolate. He ate faster, more carelessly, and then lay back on some cushions, watching through the open door as cumulonimbus creatures migrated across the pinking sky. He had the rare sensation of being the still point at the centre of the world, of everything making sense. It reminded him of moments in his childhood when there was a simplicity to his happiness. As now, these times had often been when he was removed from the fray, hidden in the woods near his home or quietly absent from his parents in the dusty attic.

A rattling sound made him sit up slowly and then lean out of the door in time to see Daphne step on to the ground below. 'Are we leaving already?' The girl pulled the ladder away from the tree house, and laughed at seeing him stranded ten or twelve feet up. He smiled. 'What are you doing?' She let the ladder fall to the grass, wiped her hands on her shorts and looked up to assess his response. 'Making you a prisoner.'

He chuckled at the amalgam of mischief and innocence. There were several games in play. 'Well, I'm perfectly happy to be here, so maybe that doesn't count.' It was slightly too far to jump down safely. He didn't fancy a sprained ankle.

'It might not be so nice when it gets dark and cold,' she challenged.

'Oh I'm fine. I love sleeping outside. And it's cosy in here. So long as you bring me some supper, and of course breakfast in the morning. We could have a basket on a rope and I'll move in quite happily.' The girl walked back towards the house and, a few minutes later, two faces – the teenage boys – looked out of a second-floor window and laughed before disappearing again.

Ralph slumped back on to the cushions and waited. She was enchanting. And he was certainly her prisoner. The sun sank lower, leaving the garden in shade and bringing a chill to the air, but he didn't mind. He was planning music for Ed's project and this was not a bad place to think about it. He even managed to jerk off, something he associated with tree houses since childhood. The smell of damp planks and mouldy curtains was perversely aphrodisiac. He leaned back against the wall, a blanket over his knees in case anyone appeared, and closed his mouth to muffle the cry that came as he finished. Twice, pleasure boats went by and the jingling of pop songs grew louder before passing off upstream towards Richmond.

It wasn't until about an hour later that Daphne returned, moving slowly with the taunting gait of a jailer. He suspected she was bored of the game and he asked, 'So, where's my dinner?'

'What will you give me if I release you?'

He'd forgotten the present in his jacket pocket until now. 'An ancient treasure in a box with lock and key. Is that fair?'

'Where will you get it?'

'It's right here, ready.'

'Don't believe you.'

He retrieved the wrapped packet and held it up for her to see.

'What sort of treasure?'

'That's a surprise. But it's very beautiful. Put the ladder back and I'll give it to you.'

'Daphne, hello darling!' Edmund's distinctive voice called from the terrace. Daphne waved in reply and Ralph waved too, partially obscured by foliage. He returned the gift to his pocket.

'Hello, Edmund.' There was a pause while Edmund peered in the direction of the voice. 'It's Ralph. Your daughter has been showing me this hiding place. I think I'm moving in.'

'Ralph!' There was the slightest pause of bewilderment, and then Edmund came down into the garden, bright blue bellbottoms flapping as he lolloped along, gangly as a crane. Noticing the ladder lying in the grass, he knitted his eyebrows at Daphne in mock annoyance and picked it up, propping it against the side of the tree house. Ralph made a swift descent and Edmund pulled him into a hug. 'Ralphie, my boy. Hoodwinked and taken prisoner by this young warrior-princess, eh? You need to keep your wits about you.' The three went back to the house and found the boys in the kitchen.

'Supper?' asked Edmund. 'What's the plan?' He looked at Ralph and added, 'Ellie's away for a few days. She's gone to Paris for a meeting – you know. Greeks plotting against evil tyrants. But we're pretty good at fending for ourselves.'

'There's nothing to eat,' said Daphne. 'I've checked.' The piles of crockery in the sink and pitifully empty fridge belied Edmund's confidence.

'Ed can cook one thing, but we don't have the ingredients,' opined Daphne.

Ralph found it delightful that she called her father by his name. 'And what's that?' he asked.

'Toad-in-the-hole.'

'And very delicious it is too,' chuckled Edmund happily, not realising this was a complaint.

'We're starving,' said Theo, stoking the fire of protest started by Daphne and looking at Liam for confirmation.

'Fish and chips?' Edmund smiled as though he had found a unique and brilliant solution and retrieved a five-pound note from his trouser pocket.

The teenagers were dispatched to fetch the food while Edmund opened a bottle of champagne. 'You need it to offset the grease.' Daphne lit candles and laid the kitchen table, observing the two men as they toasted their project, downed one glass and refilled. 'Can I have a taste? Please?'

Edmund let her sip from his glass and she gurgled with amusement when the bubbles tickled her nose. Before long, all five were unwrapping plump parcels of newspaper and, despite the eclairs, Ralph found himself ravenous. His sensations were heightened and, as he devoured the length of crispy cod and vinegar-splashed chips, the meal seemed among the most delectable he had ever eaten. Edmund had turned out the lights and they ate entirely by the golden flicker of candles. It's beautiful, Ralph thought. She's beautiful. He observed her, sitting opposite him at the long pine table, and wanted to pick her up and carry her anywhere she wanted to go. He would never do anything to harm her.

After dinner, Ralph seized his moment. The boys had left for their wires and transmitters and Edmund went for a pee.

'Here's your ancient treasure.' He held out the gift to Daphne and she hesitated.

'Why? I didn't give you your freedom. I'd have left you all night. It was funny.'

'I'd brought it for you anyway. I think you'll like it. But it's a secret. Just for us. OK?' He looked into her face – fearless, black-lashed eyes and determined lips. 'Open it later.' She took the package and tucked it inside a scuffed, leather satchel that lay on the kitchen floor.

When her father returned, Ralph saw Daphne's satisfaction and wondered if she was aware of this as their first act of collusion. Her pleasure must be at least that of acquiring a secret. All children liked secrets, didn't they? He had never lost the particular delight in private things, in keeping areas of life apart, in mystery. Secrets were like places where you are not overlooked, like a series of tree houses. Spaces where you could do as you liked and in which you were not accountable. He avoided introducing one friend to another and with girlfriends he was almost obsessive about keeping them separate from his social circle and, more importantly, from each other.

'Ralphie. Come and have another drink and let's go up to my study.' Edmund beckoned for him to follow, ignoring his daughter – not on purpose, Ralph thought. It's the careless egotism of the creative spirit. You have to chase the fire and let everyone else look after themselves. Edmund was already out of the room and Ralph followed him, turning momentarily to wave to Daphne. Her smile was so exquisite and so electrifying that he shuddered.

2

DAPHNE

She cut through the velvet, snipping carefully around some ornate, silver-threaded embroidery until the piece lay in her hand. The crude hole in the antique Moroccan waistcoat provoked a rush of vandal's exhilaration – she had owned it since she was eleven. It had been shabby even then but now it hardly held together, its beads gone, the tarnished, cotton lining decayed. Touching the metallic stitching brought back the thrill of holding it for the first time.

Ralph had left a note:

You need to search. Here's the clue, by a poet called Keats:

What, but thee Sleep? Soft closer of our
  eyes!
Low murmurer of tender lullabies!
Light hoverer around our happy pillows!
Wreather of poppy buds, and weeping
  willows!

The gift was concealed beneath her pillow, wrapped in creased white tissue paper and tied with twine. As she pulled at the bow, the packaging fell open to reveal something shimmering and precious. Sitting on the bed, she'd traced the intricate needlework with her finger and stroked the soft pelt of red velvet. The waistcoat felt magical, instilled with mysterious powers. Of course, she'd worn it to death. Wreathed in its spell, she shed gilded threads and buttons as she went, until it hung in shreds.

She located the box of pins amongst the sewing paraphernalia that lay strewn around and attached the silvery patch to the backdrop. This latest creation was her largest ever and, inspired by the move back across London to the landscape of her early years, she named it *Putney*. She pictured her childhood as a golden age, a marvellous jungle of a household that her parents had created by the edge of the river. There had been no rules, no constriction, no bars. No bras either. And very often, no shoes. She travelled barefoot around London and revelled in the rebellion, masquerading in her father's hats and her mother's scarves and racing across the bridge, waving wildly to passengers on boats below and trains beside.

At the centre of this outlandish Eden was Ralph. He had almost disappeared from her life, but her return to the river six months earlier had brought a new intensity to his place in her memories. She even wondered whether she should get in touch after all these years, especially given the central part he was playing in *Putney*. He had been so significant to her when she was young and yet had scarcely entered her adult life. They had occasionally encountered each other at parties and chatted like old friends, but they hadn't talked properly since ... in truth, since she was a teenager. He often strolled through her mind, but it was like remembering a dream. Recently, however, she'd begun to imagine discussing things with him – especially now that her life was something she could take pride in.

She had left behind the shame of her own Dark Ages, her abominably misjudged marriage, her twenties squandered in the mire of 'substances', her thirties climbing out of that swamp. Now she could present herself to Ralph quite truthfully as a healthy, happy adult with a beautiful child, a job and a home of her own. She was fine. She'd like him to see that.

She picked up the binoculars from the window ledge and fixed her sights across the Thames. Before she had come back to the familiar territory of her childhood and moved into Aunt Connie's flat, she wondered whether it would be alarming to look almost directly at her old home on the southern bank of the river – like looking back in time. But so far, the view had provided only pleasure. This was partly joy found in the soothing ebb and flow of the tides, the open expanses of sky and the cries of water birds. It was wonderful to have the rhythms and noises of nature alongside an urban existence. She had to admit, however, that she was also enjoying peering into her own foundations; emotional archaeology.

Focusing the binoculars, she homed in on what had been her bedroom on the top floor of number 7 Barnabas Road. In those days, the curtains were made from billowing, orange saris that tinted even bright daylight into a permanent sunset glow. Of course, as a child, she had looked out on exactly the opposite view; she might have spotted a woman spying on her from this building. The reverie reverberated like a hallucination until a man opened the window – her old window. It was almost as if Ralph had stepped in. The figure backed away and she put down the binoculars. Each time she spotted people in her old house it gave her a jolt. The previous day she'd seen a couple having drinks by the river wall, where she used to sit dangling her legs over the water.

She returned to her work and cut another gleaming whirl from the waistcoat and pinned it into position. In this depiction of her childhood, she was placing several versions of a man and a girl so they would float Chagall-style in the sky, lie on grass, go boating on the river and dance along the bridge. This hanging was by far the most personal thing she had made so far and she gave all her spare hours to working on it.

Today's job was fixing the bridge that spanned the centre of the piece and the glinting remnants of Ralph's waistcoat were perfect for its structure. She had found Victorian lithographs of gulls and ducks, printed them on bright yellow silk and had assembled feathers and tiny bones to sew around them. As a homage to things she loved in her youth, she had laminated pieces of tarot card, astrological signs and scraps from old comics, which would dangle along the bottom.

In addition to the Moroccan waistcoat, there were other secret clues – things that only she or Ralph would recognise, like a scrap of a cotton scarf printed with wild strawberries and an Egyptian scarab he'd given her. In one corner hung a shabby racoon tail from a Davy Crockett hat she'd treasured at that time. If only she could add the smells of those years: Ellie's musky perfume; burning cones of spicy incense; the vegetal reek of river mud; her leather satchel that stank of camel hide; the chemical tang of cheap sweets.

This was not a confession. Although her memories of being with Ralph as a girl were tender, she knew they could not be talked about openly. It had always been a secret, but not a dirty one. It was still precious to her. And *Putney* was going to be her private vision of this forbidden but genuine love, fuelled by the view from her window, a few old letters and notebooks and the carefully retained objects that symbolised a whole era. A distillation of the past.

* * *

Her mobile vibrated with an angry beetle's buzz: Libby.

'Hi, Mum. Are you coming?'

'Oh bugger!' She often found herself using the sort of dated expletives her father had preferred and that made Libby snort with laughter, though this time she groaned in annoyance.

'Sorry. I completely forgot the time. I'm on my way. Ten minutes, maximum. Where are you? Did you leave Sophia's?'

'Yeah, I'm at the end of her road, by Putney Common. But hurry, OK?'

They drove to their new favourite café – a French place off Putney High Street, with authentic baguettes and brioches and always some Edith Piaf or Charles Trenet playing. As they sat down, Daphne put an arm around her daughter, nuzzling into her neck and hair, and taking in the familiar smell of soap and fresh-mown meadow. How did this extraordinary person emerge from me? she wondered. How could all my mayhem and mistakes be alchemised into this perfect girl, with her honey-coloured hair, her legs elongating out of childhood, and her clear-eyed view of the world?

Daphne ordered coffee, Libby got hot chocolate and they ate croissants, scattering flakes across the red-checked tablecloth. They lapsed into a familiar ease; she'd been lugging Libby round cafés since she was a baby and they regularly took homework, laptops, even bits of sewing and settled in somewhere cosy for a couple of hours.

'I got my period again.' It was only her second cycle, but Libby sounded confident, even proud.

'Great. Feeling OK?'

'Fine. It's not such a big deal, Mum. Most of the girls in my year started a while ago.'

'I know. But it is *quite* a big deal. It's so extraordinary that we female humans should be linked to the moon and the tides. It'd sound like science fiction if you made it up – mysterious planetary forces making us bleed. And now you're part of that.' Libby laughed but glanced to see if anyone was listening. 'Yeah, well, you're making it sound very sci-fi. It's quite ordinary.'

'I suppose it's ordinary and extraordinary – like childbirth. I can't help it if you're such a cool cat.'

'Miaow.'

She found Libby's development oddly moving. Like a plant forcing its way up through heavy earth, her daughter's body was transforming. Daphne couldn't ignore the signs that her own body was retreating from fertility. Lately, her periods had been erratic and her first hot flushes had arrived with an unfamiliar burn that began in the face like a fever and spread down through the chest and limbs, leaving her sweaty and mildly shocked by its ferocity. The 'change of life', didn't they call it? Changes that were private, unadvertised to the world – even disguised. She was well aware that while her hair grew as energetically thick as ever, below the vibrant tint of Persian Copper it was now almost entirely grey. Libby and she were crossing each other's hormonal paths, travelling in opposite directions.

'So how did the lesson go?'

'Really good! So much better than Saturday Greek school. Sophia's great. We actually have fun. It's not like a lesson. She taught me a song and played her guitar. At the end, a friend of hers from uni came round. Aris. He's from Thessaloniki. Told some really funny jokes.'

'That's great. And I admit I got it wrong with Greek school. I think I was just trying to copy what my mother did; you know, unthinkingly pass on a tradition. The truth is I was always horribly bored there too.' Those Saturday mornings getting to grips with spelling and grammar with a pack of ex-pat Greek kids had been interminable. She'd eventually learned to lie about going, regularly sneaking off to meet Ralph somewhere instead, and then making up stories for her parents about Mr Korakis, the awkward, myopic teacher.

Libby's mobile rang. 'Hey, hi Dad.' Daphne felt a small lurch. Dad? When did that happen? He'd always been Sam and that suited her.

'Yes, I'm so excited.' Libby turned away slightly as though hiding her unmistakable elation. Daphne flicked half-heartedly through some emails on her phone while listening to Libby's enthusiastic discussion of the forth-coming trip to Greece. In vain, she strained her ears in the hope of overhearing Sam's side of the conversation; Piaf was growling too loudly from the café's speakers.

Sam was now the age she'd been when they met, but even in his late thirties he remained a boy, with smooth-skinned features, sun-bleached hair and jeans that edged down narrow hips. They'd got together one winter when she was housesitting on Hydra; he had evidently been intrigued by the prospect of a fling with an older woman. Sam was working in bars while slowly fixing up a ruin in the highest point of the town that surrounded the port like an amphitheatre. His dream was that one day he would rent it to wealthy American tourists and would never have to work again. By the time she left the island she was pregnant.

'So can we stay some of the time in Athens then? Can I help out too?' Libby's face was pink with anticipation. Daphne felt small but undignified pricks of jealousy. She struggled with Sam's increasingly significant role, though there could be no reasonable objection. This Easter would be the first time Libby was going to travel out to Greece alone. Daphne knew the life she had created with her daughter was not perfect but it had always been exclusively theirs. Now the boundaries were changing and she worried about these burgeoning familial ties.

'So how's Sam?' Daphne asked when Libby hung up. She couldn't see herself ever referring to him as 'Dad', while 'your father' sounded starchy and prim.

'Fine. He says they're mostly in Athens now, at Xenia's place. She's taking time off from the hospital to work with refugees. Dad's been volunteering too.' Libby flashed a glance at her mother, as if testing the reaction to Sam's new appellation. 'He said it's chaos, especially at Piraeus. Thousands of people arriving off the boats every day. I said I'd like to help them, so we might spend half the holidays in Athens and half on Hydra.'

'Amazing. That's such a good idea.' Daphne smiled firmly, feeling vaguely diminished in stature. Who could compete with that sort of saintliness?

They drove home and Daphne followed Libby into the flat that still felt as though it belonged to Aunt Connie. The air was not yet completely theirs. The coats hanging in the hall looked like tired friends waiting to go home. This place had shone with contemporary stylishness when she'd visited it as a child. She had loved its chocolate-brown carpets, green-leafed, William Morris curtains and the scattering of chunky ceramics and African masks. Now she had to admit that it was becoming an almost overwhelming time capsule.

'Maybe it's time we stopped collecting all this '70s junk,' she said to Libby, indicating some useless tat they'd bought at a car-boot sale that was still in a cardboard box. 'I'm afraid it's become like a joke without a punchline. A shaggy-dog story that keeps getting shaggier.'

'It's fun, though,' said Libby. During the six months since their move, she had persuaded her mother to buy three lava lamps, a pointless macramé plant hanger, a box of mugs decorated with outmoded protest slogans, and a pile of tie-dye clothes. Daphne felt unable to refuse, given that it was her idea to augment the retro look by snapping up relics from that gaudy decade of space-age plastics and hippy crafts.

It had only been a short walk from Barnabas Road to visit her father's sister on the other side of the bridge. Connie had often been a useful excuse when she was hurrying off to meet Ralph somewhere, but she'd genuinely loved her aunt. And they'd stayed close. It was in the hospice, towards the end of Connie's final illness, that she told Daphne about the bequest. 'There's enough in savings to cover the inheritance tax. I've wrapped it all up very tidily for you.' She even left her the unlovely, nineteen-year-old Ford Fiesta Daphne now drove.

They stopped at Libby's bedroom door with its 'Private – Keep Out!' sign.

'Have you got plans for the rest of the day?'

'I'll just hang out for a bit, then I've got some homework.' Libby opened the door, providing a partial view of the only room that looked not only contemporary but meticulous. She was cleverly curating her child-into-teenager collection of teddy bears, books and pop posters.

'Chloe might come over.' Libby frowned.

'Nice,' lied Daphne. It hadn't been easy changing school, and Chloe was an unfortunately pudgy, freckle-faced child whom Libby found dull – a person she was only friends with because Paige, an older, more glamorous girl, was not interested. Daphne knew there was absolutely nothing she could do; this hardest lesson in motherhood was being spelled out increasingly frequently. In fact, it seemed almost miraculous that they had made it this far without major mishap. She remembered the force of youthful friendships and longings from her own schooldays. While she often looked up to her best friend Jane as someone more academic and composed than she was, she recalled how Ralph made cruel jibes. 'You're a swallow, full of speed and light, but poor Lady Jane is more like a goose.' He had laughed. 'Geese are fine. Nothing wrong with them – after all, they lay the golden egg. But a swallow is celestial, something that makes your spirit soar.' Daphne hadn't experienced the relationship like that. Jane was her first intimate friend, with whom she crossed the treacherous seas of adolescence and who held her hand all the way. She had needed her. Now she wondered whether Jane had sensed Ralph's harsh judgements. And where would she place Jane in this new hanging?

'OK, Lib. I'm going back to my work. Shall we just make a sandwich when we get hungry?'

'Sure.' Libby waved a hand, slipped inside and closed her door. Daphne meandered back into the living room where *Putney* was taking shape amidst tangles of rags and glittering trinkets.

* * *

There was no clear point when the friendship started – Ralph was just around. He'd drop by or have lunch with her parents or wander into her room to see if she wanted to go for a walk or watch *Blue Peter*. Ralph was like a kind uncle or godfather. He took her to a concert of Indian music at the Roundhouse, swimming at Putney Baths, and he had the time to sit and talk with her about whatever seemed important to her then. It was he rather than her parents who accompanied her to see *Oedipus Blues*, the collaboration between him and her father that ran for a year in the West End and then went on tour. She hadn't understood all the references to brothels and drugs but had a visceral comprehension of the taboos that were broken by young Eddy getting involved with his birth mother after he accidentally killed his Greek father. Most exciting of all was the real motorbike that roared on to the stage.

Right from the start there were secrets with Ralph, but they were sweet things like presents or notes. There were phases when she so frequently returned home to find something from him waiting in her room that she almost came to expect it. He gave her a copy of Edward Lear's *Book of Nonsense*, marking a page.

There was an old person of Putney,
Whose food was roast spiders and chutney,
Which he took with his tea, within sight of the sea,
That romantic old person of Putney.

One day there was a pile of red petals in the shape of a heart on her desk, another time an expensive chocolate truffle in its own miniature cardboard container. She noted each episode in a diary, stuffed with scrappy mementoes and the pages stained with spilt drinks, food and tears.

For a long time she believed it was a coincidence when Ralph came across her in the street and walked alongside for a while or bought her a bar of chocolate. They established private names for each other. He was Dog; always waiting for her, he said, loyal as a hound. She was Monkey for her delicate hands and supple limbs. Or Strawberry, 'Like strawberries in winter.' And in those funny days not so long after the post-war era, strawberries were something special and seasonal – a treat that Libby's supermarket generation would never understand.

When Ralph brought Daphne a record of Stravinsky's *The Rite of Spring* and gave an impression of how the dancers moved, he said, 'You have to feel the pagan spirit.' He looked like a madman with his uninhibited jumping, in-turned feet and manic rhythms, but persuaded her to join him. 'I'll take you to see it one day,' he said when they fell to the ground, breathless and giggling. 'It's already sixty years old but it's still astonishingly modern. There were riots when it was first performed. That's what I'd like to happen with my music.'

One summer afternoon, when they sat on beanbags in her room, the sash window wide open to the garden, he explained how to listen to ambient sounds.

'Can you hear the bass notes? The rumble of traffic in the distance, that chugging getting more muffled as the tug goes away along the river? Then you've got the high register. There, like those brakes screeching.' He replicated the sound and then joined in the barks and yelps of some nearby dogs. Even more entertaining was his imitation of birdsong. He could do about twenty different species. Not just obvious calls like the cuckoo or the owl, but the sweet whistle of the blackbird, the thrush's warble, the swallow's chirp and the descending cry of the buzzard. He opened her ears to things she would not have noticed, but it didn't feel as though he was trying to educate her. Another time, when he gave her a record of sacred music by Elizabethan composers like Tallis and Byrd, he turned it into an adventure, talking her through the parts, explaining some of the Latin, and identifying the entwined voices as though they'd crept into a dark, sixteenth-century church and were spying on the singers. 'I sang that stuff as a child,' he said. 'A scrawny little choirboy in Worcester cathedral. I'd sail right up to the high Cs without a thought.'

When Daphne was eleven he took her to a recording studio to sing for his latest piece, *Songs of Innocence and Experience*. They were based on William Blake's poems and Ralph assembled a huge children's choir from several London schools and a band of Gambian drummers. For the *Songs of Experience*, he gathered up some homeless men and paid them to read the poems, accompanied by a small string orchestra. Ralph wanted untrained people rather than musicians – unpretentious voices of innocence and of experience. He was determined to have Daphne participate, and insisted she sing some solos, along with a young boy of about eight with an angelic voice. 'Like a bird singing — the sounds coming straight from the body. That's what I want.'

Singing in front of all those people was terrifying and, while she tried to do what Ralph requested, she couldn't understand what was going on much of the time. The drummers wore African robes and treated the event as a party and Ralph encouraged it, providing beer for them and Coca-Cola and crisps for the kids.

'Pandemonium,' Ed said when he dropped by one day.

> *Little Lamb,*
> *Here I am;*
> *Come and lick*
> *My white neck.*

In the end, the recording was a success. Daphne even had her photograph taken for a piece in a weekend colour supplement. The journalist who interviewed Ralph, the drummers and one of the homeless men asked her what she thought. 'It's really super. I enjoyed it,' she was quoted as saying. She never forgot her song; in fact, she had sung it as a lullaby to Libby when she was little.

> *My dear Strawberry girl,*
>
> *I* <u>*really really*</u> *enjoyed yesterday. I can't imagine who else could have done those solos or who would have given it what you did. I just felt so happy afterwards. I always hope you are happy and look forward to seeing you.*
>
> *Love and a big lick on the ear from your devoted Dog*

Daphne had been ten when Ralph met Nina. A friend of one of Ellie's many cousins, she had come from Athens to London to study painting at the Chelsea School of Art and stayed on to do postgraduate work. She was invited to Barnabas Road one weekend when Ralph was there and Daphne had immediately spotted his attentiveness. Nina had a doe-eyed face with pleasing, regular features and an extravagant amount of chestnut hair that was so long she could sit on it. She often wore it in a loose plait, and dressed in kaftans and long skirts, all of which Ralph said made her resemble an Ancient Greek. Daphne was present when he told Ed that Nina was like a caryatid – classical and timeless. He appreciated women who didn't slap on make-up or wobble around in ridiculous high heels and tight skirts. He often told Daphne: 'Don't think you'll attract the boys with lipstick and feminine flimflam.'

After Ralph and Nina became a couple, Daphne overheard Ellie gossiping on the phone about how Nina would be the perfect match for Ralph, being both pretty and intelligent but, most important, silent. This would allow him his fantasies, she said. And that's what men need. And what's more, despite her artistic inclinations, Nina would be a thoroughly traditional Greek wife, who would stick close to the hearth and the cradle and not ask questions. '*Plus ça change.*' Daphne liked how her mother's spiky verbal nails were hammered home. But in fact, Ellie and Nina became increasingly friendly. She often returned from school to find them ensconced in the kitchen chattering away in Greek about the latest political developments or the impossible nature of English weather.

Ralph never hid his relationship with Nina. Quite the reverse. Daphne was his true friend and confidante who 'should know everything'. Even his sexual escapades were not taboo in their conversations and there had always been various passing girlfriends he made fun of to her so they could both laugh about them. 'A silly, drunken fuck,' he said without compunction. 'It's like eating too much chocolate – you feel greedy before and regretful after, but nothing serious. It's just physical.' He hugged her. 'You're the one I love.' Nevertheless, when Ralph and Nina moved in together, Daphne was perplexed. This was evidently something much more serious than she'd understood, though he'd never explained it as such. He took her to see the terraced house they'd bought in Battersea while it was being decorated – a two-up two-down on the hill near the park, with a rickety extension for kitchen and bathroom. They edged past workmen sanding floorboards and repairing windows.

'This is the best part,' he said, leading her through a cramped garden to a shed. 'This is where I'll work.' There were trees hanging over the wooden structure. 'It's almost like a grown-up's tree house, even if it is on the ground.'

When Ralph announced he and Nina were getting married, Daphne felt a spasm of envy she couldn't express or even comprehend. Although she was only eleven, Ralph had already made her grasp the exceptional position she held in his life. She didn't say anything but he evidently noticed the change in her expression.

'The thing is, I feel she's like your family,' he said, as if making an excuse. 'And if there are babies, they'll be half-Greek like you!' He claimed he was getting closer to Daphne through this arrangement, becoming an honorary Greek of sorts, and Nina was as good as Daphne's cousin, even if it wasn't strictly the case in terms of blood. 'You know it doesn't affect how much I care about you.'

The wedding was held in Greece in September and, although all the Greenslays were invited, in the end only Ellie went. Ed had obligations at the university and the school term had just started. It was Daphne's first year at Hayfield and she was pleased to have the excuse not to attend the nuptials. Before he left, Ralph tried to reassure Daphne that his feelings for Nina were entirely separate to the unique attachment to his young friend. 'Nothing can change my love for my Miss Monkey,' and he kissed her hand, moving his lips in little jumps up towards her elbow like an old-fashioned suitor. Eventually she giggled and he looked relieved.

It was true that Ralph's marriage appeared to make little difference to the progression of his intimacy with Daphne. It was only a year or so later when they first kissed. Kissed properly, 'like in films', as she thought of it as a child. 'Tongue sandwich,' as boys sneered at school. She was twelve. It must have been a weekend and the weather was fine enough for a picnic. He collected her in his car, a Morris Traveller so decrepit that the timber frame had moss growing on it. Ralph had given the car a name. 'Poor old Maurice, he's trying to get back to nature. Soon he'll start sprouting trees. Before long he'll be a small, travelling wood with birds' nests and badgers' lairs. And I'll be the madman in the forest, making music only the animals can understand.' Daphne got into the front seat and noticed the back was filled with musical instruments – old gourds and goat horns tied up with twine, or a funny object hung with beads that he said was a Sudanese lyre. Never something normal, like a clarinet or a guitar, and although he'd been a violinist, he rarely touched the instrument any more. Ralph drove to Richmond Park, teasing her by taking his hands off the steering wheel and pretending that Maurice was driving by himself. 'Maybe he'll start flying like Chitty Chitty Bang Bang.' Later, she saw that Ralph was using his knees all the time.

When they arrived in the park, he handed over a paper bag. Inside were two reproduction Victorian masks made of card. 'This one's for you.' He held up the face of a blond, plumed monkey and looked through the holes, making small grunts and grinning. 'Here, I'll help you put it on,' he said and she twisted so he could tie the ribbons into a bow at the back of her head. 'Ah, what a beautiful little monkey,' he marvelled when she turned around. He stroked her hair and asked her to fix his mask – a dog with worried wrinkles on its forehead and wearing a small red fez. 'Your loyal servant and obedient hound,' he said, his eyes all dark and shiny behind the cut-outs. They stared at one another as if they'd metamorphosed into different people or indeed animals. The ability to step outside herself, to masquerade as someone else, was a skill she learned from Ralph and quickly made her own. It was a recipe for instant freedom – as simple as changing your trousers or putting on a hat but being transformed by it.

'Shall we go, Miss Monkey?'

They left Maurice in the car park and made their way towards a wooded area. A number of walkers stared at this odd pair. She felt vulnerable – a fox slinking across the open space – until they reached the green shade. After following a narrow path through the trees, they reached a clearing that was almost like a room; apart from a discreet opening, it was surrounded on all sides by bushes and trees.

She watched as Ralph put the picnic basket on the ground, unfolded a plaid blanket and stretched out on his back, his hands under his head. She lay down too, and gradually he turned towards her and caressed her face very slowly and gently underneath the mask. It felt nice. Any potential awkwardness was removed by their disguises.

'We're like animals in the enchanted forest,' he said.

Inside the basket was a bottle, which he opened using the corkscrew on his penknife. Pulling off his dog mask, he took a swig and handed it to her.

'I like drinking,' she said, removing her mask too and tasting the slightly sweet white wine.

'So do I.'

'Sometimes I smoke too. I nick them from Ellie and she never notices.'

He leaned over and kissed her very gently on the lips. She didn't respond, but nor did she draw back. Pulling away a few inches, he said, 'I love you so much.' Then he kissed her again, warm mouth just opened.

Looking up through the fluttering layers of green leaves made her feel reverse vertigo. Ralph lay on his side and looked as though he was examining her, lightly running his finger along her eyebrows. His face was deeply familiar; kind dog eyes, mobile features, and though he was much larger, his size was not imposing. 'You're the boss,' he repeated. 'I like it when you tell me what to do.' She knew him, trusted him. A friend. 'A special friend,' was his expression. Not like the others – that was clear. He was free to pass between the age zones. She liked what was happening and was intensely curious about this man who loved her. Soft and dangerous. His skin hot against hers and slightly scratchy on her cheek. When he tried to slip his hand inside her shorts, she pulled it away. It gave her another sort of vertigo. They went back to kissing, long and slow and new, his tongue diffident, just inside her lips and along her teeth.

High above their heads, a parakeet with emerald plumage landed on a branch and began chirruping. 'A love bird,' said Ralph, 'escaped from its cage. Come to serenade us.' He squawked and chirped until a strange aria emerged between man and animal.

'You won't tell anyone,' he said. 'It's our secret, isn't it?'

'Course!' It seemed slightly insulting that he needed to say this. It went without saying that none of it could be spoken about. In any case, she didn't have the words.

They agreed to meet on the train-bridge after school the following week, but by Wednesday there was no sign of him and she was getting worried. She dawdled in the middle of the walkway, leaning over the railings, staring down at the fast-moving river. The bridge's structure was deeply familiar: ochre brickwork at either end sprouting tiny plants from the cracks; grey-tiled steps up to the ledge where she and Theo had sat and thrown pigeon shit on passers-by; garish yellow flowers that grew up between the train tracks. She enjoyed feeling the tarmac walkway shake and tremble as each train monster passed. The distant rumble became a roar, metallic slashing and gnashing of teeth against the rails, a breath like a wheeze and it was gone. She made a bet, like an appeasement to the gods: I'll run to the next lamp post and if I get there before the train passes, he'll come. Just before the last carriage went past, she saw his familiar figure in the distance, hurrying up the last steps, two at a time. Her chest thumped with guilty, bewildered pleasure and she looked away, pretending to be concentrating on the view. Out of the side of her eye she noticed him decrease his pace to a saunter.

'I'd say snot-soup, today,' he remarked casually, continuing their running competition to find the best description of the khaki-coloured water down below.

'Decomposing diarrhoea,' she countered.

'Fetid putrefaction.'

He looked quickly up and down the walkway, established that nobody was about and pulled her against him. They kissed, harder this time than in the woods. As the faint rumbles of a distant train approached, they broke apart.

Ralph gripped on to the rail and looked out like a captain on a ship. '*Panta rhei*.' He had done enough Ancient Greek at boarding school to put him off it for life. 'Everything flows. You never step into the same river twice. Everything is changing all the time.'

'Oh yeah, yeah, very clever. Of course everything is changing. Just look at my body, for a start. *Panta rhei*, pantaloons.'

'Your wondrous body – exactly. And you should wear that sweater more often. Just like that, with nothing underneath.' She knew her jersey revealed her tender nipples that were just starting to swell.

She and Ralph leaned against one another as they walked over towards Barnabas Road, not daring to hold on for fear of coming across someone they knew. But this anxiety was not enough to eradicate the invisible, magnetic pull of their bodies that diminished distances as if by a natural force.

After 'the leafy bower' (as it became known), their meetings took on a new intensity. The secret became darker.

Ralph composed a piece of music for woodwind ensemble called *Into the Woods*, with squawking oboes ('the green love bird,' he explained) and strange percussive honks of the bassoon. 'It's for you,' he said. 'I wrote the whole piece in D minor – D for Daphne and minor for the mystery of your melancholy eyes. I can't actually dedicate it in public, but you know.'

His notes to her became more urgent in tone, scrawled on scraps of paper as though his emotions were pouring out too quickly.

My dear sweet child, my lovely girl, my Angel, and many other ways of describing you that would fill a page, a book, a whole library!

Seeing you yesterday was fantastic and I was sad leaving you afterwards. I know I go a bit crazy when we're together, but it's like a dream.

I will try to come over with Maurice on Thursday after school and we could go somewhere.

Maybe you should throw this away? Be careful.

Love your devoted friend

She didn't throw away his notes, placing them instead in a small tin trunk he'd given her, along with a padlock and key on a length of string. It was also a store for some of his gifts – precious items full of meaning that became like talismans: an empty box of Balkan Sobranie Turkish cigarettes containing a dried sprig of wild strawberries; an Egyptian ankh; a stone skull pendant with green gem eyes; a trio of brass monkeys; a red paper heart; a matchbox with a sharp tooth inside. There was also a bronze snake with a label tied round its neck saying: *Leave me in the trunk.*

A token of my love and hope. Anyone trespassing will die by my bite. These objects were like evidence of things that might otherwise have been imagined, of events not witnessed by anyone else and feelings that must not be mentioned.

In her memory, the woods marked the point where a childhood friendship turned into something more exciting. There was a new fear of being found out. Without discussing it, they both assumed that even Ed and Ellie's tolerance would have limits if they learned what was going on. It was true that her parents were frequently absent or at least absent-minded, but the simplicity of their earlier meetings had disappeared. Daphne loved her mother and father and she had no doubt about their affection for her, but she didn't feel at the centre of their worlds. True, Ellie had given up working soon after the junta seized power in Greece, but it was to concentrate on the political fight, not to be with her children. Daphne pictured the colonels with bulbous noses, waxed moustaches and red eyes, like the baddies in comics. Helping bring down a dictatorship was more important than building a career in some stupid London legal firm, Ellie said, and Ed earned enough to provide for the whole family. However, her mother became even busier than before, taking up many cases on a pro-bono basis to help exiles and supporters of the cause. There were interminable meetings, often held in the kitchen, which filled with the shouts of angry people and their fug of smoke and coffee fumes.

Ellie's preoccupations did not change much when, after seven years, the colonels were locked up and Greece was free. Her trips to Paris continued and she attended an apparently endless stream of protests with radicals, feminists, anti-apartheid groups and CND. 'What will you do with me and Theo when the nuclear family is abolished and women are finally free?' Daphne once asked her mother, half-teasing, half-concerned.

Ed was more predictable as a parent, though he too was wrapped up in his own concerns. He claimed children should find their own way to grow up – a philosophy that suited him. When he was writing a book, he was so distant as to be almost like a ghost in the house, forgetting meal times and spending half the day in his dressing gown, which was so extravagantly embroidered he resembled a walking tapestry. 'Be a darling and pipe down,' he'd say to Daphne or Theo if they were making too much noise.

Daphne was never quite sure what Ed's academic post at King's consisted of, but there were references to students' theses and to colleagues. Various people (predominantly rather attractive young women, as Ralph pointed out) came to the house carrying sheaves of typed pages and pensive expressions. So although Daphne couldn't be sure if her father would be closeted in his study and refusing to emerge, hosting a group of writers and students in the kitchen, or away at work, she was less worried about him interfering with her plans than about her mother.

She knew both her parents had affairs. Even without eavesdropping, she was sure that when certain 'friends' of both Ed and Ellie made a fuss of her, it was because she was their lover's child. She saw letters and witnessed rows. None of it surprised her. On the other hand, Daphne felt increasingly wary of Nina, especially when she had a baby a year or so after the wedding. Sometimes, on returning home from a furtive encounter with Ralph, Daphne found Nina drinking coffee with Ellie.

'Come and see darling little Jason,' Ellie would coo. 'Would you like to hold him?' And Daphne would say she was too tired or had homework and tried to keep out of the way. She didn't analyse her discomfort or admit to jealousy.

Although Ralph never appeared to feel a conflict between his love for Daphne and his family obligations, it became harder to find time together. They were both imaginative in finding solutions. One day after school, when she was nearly thirteen, he took her to a barber in Battersea. Before the appointment, they sat in Maurice, holding each other across the seats and kissing. The gearstick dug into her leg, but she didn't care. She wanted to kiss him so much it gave her a tummy ache. Sometimes it was all she thought about for an entire day.

'You'll look so beautiful. It suits you to be brave and unusual,' he said as they walked to the small barbershop, with its red-and-white-striped pole and photographs of men with bushy moustaches, sideburns and puffed-up quiffs. She didn't need persuading. She liked the idea of being daring, revelling in the fear and excitement as when jumping from the highest diving board into the pool. The barber hesitated before cropping her mass of hair, but then enjoyed himself getting the short back and sides just right with his clipper. Afterwards, Ralph stroked her scalp up and down. 'Like an animal's fur. You're my otter,' he said, sniffing her as though she'd been transformed into another species. 'A sleek, water animal.' When she got home, Ellie and Ed were shocked to see their daughter shorn and boy-like. But they came around to it, appreciating a radical gesture. At school, people laughed and mocked her. 'You should use the boys' toilets now,' jeered one girl. 'Lezzer, lezzer,' chanted a group of boys with shoulder-length hair.

Ralph was ecstatic about Daphne's new appearance and treated the haircut like another of their secrets.

'Do you really like it?'

'Ah, my darling girl!' He smiled at her, pulling her in close to him and smelling her hair.

'Then why do you like Nina's hair so long?' She had noticed him stroking Nina's lustrous mane absent-mindedly when the previous weekend they came over to lunch at Barnabas Road with little Jason. He looked puzzled for a moment. 'Your hair is the most beautiful thing. You're a spirit from another world, my Daff. You are magical and mysterious. You can't be compared with anyone. Don't even think of it.'

He kept some long locks of her hair, picked up from the barber's floor and plaited into a tight, dark braid. Sometimes he put it in an inside pocket of his jacket and carried it around with him – a risky memento. Once, when they were together, he brought it out with a flourish. 'It's like having you with me,' he said. 'Or at least a tiny part of you.' He held it to his nose, inhaled deeply and, exaggerating the impact, swayed as if he was about to swoon. 'I love you, Daff. Damn it. I love you.'

3

JANE

She turned on the hot tap again, keeping the temperature in the bath at the maximum she could bear, a wasteful trickle draining out through the overflow. Beyond the steamy scent of sandalwood oil, she could make out onions being sautéed, the aroma floating up the stairs and under the door. It was Michael's week for shopping, cooking and washing-up and she was taking full advantage of his dogged preparation of a mushroom risotto.

Despite being submerged to the ears in her scalding bath, she couldn't relax. The unexpected communication from Daphne after such a long silence had been a shock. She spotted the Facebook message that morning on the bus as she travelled slowly across rush-hour London towards the lab. It gave her such a jolt she let out a noise. The man next to her turned curiously, so she had to smile at him and show there was nothing wrong. And she wasn't clear what exactly *was* wrong. Yet she was disturbed by this casual reaching out across the years. It had dug up complex memories she'd taken a long time to entomb and cover with a heavy slab of stone. After all, she and Daphne had been so close. She was always hearing from colleagues and friends about the mild gratifications of middle-aged reunions enabled by social media. And yet she still couldn't make up her mind how to reply.

Jane looked down at her body as it pinkened in the hot water. She was happy with what she saw – so much happier than she'd been when she was young, when she had been close to Daphne. The long-standing regime of daily, lunch-hour swims had tautened her limbs and even a fifty-year-old abdomen that had stretched through two pregnancies was smooth and flat. She had hardly noticed when the menopause came and went, only glad that the inconvenience of periods had ended. At weekends she ran, and was even considering training for the London Marathon, maybe with Michael, if she could persuade him. She liked what she'd become. Strange, then, that this rush of memories about Daphne had thrown her into the kind of mental turmoil she associated with the agonies of her podgy, lank-haired adolescence.

'Death baths,' she and Daphne had called the scalding, perfumed immersions that they frequently shared. Until Jane met the Greenslays, bathing had been something functional, associated with the practicalities of hygiene. It was only with Daphne that she learned how to take a brim-filled bath so hot you turned feverish crimson and needed to rest afterwards. A drink, a book, a candle, or someone else at the other end of the tub were regular Greenslay variations on a theme that was all about indulgence and only incidentally about washing.

They had found each other in the first days at Hayfield, attracted by a sense of belonging, mocked as posh girls. Physically, they were not well matched. Daphne was compact and lithe, Jane was tall and physically 'mature' for her age. At eleven, her breasts had already expanded.

Actually, everything had expanded. Puberty arrived like a shocking, foreign invasion, and while many of the other girls had not begun the whole bloody process, Jane was obliged to deal with the humiliating embarrassment of sanitary towels and bras, not to mention being the galumphing Gulliver of a girl in a class of Lilliputians. At the start of the first year, almost all the boys were smaller than her. They were still children, but they knew how to inflict pain. They sniggered when her name was read out during class register (Jane Fish came right before Daphne Greenslay), they stared at her chest and at break time they made rude remarks, like 'Big Fish' or 'Chips', and pretended they could smell a fish shop.

She wasn't fat. She could see that now in the old photos. But she felt chunky. Hefty. Even her hands and feet were meaty. The feeling of the words pursued her, even if none of these adjectives applied to her in adult life. It was as though the early comparisons to her friend had been fixed. Daphne's skin was always slightly gold – intensified by summers in Greece – whereas Jane felt white and pink, almost swollen, in comparison. True, the glasses were unfortunate, with their ice-blue, NHS frames. As she grew taller, not stopping till she reached five foot eleven, she hunched and stooped as though apologising for taking up too much room. It was like an elephant running around after an antelope, she thought, always able to be unkind to herself.

It didn't make any difference that she'd been the clever one at school. She won prizes and was often top of the class, whereas Daphne was always getting into trouble for poor schoolwork and failed exams. It was Jane who helped her with essays and gave her the answers in tests, who tidied her room when it was so messy she couldn't find any clothes to wear, let alone locate her schoolbooks. But it had been the physical, bodily things that loomed large. She always hated the game where you must choose in order of preference to be beautiful, good or intelligent. It was so obvious that beauty must come first; people believed you were good and intelligent if you were beautiful. Her stooping, bespectacled years were left behind after her mid-teens, and by the time she was eighteen there were enough well-meaning wankers talking about ugly duck-lings and swans for her to realise that she'd changed.

She didn't want to think any longer about those days; there were still episodes she refused to revisit. Jumping up, she showered with icy water, putting an end to the wallowing in overheated thoughts. It was fine. Of course she would see her old friend. She was actually curious about what had become of Daphne after all the early disasters.

Michael made an affectionate fuss about getting her to come to the table so the Arborio rice was perfectly done, and he grated Parmesan over her plate with a flourish. He had the inexpert pride of the new enthusiast, but all the cookery books and his manly butcher's apron could not disguise the fact that he was a late starter and his culinary skills were still developing. To compensate, Jane made more compliments than necessary, even though the risotto was slightly underdone. She had no doubt she was a fortunate woman. They drank Italian red wine – Saturday tomorrow – and Michael listed a few of the day's horrors at school: the same old stories of dwindling funding, swell-ing class sizes and overworked teachers. 'And to cap it all, the school governors didn't agree to our refurbishment spend.' He had almost run out of outrage and she could only commiserate.

'I got a message from Daphne Greenslay today.'

'Ah.' Michael looked distracted, finishing off the salad, half-listening.

'Do you remember her?'

'Um, was she ...' He paused, paying more attention. 'Oh, the one who came to our wedding?' He grimaced. Daphne had turned up late and was clearly drugged or deranged. Horribly emaciated, she had dirty hair and didn't appear to have changed her clothes for days. When Jane kissed her at the reception, she noticed a rancid smell. She was like a bad omen – a sick bird flapping over the festivities.

'That's the one.'

'Went off the rails? Didn't she move to Greece?'

'That's right. She's half-Greek. Was married to a Greek for a bit. We were at school together. Best friends. You remember. The thing is, she got in touch again. Says she's moved back to Putney Bridge. She wants to meet.'

'What do you think?'

'I'm a bit nervous. I haven't seen her for decades.' She laughed to make the comment appear lighter than the strange, internal electricity that was sparking compulsion and fear. 'I'm not really sure why. For so long it felt like the right thing to keep my distance, almost as if her chaos might be contagious.'

'Maybe you can just send a polite reply and leave it at that? It doesn't have to be a big deal, does it?' Michael began stacking plates, his movements expansive from the wine.

'Yes, but then I expect she's settled down now. She's got a child. I suppose I'm intrigued.'

She helped clear the table and put her arms around him from behind as he stood at the sink. He jumped slightly, then turned and kissed her full on the lips before breaking free and going back to the washing-up. She said, 'Shall we watch another episode tonight?' Their tranquil evenings on the sofa watching streamed television series were an enjoyable feature of the empty nest. They'd probably fall asleep there, especially after the wine, and there would be a blurry-mouthed stagger up to bed in the room they'd shared since they were first married, where she'd breastfed their babies in the night, where they'd stifled sounds their sons shouldn't hear, where they'd been ill, had Sunday breakfasts in bed, and where, with any luck, they would grow old.

* * *

She woke to a brilliant morning, sunshine streaming in through the gaps between the curtains. It must be late – at least eight – as there were the sounds of tennis being played in the nearby courts and Michael was already up. In fact he'd probably left, as he did nearly every Saturday, to join his friends for a fry-up at a café near the common before football practice. Looking out of the window it appeared that, after so long waiting for the end of winter, this April day was everything you'd want from the tender season of hope. The row of back gardens was brimming with evidence: leaves sprouting every shade of green and spring bulbs that had pushed up their colourful, scented offerings through city soil.

Her uneasy dreams had been filled with Daphne. Sitting at the kitchen table in her dressing gown, she drank tea and logged on to Facebook. There it was, the banal little message accompanied by a photograph of her old friend, tousle-haired, laughing and bathed in golden light that could only be Greek.

Hello Jane, old friend. It's been too long. I've moved back to the south-west – right by the river, opposite Barnabas Road, and I thought of you. I'm here with my daughter Liberty. Are you still in this part of London? Shall we meet? Lots of love, Daphne

Proceeding before she could regret it, Jane tapped 'confirm' for the friend request and typed her reply.

Hi Daphne. Great to hear from you. It certainly has been a long time. Yes, I'm still around. Still Wandsworth. All good.

She deleted the next sentences — How strange that you are back in our old haunts. I often think about Barnabas Road — instead finishing off with a simple, Love, Jane.

Before she had taken another gulp of tea there was a jovial ping from the laptop as a new message popped up from Daphne. Janey! Good morning!!! How amazing. Can I call you? What's your number? This was going much faster than Jane had imagined. Slowly, she tapped in her house phone number, and again the response was almost instantaneous. Jane let it ring several times before picking up.

'I can't believe this,' Daphne said. 'I've been reminiscing about our times together. I was so excited when I found you on Facebook.'

'Yes, I'm sorry about the delay. I don't use it much and I only … wow, Daphne, it's so strange to be talking with you again. As if we were still fourteen or something.' She had wanted to keep a distance, place markers of her limits, but she already felt herself being pulled into Daphne's seductive orbit.

'God, you can't imagine how much I've been thinking about those years,' Daphne said. 'I'm living in this flat that's literally on the other side of the river from our old house. It's crazy. Like tripping down memory lane each time I look out of the window.'

There was a brief silence then Daphne said, 'Are you busy today?'

'Um. Well, I'm about to go running, but ...'

'After that? Could we meet? Oh do come over here and see my new flat, my new life. Please. I'd love to see you after all this time.'

Jane didn't reply immediately, giving Daphne time to fall into her old role as the daring, dashing one. 'Oh go on, Janey. Live dangerously! Take the risk. What do you have to lose? If it's a failure, we never have to meet again. I'm a reformed character, I promise.'

A flash of annoyance nearly led Jane to say she was busy all day, but the truth was that she was completely free. In the past she often worked over weekends, and even now she and Michael both frequently brought back some paperwork. But since Josh and Toby had left, hers was fitted in easily to a couple of hours on Sunday evening. Without the boys around time had expanded, and she found whole swathes of it at weekends, reminding her of her student days.

'OK. Shall I come for a coffee then?'

Daphne's response was touchingly sweet. 'Oh, that's wonderful. I'm so happy.'

* * *

Sitting in the front seat on the top deck of the 220 heading into Putney, she looked out at places that were familiar from a lifetime living in south-west London, but that had also been the backdrop to her friendship with Daphne. Her entire body was stiff with anticipation and revived reminiscences. The first time she'd visited Daphne's house had been a revelation. It must have been in the spring term of their first year, so they were just about twelve. They sat in the same place in the bus as she was now, but enveloped in a miasma of cigarette smoke spiked with odours of bubble gum and salt and vinegar crisps. Jumping off at the traffic lights near the bottom of the High Street, they walked to the corner shop on Putney Bridge Road to buy sweets. With lips green-tinged from sugary, glutinous worms, they stopped to ring a random doorbell on Maresfield Road and then sprinted off, giggling, short blue skirts flapping, schoolbags banging.

By the time they reached Barnabas Road they were panting and clinging to each other's arms with excitement. Naturally, Daphne was the fast one – the girl who won the 100 yards at school almost without trying. Following her friend downstairs to the kitchen, Jane's first emotion was bewilderment at finding so many people there. A tall man with a long nose and straggly, fair hair was leaning back precariously on his chair and waved extravagantly at Daphne, almost losing his balance. 'Hello, darling. Who's your little friend?' He looked mad to Jane – turquoise velvet trousers, bare feet and a large, multicoloured scarf wrapped around his neck – but she appreciated the 'little' part of his question.

'Hello, Ed. This is Jane. Jane, this is Edmund.' Daphne sounded rather firm, like a mother talking to a child. 'And don't be patronising. We're not little.' Daphne was good with the quick retort; Jane envied her that, generally finding the reply she required only hours later. The man looked amused rather than chastised, and held out his arm to Daphne, who meandered over to give him a casual kiss on the cheek. It took some minutes before Jane realised that this was Daphne's father – it was the first time she'd witnessed a child calling a parent by their Christian name.

There seemed to be no sign of a mother, but there was a handsome, imposing woman in floor-sweeping skirt who turned out to be an opera singer. Also sitting at the table was a pretty research student of Edmund's called Dizzy. It was not Edmund but a younger man who jumped up on the other side of the room and came to speak to the girls. He was slim with a smallish build and wore a baggy, collarless shirt and battered lace-up boots.

'What have you girls been up to then? Lurking with intent? Didn't Miss Driver deal out a detention today, Daff?' He seemed to know a great deal – even the name of their mean-spirited form teacher, who enjoyed keeping pupils behind after school.

'Yes, but we're bored with lurking now. Come on, Jane. Let's go to my room.' Daphne turned and led the way out of the kitchen. The man came to the foot of the stairs and then followed them halfway up until Daphne stopped.

'I got you something.' Jane saw the man smile as he extracted a little package from his pocket. Her friend took the gift and pulled off the wrapping paper. It was a brass model of three tiny monkeys and the man showed how their paws were placed to cover eyes, ears and mouth. 'See no evil, hear no evil, speak no evil.' As he spoke, he held on to Daphne's wrist with one hand and pointed out details with the other.

Daphne's hands were already familiar to Jane – small and wiry, they were hands to pick locks or tie complicated knots. Her nails were bitten and sometimes coloured with felt-tip pens or patterned with matt-white corrector fluid – something she did when bored in class. She had several cheap silver rings, including a puzzle ring that Jane coveted.

'Thanks.' Daphne sounded as careless as though he'd just passed her the bread at table. But her expression was one of pleasure and of power. 'Come on!' she gestured to Jane. Then in an exaggerated American accent, 'Let's get outta here.'

* * *

The last time Jane had spoken with Daphne must have been at least twenty years earlier when she was living in some sort of experimental cooperative outside London. So it was odd to make her way to the entrance of an old-fashioned, redbrick mansion block with well-trimmed gardens and polished brass door furniture. But then nobody had gone through more transformations than her old schoolfriend. Maybe it should not be surprising to find her ensconced in this haut-bourgeois residence.

Daphne was waiting in an open doorway at the end of a muffled, non-descript corridor on the fourth floor. As they hugged, Jane smelled a rich, amber-scented perfume and noticed how like her mother she had become. Ellie had been beautiful in the way that aged well – with olive skin and a face so mobile with expression and with such intensity of gaze that you'd never notice if there was a wrinkle.

'Who'd have guessed? When we were young, I could never imagine being this ancient.' Her low, throaty voice still cracked up into raucous laughter that Jane remembered from their teens. 'Well, what the fuck, eh? Anyway, look at you! You look fantastic. I love your cropped hair – all spiky. When did you chop off your Rapunzel tresses? God, you must tell me everything.' She spun around lightly and gestured for Jane to follow her, which she did, immediately feeling large-boned and leaden-footed.

The flat was painted odd, uncoordinated colours – turquoise in the hall, purple in the sitting room and mustardy ochre in the kitchen – and it was as messy as the rest of the building was orderly. Piles of books and clothes were strewn on the floors, food-encrusted plates and mugs were abandoned on shelves and tables and the layer of dust that covered most surfaces was so thick that Jane only just refrained from running her finger through it to make a mark.

'Coffee? Tea? A glass of wine? A vodka shot? What would make you happiest?'

'Oh, just a coffee, thanks.' She smiled politely. They moved into the kitchen and Daphne put water and coffee in a battered stove-top espresso-maker.

'You know, I'd never seen one of those until I went to Barnabas Road. I thought it was so exotic.' Jane laughed, then regretted that she was revealing too much. She remembered the vaguely threatening hissing and bubbling as the black liquid entered the top chamber. Be careful, she thought.

'So it's a bit like stepping back into the '70s here, isn't it?' Jane gestured to a throw on an armchair patterned with bold orange flowers and a collection of publicity photos and postcards of Marc Bolan, David Bowie and other stars from their youth. Daphne chuckled somewhat bashfully. 'Yes, we thought we'd go the whole hog. Seeing as the place was still almost exactly as it was forty-odd years ago, we're continuing the theme. Saved me having to redecorate. Libby and I are planning an evening where we get rigged up in Lurex tank tops, flared cords and Day-Glo wigs and dance to old recordings of Abba and *Top of the Pops*.'

She laid out some of the brashly patterned 'vintage' crockery on a tray with the coffee. 'So! You must tell me everything. Still pushing the boundaries of science? Curing the world of cancer? I imagine you're heading for a Nobel by now.'

'Yup, Nobel Prize any day now. But yes, still working in cancer research. Still just as obsessed.'

'And what about ...' Daphne hesitated. 'Your husband?'

'Oh, Michael's fine – a head teacher now. The principal at Redgrove Academy. In Southwark.'

'Such high-fliers! I expect your boys are geniuses too.'

Jane laughed at the exaggeration. 'Well, they're all grown up now. Josh is finishing a PhD in physics at Imperial.'

'Wow. Following in his mother's footsteps then?'

'Yes, he's firmly wedded to the sciences.' She tried not to appear too proud, disapproving of boastful parents and knowing she could easily fall into the trap. 'Toby's taken a different path, though – halfway through a degree in English and drama at Birmingham.'

'Amazing. So since I last saw you, you've brought up two brilliant sons. You must be so proud. It sounds like the perfect family.' Jane scrutinised Daphne for a sign of irony, but detected none.

'Of course, I'm convinced that Libby is the best, most brilliant, prettiest girl that ever existed, even if she is only twelve.'

Daphne flushed slightly from enthusiasm and produced a picture on her phone of a sweet if fairly ordinary, blue-eyed girl who looked nothing like her mother. 'It's so sad you can't meet her today,' she continued. 'She's at a Greek lesson, then going straight to a friend's. Next time, though – definitely!'

'So it's the two of you living here?'

'Yes, no man.' Daphne had always favoured directness over the evasive, characteristically English 'beating the bush', as she called it aged twelve. 'It's better that way. I've tried to keep my relationships separate from home life with Libby – certainly in recent years. And at the moment there's nobody anyway. I wouldn't marry. Not again. Constantine was enough to put me off that for life.' She looked away for a moment. 'It all got quite scary and out of control. Not just the drugs and all sorts of unmentionables, but he got pretty nasty. Often on the verge of violence.' She turned to face Jane. 'You know I had a miscarriage? It was quite late. I think that all set me back years – in terms of sorting myself out.'

'I'm so sorry. I didn't know.' She's still so pretty, thought Jane. You wouldn't guess what she'd been through.

'Yeah, well anyway, long-gone and all good now. The last guy in my life was Kit and he was away on assignment most of the time. A photographer. Wars and any other available horrors – you know the sort of thing.' She laughed. 'That ended last summer. I'm quite content, though. It's actually rather peaceful.'

Daphne led the way out of the kitchen. 'Let's go through to the living room. You must see the view.' It was just as she'd said – the south-facing windows gave on to the river and looked straight across to the backs of the tall, narrow, semi-detached houses on Barnabas Road.

'Your old place has changed colour. It's the pale grey one, isn't it? Wasn't it dark green in your day?'

'That's right. Here, take these.' Daphne handed her some binoculars and Jane focused on the building that was so significant in her youth that she still revisited it in dreams. A Tube train crossed the bridge, sending gentle tremors through the room like a milder version of the regular rumbling that was part of life in Barnabas Road.

'Wow.' It was almost too much. Perhaps I should leave, she thought. I'm not sure I can do this.

'So, are you working?' Jane pulled herself back into the present with the question.

'Yup. Too many years now at a crappy little travel agency called Hellenic Heaven! Or Hell, as it's more commonly referred to. Could be worse. Pays the bills. And it's the first place I've actually managed to stay in for longer than a few months.' She shrugged. 'Still, I always hope it's not for too much longer. Especially now we've gone up in the world and for the last six months have been proud homeowners. It's quite a change from our rented "garden flat" dungeon in Camden and all the other shitholes we've passed through or been evicted from. The neighbours here are by far the quietest, most genteel, well-heeled I've ever had! Libby says it's like a posh hotel.' They both laughed.

'The only annoyance is that my dear old Aunt Connie made a clause in her will – I'm not allowed to actually sell this place. I suppose she deduced from all the early fiascos and failures that I still need some external control. She apparently hadn't appreciated how much I've changed. A bit insulting, but there. Never mind. Anyway ...' She shook her head as if it would rub out that train of thought.

'Here, sit down. I'll just move this.' Daphne cleared some of the rag-and-bone clutter off the armchairs. On the opposite wall hung a large collage made from textiles.

'So I'm very involved with making these hangings now. I haven't made my fortune – yet – but I love doing it. Almost a compulsion. The one thing in my life these days that's completely absorbing and all-consuming. Apart from motherhood, of course.'

'What's the story on this one?' Jane already felt uneasy.

'It's called *Putney*!' Daphne laughed. 'It's a riff on my life across there. Doffing my cap to my childhood, I suppose. And, Jane, you were such an important part of that time – such a good friend to me. So loyal. See this long-haired girl in the garden here? That's you! And inside the windows, those faces are Ellie and Ed. And that's Theo leaning out with all the wires draped around.'

A swell of nausea rose inside her as Jane examined the hanging. She understood immediately. It was unmistakable who the male figure was – repeated over and over, cavorting across the canvas with a wild-haired scamp that could only be the young Daphne.

'So I started off with lots of cushions and throws and things,' said Daphne. 'You know, selling them in stalls and to shops. But I gradually got more daring. And there's this guy Adrian, with a gallery in Shoreditch. I've had two shared shows there now – one with a mad yarn-bomber, who knits her way around bikes and musical instruments till they're covered!'

Jane pointed to one of the male figures. 'So is that Ed and you?' She wanted to test Daphne.

'Um, no.' Daphne smiled. 'It's sort of secret, but as you knew anyway ... it's Ralph.'

It was jarring to hear his name. Horrifying to see this awful man glorified and honoured. Almost unbearable that Daphne should be celebrating something so appalling. 'Isn't that a bit ...' Her words hung suspended.

'What? Subversive? Wicked?' There was a hint of taunting in Daphne's reply.

'A bit inappropriate. You were a kid.' Her voice came out small, whiny as a child's.

'Yes, but it didn't damage me. I loved him. And he loved me. What happened with Ralph was one of the many complicated things in my life. Actually, probably one of the less traumatic. It was an intimate relationship with someone older. End of story. Not everything fits into the tidy boxes society lays out for us. We both know that.'

'Have you seen him?' She could hardly bear to ask, dreading that Ralph retained a hold over Daphne, even into her middle age.

'No. Haven't clapped eyes on him for years. In fact, I was thinking maybe I should contact him. Especially now I've seen you! I've bumped into him at the occasional party, but we've never really spoken. I've got fond memories, but I know very little about his life now — apart from what I read in the papers.' She laughed as though relishing her association with someone famous; like a groupie, thought Jane, reminiscing about backstage conquests.

Jane stood up to avoid continuing the disquieting conversation and moved closer to the complex, layered landscape that filled almost an entire wall. One of the doll-like Ralph figures had red flowers wreathed in his hair. He was leading the miniature Daphne across the bridge; a romance or an abduction?

She began to identify more elements, recognising fragments of an oriental waistcoat Daphne had worn obsessively. Stitched into the riverside garden like a turquoise tortoise was an Egyptian scarab she knew was a gift from Ralph. It was kept in a box, which Daphne sometimes unlocked to show off her secrets. Then Jane approached the manky racoon tail dangling like a dead thing in a corner of this disturbing handiwork. Recollections returned too quickly, making her unsteady as the passenger on a heaving ship. 'Could I pop to the loo?' she asked, trying to keep her voice casual.

She gagged and almost threw up, then washed her face in cool water and looked into the mirror. It had been a mistake to come. She should have trusted her first instincts and stayed away. Thinking about Ralph made her angry. All that sniffing around a child like a horny goat, ready to do anything Daphne asked. Yet she remembered how compelling he had been, how much she wanted him to twinkle his eyes and honey his words at her too. As she got to know the Greenslays, she noticed how the atmosphere at Barnabas Road changed whenever he arrived, as though his charm carried an electrical charge that affected everyone and turned the light a rosier shade. It was seductive to man, woman and child, and she could see him using it like a tool. He showed up with unusual offerings – a box of small, aromatic mangoes from an East End market or some Beaujolais Nouveau that needed to be drunk there and then. And he made them all laugh. A slow-motion hunt so gradual that the prey didn't even realise it was being pursued, and would eventually just lie down to be mauled. It had been so obvious to Jane and so disgusting, and yet nobody ever said anything about it.

Ralph had never shown remorse for that or what followed. Worse perhaps, Daphne, with her talk of love and emerging unscathed, was like a bloody, one-woman paedophiles' charter. Of course, when you took the rackety elements of her life – the broken relationships, the substance abuse and who knew what else – she didn't appear unscathed. Jane felt sick when she thought about Ralph. Sick at her part in the whole sorry business.

Returning to the sitting room, she attempted to strike up another conversation – anything to get her away from the thoughts about Ralph.

'So what about Libby's dad? Where's he?'

'Sam's in Greece, which is where I met him. A San Franciscan mooching about with a guitar, channelling the spirit of Leonard Cohen. And such a great name: Sam Savage. He was working bars in the summer – mostly serving drinks but performing a bit with his guitar. Still, I have to admit he's got his act together now. Anyway, when I said I was going to have the baby alone, he was completely cool. He came over to London to visit us at the hospital, but kept his distance, as I requested. I named her after my mother really – Liberty, the English version of Eleftheria.' She paused briefly and Jane pictured Daphne's face after Ellie died. The devastation seemed to change her very features as well as her pallor.

'Anyway, Sam's a good boy. And things worked out for him. He's got this Greek girlfriend, who's not only beautiful but a doctor, and his mad plan to renovate a ruin on Hydra actually succeeded. As far as I can tell, he's making a fortune now, renting it out to rich Americans. There's a fancy website. You know the sort of thing, picturesque donkeys carrying your luggage from the port up cobbled alleyways to the "hidden paradise"? And he's even kept an outhouse for himself. So the really good part is, he's started paying regular upkeep for Libby. Even funds her Greek lessons in London and her plane tickets to Athens. What more could I ask?'

'Sounds great,' said Jane, unable to concentrate well on what Daphne was saying. She wondered whether she was coming down with flu, such was her physical discomfort.

'Listen, Daphne, I'm afraid I really need to get going.'

'So soon? Oh do stay a bit. I feel we've only just begun.'

'I would, but I'm meeting Michael and some friends for lunch – it took longer getting here than I imagined.' It was easier to lie. Get the hell out of there and don't look back.

'But there's so much we haven't discussed yet. Can we meet again? I can't tell you how happy I am to see you. And I'm so pleased that you're flourishing – that life has been good to you.' Daphne appeared sincere. 'I've moved on so often from so many different sorts of mess that I don't really have friends from the old days. Or not ones I want to know. It's incredible to think that we met ... how many years is it?' She paused, calculating the numbers. She'd always been hopeless at maths.

'Thirty-nine,' Jane said.

'So? What do you think? Shall we make a date? Have a proper reunion? A weekend lunch or a walk, or whatever suits?'

'Great.' Jane gathered up her bag and jacket, thinking she never wanted to see Daphne again. It was too upsetting.

'Here, let me give you this.' Daphne picked up something decorative and glistening, made from bits of vintage jewellery and minuscule pieces of needlework. 'I make these brooches and they do quite well – they're sold in several shops.' She pinned it to Jane's shirt. 'There's a little

68

Greek eye bead in there. It'll protect you – keep away the evil eye. They work, you know.'

As she waited on Putney Bridge for the bus home Jane glanced down at the bright-blue Greek eye staring out from her chest. She would never normally wear something as quirky and conspicuous as this. The panic had dissipated, but she felt as disoriented as if she'd been flung back in time and now inhabited the plump, hormonal flesh of her teenage self.

4

RALPH

His body was turning away from him, poisoned, sliced and wrenched from the easy familiarity he'd taken for granted. New aches and shooting pains, biliousness and constipation, gauzy eyes and dry mouth; betrayal. He was an old crock of blood and bones. Returning home from the treatments, he caved in, lying in the bath for hours, not reading or planning music or doing any of the things he was accustomed to when cradled in warm water. Now he found he could just let his mind wander, knowing the direction it would take, back to when he was so young and vigorous he was unaware there could be anything else. His mind frequently snaked away to his childhood: the boys at school he'd kissed, with knee scabs smelling of TCP and necks as tender as goslings; trees he'd climbed and sat in spying from green hiding places; but most of all it blurred back to Daphne.

In truth it wasn't just Daphne, but a whole package. These days, he rarely saw any of the Greenslays, but back then they were like a substitute family – friends, comrades, collaborators, lovers. His work with Edmund on *Oedipus Blues* was followed by their show for children based on *Aesop's Fables*, with young dancers dressed up as foxes, crows, grasshoppers and ants. The music mixed Indian ragas and jazzed-up English nursery rhymes in a way that was 'outrageously eclectic but breathtaking', as *The Times* critic put it. Edmund's established reputation was helpful to Ralph and he was introduced to producers, managers and influential types in the media world, whose reviews could make all the difference. It was also undeniable that Ralph's youth and animated vigour reflected a flattering light on to Edmund, perhaps lending a wilder element to his reputation.

These collaborations had the added advantage of making it much easier for Ralph to drop by Barnabas Road without it looking odd. He could leave a note hidden under Daphne's pillow or time a visit to coincide with her return from school. And if neither Edmund nor Daphne were around, Ellie had also become a friend who enjoyed the company of the young composer. She was mercurial like her daughter – you didn't quite know what you'd find. They never repeated the madly risky fuck (locked in the bathroom at Barnabas Road, while a party was taking place downstairs), but it left an air of intrigue between them. 'Write us a revolutionary song,' she repeatedly demanded, though he never did. 'Leave Edmund's myths and monsters and give us something to march to.'

He knew it had been 1976 when he went to Greece with Daphne because it was that bizarrely hot summer, when a seemingly endless series of cloudless days baked the country into an almost unrecognisable landscape. Londoners cooled off their feet in public fountains and had picnics in desiccated parks, their character transforming into something lighter and more appealing. It was like witnessing the marvel of adding heat to yeast, flour and water and finding you have bread. As the city took on a Mediterranean atmosphere, the accustomed odours of damp stone and muddy gutters were replaced with grass turning to hay, melting tarmac and unlikely whiffs of Ambre Solaire.

The plan proceeded so smoothly it was as if a natural order was merely falling into place. He could scarcely believe how easy it had been. Daphne's parents needed no persuading; they were grateful when he offered to take their daughter to Greece and deliver her to some cousins. Ed was already away in Germany giving some talks, Theo had just left school and was travelling in Scotland with Liam, and Ellie was going to Paris as soon as a solution was found for her daughter. 'How's your pet existentialist, Jean-Luc?' Ralph asked her when they spoke on the phone. It was abundantly clear why she was always rushing off to France.

It did not feel like lying when he told Nina he would join her and the baby in Greece and gave her a date three days after his scheduled arrival. Nina had already been at her family's house in Pelion for a month. She wrote letters annotated with charming cartoons depicting her tranquil days taking little Jason on expeditions to the beach and for evening strolls around the village. When their son was asleep she painted. She described her landscapes as full of colour and hope, like distilling everything that was good around her and putting that on the canvas. He was pleased to hear this. It calmed him. Ralph adored Jason, but he admitted never actually suffering when they were apart. It was enough to know that his son was safe and well.

'I'll be chaperoning two terrible teenagers – Daphne and her friend,' he told Nina. 'A nightmare, I expect. But I want to help out Edmund and Ellie.' A few more days without him would make little difference to her, he reasoned.

Compartmentalising his life allowed Ralph to lead separate existences, each with its own truth. He pictured it like the old-fashioned train carriages that were just being phased out, where there was no corridor or link between compartments; you merely entered and left at the platform. Using this model, his obsession with Daphne had no impact on his love and commitment to Nina and Jason. He would never abandon them and he explained this to Daff. It was entirely possible to love more than one person at the same time and neither relationship had to compromise the other.

He didn't tell Daphne (or Nina) his train-compartment theory, but he found it helpful to think of leaving one carriage before entering another; it kept things discrete. Daphne once told him she hated those closed carriages on trains – they hadn't quite been discontinued. 'You feel trapped,' she complained. But he considered them the best and certainly the sexiest form of transport – apart, of course, from sleeper trains, which were almost too much of a provocation. If you were lucky enough to get such a carriage to yourself and the object of your desire, you were free to exist totally and exclusively in that space – at least between one station and the next. He told Daphne how he once kissed a fellow schoolboy while hanging from the luggage rack. His fingers had hurt from pulling so tightly at the maroon string netting. In truth, it had been more than a kiss and they'd yanked off a white antimacassar from the seats afterwards to wipe themselves. But by the time a plump mother and two young children got in at the next stop, both boys were sitting in a red-cheeked daze, staring out of the foggy window with seraphic calm.

It was clearly going to be another 'scorcher', but the morning was still pleasantly cool when he took the train from Battersea to Putney station and walked down the hill to Barnabas Road. He noticed that he was smiling, as though his face had arranged itself into that shape without his knowledge. His pace, always brisk, was so buoyant he almost floated along the pavement, despite the large rucksack on his back. Young and fit, he was ready for anything.

When she opened the door, he saw immediately that she was Elusive Daphne today – not Wild Daphne or Teasing Daphne and certainly not Soft Daphne. She kissed him carelessly and turned on one foot with dancer's control to pick up a rough, ex-army duffel bag almost the same size as she was.

'Where's Ellie?'

'Oh, she left for Paris yesterday afternoon. There's nobody here.'

'Off with that anarchist Prince Charming, is she? I don't know what she sees in the nincompoop, with his overcooked Gallic charm and unreadable little magazine. Christ, he even wears a beret – so we won't forget he hails from the centre of the civilised world.'

'Are you jealous?' she said and he laughed, pulling her into an embrace, nestling his nose in her hair and inhaling deeply. Nuts, squirrels, summer-green trees. In normal circumstances it would be easy to get carried away; the opportunities presented by an empty house were tempting. But they would miss the bus. 'Control yourself, man!' he muttered as though to himself, but to indicate his desire. He cleared his throat, as though changing emotional gear. 'Are we off then?' Mustering a bluff, scoutmaster tone, he detached himself. 'All present and correct? Passport? Swimming costume? Sola topi? Clean underwear?'

'OK.' She looked like a child today. Where was the wicked teenager he was accustomed to?

He heaved the soldier's kitbag on to his shoulder. 'What the hell have you got in here?' It was surprisingly heavy. She laughed and they walked out of the house and up the steps on to the train-bridge. His pace was less buoyant now. The kitbag dug into his shoulder and the increasing heat of another boiling day was making him sweat. But seeing Daphne's light step by his side kept his spirits high and the prospect of this time together was creating an electric excitement.

'Dysentery-drain-coloured today, I'd say.' He indicated the gravy-brown river that was emptying itself out towards the sea and heading for low tide.

The Tube was crowded with people travelling to work and they stood by the door, bags propped up, fingers touching as if by accident as they held on to the warm metal handrail. She wore a thin blue dress that showed the outline of her pointed breasts. Her arms were already brown from London sunshine, her eyes were lined with black, and an assortment of silver bangles emitted small tinkling sounds. 'Rings on her fingers and bells on her toes, she shall have music wherever she goes,' he sang quietly into her ear and winked.

When discussing the matter with the relevant adults, he had defended his choice of the Magic Bus to Athens on the basis of it being cheap (under £30) and fun. Actually, the real motivation was the prospect of having three undiluted days sitting with his love and not needing to deal with anyone else. However, boarding the small, dilapidated vehicle at Victoria Coach Station brought a depressing burst of realisation that the journey was going to involve much more than merely proximity to Daphne. The driver and another man who turned out to be the second driver were leaning up against the outside of the bus, smoking and arguing in Greek. They didn't appear to speak English and gestured carelessly to where luggage could be stowed.

Many of the seats were already occupied by a predominantly young, unwashed but colourful collection of people who seemed to know what they were doing; Indian bedspreads rolled into pillows, bags of fruit, battered water canteens. He grabbed two seats behind a heavy, middle-aged Greek woman and a youth who was evidently her son, and who leaned away from her towards the window as if he wanted to break through it.

By the time the bus was loaded and pulled out on to the street, there was already an animal reek of humanity, despite the open windows. The vibrant chatter of the travellers was overlaid by Greek music turned up loud – a rudely honking clarinet and a male singer whose misery was so vocal you thought he might start sobbing. Ralph winced then smiled. A voodoo assemblage of beads, Orthodox saints, crucifixes and evil eyes was hanging off the driver's mirror. The woman in front of them opened a plastic box reeking of meat and garlic. She was pressing the boy to eat – evidently a never-ending maternal–filial dialogue, as he repeatedly refused her offerings and she only waited a short time before pleading once more.

Ralph traced outlines with one finger on the side of Daphne's thigh, careful that nobody could see him, though he quickly realised that no one was interested. The story they'd concocted about him being her uncle taking her to join the family in Greece was manifestly unnecessary in the face of this seething mass of people. They were merging like elements in a single organism, contained within the bus's tinny membrane.

The domineering mother offered slices of pie through the gap in the seats and Ralph thanked her so warmly that her face transformed into something almost attractive. Keep her sweet, he thought. If there's trouble from anyone it'd be from this Greek mama. Daphne took a small nibble and grimaced. 'Ugh. Spinach.' She looked like a toddler about to have a tantrum.

'Oh, eat your greens!' He gave her leg a small playful slap. 'Don't forget Popeye – you need your beautiful muscles.'

Daphne didn't let on that she spoke Greek, though she whispered translations of the absurd conversations that took place ahead of them. Over the next days they laughed heartlessly at the miseries of poor Yannakis ('Little John'), whose mother had come to collect him from university, not trusting him to make it alone. As the maternal humiliations continued, the boy sank progressively lower into his seat until he almost disappeared.

The passengers dispersed on to the ferry for the crossing to Calais and there was a new, more relaxed atmosphere when everyone returned to the bus at the port, like rejoining a party. Two young men across the aisle from them passed around a joint and Ralph took a quick drag, holding his breath to keep the smoke in, and then laughing and releasing it when Daphne held out her hand to take her turn.

'Just a tiny puff?' she wheedled, seeing his expression.

'No, Daff, I don't think so. You're too young.'

'OK, Uncle Ralph. You know best. And you set such a good example.'

'Oh go on then, but just a very little one.' She coughed before she could inhale properly and he quickly passed it back to the owner.

A couple who had been locked in furious embrace on the way to Dover lay down at the back of the aisle, covered themselves with a torn blanket and went for it, thrusting unashamedly as animals. The second driver was laid out snoring just above them on the back row of seats and didn't wake during the spectacle. Ralph veered between shock and curiosity. Initially, he tried to prevent Daphne from witnessing the scene, but when she eventually noticed, he was turned on by her avid attention to the eternal rhythms being played out, as they bowled along French provincial roads, the lines of trees creating strobe-like flashes.

Daphne went to sleep leaning against him as he stroked her hair. He was so alive, he was fizzing, his mind light, his body alert. Nothing about what they were doing was wrong; quite the reverse, it was as right as anything in the universe could be. Otherwise it wouldn't feel as if everything fitted together, as if the planets had all aligned and were beaming down on them alone. He realised that others might not understand their unusual relationship, but this only indicated that it could be added to the long list of literary and actual lovers who were forced into shadowy hiding places. There was only beauty in this thing that had engulfed them.

He woke to find himself comfortably slumped in her lap and was touched to observe that she'd placed a scarf under his head. Periodically, the battered bus stopped and they bought drinks and sandwiches and did jumping exercises to stretch their legs. Daphne accepted a cigarette from the 'copulating couple', as they'd named them, and stood smoking in the radiant red skies of the sunset, proud as a young lioness surveying her territory. He wanted her to stay like that – untameable and unconstrained by adult rules.

After dark, they cocooned themselves under a cotton blanket and he kissed her long and slow, stroking her until he groaned from frustration, his cock pressing painfully against his trousers. Daphne laughed, though he could tell she wanted more too. The bumping bus had a lulling quality to it and, at a certain point, Daphne appeared to tire of his tender attentions and pulled herself up the seat, removing his hand. What must it be like, he wondered, to be a female with the mysterious ability to be aroused and then grow tired of it? So different from boys, with our aim-and-fire simplicity, even when we are half-mad with love.

In Switzerland, he drank a beer, staring out at the looming, moonlit mountains. Daphne tasted her first cappuccino in northern Italy. In Yugoslavia they stopped at a roadside cafeteria outside Ljubljana that offered clean, spacious cloakrooms where they could wash. Beside the entrances to the men's and women's areas sat a beady-eyed crone under a framed portrait of Marshal Tito. She handed them a few pieces of lavatory paper each and Ralph gave her some small change. He washed using a lump of hard soap and dried himself by putting his shirt back on.

After their passports were inspected at the Greek border and the bus was waved through, there was a subdued cheer from the passengers, despite the fact that it was dawn and they had now been on the road for three days. A camaraderie had grown up amongst this disparate collection of people; they had seen each other sleeping and singing, eating and vomiting, quarrelling and kissing. Ralph and Daphne had sometimes spoken to their fellow travellers, but nobody quizzed them about their relationship or what they were doing there. Their cover story had been redundant. Ralph took photographs in the soft morning light, adding to his collection of Daphne asleep, Daphne with sunbeams in her hair, Daphne looking directly, provocatively into his lens. 'I'm your slave,' he told her. 'I would do whatever you tell me to.' She mocked him, 'OK, slave, jump off the bus,' but he saw her receive and comprehend his obeisance.

It was abominably hot in Athens and the bus station stank of exhaust fumes and roasting meat. The hippies, students, and even the Greek mother and her son, looked like refugees leaving a boat after a long voyage. They staggered slightly, as though their sea legs couldn't adjust to dry land and peered around in bewilderment. Ralph felt exhausted and suggested they take a taxi to their hotel. Daphne gave the address to the driver, who drove frighteningly fast, swerving to avoid dogs and pedestrians and jumping red lights. The small hotel in Plaka was like a sanctuary, with its dark, cool reception hall and chlorine-mopped floor and an uncurious young man, who checked them into a twin room on the top floor. From their tiny balcony, a section of the Acropolis was visible between two neighbouring buildings. They pushed the single beds together, turned on the ceiling fan, closed the shutters and collapsed on to the coarse white sheets, plummeting instantly into magnificent sleep.

When he woke it was almost dark. Daphne was reading a book – he couldn't see whether it was *David Copperfield* or *The Exorcist*, both of which she'd brought in her pack (his ambitious choice of *The Idiot* remained almost untouched at the bottom of his luggage). She had evidently taken a shower as her hair hung in damp curls and she was wearing a pair of utilitarian white underpants (her 'no-entry knickers', he teased) beneath a disintegrating Victorian lace camisole. She smiled at him. 'I'm starving. Are you going to have a shower? Then we can go out and eat.' There was a dingy bathroom along the corridor with a temperamental supply of water, but he returned from his cold shower renewed. He felt like a demigod – like Odysseus after he had bathed in a river and anointed himself with oil. Ready to fight or to fall in love with a sorceress.

The streets were crowded with people strolling slowly and they adopted the pace, ambling without a destination. The day's burning heat had transformed into something gentler, though the paving stones and walls were still releasing their absorbed warmth into the cooler night air. They chose a small restaurant on the lower slopes of the Acropolis, and Daphne translated the waiter's instructions to go through to the kitchen to look at the food. After some deliberation, they ordered stuffed tomatoes, fried calamari and some boiled bitter greens. The waiter brought retsina from the barrel in a tin jug, the yellow liquid pungently resinous and redolent of sun-warmed pine forests and petrol cans. 'It improves with each sip,' said Ralph, wincing.

Daphne drank some wine too, and on the way back to the hotel he watched her weaving to and fro across the narrow roads as if following her own invisible path. He admired her swaying, narrow-hipped figure and the muscular lightness of her limbs. She reminded him of a young leopard that was no longer a cub but hadn't yet acquired the weight and bulk of an adult – poised at a fleeting yet perfect point. His pursuit of her and their union had the power of one of nature's wonders, like salmon swimming upstream against the crashing river or birds flying thousands of miles. These things appear impossible, but they are not.

His hope was that this trip would be the opportunity for them to make love for the first time, but he suspected that tonight was not the night. It would be hard to summon the requisite patience he presumed this operation would require – not that he was highly experienced in deflowering virgins. He certainly didn't believe in the sanctity of the maidenhead, but the prospect was daunting in its way. Loving Daphne enabled him to share experiences that were brand new – bright, shiny, unsullied – and this was intoxicating. It was like a return to his own youth and initiations. First orgasm, first travel abroad without parents, first time with a girl. Three days of messing around together on the bus had left him urgently in need of resolution, even if there had been a quick solitary wank in an unappealing lavatory in southern Yugoslavia.

Back in their room, she looked shy as though avoiding a moment of reckoning. She was often awkward before they began anything sexual and, to distract from this, he picked her up and bounced her like a bundle on to one of the beds. Tickling sometimes proved the way in, but today that didn't seem necessary and he entwined himself in her smooth boy's legs and drew her close. He pulled off her clothes and examined her breasts before he licked them – so recently swelled out of flatness, like an illusion. She didn't resist when he removed her knickers. He rubbed his cock against her thigh, hoping she'd remember how he showed her. Her beloved monkey hands, so pretty, with their bitten nails and adorned with silver rings, sent him into a delirium. He realised it was selfish, but he allowed himself to forget about anything apart from speeding towards a final ecstasy. Nothing else mattered – not even Daphne.

When he opened his eyes, she was sitting upright, dark tresses around her face, cheeks prettily pink and an analytical expression as she examined the white spill rolling down her hands and dripping on to the bed. He clutched her wrist and smiled gratefully. 'God, you're lovely! I was like a volcano. Vesuvius erupting.' Later, 'Vesuvius' became another word for their private lexicon. He lay back and heard her get up and leave the room, presumably to go to the bathroom. Before she returned, he had sunk to the ocean floor of sleep.

5

DAPHNE

A luminous spring morning drenched the dull rows of semi-detached Edwardian houses in a rosy blush. Although she didn't look forward to work, she enjoyed cycling there along the quiet back roads. There was enough of the incredible in her daily routines to make her thankful. She even appreciated school mornings with Libby, when she stumbled around in a muddle, attempting fruitlessly to assist her methodical daughter. For so long she had lived in dread of the unknown disaster that was sure to be lurking like a mugger around the next corner. In the past, tranquillity itself was a trigger for anxiety. So much did she expect disasters to befall her that she walked under ladders and stepped into roaring traffic, as if that would confuse vengeful gods. That was before Libby. Now, she admired the blossom in modest front gardens, inhaled the damp city air, pedalled hard and gave thanks.

She arrived at work energised and warm. Locking up her bike, she waved at some drivers standing outside the minicab company on the other side of the road. Jelly was already in and, as Daphne came through the door, mouthed 'Morning' from her desk where she was making a phone call. 'Good morning, Angelica Frank here from Hellenic Heaven.' They had a loyal, if ageing clientele who appreciated the 'bespoke' touch when searching for villas or cruises in the Ionian Islands. None of them would guess that this groomed professional with strawberry-blonde curls, azure eyes and perfect skin had once had a ferocious heroin habit. And they would certainly not imagine that Daphne had originally been Jelly's sponsor at a Hackney branch of NA. They had spent some long, testing nights together.

Computer on, shuffle some papers, listen to phone messages. She did all this without thinking and forgot to write down the details of the messages. It was hard to summon any enthusiasm. As soon as Jelly was off the phone, she'd give Daphne a list of tedious tasks. There was just time for a quick message to Jane.

Good morning, Janey

Thank you for taking the risk and coming. I loved seeing you again after so long. I feel we have so much to say. Shall we concoct a plan?

Lots of love, D

This burgeoning friendship looked full of promise to her, as though their distant past gave it extra heft and value. Over the years, she had fallen out of touch with a number of friends, especially after Libby was born, and while she'd once been close to Jelly, the daily grind of following her orders at work had eroded that. Given Daphne's potential for calamity, she had to admit she did pretty well out of the agency, even if it was dull as congealed porridge. Her boredom sometimes had the urgency of an unbearable itch, but she usually had some sewing squirreled away in her bag. Today, there were some small pieces of fabric to stitch in quiet moments – yellow, silken sunrays, which would pierce the clouds in *Putney*.

'See if you can sort out our listings for Corfu and Paxos today, OK? We need to know if the Thalassa apartments are going to be available.' Jelly was striding about in heeled boots. 'We've already got so many bookings there, you're definitely going to have to be around as back-up.' Apart from a salary, Hell provided another advantage. Each summer she spent several weeks in an unused flat or even a small villa, so as to be on-hand for clients. Libby went along too. They had fun, even if morning beach trips and afternoon siestas were liable to be interrupted by someone calling about a septic tank overflowing. There were occasional disasters that required the police and even the British Consulate in Athens – an elderly woman who had died on a yacht or a husband who had scarpered. Daphne had heard Libby tell Chloe that she had already lived in seven different homes around London by the time she was twelve, not to mention dozens of places in Greece in the summer. Well, nothing wrong with seeing a bit of the world.

It was during recent Hell-subsidised, 'working' summers that Daphne realised she had completely recovered from Constantine. She no longer broke into a feverish cold sweat when she thought of him. Memories of his cruelty no longer gripped her like migraines. She gradually regained her affection for Greece from before her marriage, and a couple of times she and Libby went to Aegina to stay with one of her three maternal aunts who had taken over the family's holiday house.

Occasionally, the secret trip with Ralph would flash into her mind, provoking a physical quiver of excitement.

After their Greek journey, he had written *Ithaka*, a piece for orchestra and six bouzoukis. It was based on their time together, he said. On the sense he'd had of arriving home when they got to the island – like Odysseus after his long voyage. It was all about his longing for her. 'I couldn't call it *Daphne on Aegina*,' he laughed. 'But that's what it is.' He and his music were part of her. The notes had fused with her growing body. Travelling to Greece with him was also something that had formed her. It was internalised, essential as bone marrow.

* * *

The early-morning sun was already turning savage as the taxi hared down Syngrou Avenue towards the silver glare of the sea. Ralph held her hand, tracing patterns and beating gentle rhythms she imagined were some tune he was remembering or creating. A lack of breakfast and the smoke from the driver's cigarette were making her queasy and she was nervous at the potential for mishap in the plot to use her grandmother's house on Aegina.

They tried to get the story straight in case her relations got in touch: they would say that Jane had been travelling with them on the Magic Bus and had left to join her family in Corfu. Daphne had rung *Yiayia* from London. They still weren't quite sure of the dates, she told her, but would it be all right if the three of them went to Aegina? It would be for a couple of days. *Yiayia* was unconcerned. 'Just contact *kyria* Lemonia and she'll leave a key under the stone.' She herself would be in Crete with relations and would see Daphne later in August. They were all to meet up on Poros, where Aunt Athena, the oldest of Ellie's three sisters, had a house. Daphne experienced a mix of guilt, dread and pride from her involvement in this web of deception and adultery. She wondered whether it *was* technically adultery. If not, it probably soon would be.

It was still before eight when they reached the port at Piraeus and their ferry was not due to leave for half an hour. A salty breeze brought whiffs of ship's fuel and rotting rubbish, but even the less appealing odours summoned memories of other summer departures and expanded Daphne's spirit. This time, the familiar anticipation of sea travel was combined with the dangerous elements of love and desire – a new game of joy and pain that was so intense it sometimes frightened her.

They sat on a bench under a dusty tree, legs pressed together, and she looked at him, wondering if she could ask what would become of them. She longed to discuss this incredible thing that was happening, but Ralph never tried to analyse their relationship. There was no attempt to put it within a larger context or make sense of it. They just existed. The secrecy and the lack of vocabulary to describe what they were doing made it all the more powerful, as if the concentrated emotions were never diluted by being spoken about or revealed. Even Jane (the only person who knew something) was hardly sympathetic to the subject and Daphne avoided confessing more than necessary.

Daphne bought *koulouria* from an old man standing unsteadily by his barrow and they ate them, shedding crumbs and sesame seeds on their clothes. A dusty, mustard-coloured dog dragged itself over and sat staring at them, close enough to be obvious, but far enough away that it couldn't be kicked. She threw pieces to their observer, which caught each one with an accurate snap and trembled with anticipation for the next. A couple of itinerant salesmen meandered up touting cheap sunglasses and plastic cigarette lighters in unusual shapes. Daphne copied her mother's reaction by holding up a hand, raising her eyebrows and making the 'Tsssst' sound for 'No'. Surprisingly, it worked and they drifted away.

After being allowed to board, they established themselves on the ferry's upper deck, placing their belongings under a slatted bench and spreading out along its length. Seagulls looped and flicked between the two blues of sea and sky. On leaving the port, the ferry let out a large hoot and Daphne screamed, nuzzling into Ralph's side, holding on in mock terror longer than the real fright lasted. She wanted to be engulfed, swallowed up, to never let go. It hurt, even if she would not admit that to him.

The years of easy friendship had transformed with shocking rapidity into love. A couple of months before her thirteenth birthday, she woke up and said aloud to herself, 'I'm in love.' Almost like a decision or a spell. Of course, she loved him before that. But this overwhelming emotion that dominated everything else and coloured each moment was only six months old. Desire thrashed about blindly – powerful and chaotic as a bull escaped from the arena. These were longings she didn't know how to control or follow through.

Ralph said he'd search out some coffee and she pulled her diary from her bag. She made at least one entry each day in the blue hardback notebook from Smith's, decorated in biro with skull and crossbones and threats of revenge to snoopers. As she flicked through pages covered in doodles and drawings she pondered how to write about 'Vesuvius' without it sounding disgusting. She momentarily recalled the flasher who opened his coat as she walked along Barnabas Road one afternoon when she had just started at Hayfield. It had been her first sight of an erect penis, emerging like an angry, red animal from the man's trousers and pointing its bald head at her.

Thinking back to Ralph's orgasm, she realised she was not sure whether she had ever had one herself. How exactly could you tell? It was clear that she could be engulfed by longing. At times, this was so powerful that everything else became irrelevant and annoying – mosquitoes distracting from the only thing that mattered. The world shrank, so only she and Ralph existed and all she needed was his embrace – hot breath, deep kisses, his weight pressed against her. Nothing else. However, when it came down to her own body's mechanics, she was less clear. She had read about women 'coming', about vaginal spasms, but this wasn't something she had discussed with anyone. Ralph didn't provide words for what they did together.

He returned carrying a plastic cup of Nescafé, a carton of Choco Milk for her and two toasted sandwiches.

'My God, food tastes good when you're at sea.' He ate fast, standing on the lower rung of the rails, looking out towards the distant outline of the island with its pointed mountain. She nibbled at the melted cheese and ham, leaving the crusts, and watching him. He moved constantly, giving the impression of an impatient boy, and she fantasised about how perfect everything would be if they were the same age, if she could fast-forward into womanhood or he could rewind to youth. Sometimes, especially when the pressure of secrecy and pretence was overwhelming, she longed to be a girl with a normal boyfriend. The previous evening, walking through Plaka, she had felt almost a physical ache from wanting to hold his hand and from refraining for fear it would not look right. If only Ralph was seventeen, she thought, picturing them as a carefree couple that could walk arm-in-arm along the street.

The salty sandwich and rich chocolate milk battled inside Daphne's gut, resulting in an urgent need to find a toilet. She walked off casually, without explaining anything to Ralph, preferring to pretend she existed in a world free of excretion and, above all, menstruation. She had already decided never to mention her periods to him. The previous year, some time after the leafy bower, they had pricked their fingers with a needle and smeared the red drops together, swearing allegiance and eternal friendship. Afterwards, he sucked her finger clean and kissed it. 'Everything about you is perfect,' he said. 'Even your blood. You know, I can be quite squeamish about it – with other people. Especially, you know, women's ...' He didn't finish his sentence and, still premenstrual, Daphne felt mildly superior to the bleeding females who revolted him. Six months ago, she had joined their number and now dreaded provoking his disgust.

The rise and fall of the ship on the swell was more apparent inside the cramped toilets, which smelled of engines and gloss paint. One of the two cubicles was occupied and, as Daphne locked the door and sat down, she heard a long fart followed by a stream of piss. The edge of a polished shoe was visible under the cubicle division. She froze in awkwardness at the intimacy, but there was no way to be genteel about diarrhoea. Her intestines writhed and cramped as they expelled their watery contents. She delayed emerging, hoping the other woman would depart, listening to the unhurried washing of hands, unzipping of handbag, clicking as lipstick or powder was opened and shut. Eventually, bored of hanging around, Daphne came out as a stout, elderly woman turned away from the basins to leave.

'Daphnoula?' Daphne understood the query in *kyria* Frosso's voice. Seeing her own reflection in the mirror demonstrated to Daphne how she'd changed since they'd last met: smudged eyeliner, skimpy top with no bra, ripped shorts and mismatched earrings. *Kyria* Frosso looked her up and down. Last time, Daphne had been a child. Now she definitely was not. Frosso was a friend of her grandmother's – top-heavy, with a platform of a bust encased in a short-sleeved summer suit.

'Daphne *mou*. Unbelievable. How are you? Are you here with your *Manoula*? Your brother? Oh how lovely.'

'Um, no, they're all abroad.' To give herself time to think, she listed the disparate places where each member of her family was located. But the old woman was not distracted by the mention of Germany, France and Scotland, and Daphne knew she must explain why she was travelling alone with a man. 'I've just come out to Greece with my schoolfriend Jane, and we were brought by an English uncle. He's here on the boat. And then I'm going to my aunt's place. And my grandmother is coming. Oh, and Jane is coming to Aegina on the next boat.' She felt ashamed to be gabbling and creating traps for herself. *Kyria* Frosso looked amiably puzzled. 'Well that's very nice. Won't you introduce me to your uncle?'

They progressed slowly along the deck, *kyria* Frosso's shiny shoes clicking on the boards. Ralph was stretched out on the bench. His blue espadrilles off, he was rotating his feet as he jotted something down in his 'ideas book'. He didn't notice them until Daphne coughed and then quickly repeated her series of lies to 'Uncle Ralph', to put him in the picture. He jumped up and, taking *kyria* Frosso's plump hand, kissed it. 'Delighted to meet you, madam.'

'And I am,' she beamed.

Unfortunately, she had enough English to be able to limp along in a conversation with him. He got in first: 'Don't you find being at sea is one of the greatest pleasures in life? But here, in the most beautiful country in the world, it's like heaven.'

'So, you Daphne's uncle?'

'Well, my wife is Greek and she's practically a cousin of Ellie's, so yes, I'm her uncle. I'm joining my wife after I leave young Daphne here with her relations.' He said it quickly, evidently hoping to lose his inquisitor's concentration somewhere along the way, and turned to give Daphne a conspiratorial wink. 'Now, you must tell me about Aegina. I'm sure you know the very best places to visit. The Temple of Aphaia must be first, no?' He gazed into *kyria* Frosso's face and Daphne saw how easily he had taken the focus away from the conspiracy and how the ageing lady became almost coquettish.

'A real English *tzentelman*,' she confirmed to Daphne in Greek, before returning to her companions.

Daphne was left feeling exposed and shamed. It had been bad enough having to shit so close to someone else, but to find that it was *kyria* Frosso turned her stomach in a different way. Ralph was more sanguine. 'Don't fret. Just believe in your story when you're with her and she'll believe it too. It works!' They delayed disembarking, hoping to preclude another encounter, but Frosso and two portly friends were moving so slowly that they passed them on the long jetty. *Kyria* Frosso gave an amicable wave and called, 'Be seeing you.' But Daphne noticed a narrowing of her eyes, as though the old woman was doing sums in her head.

It was less than five minutes' walk to the house, starting out along the port with its ouzo cafés.

'Like hanging out the washing,' said Daphne, gesturing towards the purple octopuses draped on lines, their dangling tentacles stiffening in the sunshine.

'Rather a macabre load of laundry they've done today. Though I can see you in an octopus bikini …'

They passed the tourist shops crammed with mocked-up ancient relics and silver jewellery, and along one of the cobbled alleys by the fish market, with its piles of small, reeking corpses. She had known these streets since babyhood and now feared it was wrong to come here with Ralph. People would recognise her or Frosso would call her grandmother. All this subterfuge was exhausting. She was hot and bothered and annoyed with the whole world and this was exacerbated by her savage hunger for Ralph. She could hardly wait to tumble into their private darkness.

Her grandmother's house was an elegant, neoclassical building painted creamy ochre with dark green shutters and terracotta roof tiles. As arranged, the keys were hidden under a stone between pots of geraniums and she opened an imposing green door that led into the courtyard.

'Christ, that's lovely.' Ralph dropped the bags on to the honey-coloured stone paving and she watched him take in a place that was so familiar she hardly saw its beauty — lemon trees, scented jasmine plants and the marble table beneath a vine canopy where they always ate in the summer. He walked past the well in the corner and then hurried up the stone staircase to inspect the loggia draped with shocking-pink bougainvillea. *Kyria* Lemonia had evidently prepared for them as there were cushions on the chairs and everything was immaculate.

'It's so private and secluded,' Ralph marvelled as he came down. 'You come in off the street and there's another world, like a secret garden. Nobody can see you here.' He took off his sweaty shirt and ran across to the tap in the corner, dipping his head under the cold water. 'Aah, that's better. You should try it, Daff.' She couldn't help being infected by his good mood. He shook his head like a dog after a bath, scattering droplets around him, and she removed her top too, taking his place at the tap and yelping with delight as the cold water hit her scalp and splashed over her body.

Dressed only in her shorts and still dripping, Daphne used a second, ancient-looking key to enter the house. The hallway was shady and cool and smelled of polish. A pale-skinned gecko raced up the wall on Spiderman-sticky feet. Ralph came up behind her, putting a hand on her bare shoulder.

'Now, sir, let me show you the accommodation,' she said in estate-agent tones. 'Here on the right, the *saloni*. Only for special occasions.' The dark room was cluttered with uncomfortable-looking chairs and glass-fronted cases of ornaments, its heavy mahogany sideboards topped with lacy cloths. 'And over here the dining room.' More mahogany and lace was visible in the dim light. 'And the kitchen.' She unlocked a door giving on to another small, more workaday courtyard and opened the green shutters, letting in a dazzle of sunshine. On the table was a baking tray filled with a sweet pastry, and she got out plates and small forks as her grandmother did, and poured two glasses of chilled water from a bottle in the fridge.

They sat shirtless at the scrubbed wooden table and ate two pieces each of the *galaktoboureko*, the syrup-laden custard pie slipping down like nectar. Ralph gulped a whole glass of water and leaned across the table to kiss her lips.

'We did it, eh Daff? I can't believe we've actually arrived. We're completely free. We can do anything. Nobody knows where we are.'

'Apart from fat Frosso.'

'Well that's nothing to worry about. Anyway, your grandmother knows you might stay. It's all OK.'

'Won't Nina wonder where you are?' Daphne wasn't sure if she should mention Ralph's wife, but curiosity won the battle with discretion.

'No. She's fine. There isn't a problem.' His breezy reply didn't satisfy.

'Do you think she knows? About me? Isn't she jealous?'

'What?' He didn't look pleased and, with greater emphasis than was necessary, repeated his earlier response. 'No!'

'No, she isn't jealous or no, she doesn't know?'

'Both. Neither. It's not an issue.'

Daphne didn't show her discomfort and pretended, even to herself, that she didn't feel any. Why should she? she reasoned. She didn't own him? But she couldn't help wondering what would happen to her and Ralph if Nina disappeared or died. Perhaps they would live together when she was old enough? Even get married?

'Nina knows I'd never leave her. She's happy. It's all fine.' Ralph jumped up as a physical method of changing the subject. He liked to keep a well-defined space between his wife and his special friend and he looked uncomfortable. 'Why don't you finish showing me around? Where will we sleep?'

She felt like an obedient dog dropping a bone and she led him upstairs to the landing that opened at one end on to the loggia. There were three bedrooms.

'This is *Yiayia* and *Pappou*'s room.' She held the door but didn't go in. There was no way they'd use this room filled with the framed and unsmiling faces of generations of family members wearing their best clothes in photographic studios. It seemed to retain *Yiayia*'s perfume. 'Then there's this room with a double bed, where Ellie and Ed usually go, and the one at the back there with two single beds, where me and Theo sleep.'

The clock from a nearby church struck so forcefully they both jumped, then as the chimes continued to mark eleven, they smiled with relief.

'I'll put my bag in my usual room and mess up both single beds so it looks like Jane and me slept there. Let's put your stuff in the double room.'

She suddenly felt timid and young with this talk of beds. Her overwhelming wish was to be entwined with Ralph, but she hated the time before it happened, the stark light that made it seem calculated. Having a drink or being in the dark often simplified the process. She hadn't worked out how to make the awkward transfer from the ordinary world into the other one of sex, of becoming those different people.

They decided to go swimming and bought a picnic of bread, cheese, olives and white peaches. Walking away from the port, they passed the sandy beach and the ruined Temple of Apollo, with its single, slim column sticking up on the headland. They continued along the coast road until they reached some steps leading down a steep slope to a rocky beach. Skirting a few bathers who were preparing to leave, they took over a small section at the far end, made private by some large, russet-coloured boulders.

'Bliss,' said Ralph, as they placed their towels and bags down and changed into bathing costumes. The stones burned her feet as she scampered into water so cool and refreshing it was almost effervescent. Ralph whooped from happiness and she imitated him, feeling wild as a sea wolf. She swam out as fast as she could, only stopping when she ran out of breath. He was still floating near the shore and waved. The sea had transformed her from sulky teenager to woman in love.

She stayed in the sea long after he got out, diving down to pick up curvy, mother-of-pearl shells, turning underwater somersaults and basking in weightlessness. Afterwards, she lay flat on her towel as the sun burned the water off her back and the salt tightened her skin. It was the first time she'd consciously felt beautiful, as if she had become what he saw. Out of the corner of her eye she watched Ralph pull food out of the knapsack and use a penknife to slice hunks of bread and cheese. They ate in silence, looking out to sea, throwing the olive pits as far as they could. The peaches made such a mess that they went back into the sea to clean off. Then, finding a shady area amongst the pines and eucalyptus trees, they slept with T-shirts over their heads.

When they woke, they shared Ralph's last Gauloise and he licked her salty shoulder. 'You could make a scent called Summer Beach,' she said, listing the ingredients: 'seawater, hot pine trees, suntan oil. And a tiny bit of cigarette smoke.'

'Genius girl. We should do it and become millionaires. Imagine a bottle of that in London in February. People would die for it.'

On the way home, Ralph bought some vegetables, using Daphne as his interpreter.

'I love hearing you speak Greek here. It's so different to when you do it in London. You make sense as a part of this place.'

'He's my English uncle,' explained Daphne to the curious greengrocer, *kyrios* Kostas, who made deliveries to her grandmother's house and knew the whole family. 'My aunt's at home with the baby.' Daphne wasn't sure how far to go with the lies; it was easy to get caught out on an island. And *kyrios* Kostas did start asking about the baby, and how long they were staying, and was the aunt English too, until Daphne changed the subject by requesting bunches of spearmint, dill and parsley as Ellie always did for a green salad. He went out to the back to fetch them from the coolroom.

'Maybe it wasn't such a good idea coming here,' she said. 'We should have gone somewhere nobody knows us. I hate all this.'

After they showered, Ralph made them both tea.

'Tea! In this heat? Ach, thees Inglees *tzentelman* must have his cup of tea,' Daphne teased in a Greek accent, echoing Frosso's remark.

'It's the most refreshing thing when the weather's hot. Surely you know that? You greasy little Greek!' Daphne threw a glassful of water at Ralph's head in retaliation for the insult and squealed as he yelled and chased her in mock anger. Racing up the steps to the loggia she felt a stab of actual fear, as though her pursuer wasn't the man she knew, but an attacker. She made it to the upstairs landing and ran into her grandparents' room, locking the door and leaning against it, heart drumming. Hot tears slipped from her eyes.

'Little pig, little pig, let me come in. Or I'll huff and I'll puff and I'll blow your house in,' Ralph called. She didn't answer and tried to smile, but it still didn't feel like fun.

'Fuck off, Wolf! You can't come in, not by the hairs on my chinny chin chin.'

'Just a little kiss for your wolf?'

'No!' Her voice wobbled and, after the briefest pause, he said, 'OK, my lovely little piglet. You win. I'll see you downstairs. I'm going to prepare supper.'

She mooched around the room, picking objects off her grandmother's dressing table, examining boxes, bottles, hairpins and tweezers and sniffing the rosewater and cold cream. The wardrobe smelled of mothballs when she opened it, and she slid the clothes along the rail, finger-ing the old jackets and slithery dresses. She recognised the housedress in blue and white sprigged cotton, worn so thin it was delicate as muslin. Removing it from the hanger, she took it into her bedroom and tried it on. As she did up the buttons and felt the fabric skim her ankles, there was a peculiar transformation, as though she was leaving behind the vulnerable, fearful girl and becoming a confi-dent woman. She decided not to go down for a while, but to stay in her room and write.

It was clear to her that tonight was likely to be the night they would make love. He had shown her the packet of 'French letters' in his rucksack and, though she approved of the plan, she was nervous about going through with it. She was spilling over with emotion and desire, but it was definitely 'weird', as she wrote. There was such a fuss about 'losing' your virginity, but where did it go? Why are you one moment 'intact' and the next penetrated, pierced, different for evermore? And would it hurt? she wondered. More than almost anything, she hated the idea that there would be blood, especially given Ralph's fastidiousness. She pictured his expression of revulsion when confronted with the gory flow produced by a punctured hymen. Would it pour out? It all sounded so medical.

For a brief moment, she felt out of her depth and wanted her mother. She pictured Ellie's strong, tanned arms holding her tight, her comforting maternal smell and the things they would talk about if they did that sort of thing. It was true that Ellie had always been open with her about sex: 'You can ask me anything you like,' she'd said when Daphne was curious about the subject as a young child. But although she asked her mother a few questions, they'd never had a serious discussion. She didn't know what Ellie thought about the value of virginity, let alone what she would advise her to do – or not do – that night. It would probably be her usual recommendation (in Greek) to 'Find your own road.'

When she reappeared downstairs, she was wearing her grandmother's old dress. It was much too large for her, but she'd tied it with a belt and had wound a silky scarf around her head. She'd also found an ancient lipstick and her lips were a provocative, pillar-box red.

'So who are you now, my darling Daff?' he laughed. He was in his element in the kitchen. A bottle of red wine was open and he was chopping onions and herbs and singing something very uncatchy. Daphne poured herself some wine and took a couple of large gulps.

'Steady on, old girl,' he said in the tones of a bumbling military man.

'OK, Sergeant.' She reached for a cigarette from the packet of Karelia they'd bought at the kiosk, and sat on the edge of the table, enjoying the rush.

The alcohol and nicotine transported her somewhere away from fear and broke the anxious chains of inexperience. They allowed her to stop observing.

Ralph didn't comment and continued with his cooking, throwing together an omelette, jazzy with tomato, green pepper and feta. When he had dressed the herb-filled salad with olive oil and lemon, they carried the meal into the courtyard. She made the marble table pretty, lighting candles and bringing out her grandmother's white napkins; then, sitting opposite each other, they clinked glasses. His face was the most beloved thing in the world. The air thrummed with a shrill cicada buzz and was heavy with jasmine.

The evening cooled and quietened, despite the rhythmic thudding of an open-air disco in the distance.

'The cicadas are going to bed,' said Ralph. He rose, drained his wine glass and, like a prince in a fairy story, stood humbly before her, holding out his hand until she took it. He helped her get up and, holding on to her waist, led her into the house and up the stairs. She was drunk enough to be relaxed and sober enough to be glad the lights were off. The moon lit their way into the bedroom.

She sat on the edge of the bed, the crocheted cover lumpy under her legs, and observed Ralph as he unbuttoned her borrowed dress and kissed her breasts.

'I want you so much.' He looked directly at her. 'Do you still want to?' She nodded and he delayed tactfully, before digging out the dreaded packet and placing it on the bedside table. They continued kissing and he put her hand on his cock. 'Like that.' When he ripped open the wrapping and started rolling on the condom, it was as though he was masking a strange animal. Fascinating but bewildering. He climbed on top of her and pushed between her open legs. 'I don't want to hurt you.' She didn't reply. More pushing against something that felt closed.

After a few minutes of stubbing himself hopelessly against an impassable door, Ralph groaned and rolled off, peeling away the sticky layer of rubber.

'I can't stand this awful thing,' he said, flinging the offending item on to the floor. 'I love you, Daff.' She felt a failure. This prospect was worse than the discomfort she had experienced and it was miserable to leave it like this. She put her arm across his chest, moving her body against his, and then laid herself on top of him. This provoked a sudden change of tempo. He flipped her over and, with new determination, entered her.

It hurt but she didn't make a noise.

'I'll be careful,' he whispered, moving more gently now he was inside. She gripped his shoulders.

'You OK?'

'Mm.'

'Should I stop?'

She shook her head. It felt strange, this big thing right inside her. Big but fine. She observed the scene as though from above, pleased but detached, noting the intensity of Ralph's pleasure. His mouth pressed against hers and then, 'Christ ...' He arched upwards. 'Daphne, I ...' The sentence never finished. He pulled out and made a noise that sounded like disappointment or pain, but was obviously Vesuvius.

'Oh my God!' He exhaled as though shocked by what they'd done. 'Are you all right?'

'Yeah.' She looked at him, but he was already retreating. 'You?'

'Unbelievably, incredibly, blissfully well.' His breathing slowed as he lay beside her and before long he was asleep. So there we are, she thought. I did it. It's lost. That's good.

The bedroom window was open and through the slatted green shutters she could still hear the far-off disco beat throbbing in the darkness. It took her ages to get to sleep but she didn't mind. It was an unusual luxury to spend the night in a bed with him. She put her arm across his chest and, pushing up close, smelled soap and sweat from his armpit, the warm, vanilla skin of his neck and the animal fur of his hair.

When she woke, the bedroom was striped with bright daylight slicing through the gaps in the shutters. Ralph wasn't there. Crouching motionless on the floor was a grasshopper, the size of a well-nourished mouse. It was a similar non-committal yellow to the shrivelled rubber that lay next to it. Ralph came into the room, a towel wrapped around him like a loincloth.

'You OK, Daff?'

She smiled but didn't reply, following his gaze to a dried bloodstain on the sheet. It was uncomfortable to see this evidence – exposing.

'Oh! Oh dear.' She got up, pulling bedclothes over the offending area. 'No. Yes, I'm fine.' She pointed at the large, spiky insect. 'But what about him?'

'Christ, it's a monster.' He leaped up on to the mattress next to her and, as if in response, the armoured creature moved towards them unhurriedly but efficiently as a mechanical toy, and ratcheted itself up the cast-iron bed leg. Daphne screamed.

'I'll get a broom from the kitchen,' he said and ran out.

While he was gone, she quickly pulled the dirty sheet off and took it with her to the bathroom, holding the bloodied part under the tap. She scrubbed at it but a mark remained – a faded brownish proof of the night before. It reminded her of Bluebeard's wife with the bloody key, rubbing sand in desperation, unable to remove the red evidence that would betray her curiosity about the forbidden rooms. She half-filled the bath with water and threw in the whole sheet. The previous summer, Evgenia, her older girl cousin, had described the tradition of hanging the bridal sheet from a balcony the morning after the nuptial deflowering. 'The whole village would come to take a look. Frightful.'

When she returned, Ralph was sitting on the bed, holding the broom, triumphant as St George with his spear, having just killed the dragon. 'That took some doing,' he said proudly. 'He refused to die. He leaped from the bed right up on to the wardrobe. But I got him in the end.'

'Where did you put it?' She didn't want to see the yellow corpse and noted that the rubber Johnny was gone too.

'Straight out of the window and into the bushes.' He smiled heroically. 'Right, I'm off to get breakfast going.'

When she joined him in the kitchen he had already made coffee and was slicing a melon. 'My darling girl. Come here.' He gripped her shoulders in an almost avuncular way, kissing her forehead as if anointing the non-virgin.

'Do I look different?' She laughed.

'Transformed by love. More exquisite than ever.'

The coffee was strong and she struggled to drink it, even with dollops of Nounou evaporated milk. In truth, she hated coffee, but she viewed the habit as a challenge, believing that if she was able to smoke and drink alcohol, not to mention doing what she liked with a man, then surely coffee should not confound her. It was shaming to drink milk for breakfast at her age. She wanted to be the sort of person who needed the dark, poisonous-tasting liquid first thing in the morning, perhaps with a cigarette; someone like her mother.

As she gave up on the coffee and spread honey on a slice of bread, the house telephone rang, loud and improbable. They looked at one another puzzled, then alarmed, as though they'd been caught.

'Don't answer. It's probably for your grandmother.' Sure enough the ringing stopped and they continued their breakfast. It wasn't long, however, before there was a knock at the door and a woman's voice calling for Daphne.

'Fuck, shit, bugger, wanker!'

Daphne managed a smile. 'I think it's *kyria* Lemonia.'

'Bloody bastard, bollocks, cunt, arse,' Ralph continued with a grimace.

'What shall we do?' She was tempted to ignore this intrusion, to sneak upstairs and hide until it was over. Perhaps her grandmother's housekeeper would leave. The knocking continued and the strident voice was clearly audible. 'Daphnoula, I need to speak to you.' By the time Daphne had traipsed into the courtyard towards the door, *kyria* Lemonia was letting herself in; she must have had a spare key.

'Ah, thank goodness, praise the Lord.' She crossed herself three times, resting a weathered hand on her chest. 'I didn't know what I'd do.' She sniffed and wiped a tear away, smoothing hair that was pulled into a tight, grey bun.

Daphne waited, observing the wiry-framed woman she'd known all her life. 'Is something wrong?'

'Ah, my sweet.' She came towards her and took Daphne's hand. 'Condolences, my dear. Your beloved *Pappou* has died. Life to you. May we remember him.'

Daphne's first reaction was relief that it wasn't something worse; her grandfather had been unwell for as long as she could remember. Poor old *Pappou*, with his lopsided face, tear-leaking eyes and sluggish drawl that mangled words. She was always impressed that he'd been born in the last year of the nineteenth century. So he was seventy-seven. It was sad, but not a disaster. However, no words came, as if she was hollowed out and struck dumb. *Kyria* Lemonia embraced her and then held her at arm's length. 'He was an honourable man.'

Daphne wondered how she could keep Ralph out of this, but the chill of planning how to explain what she and her lover were doing on Aegina was quickly supplanted by a hot rush of guilt at her heartlessness.

'You must sit down. You've gone pale. Let's go inside.' The bird-like old woman put her arm around Daphne and led her through to the kitchen, helping her to a chair. Ralph stood up, but despite his best efforts it was apparent that *kyria* Lemonia was nonplussed to find a half-naked man taking breakfast with young Daphnoula.

'*Kalimera*,' she said without a smile.

'Good morning,' he replied.

'And your other friend? Is she here?' she said in Greek.

Daphne suspected that everyone on Aegina already knew there wasn't another person with them – this was a small island. 'No. My friend Jane had to go. This is my uncle.' She turned to Ralph. 'My grandfather died.'

'Oh!' He stood rooted, awkward, unable to come to her. 'I'm so sorry.' By now, Daphne was crying. He knows we're in deep shit, she thought, as he looked at her, trying to understand. How will we work this one out?

'Now, my Daphne, you need to call your mama. She tried to ring the house but there was no answer. She's so worried. I have a number in France here.' *Kyria* Lemonia produced a scrap of paper with a laboriously long number and 'ΕΛΛΗ' in blue biro capitals. Her eyes were flitting round the kitchen as if the bizarre presence of a bare-chested man at the table implied there might be a stowaway in the cupboard. Daphne went into the hall to the small table where the phone was kept, sat on the hard chair by its side and dialled.

'Ah, Daphne, thank God!' It was Ellie. Her voice was thick. 'My darling, I …' The line crackled and hissed. '… Just left in his sleep. Very peaceful. But still, such a shock. Maro found him this morning when she went to make his coffee.' Her mother's voice rose in pitch, unable to prevent tears. Then she gave a loud sniff and continued. 'She said he looks very handsome like in the old days. *Yiayia* is on her way back from Crete and I'll fly out later today. Ed's trying to get a ticket from Germany. The funeral will be tomorrow, in Athens. Ah, Daphnoula, at least you'll be able to come.'

The line cut just as Ellie began asking her daughter a question. 'Daphne, why …' Ralph was leaning against the doorway, observing her, while *kyria* Lemonia was making herself busy in the kitchen, soaping cups in the marble sink. The gap in the conversation with Ellie was like a mischievous offering from the gods.

'Quick. What do we say?' she asked him, hopelessly incapable of creating a good excuse. 'How do I explain that you didn't go straight to Pelion? Shit.'

'Shit, fuck, bugger, cunt,' he whispered, biting his lip, mustering ideas. 'I suppose we'll say we left England earlier than we thought and ...' He paused, extemporising. 'And you ... you wanted to show me Aegina – just for one night. We'll say we arrived in Athens yesterday and that we'd arranged that I'd drop you off with the cousins on Poros today or tomorrow – it was only going to be the day after that anyway. They'll never focus on the dates, given what's happened. What do you ...?'

The telephone's brash trill broke into his words. 'OK? Don't panic. Nobody's going to worry about us. They trust me. This is a sideshow now – the attention is elsewhere. It's all fine.'

'Daphne, why are you at *Yiayia*'s house?' Her mother's voice was sterner. 'And where is Ralph? Has he gone to Pelion? Are you there alone with Jane?'

'Uh, well, we thought ... No, not alone. I wanted to show Ralph Aegina. I mean, he is here now and we ... we were going to take the boat to Poros today or tomorrow and then he's going to Pelion.' She paused and changed tack. 'How is *Yiayia*?'

'She's a very strong woman. She'll be OK. But Daphnoula, you should have told someone. I was so worried about how to find you.'

'How did you know I was here?' Daphne regretted the question immediately.

'When *Yiayia* called me from Crete she said she didn't know if you were there but she rang *kyria* Lemonia. Are there other people there too?'

'No, just Ralph.'

'So you've seen *kyria* Lemonia?'

'She just came round. And she'd already left us some *galaktoboureko* and made up the beds.' Daphne also regretted the word beds, but Ellie didn't ask about sleeping arrangements.

'OK, my sweet. Will you go back to Athens by tonight? We'll all gather in Maroussi at *Yiayia*'s house. Athena and the girls are already on the boat. The funeral will probably be tomorrow morning or early afternoon, but we're waiting to hear from the priest. OK, *agapi mou*?' Daphne began to cry again, mostly because her mother was being so kind, calling her 'My love' and not cornering her with the flagrant irregularities in her story.

After she'd rung off, she and Ralph moved into the shadows at the end of the hall and he took her in his arms. She closed her eyes, feeling like a baby against its mother's breast. Their experiment to create a miniature, private version of paradise was over. What had seemed an idyll, as contained as an island, was invaded on every side. They heard *kyria* Lemonia's footsteps in the kitchen and broke apart.

'You need to eat something,' Ralph said in a public voice. 'This is a shock to the system.'

Daphne felt sick and exhausted. There was a bloody sheet in the bathtub upstairs. It was like being caught in a net, caught in the act.

'We're going to leave later today, *kyria* Lemonia. I'll put the key under the stone again, shall I? Thanks for coming round. I need to go and pack now.' Daphne didn't care if she sounded abrupt. This awful scene needed to be terminated. She wanted to go home, to get under the duvet in her cool, orange-tinged, Putney bedroom and forget all this.

'Fucking shit,' she said as soon as the interloper had left.

'Bloody, bastard, bollocks, pools of poxy piss,' he responded, the hint of a smile emerging as he looked into her eyes.

She managed to turn the bloodstain a faint beige colour and hung the sheet over some chairs on the loggia – it would dry quickly and then she would fling all the used sheets and towels in a pile. From the upstairs landing she heard Ralph call Nina and stood still to listen.

'Yes, darling ... Yes, Aegina, at Ellie's mother's house ... No, but we're leaving now because Ellie's father died in the night ... Tomorrow, in Athens ... Yes, because we were able to leave earlier than we thought ... Yes, yesterday. Sorry, but it was chaotic, I was exhausted, you know ... In the end, I had to take her to Poros, so Aegina's on the way ...' He laughed and replied, 'Well you know what teenagers are like ...'

Daphne scowled at the cliché of 'difficult teenagers', and pictured Nina in the house in Pelion. She'd stayed there with her family a year earlier and had witnessed Nina as a hostess – quiet but gracious and generous. Wonderful meals appeared, 'As if from nowhere,' Ellie had remarked in admiration. It was true that, in a group, she was unobtrusive. 'A peahen to Ralph's peacock,' Ed said to Ellie, and they both chortled, unaware that Daphne was listening. 'I'm not so sure,' replied Ellie. 'That bird has a glint in her eye. And she has him exactly where she wants. He might be preening his fancy feathers, but he needs her. She's a marvellous mother. And she's strong.' Daphne had also perceived the underlying strength, even ferocity in her rival. While everyone else was sleeping, Nina got up at dawn to go and paint in the woods, returning before breakfast with incomprehensible but vivid, abstract pictures in a million shades of green. Nina might not gabble away like lots of grown-ups, but Daphne didn't underestimate her power and avoided too much direct contact.

'No, don't come to Athens,' continued Ralph on the phone. 'There's no need ... Better to stay and be quiet. No, I'll see what it's like when I drop her off, but I don't think so. I'll check out the timetable in the late afternoon ... No, thank you. I'll make my own way from Volos. How are you coping with the heat? And our little man? I know ... I can't wait to see you both ... Yes, me too.'

She noted Ralph's easy lies, but also perceived the genuine tenderness; Nina was pregnant again. She walked slowly into the room which contained two unused single beds and flopped face down on to one. She wondered whether she was sad about *Pappou* and a tear rolled from her eye, but she knew the main cause of her misery was not due to this loss. Ralph's division of life into different spheres came so naturally to him, but it wasn't like that for her. There was no husband and child waiting for her.

When Ralph came upstairs, she was still lying spread-eagled. He sat at the end of the bed and stroked her feet, sweeping the dust from her soles and pulling each toe with matter-of-fact practicality. 'I love you completely and utterly, Dafflings. You are my muse and my inspiration. Nothing can change that.' She didn't react, but lay breathing in the clean linen scent of the pillow. 'But that doesn't mean I don't love Nina and Jason. They're different.' He patted her feet in rhythm with his words and appeared entirely confident with his system. 'With you it's another thing. We're not bound by old-fashioned morality or small rules made by churches or by leaders who want to keep you under control. We're free. You're a free spirit.'

She paused, then nodded, believing him. Maybe she was free, even if it was unclear what this meant.

Ralph's bedside manner gradually altered from inspector of feet into something slower and more intense as he massaged her legs and then he squeezed alongside her on the narrow bed. She turned to face him and they kissed hard, as though it hurt. Teeth, tongue, lips pressing as if they were becoming one welded creature. I *am* free, she thought. And this is what I want.

She enjoyed it more this time, as if she'd grown up since yesterday and was getting the hang of this sex business. It didn't hurt nearly so much. Once more, it didn't take long from start to finish. 'I'll be careful,' he said before finishing on her belly like the night before. Afterwards, she lay there, feeling the wet turn dry. Yes, I like it, she thought. This is a whole new world I've entered.

She remembered the return to Athens as a series of disappointing snaps. The crowded boat to Piraeus that left their faces spotted with black soot. The obese driver of a rusting taxi, who refused to open the windows for fear of catching a chill. The perfunctory goodbye when they dropped Ralph at the KTEL bus station. Her angry tears on the road to Maroussi.

Yiayia's house was airless and shadowed, curtains drawn against the blinding light and insupportable heat of an urban summer afternoon. *Yiayia* was stiff-backed, black-dressed and tearless. She was clear about the protocol, imposing order in the chaos of death, welcoming people, accepting their condolences. She held Daphne's hands and said, 'He loved you very much,' though Daphne doubted it was true. Mourners moved from room to room, voices hushed. It was her first sight of a dead person and there was a strange fascination in *Pappou*'s waxy face in the coffin, skin pulled tight over his pointed nose that jutted ceilingwards.

Ed arrived before Ellie, having caught an earlier plane from Germany. He looked outlandishly tall and pale beside the Greeks and was dressed wrong, with a flowery shirt and silky scarf. Daphne held his hand when he paid his respects to his father-in-law and heard him emit a small groan of sadness. 'Poor George. All over now,' he whispered.

It was early evening when Ellie entered the house, face swollen, eyes hazy, and wearing a black dress. Daphne ran to her, horrified by the sight of her mother in disarray. Ellie rarely showed anything but strength or anger in a crisis, yet she looked like a forlorn child. Daphne held her tight, not wanting to let go, breathing in the soothing mother smell tinged with aeroplane and competing with ambient wafts of coffee, cigarette smoke and burning incense. Yet even now, her mind returned to Ralph and what they'd done together: the hot joining of bodies, the smell of his sperm, falling asleep in bed with him, the bloodied sheet. Nobody there knew she was changed.

* * *

She finished tacking the silk sunbeams to the backcloth so they sliced through the *Putney* clouds, then she went into the kitchen to ponder the puzzle of supper. It was one of the daily challenges of parenthood, this providing of meals. The dull contents of the fridge gazed back at her as though there was a camera lurking inside and this was a crude TV game show she was doomed to lose. Not that she didn't like eating good food, she just hated the planning and preparation. Nobody had taught her. As a girl, she didn't notice; after she married Constantine, they ate out or were too high to care; and then, in the dreadful years, she didn't eat. Not quite true, she thought. Of course I ate, but I didn't give a damn. Probably too many fried eggs. There had been some bad times. In the worst phases, she had resorted to 'dumpster diving', before eco-warriors gave it that quaint label. The memory still provoked a quiver of shame.

That was all long ago. These days, she was accomplished at the art of culinary cheating. She'd buy a ready-made pizza and throw on some fresh mozzarella and tomato before it went into the oven, or she'd make scrambled eggs on toast and chop some herbs or smoked salmon to go with it. Anything on toast was the best bet.

She was still standing before the open fridge hoping for inspiration, when Libby joined her.

'Toasted cheese? We're clean out of *boeuf en croute*.'

'Yum, with mustard on the toast? And baked beans?' Sometimes, Libby's tender appreciation of these meagre efforts made Daphne feel worse.

They ate the toasted cheese watching television. It was companionable and undemanding. This might not be what ideal mothers did for supper, thought Daphne. They probably laid tables and had instructive conversations. But this was startlingly precious. It was ordinary. And for a long time she'd feared she would never have that in her life. There was no doubt that her existence was divided into before-Liberty and after and, despite all the tests of motherhood, it was like the difference between dank darkness and brilliant, warm light.

6

JANE

She slept badly the night after the reunion with Daphne. Their conversations ran through her mind on a loop and the creepy collage became a nightmare. These were mementoes from a time she had managed to forget and it was harrowing to be confronted by them again. At five thirty, sleepless and drained, she rose quietly, trying not to wake Michael.

'OK?' he mumbled, reaching out a hand that would have held her if she'd been close enough.

'Fine.' She had avoided talking about Daphne the previous evening, unable to find a way of explaining her wretchedness to him. 'Fine,' she had replied, when he asked how it had gone. 'But I don't know if I'll see her again.'

Running was often a way of solving problems and she set off into a leaden dawn so damp she couldn't tell if it was raining. After reaching the river, she turned eastwards along the empty Thames Path and arrived at Battersea Park just as the gates were being opened. She did a circuit, hardly noticing where she was, tormented by Daphne's blind insistence that a child can be happily raped by an adult – for that is what Ralph did. How could she blithely claim there had been no negative consequences? It made

Jane want to kick and scream, almost as incensed with her old friend as she was with her abuser. It was only on the way home that the regular drum beat of her feet on tarmac calmed her and her spent physical energy brought a feeling of greater control.

By the time she opened her front door, she was drenched in sweat and aching, but she had the beginnings of a decision. Her anger would be channelled and turned into a force for good. There was a way of doing the right thing. Instead of fleeing, she could fight. She could help her old friend, make Daphne realise how misguided she was. She would persuade her that child abusers should not be garlanded in roses and displayed on the wall, but reported to the authorities and put behind bars.

Michael was in the kitchen. The room was warm and comforting, aromatic with coffee and toast. A low rumble of polite, Sunday morning voices burbled from the radio. Jane fetched a glass of water and sat down at the table opposite him. She should have taken a shower and changed her clothes, but this moment needed grasping. Her plan would be made real by declaring it. She had to tell him.

'That's very bright and early for a run,' said Michael, crunching toast and briefly glancing up from the *Observer*. 'Impressive. Coffee?'

'No thanks.' She wiped her face on her sleeve. 'There's something I want to talk to you about.'

'Oh yes?' He only put the newspaper halfway down, evidently hoping this would be something easy – a plan with the boys or a work trip.

'I've been quite upset since yesterday. Since seeing Daphne.'

'Oh?' Realising this required attention, he folded up his paper and the three vertical lines between his eyebrows deepened with apprehension. 'What happened?'

'Nothing happened exactly. But we talked about the past. She had this ... she was sexually abused as a child. I knew him. It was Ralph Boyd. You know, the composer?'

Michael nodded. 'Oh God.'

'She was so young when it started – only twelve or thirteen – and he was married with children. And the awful thing is that she still doesn't think he did anything wrong. In fact she's making a huge artwork about it, as though it's something to be glorified.'

'That's appalling.' Michael got up and switched off the radio.

'I know. He's a monster. And it's brought it all back, how I was part of it. I was there, witnessing the whole thing, complicit.' Her voice broke momentarily and, though she tried to disguise it by coughing, Michael came round to her side of the table and put his hands on her shoulders. 'He didn't ...? Not with you?'

'No!' It came out louder than expected. 'No, it's not that. But I can't bear that she just smiles about it as if it's not a crime. Just because he's cultured and charming, there's no reason he should be treated any differently to Jimmy Savile or Gary Glitter. He deserves to be arrested along with all the other child molesters.'

'I don't know how people can do that.' His reactions were so familiar to her that she knew he would run a hand through his hair, as he often did when stressed. He'd gone completely white now, though when they were first together his hair was like hers – a mousy blonde that turned flaxen in the sun. 'So what will you do? Will you report him?' His fingers were already touching his scalp.

'No, it needs to come from her. I have to make her see there's been a crime committed and that she's the victim. I'm not going to just leave it. People should know he is a child rapist.'

* * *

When Daphne returned from her sneaky trip to Greece with Ralph, she'd changed. Even before she admitted she'd 'done it', there was something different about her. After the summer she always looked smooth and brown as a polished nut, but this time it was as though the small, internal piercing made her walk with a new looseness, a voluptuous sway. After she confessed, Jane quizzed her. 'What was it like? Did it hurt?' She was hungry for knowledge. This seemed only fair for agreeing to pretend, whenever required, that she was going to travel to Greece with Daphne and Ralph on the Magic Bus. 'What about foreplay? Did you do 69?' She knew the theory, but sexual intercourse was as distant as a far-off continent. And now Daphne had been there and was annoyingly stingy with details.

'You can't describe it,' she claimed conveniently.

Just before school started in September, Daphne asked Jane to go with her and Ralph to Brighton. At first, it sounded appealing, despite the subtext that she was merely a suitable chaperone, though even after the shenanigans of the summer, Daphne's parents were more bemused than suspicious.

'We'll have fun. Oh go on,' pleaded Daphne when Jane said she didn't want to be a gooseberry. 'Please! We'll mix you up with cream and sugar and turn you into a goose-berry fool. It'll be great. You need some sea air.'

'I bet Ralph doesn't want me there.'

'Course he does,' Daphne replied, not convincing Jane, but evidently believing herself at that moment. 'We both want you.'

Jane realised it would be awkward when Ralph turned up at Barnabas Road in Maurice, and there was a baby on the back seat.

'Jason's come along for the ride,' Ralph said, smiling as though that was normal. 'Nina's got an exhibition and she's a bit exhausted.'

'She's about to pop,' explained Daphne in a cold voice, as though 'pop' was a medical term.

Ralph ignored this, adding, 'Anyway, it's high time this young man had an expedition with his father.'

It was still early – about 8 a.m. – and Ellie came out on to the street barefoot and wearing a fragile, silken kimono with nothing underneath. Her dark, curly hair fell loose around her shoulders and Jane stared in wonder that you could have a mum like that. Ralph bounded over, kissed her, whirled her around as if they were going to do ballroom dancing and then went on one knee and sang something in Italian. '*Madam Butterfly*,' he clarified afterwards to the ignorant girls. Jane was horrified: how pretentious can you get? Ellie appeared delighted by her serenade, which was obviously the whole point. She smiled absently as the girls piled into Maurice.

'Be good, children,' she said, which might have been ironic. She was often hard to gauge.

Jane took the back seat without asking – second-class citizens know where they belong. The car reeked of a milky, nappyish aroma from the baby next to her. Her period had started the night before and she felt like a giant baby herself, with a bulky, thigh-chafing sanitary towel wedged between her legs and an abdominal ache pulling like overweight gravity. She watched miserably as Ellie waved and made some Greek coo-y noises through the window at Jason. Daphne got into the front seat, as lady-like and refined as if Ralph was her chauffeur and Jane and the fat baby were bags of shopping dumped behind.

The cool of the misty morning gave way to intense heat and they got stuck in traffic leaving London. Having slept for a while, the baby began wailing and its jowly face went puce. Ralph called instructions to Jane about how to calm it down: the dummy was spat on to the filthy car floor, the rattle was ignored and the bottle of milk was drunk in a trice before the crying began again. Then there was an awful stink and, despite the girls' attempts to breathe through their mouths and cover their noses, it became necessary to stop. Ralph turned down a country road and found a field in which to change the nappy. Daphne and Jane went to have a pee and eventually found some bushes where they squatted awkwardly amongst prickly, thistle-laced grass. On their return, Ralph handed Jason to them and announced, 'I'll just take a leak too.' He walked a few steps, turned his back and, legs slightly splayed, shoulders squared, let out a golden arc. Nothing was said, nor was it necessary, but it was a moment Jane always remembered – how the easy pride of a man urinating signified so much more than pissing. It remained as a moment she'd seen the inequality of the sexes laid bare.

In the car once again, Jane noticed Ralph's hand sneaking across and stroking Daphne's fingers, while singing more bits from *Madam Butterfly*. 'It's pop music really,' he said. 'But it proves the power of a good tune. Pure emotion – that's all most people want. Isn't that right, Lady Jane?' She didn't answer. Occasionally, he shouted jovially, 'Everything all right back there?' Jason munched his way through a packet of Farley's Rusks and Jane sneaked one for herself, nibbling it cautiously while pretending to look out of the window at the green rise of the South Downs in the distance.

'So, girls, the delights begin. Where shall we start?' Ralph radiated geniality as they walked towards the sea and turned along the promenade. The front was packed with noisy day-trippers strolling or sprawled in lines of striped deckchairs. On the beach, people had established their territories with towels, umbrellas and folding chairs and the sea was rimmed with others paddling. Some braver souls were swimming and playing with rubber rings. The baby – actually a toddler, Jane and Daphne agreed – tottered unsteadily along the pavement for a few yards before being strapped into a pushchair, a sunhat plonked on his head and another rusk thrust into his hand.

'I'm starving,' said Daphne.

'Nothing like the sea for giving you an appetite,' agreed Ralph, with an expression Jane supposed was meant to be suggestive. He's so babyish, she thought. And he's only six years younger than my mum. It wasn't nearly lunchtime, but they bought cod and chips and sat on a bench overlooking the beach to eat them, blowing on the chips and handing them to the baby when they'd cooled down.

After they'd eaten, they bought tickets for the pier. It was horribly crowded and they were drawn along its length by the throng, the wooden boards vibrating below their feet.

'Hoi polloi,' said Ralph, gesturing at the hordes. 'The multitudes. Just like the Roman crowds in the Colosseum – in search of cheap thrills.' He likes raising himself above the crowds, and acting like someone special, she thought. And sure enough, he edged himself to the front of the queue to buy tickets for the merry-go-round, leaving everyone else to wait in line like the hoi polloi they were. Still, it was fun on the old-fashioned carousel with its painted horses, which rose and fell like decorous dolphins. Jane sat on a pink and gold pony next to Daphne, and Ralph was behind them holding Jason and clinging to the barley-sugar pole. Afterwards, they had to hang around while he got out his tape recorder for the tenth time. He'd already done it next to someone busking with a banjo, and he kept stopping for another little session – it was evidently the excuse for the trip.

They all took turns in pushing the baby – he wasn't bad, Jane agreed, when Daphne said he was sweet, though she found him at best irrelevant. The pier became over-heated and even more congested and she felt trapped and angry. To add to the misery, the stabbing period pains were becoming worse. If she didn't change her sanitary towel soon there would probably be a leak. She'd been through this particular mortification and walked around for ages with a great red stain on her jeans before a woman at a bus stop told her. Her body seemed designed for treachery – a vehicle bringing public and private shame. Three spots on her chin throbbed in the heat and her T-shirt was damp with sweat despite much rolling with Mum deodorant. It was a great injustice that Daphne never appeared to be brought down by these biological weaknesses; she'd only ever had one spot and didn't appear to sweat, or at least not in any quantity. Jane's mother said, 'Horses sweat, men perspire and ladies glow.' Daphne only ever glowed. So I am a horse, thought Jane.

They stopped to lean over the cast-iron railings, squinting at the sunlight that turned the sea silver. A father and son were fishing and had boxes of live maggots wriggling by their feet.

'Listen, if any of us get lost, shall we say we'll meet right here at this bench?' Ralph said like the leader on a mountaineering trip. 'Opposite the candyfloss stall, if you forget. OK? There are so many people, you never know. Best to be safe.'

Yes, Ralph. Whatever you say, Ralph, she thought and nodded obediently.

It did not take long before she found herself alone. She'd seen Ralph whispering in Daphne's ear earlier – that was nothing new – but she didn't imagine her friend would conspire against her. For about ten minutes, her anger at this abandonment brought on a renewed energy and she strode past the bench where they'd agreed to meet, where naturally there was no sign of Daphne or Ralph with his stupid baby. Giving up on them, she went to find the toilets, changed her ST, placed the old one in a paper bag provided and took it to the special bin by the basins. Deciding to teach them a lesson, she left the pier and walked down to the beach. This brought temporary relief. She shuffled along in the shallows, holding her shoes and letting the sea splash on to her turned-up trousers. I hate him, she thought, kicking the water with irritation rather than joy.

She persuaded the ticket seller to let her back on to the pier and returned to the assigned meeting place, hoping the others would be waiting. Nobody. Now she hated Daphne too. The cool reprieve of the sea was soon forgotten as she sat on the appointed bench and began overheating again. Her arms were red from the sun and her glasses were slipping down her painfully hot and presumably burnt nose. An elderly couple sat next to her eating ice-cream cones, licking slowly, gazing out past the screaming gulls that dive-bombed down to pick up pieces of discarded food. When the pair got up in silence and trudged glumly in the direction of the pier's end, Jane wondered whether they were going to jump off and drown themselves. And what about me? What am I going to do? What if the others don't come back? How long would I wait here? What if they've run away, eloped?

Half a dozen teenage boys walked past, holding bags of sweets and ridiculously large sticks of pink Brighton rock that they thrust and jabbed at each other like swords. They stopped to buy some candyfloss and one of them, lanky and narrow-eyed, called out to Jane. 'Oi, feeling hot?' He fell against his friend crowing with laughter. 'Fancy a snog?' he shouted, looking at his small gang for approval as they yowled like hyenas.

'Fuck off!' she said too meekly, realising immediately that this was the wrong approach. The boys gathered round. 'Oooooh,' squealed the lanky boy, in mock horror, closing in. 'Don't mind if we do ... if you fuck off with me.'

He swung himself over the bench so he was sitting on the back, his feet on the seat next to her, and leaned down. 'Fancy a bit of my candyfloss?' She could smell him – an animal pungency and cigarette breath joining the warm chemical sweetness of pink, spun sugar. He was leering, emboldened by his mates who circled round them. Jane turned away from him, striving for haughtiness, but the boy jumped off the bench and leaped into a crouch at her feet. 'Here, try a bit. It's really nice. Sweet. Like you.' He turned to his mates with a grin.

She edged along the bench and looked in the other direction.

'What's your name then?'

She didn't answer and stood up, looking for a way out, but the boys all moved so they surrounded her in front and the bench blocked her escape from behind. 'Come on, no hurry. Sit down again?' The boy patted the bench and sat down himself.

'Jane!' Ralph's superior tones sounded clear and incongruous as a bugle. He and Daphne were hurrying along the pier towards her, the pushchair bumping along before them.

'So, Jane, give us a quick kiss then before we go,' said the boy, weighing up the options and preparing his exit. 'That your dad, then?' he asked, gesturing at Ralph.

'Yes, and he'll kill you,' replied Jane.

'What's going on here?' demanded Ralph, providing a good approximation of an angry dad.

'Nothing. Just talking.' The boy paused for effect. 'She's gorgeous, your daughter.' His mates snorted with mirth and their eyes flitted between the risk of an irate father and the fun of teasing a bespectacled girl with spots and big tits.

'OK, off you go now,' Ralph countered sternly, having evidently considered and then decided against denying his paternity. 'Go on, scat.'

'Ooh, keep your hair on,' retorted Jane's lanky tormentor. 'Come on, boys, we're not wanted around here.' And he turned and sauntered off, his hyenas following with a look of satisfaction as they tore pieces of candyfloss from their sticks and stuffed them into their mouths.

'Where were you?' Jane whimpered. She addressed Daphne. 'Why did you leave me?'

Daphne didn't meet her eyes. 'We couldn't find you ... and then we went for a walk to find some shade.' Daphne's lips were red, her hair mussed. You could see her pointy breasts through her shirt. She looked as though she'd been getting off with Ralph. What kind of friend abandons you to go off with an old man? An old man with a baby! Jane pictured them in the damp shadows beneath the pier, hiding behind the wooden supports. There was a strand of green seaweed tangled in Daphne's hair.

'Are you OK, Jane?' asked Ralph. He was clearly anxious, his eyes flicking in the direction of the boys who had now disappeared into the crowds.

'No. Yes. I'm fine.' Jane looked away. Her anger was slightly assuaged by Ralph's alarm. He was evidently aware that he was at least partially responsible for the incident. She glanced back at him and felt the intensity of his gaze upon her.

'Nasty little buggers. Were they here long?' The comforting arm he placed around her shoulder transmitted such power that she felt suddenly much better, as though miraculously healed from her recent humiliations.

She shook her head, wanting to appear brave and worldly. 'No, hardly any time at all.'

Ralph bought them ice creams in a cone with a chocolate flake.

'You know it's made from whale blubber,' said Daphne, licking like a cat. 'What a waste of the biggest mammal in the world – turning it into fucking ice cream.' Jane suspected Daphne liked swearing because it made her feel grown up or sexy, especially if Ralph was there. On the way back to the car, Daphne stopped in front of a small kiosk. Madam Julia, daughter of Almena Lee. Palmist, Clairvoyant and Spiritualist. 'Fuck! I've got to go in,' she pleaded, pulling on Ralph's arm. 'Please. I've never met a proper clairvoyant.' Jane expected Ralph to capitulate, but he was rather gruff. 'Definitely not! Load of codswallop. Come on, we need to go now.' He almost dragged her, but then tried to make it up, buying several sticks of Brighton rock and some saucy seaside postcards, which he dealt out to the girls. *You've got a couple of nice handfuls! Slice of rock, cock.*

Daphne insisted Jane sit in the front on the way back, and Ralph agreed. 'Come on, Lady Jane. Your turn.' She felt pleased and then annoyed at herself for being so easily pacified after the betrayal on the pier. As they edged out of Brighton along traffic-clogged roads, Ralph asked her about her dreams and what she hoped to do in her life. Stopping the car at some traffic lights, he looked straight into her eyes. 'What do you feel truly passionate about?' And she suddenly felt shy that this handsome man was taking an interest in her. She remembered his hand sliding across to Daphne's on the morning's drive down, and wondered how she would react if he did that to her. The thought was thrilling and terrifying. What, she wondered, did Daphne feel when she was with him? What had they done under the pier? Placed physically between the two lovers in the car, she sensed the intensity of their connection as though it was palpable. She felt connected to them both, part of their secret and almost aroused by it.

They had all the windows open but it was still baking hot, and the journey home was interminable. Ralph's attempt at charming her gradually petered out and, as they snaked through London's southern suburbs, he was mostly silent. The car made odd coughing sounds and the engine stalled a couple of times. 'Shit,' Ralph muttered and then cheered up when the car started again. 'Good old Maurice.' The baby dozed for much of the way and Daphne slept too, curled up next to him on the back seat. Unlike the sexy femme fatale she'd been impersonating in Brighton, she now looked like a tired child.

* * *

By the time Jane received Daphne's friendly email on Monday morning, she had a plan. It was not an easy project. Jane had spent the last decades removing herself as far as she could from this story. It was like returning to the Minotaur's labyrinth; she must sharpen her sword and take a strong length of thread with which to make her way out again. But justice must be done. Daphne would eventually realise this.

At the lab, she was distracted. She forgot an appointment to interview candidates for a technician internship and was located in a distant part of the building, devouring a spicy hummus sandwich for a late lunch, her hair still wet from the swimming pool.

When she got home she phoned Daphne. 'It's your birthday this Friday, isn't it?' Dates learned in childhood remained a fixture and she always remembered Daphne on

May 2nd, even if she had not been part of her celebrations since they were teenagers.

'Shit, that's clever of you. Well, you always did have a brain. Yes, an undistinguished fifty-one and I'm not going to do anything about it. Libby's off to Normandy on a school trip and I'm planning to sew my way through the weekend. That's my idea of fun now!' She let out a girlish giggle.

'Oh why don't we get together then? You can't be alone for a birthday. Michael's away at a conference the whole weekend, so I'll be alone too. Come for a little birthday supper at my place. Nothing elaborate.' She pictured Daphne weighing up her options. Maybe she had been lying and was having a party and just didn't want to invite Jane. Her response, however, gave no hint of this. 'That's so sweet of you. Are you really sure?'

'Of course!'

'Well, great. I'd love to.'

On Friday she hurried home from work. Having prepared the stuffed aubergines the previous day, she placed them in the oven and chopped up sweet potatoes, parsnips and onions to roast with olive oil and rosemary. For a first course, she assembled a salad of quinoa with halloumi, coriander and lime. Sitting ready in the freezer was the Arctic Roll she'd bought at Sainsbury's. It had been Daphne's favourite and they'd sometimes worked their way through an entire cake, sawing at the hard, frozen log at the beginning and scooping up melted ice cream by the end. Only one candle today; fifty-one wouldn't have fitted and two digits might have seemed like a dig. A present was waiting, nestled in tissue paper in a glossy blue bag: a bottle of Floris's Stephanotis bath essence. She believed

Daphne would understand the reference, and not think it was merely a conventional gift. Just in case she'd forgotten, Jane wrote at the bottom of the birthday card, 'For death baths only!'

Daphne arrived late. 'Sorry, sorry! I'm Greek!' It was the perfect excuse, not only because it was half-true, thought Jane, but because it charmed. Dippy Greek was probably a useful ploy. Perhaps she really was becoming more Greek with age, Jane mused as her friend entered the hall – effervescent and laden with a bottle of chilled champagne and an extravagant bunch of fragrant, blue hyacinths, as though it was Jane's birthday. She wore jeans dressed up with daintily heeled boots and a green silk shirt that rippled.

They drank the champagne, toasting the mysterious joys of middle age. There was a nervy volubility to Daphne, who couldn't stay still, almost dancing over to inspect the food sizzling in the oven, or to peer at the photographs of Jane's sons proudly plastered on the fridge, their mop-haired faces grinning out from ski slopes and school sports events, Toby in wig and breeches for a play, Josh in graduation robes. Jane knew she must take things slowly rather than barge straight in with talk of exploitation, abuse and rape.

The room sparkled from the candles on the kitchen table, but also, it seemed, from Daphne's presence. As they sat down to eat, there was a small silence and slight tension.

'You're so clever, so accomplished,' said Daphne. 'Just look at you, climbing the heights of the scientific world, opening up the frontiers of medical research, *and* cooking this perfect meal.' Her overgenerosity meant you couldn't be sure what to take seriously. Still, the food *was* perfect, Jane thought. And nothing wrong with boosting morale.

They talked of their children and then their parents.

'Not much to report,' said Jane. 'Still in the same house. Dad retired, but apart from that, everything's almost exactly as when you knew them. What about Ed?'

'Oh Ed's in the Dordogne, but you probably knew that. I suppose it's been about twenty-five years. I hardly ever see him.' Daphne looked wistful. 'Still with Margaret – his Canadian wife.' Her expression turned mischievous. 'Mags was a fan. Went to one of his lectures and started writing to him, bombarding him with adoring letters. No aphrodisiac like flattery. You know how it goes. Anyway, they've been together ever since.'

'Do you like her?'

'I hardly know her. I suppose she's a good person. Solid, reliable, keeps an even keel. Nothing like Ellie. But then nobody could have her *joie de vivre*.'

'Ellie was such a remarkable mother,' agreed Jane. 'I always wished mine could be a bit more like her – both the glamour and the unpredictability. I loved the way she'd organise a huge picnic for us all and then the next day she was leading a battalion of protestors into a line of French policemen.'

'Yeah. Or fucking a Frenchman.' Daphne's tone was suddenly peevish.

'Do you think she was away too much, that she should have defended you more?' Jane grasped the opportunity. 'Safeguarded you?'

'Safeguarded? From what?'

'Well … from Ralph.'

Daphne looked interrogatively at Jane before answering, but she didn't say, 'Oh leave me alone.' Instead, she responded reasonably, 'Well, Ellie's approach was absolutely of its time. But it's like I said when we met before, the thing between Ralph and me wasn't something I wanted safeguarding from. Of its time too, of course, but wonderful in its way.'

'You don't think it harmed you? That it affected your life at all?'

'No. I really don't.' She shook her head. 'I'd know if I was harmed, wouldn't I?' She didn't expect an answer.

Jane knew she must be cautious but couldn't resist taking up the challenge. 'So you're saying what Ralph did was fine?'

'Oh God, Janey, I don't know. It was a very specific thing. He fell for me and I happened to be a child. He wasn't in love with other girls. And then as I grew up … I wanted it. I loved him. You remember. It was exciting.' She beamed and glinted. 'Why should there be such a specific age placed on what young people can and can't do? It's so puritanical. No one's allowed to break the rules or have fun.'

Jane moved in closer. 'What would you do if a man made Libby love him?' A flash of puzzlement crossed Daphne's face, and then she appeared to resolve the question by some sort of internal reasoning. She was so easy to read.

'It's a different era now. I mean, think about what was going on in those days. Do you remember? You couldn't behave like that today. Everyone was so busy having fun and getting liberated, it was only fair for kids to … I don't know. I suppose we're all children when we're in love. I don't know anyone of my age who didn't have some sort of inappropriate fling or grope or … something in those days. You expected it. It didn't *seem* wrong at the time. And you saw how both my parents were behaving. It was in the air.'

It was true, thought Jane. An image flashed of a day when she went home with Daphne after school and Edmund was there with Dizzy, his research student. The girls sat in the kitchen and watched them prepare a bottle of wine and two glasses to take upstairs. 'Sustenance – we've got a lot of correcting to do,' announced Ed. Later, Jane followed Daphne to her attic room and, pausing on the top-floor landing, they heard the unmistakable sounds of sex coming from behind the door to Edmund's study: deep male outbreaths in a furious duet with female sighs. It was monstrous and fascinating, as though there was a danger-ous animal on the other side.

Jane was so shocked and embarrassed she looked away, pretending not to hear. She thought Daphne was also ignoring it, as she turned and ran back down the stairs, but when they got to the kitchen, she was laughing. 'Ralph said he thought Ed was having it off with Dizzy. Yuck! They're terrible, my parents.' Perhaps she was pretending she didn't care, thought Jane. It was an upside-down world.

'Does your mum know?'

'I'm not sure. She's probably doing the same thing.' Daphne gave a harsh laugh, as though her parents were wayward children and she was the tolerant minder.

'You must remember what it was like then?' Daphne's adult voice forced Jane back to the present.

'Of course I remember,' replied Jane, noting an annoy-ing touch of the schoolmarm in her own voice. It had been as though the cloud of steam from all the sex people were having had been located somewhere above Barnabas Road. It certainly wasn't in Wimbledon.

'Everything was hanging out – it was so ... hairy,' said Daphne.

'Hairy?'

'You know, hair grown long, hair gone wild, hair not shaved. Like *Hair* the musical. Like when we found Ellie's copy of *The Joy of Sex*? God that was hairy! The woman with unshaved armpits ... and that bloke with his beasty, black beard and greasy locks. And testicles viewed from absurd angles. Ugh.' Daphne chuckled as though she was still the kid with the naughty book in her hands.

At the time, it was all dizzily distant, desirable yet dangerous, and far removed from the codified progression that was used by young teenagers after parties: 'How far did you go?' Jane couldn't quite remember how it went. Was it number 1 = kissing, number 2 = hands on breast outside clothes and 3 = outside down there? At least it defined things and implied a logical system, whereas Daphne had led her into hazardous confusion. Their emergence into the irrational land of adolescence coincided with an era that reinvented notions of what it meant to be free. Entering Daphne's sphere was like setting off along the yellow brick road. Everything was suddenly in Technicolor; Wimbledon was the black and white Kansas. She knew that even then.

'It's all very well to think of the fun and games.' Jane noticed that Daphne hadn't answered her question about Libby. 'Course it's fun to think you invented freedom and to rush around pushing back boundaries. But you're ignoring the dark underbelly. The *hairy*, dark underbelly of those times.' She was trying to make Daphne smile, though it wasn't funny. 'You know? Things like the Paedophile Information Exchange? They campaigned for the sexual rights of children, as in the right for kids to enjoy sex with adults. It was lined up alongside gay rights as though it was the same sort of deal. Sickening!'

'Oh God, I don't know.' She kept saying that, noted Jane. 'You can't compare things then and now.' Daphne appeared relaxed and comfortable. 'I mean, in some ways we're more liberal, like not locking up men for being gay. But with teenagers, they're called "children" almost till they're able to vote and fight in a war. It's all mad.' She leaned back, stretching her arms and running her hands through hair that was luxuriant as ever, even if these days it was tinted a bold, mahogany shade. Just as they'd always done, bangles jangled on her wrists and Greek, hammered-silver earrings swung and glittered.

Jane brought out the Arctic Roll and sang 'Happy Birthday, dear Daffers'. The lone candle was blown out and Daphne cut two thick slices, exclaiming about the generosity of her friend, whom she kissed. The present was ideal. 'You're a darling, Janey. My old favourite. I'll have scented death baths. Nothing like those to raise morale on a cold London evening.' They ate another two slices of the roll and Jane was bewildered to find herself enjoying it. She hadn't tasted the synthetic sponge and cheap vanilla ice cream since she was a girl and the combination transported her straight into the kitchen at Barnabas Road. 'Looks like we're going to polish the whole thing off, like in our misspent youth,' she said.

After Daphne left, Jane felt wired, as though she'd drunk too much coffee. Clearing up, she knocked a glass on to the floor and went through the rigmarole of picking up dozens of jagged slivers. She was relieved the evening had gone well but she was still uneasy. Their friendship had always been like that, she thought, characterised by opposites. As a girl, she had loved and hated her simultaneously. Affection and admiration were threaded through with envy, but also exasperation and sometimes despair. As far as the Ralph business went, she would have to lead her gradually in the right direction. It was impossible to be frank or tell her everything.

She spent almost two hours in bed with her laptop, researching historical child sexual abuse. The amount of data available was almost overwhelming. All across the country, women (and some men), many of her sort of age, were emerging to divulge their grim stories. Unspoken for decades, the words had begun to gush forth with details of sordid events that had been hidden in shame and were finally now being revealed and recognised as crimes.

7

RALPH

It was only when he heard Nina's key in the lock and her tentative call that he realised he had spent nearly forty-eight hours on the sofa. Following his fourth visit to the hospital, the sitting room looked like a tempting place to rest – the view of freshly born April leaves outside the window was soothing. Then he became rooted there, barely able to stumble to the kitchen to get a drink or some crackers. He'd been told to expect fatigue after the chemo, but this was beyond any tiredness he'd experienced.

'In here.' His voice emerged as a croak. He could only imagine what he looked like from the alarm on Nina's face. She said something incomprehensible in Greek before switching to English. 'Oh my God. What's going on? Are you ill?' She put her hand on his forehead, checking for a fever.

'No, I'm OK. Well, a bit. Maybe I'll go and take a bath.' He suspected he didn't smell too appetising, having failed to wash or clean his teeth during this period. Upright, it was hard to get a balance.

'Sit.' Nina had evidently never realised that, in English, it sounded like an instruction to a dog, but he took her advice. After she removed her coat and gathered up the accumulated mail on the doormat, she returned. 'OK, let's get you upstairs.'

While he lay in the bathtub, Nina came back with a mug of camomile tea – her notion of a panacea, and it did make him feel better.

'Angel of mercy. Thank you, darling.' He looked up at his wife from the steaming water. Not many marriages lasted this long – forty years in October. Nina was planning a celebration with children, grandchildren, friends gathered across all these decades and from various places. It hadn't always been easy (find me an easy marriage, he thought), but they'd made it through this great span of existence together. Even in her mid-sixties she looked good: a gentle, pleasing face with kind, brown eyes, and she still had long hair, now mostly grey and wound into a chaotic bun or loosely plaited.

She knelt down on the bath mat and kissed him on the forehead. 'You should have told me. What's the point otherwise?' Nina had become increasingly independent during the years since the children left. She was painting almost fanatically, ever smaller pictures, almost miniatures, which could be pieced together to create something like a mosaic. Wherever he found her, she'd be bent over some tiny creation, using a paintbrush as fine as a butterfly's antenna. But she was deeply loyal to him. Steadfast. He couldn't just shut her out. So he told her about the hospital, playing down the return of the illness. 'A top-up to keep it under control,' he said. 'I'll have a few more sessions over the next months and then it'll all be fine.'

His system of hiding things was now more often a habit than a vice. The shed in the garden still offered the sense of retreating from the world that he needed for equilibrium and for his composing, but with the house often quiet and unoccupied by anyone but himself, this had become a luxury rather than a necessity. These days, Nina was frequently absent, visiting one of the children, or going for weeks, even months to Greece, where she could work and keep an eye on her old mother. True, she was still remarkably supportive of his music, even after all this time – she never missed a premiere or an important concert of his. And she had always been a guard dog for his composition, keeping people out of his way, taking his phone calls, or organising the practical elements of his life. She had filled books with cuttings about him and his music, going all the way back to when they first met. As he'd become better known, she'd bought larger albums to fit the proliferation of interviews and reviews. He had enjoyed witnessing her pride.

Nina took charge of his convalescence with generous efficiency – mother, nurse, handmaiden and wife bound into one. Nourishing broths simmered on the stove, pots of spring flowers were placed around the house, and within a few days he was edging back to something like normality. It never surprised him to be the centre of attention. When he was young, his mother had joked that all the parties and firework displays on November 5th were a countrywide celebration of his birthday, and he had half-believed her.

If his own mother had been devoted, Nina was many times more so to their children. He recalled how she'd tended to them through their childhood illnesses, staying up all night, strong as a rock, fiercely loving. She never asked him to help, perhaps, as she said, because he needed his sleep and had to work. She had flung herself into maternity, so it hardly mattered if he was away or busy or up to some escapade. He only really noticed this had happened afterwards, when it was too late for him to rethink his approach to fatherhood.

Nina evidently told the children something, as they each made contact, showing signs of mild concern. Jason called from Madrid and made Sydney (now four) come and say 'Hello to Grandpa'. Ralph loved his grandchildren, but wished they could avoid calling him this name; he still felt too youthful for it. Lucia caught the train up from Brighton for a flying visit with her little girl Bee, who looked almost identical to her mother at that age, with her solid step, pouting mouth and surprising, green-flecked eyes.

He had doted on Lucia when she was young. He remembered lying on her bed at night and telling her stories or singing songs while she snuggled against him, her breath slowing as she fell asleep. Somehow, they had drifted apart. He was away so much, and then she grew up and was suddenly a teenager who couldn't be bothered. Or perhaps they were never as close as he had thought. There was one evening where he had offered to take over the children so that Nina could paint. She was very grateful and it was all going fine until the phone rang once, then stopped – the signal he'd arranged with Daphne if she needed him. He called her back at Barnabas Road: he couldn't even remember now what the reason was for her distress – nothing significant – but he'd abandoned Lucia's story halfway through, hurried downstairs and given Nina some half-baked excuse about a conductor needing a pre-rehearsal drink. She hadn't complained, just washed her brushes, and picked up the tearful Lucia at the top of the stairs. His last sight as he slunk out of the front door was of his wife and daughter's hair mingled like a tawny forest animal.

Lucia brought a bag of turmeric roots with her from Brighton, and a pair of smooth crystals.

'I could give you a bit of reiki if you like? It's such a powerful treatment, you know. We're finding it's the most popular therapy at the centre these days. If it works for you we could even do some sessions by phone.' He tried to appear grateful. Bee sang him 'Greensleeves', which she'd performed in a school concert. 'My Honey Bee', he called her, and crooned a bit of Louis Armstrong's 'Honeysuckle Rose'. He'd sung it to other people, including Daphne, in rather different circumstances.

Alexander sent an email from Seattle, where he'd been doing something complicated in cyber technology for the last five years. Take it easy, Dad. Look after yourself. He was still the baby, even if he was thirty-four. He had been born in America, during the excruciating year when Ralph accepted a residency at Columbia University.

He'd done it when he realised he could no longer contain his feelings for Daphne. Daff was fourteen. Or perhaps a bit older – he couldn't remember. Certainly, Nina had two babies and another on the way. How on earth had they managed that? What about the pill? Well they *had* managed it. The offer of composer-in-residence looked like a solution to a desperate situation. His composition work was overwhelming, his family needed him and yet he was hanging around Putney train-bridge in the hope of glimpsing a schoolgirl. It was beginning to feel like an addiction.

He hoped the distance would be like medicine for him. And for Daphne, of course. 'You should spend more time with your young friends,' he told her, though the idea of other boyfriends tormented him to the extent of a physical ache. He imagined spotty youths pawing over her perfect body and felt murderous.

They left England in 1977, crossing the Atlantic on a jumbo jet. He drank five brandies with ginger ale, which left Nina in charge of three-year-old Jason – already a flirt, running up and down the aisles, stopping to speak to the prettiest women. Little Lucia, milky and soft, ringlets in her hair, snuggled against the modest protrusion from Nina's abdomen that would one day be Alexander.

The family moved into a spacious apartment provided by the university and Ralph was not expected to teach or commit to much, apart from an occasional seminar and a few social events. It should have been a dream, yet looking back he remembered it as one of the saddest times in his life. There was an excellent crèche for the children, Nina was filled with new energy and looked spectacular. He saw her through American eyes – exotic and different, with her yard of flowing hair, colourful robes and burgeoning body. She was painting huge canvases (now he thought of it, they'd been getting gradually smaller ever since) and even had a show on the Lower East Side. Together, they were treated like a golden couple – feted as beautiful young artists, fresh from Europe, embracing the new world and at the height of their powers. He felt dejected and bereft.

Dearest Daff,

I keep writing long, boring letters to you trying to analyse why and wherefore and then give up – my mind is too fuzzy. Why do I love you when it's so obviously hopeless? Hopeless? Maybe it's not, in the sense that it's not about hope or lack of it, it's about loving you. You're a great strong wilful force in my life. Even when I'm not with you, you are with me every minute. How would I have survived without you? I wrote that damn violin concerto for you — all for you.

I think I'm still drunk from last night. Or at least so hungover it's hard to tell the difference. Nina had some paintings in a gallery on a road called the Bowery. I got slaughtered — pissed as a rat, a dirty dog in the gutter. There was a rumour that Andy Warhol was going to come so everyone was overexcited. He didn't. I hardly noticed. I was picturing your dark eyes with those long lashes, your hair growing back into its old tangles, your breasts. Christ. It's much worse here than I imagined.

I hear your derisive laugh — if I do put you on a pedestal it's because you're worth it. You inspire all my work. Ridiculous? Am I mad, foolish, or just childlike? I love my family and I love you. Love you differently. You are like a stove that my fire must warm — see, I cannot express myself in words. The fact is I cannot explain it. I cannot stop my passion. As you have grown older it has only increased. Does it hurt you? I don't believe it. All I know for certain is that I love you — that you make my life possible.

Meanwhile, I surround you with love like a great cloak.

I love you.

R

Later, he regretted sending her a letter so soaked in self-pity and, the next day, wrote another, more jaunty one.

Dear lovely old Daff, how are you, my Strawberry?

Sorry about raving like a lunatic in that last dispatch. Destroy it at once!

I've been working all day on my Three Songs, sitting in my new study in the university. I miss you so much sometimes I think I'll just jump on a plane and come back to see you, even if it's only for a day. Maybe I will.

America still feels like a very foreign country and they find me rather quaint — ye olde England bollocks, and making a fuss about my accent. The only solution will be to work as hard as possible and write so much music that this time away from you will at least be productive. You are at the centre of my creativity — like a fire that is always alight.

Please write and tell me how you are. Do you ever think about me or have you completely forgotten your loyal Dog, you fickle little monkey? How is Lady Jane? How are the snogging parties? Do I want to know the answer? Have you had more trouble at school?

I've been very secret about your letters and nobody knows you've written to me. For Dog's sake make sure you lock mine away. Your parents may be wrapped up in their own affairs (joke) but Ellie will be bound to sniff them out and read them if you're not careful — except the enclosed one which you should leave lying. It's super-innocent and designed especially to allay suspicions!

My lovely girl, my beloved one. Try to be happy. Know that I love you.

Your old Dog

The communication for public consumption was folded up alongside the love letter.

My dear Daphne,

Everything in America is so large it makes us feel like dwarfish Europeans. When we go out to eat the plates are like cartwheels, the hamburgers like birthday cakes, and Coca-Cola comes in pint glasses with buckets of ice. If you want a bottle *of milk, you buy a giant carton that you can barely lift and Jason and Lucia love the boxes of multicoloured cereal that are almost big enough for them to crawl into. As to the cars, well poor old Maurice looks like a crumbling chariot unearthed from an archaeological dig compared to the shiny spaceships on the streets here. I wonder if you'd like it. I'd like to walk through Central Park with you one day and take you to see the monkeys in the zoo, who are not nearly as well behaved as dear departed Hugo.*

Love from all of us,
Ralph

He often said to Daphne that he could tell her anything, but there was actually quite a lot he omitted from the letters. He mentioned the cocaine in the hope that she would make confessions in return, but he made it sound more like a one-off experiment. Tequila was also a new discovery, but the white powder was his favourite anti-dote to desolation. It made him feel powerful, fearless, like dancing all night, which he sometimes did. As Nina neared the end of her pregnancy, he took to going out with people he'd met through her gallery and they went to clubs where girls were boys and vice versa. Initially, it was the drugs that allowed him to appreciate the music playing in the dark cellars and flashing dance floors; he had rejected the flimsiness of pop until then. But the mad rawness of punk and the chest-thumping power of rock now provided something he could embrace. He adopted elements in his own music and included an electric guitar in one of his orchestral pieces.

Usually, he managed to get to the morning post first, in case there was something from Daff. On the whole, it was easy. Their letter box was downstairs in the building's entrance, so he made sure he got there before Nina left the apartment, nipping down 'in case the contract has arrived' or some such excuse. One morning, however, he failed. Shattered from the excesses of partying and having returned in the small hours, he felt deeply depressed and physically crushed. He would have liked to sleep it off but the children were shouting and he had a mid-morning appointment at the university. Much of the night had been spent with Candy, a young singer with an extraordinarily visceral voice – Nina Simone meets Patti Smith. She was the first black woman he'd ever slept with. He already had her in mind for his *Lullabies for an Unborn Child*. The three short songs were one of his greatest successes, especially in America, where they premiered that year, just after Alexander's birth.

As he shuffled into the kitchen, exhausted, fur-tongued and desperate for coffee, Nina handed him an envelope with a recognisable, juvenile script in purple ink. She was not interested in spying or checking up on his stories, but there was a methodical side to her character. She was not stupid.

'How is young Daphne?' She didn't sound as though she required an answer. He knew there had been some discussion between Ellie and Nina about visiting New York. Perhaps she would bring Daphne. It was shocking to hear this idea posited so casually by Nina a few days earlier. He longed for that but also dreaded it. What was the point of making this break if his darling monkey girl was going to follow him across the Atlantic and throw him into even deeper turmoil? He imagined introducing her to Candy and groaned. He put down the unopened letter as nonchalantly as possible – he would read it later in private – then, squinting with irritation at the sunshine that streamed through the windows, he poured himself some coffee and grunted the guttural moan of a vampire caught in daylight.

* * *

A few days after Nina's return to London and her dauntless Florence Nightingale act, Ralph went back to his garden workroom. His agent wanted the corrections completed on a recent composition and he sharpened several 2B pencils, clipped the manuscript to his adjustable, architect's drawing board and got on with it. The work wasn't too challenging and it helped to think of something other than his body's fragility. He loved his shed that smelled of wood like a tree house, but was filled with comforts and small luxuries like his custom-made desk and a chaise longue modelled on Ed's old one in Putney. The shed had been strictly forbidden to anyone – when the children were young he'd locked the door and Nina understood him well enough to avoid even crossing the threshold. These days, he made an exception for their cleaner Anka's occasional hoovering sessions, but even then, he'd watch over the pale-eyed, lip-chewing Polish girl and close the door on her with relief.

While Ralph worked, Nina cooked: *avgolemono* soup with chicken, stuffed peppers, baked butter beans. She made sure he ate yogurt and drank freshly squeezed orange juice. In the afternoons, she took him for slow walks down Primrose Hill and into Regent's Park. London looked like a green city, with every possible shade bursting forth from the newly grown leaves, the scent of wisteria and fresh-ground coffee in the air. She linked her arm through his and relayed news about their children that they themselves didn't get round to telling him. He felt she was treating him almost like a fourth child now. Any erotic spark between them had been dampened so long he could hardly remember what it had been like when they'd been lovers. It hadn't appeared to bother her. Better, in her opinion, to be bound by the bonds of familial affection. Once or twice, he'd wondered whether she might be having an affair – not for evidence of awkward phone calls or indeed anything suspicious, but because she would glow with an internal energy that reminded him of how she'd been as an art student when she fell in love with him.

Periodically, he was overwhelmed by exhaustion, and had to lie down to recover. He took long baths, soothed by the gentle warmth and by the comfortable tones of BBC voices on the radio. It was not always calming. Indeed he experienced a sliver of anxiety when the news reported some retired teacher or scoutmaster hauled off in handcuffs for sexual abuse in the 1970s or '80s. There was regularly a new bout of shaming some seedy, long-forgotten pop singer, now reincarnated as a molesting predator, an evil fiend. One man of ninety-six was jailed for abusing two children, who were presumably pensioners themselves by now. It would be a comedy if it weren't so grotesque.

There was one report that disconcerted him more deeply than the others. An art teacher had run away with a pupil of fifteen, and they had travelled incognito to France. The man was eventually arrested and the girl was reported to have said, 'We are in love.' Ralph recognised something of his own experiences in what he heard on the radio, but sought to distance himself. The teacher was probably chasing after lots of young girls, he thought. Whereas I worshipped Daphne, body and soul. I wasn't some Humbert Humbert obsessed with nymphets. And it's not only that I never did anything against her will, it's that we met as spirits, Plato's twinned flames. It was genuine and pure.

Ralph recognised that something had been out of control. Of course it was. We were all changing the world. But now we're expected to conform like robots or lemmings. Everyone is so conventional. It's ghastly. Yes, Daphne was young, but so was I. It was *my* youth too – not just hers. Our story had nothing to do with abuse. To link them is like pouring filth on flowers, like denying the power of love.

8

DAPHNE

It was after eleven and she was sewing and drinking her third coffee of the morning when Libby meandered in. She was beginning to need the incredibly long sessions of sleep that Daphne remembered from her own adolescence, when Ed called her Sleeping Beauty.

'Hi, Libs. How are you today?' She secured the needle in the fabric and got up.

'OK. Did you remember that Paige is sleeping over after Caroline's party? We'll get out the mattress, OK? And we're going shopping first.'

'Fabulous. What about Chloe? You haven't mentioned her recently. Is she going to the party? Maybe you shouldn't just drop her altogether?'

'Chloe's fine, OK?' Libby laughed and Daphne sensed that Chloe's welfare was the last thing that mattered to her in the guerrilla warfare and tribal alliances of school friendships.

'Glad to hear it. So, should we order pizzas this evening?' This was an easy way of getting some appreciation and, sure enough, Libby beamed with innocent pleasure.

'I'm going to meet her in Putney this afternoon. We wanted to see if we could buy something for the party.'

'Great. Have you still got some savings from Sam's Christmas money?'

'A little bit. But I wouldn't say no to some more ...' Libby smiled winsomely.

Daphne enjoyed these little negotiations. She acknowledged that her life consisted of simpler satisfactions than the extreme situations of her youth. Internally, however, she heard a needling echo of Jane's comment: 'What would you do if a man made Libby love him?' The answer was obvious: Libby was far too sensible!

As she worked on *Putney* she remembered the parties she had been to as a girl; in particular, a celebration she had given on the day her O levels finished, which was coincidentally the summer solstice. Ed and Ellie went away for the longest night of the year, and friends started arriving from late afternoon to rig up speakers in the garden at Barnabas Road. By the time the sun was setting there were about fifty teenagers dancing on the grass, jumping into the hot tub in their underwear or climbing up to the tree house, taking turns for a few minutes of privacy. The rule of entry had been 'bring a bottle' and, as nobody had thought of getting plastic cups, they were all drinking directly from bottles of beer, cheap wine and rum.

She hadn't invited Ralph. Why would she? Not only was he separate from the rest of her life, he actually encouraged her (in tones of noble self-sacrifice) to 'get a little boyfriend'. She agreed it was only fair to juggle him with boys closer to her age, just as he had always juggled her with his family. Her favourite boy of the summer was Martin. It wasn't love, but she liked his hot white skin and hair dyed sooty black. He smelled of glue and Mars bars. He and his two best friends looked a bit like Johnny Rotten's gang, though they had just taken their A levels, would get good grades, and were destined for university. It was Martin who lured her and Jane into their brief punk phase, giving them the hair colour he used (very dramatic in Jane's case) and encouraging them to wear clothes covered with chains, zips and safety pins. They went to concerts where the band spat on the audience and they wandered along the King's Road making eyes at boys with green Mohicans.

She pictured herself dancing on the grass with Martin, so stoned they couldn't stop laughing – bending and swaying to the music and buckling at the source of a shared, if unidentifiable, joke. When the tide went out, they clambered down the ladder to the mudflats and Martin fixed up an improvised brazier and lit a fire. They kissed, slipping and grasping on to one another, and then danced, besmirched with sludge, as the party took on the atmosphere of a pagan celebration. By chance, she glanced up to the garden wall where people were gathered, and there was Ralph. He gave her a small wave and a pained expression. By the time she had climbed back up the ladder to find him, he was dancing flirtatiously with Jane – presumably his idea of provoking her. Certainly Jane looked pleased.

A gentle rain began to fall and Ralph asked her to go inside the house for a minute. She looked around but couldn't see Martin anywhere. In the kitchen, she noticed herself in the ornate mirror hanging behind the wooden sofa. Her hair had sprung up into an explosion of curls, her arms and legs were slicked with river mud and her eyes were blackened with smudged eyeliner. 'Wild girl,' Ralph said, as if offering a challenge. They kissed drunkenly, mouths tasting of cigarettes and alcohol. He looked sad and she felt she had the upper hand; she could choose to reject him, or they could go and screw each other. She knew it wasn't about being in love any more – it was different now, however much they cared for one another. She thought, I can do this. I'm playing this game and making up my own rules. I'm not a kid. They went up to Ed's study and did it standing against the door, fast, almost angry. Then Ralph left and she went back to the garden.

She might have felt like a woman of the world, aged sixteen and allowed by law to choose her lovers, but she had not yet experienced an orgasm. Ralph had not enquired. They had also been wantonly careless about contraception – the 'French letters' were never produced again after Aegina and they didn't discuss the subject. She had numerous pregnancy scares when her period came late and she fantasised about the ensuing catastrophe – Ralph, shocked and concerned at her hospital bedside after an abortion, her parents confused and miserable.

* * *

It was late afternoon when Libby and Paige returned home from their shopping expedition.

'Hi, Daphne. How are you? Thanks for having me over.' She was very confident and pretty, hair woven into corn-rows ending in beaded braids and wearing a tight top that revealed a pierced belly button. Her manner was more sophisticated than Libby's. She reminded Daphne of the older girls at Hayfield, whom she admired and feared in almost equal measure, whose world was impenetrable.

'Look what I bought!' With the aplomb of a conjuror, Libby whisked out a pair of shiny, black, spike-heeled shoes. 'They're for tonight,' she said, before Daphne could speak. 'We're going to dress up. I'm so excited.' Until recently, Libby's parties meant balloons and jelly; all of a sudden, they included fuck-me shoes.

'They were really cheap – on sale,' said Libby. 'I love them.' She put them on and wavered on spindly legs, precarious as a newborn fawn.

'Hey, Mum, can you make us some of that popcorn with honey and chilli?' Libby liked offering Daphne the chance to appear like an improved version of herself – more conventional and orderly, matriarch of a household with charming traditions like unusual popcorn. They were able to present something more substantial than an alliance of two orbiting females – something resembling a family. If they'd been alone together, Daphne would probably have said, 'Oh come on, Lib, make it yourself,' but she played along with the game. 'Right, but be prepared for a chilli-fest – I like it spicy.' Libby's casual acceptance of her care was part of the game too. The girls scurried off to Libby's room to get ready for the party and the merciless beat of dance music thudded through the flat.

After making the popcorn, she returned to her work. The sun had set and it was the perfect moment between day and night, the sky lit up pink. She opened the windows in the sitting room and the warm evening air brought compound scents of silty river water, mown grass and the roasting meat smoke from a nearby barbecue. Quite some time passed before Libby's bedroom door opened and the two girls made their entrance. Bright red lipstick, over-done eye make-up, teetering heels and miniskirts revealing lengths of bare, skinny legs. Their arms were covered with glitter, their nails painted bubble-gum pink. They looked like caricatures of underage sex workers. 'Wow!' Daphne tried to smile.

Gripping Paige so her wobbling heels would not betray her, Libby switched the television on to a channel with pop videos. An American singer in satin underwear and fishnet drapery was twisting and grinding, the camera angle aimed at her crotch. The video was filmed in a club where the performers had mocked up a druggy party: rough-looking men were locked pelvis to buttock with girls covered in tattoos and piercings. The dancers were fast and slick, cupping their genitals, thrusting and cutting through explicit imitations of the sex act. There was nothing ambiguous. Libby and Paige took up the beat and began dancing to the music. They knew how to do it. There was little Libby, flicking and twisting her hips, lowering herself parallel to her friend until they were almost squatting, then writhing up again. Daphne found the sight mesmerising and awful.

The previous evening, Lib had begged her mother to watch a DVD of *The Lion King* — her favourite cartoon since babyhood. She had actually sat on Daphne's lap, entwined in her arms, which she gripped at the scary parts. They'd both sung along with the familiar songs. Yesterday Libby had been a child. A baby. Today she was ... well, it was hard to say a woman. It was more as if she was veering violently and uncontrollably between one state and another.

It was only too clear that Libby was being swept along by natural forces. Attempting to prevent it would be pointless. And yet there was something alarming about the scene playing out in their sitting room. 'What would you do if a man made Libby love him?' She shuddered. The shocking question had abruptly become more plausible.

The song on the television changed and Libby and Paige abandoned their improvised dance floor, ankles quivering. Libby's cheeks were pink-sheened, her eyes brilliant blue. She was taller than Daphne in these shoes. There was a steamy gust of sweet perfume as they swayed and grabbed each other, giggled and made their way through to the kitchen to get some water. Daphne followed, half-horrified, half-fascinated, unnoticed by the girls who were laughing at the red lipstick imprints they left on their glasses.

'So, Libby, what time should we leave for the party? And when does it end? Shall I collect you at eleven?'

'No way eleven! Mum! At least midnight. Oh come on. It's the holidays. Nobody will leave before twelve.'

Daphne might have enjoyed these age-old parental negotiations in other circumstances, but after witnessing the girls dancing, it felt as though the rules had changed.

'OK, eleven thirty. But that's my last offer.' She didn't like the sound of her own voice. She had never spoken to Libby like that before.

*　*　*

When she returned home after dropping off the party girls, the block of flats seemed even quieter than usual, as if everyone else was out on this beautiful July evening. The fourth-floor corridor looked bleak and bland and, yet again, she experienced the disconcerting sense of entering Aunt Connie's home rather than her own. A wave of Saturday-night loneliness drenched her for a moment as she opened a bottle of wine, poured a glass and sipped it while inspecting the fridge. Methodically, she picked at the remains of lunch, extracting a few olives, some bread and cheese and a tomato. Pleased by this efficient means of completing her supper, she took the wine to the sitting room and looked out at its view of her past.

Threading her needle, Daphne began to sew the elements for the Thames. Instead of flat water, she was creating twisting textile tubes, stuffed so they looked like snakes or bulging entrails – a living river. Taking some gulps from her wine, she tried to understand why she had been so shaken by the dancing girls, by Libby's sudden transformation. It wasn't that she hoped to prevent Lib from becoming a sexual being – far from it. But from her perspective, it was obvious that her daughter and Paige had been performing a game of sexiness. It was not supposed to be taken seriously, not so dissimilar to boys engaging in war games. But you wouldn't give them live ammunition. With girls, however, the painted lips and shiny shoes look like the real thing, rather than the equivalent of toy guns. Of course, the sexual awakening was true too – she'd never deny that. But she now saw with clarity how adolescent awakening cuts both ways, between new bewildering longings and the playgrounds of childhood.

As Daphne made minute stitches on her writhing river, she thought about herself at Libby's age. It was impossible not to compare her own experiences to her daughter's. She'd never deny that she loved Ralph, but a bright spotlight now gave that era a different appearance. She had been far too young to understand what was happening when she was swept into the deep waters of a love affair. Unlike Libby, Daphne hadn't used the props of make-up or stripper's gear for her game but, looking back, she could see that twelve or thirteen or even fifteen are not ages for being taken seriously by men of thirty. And certainly not for being taken into their beds. Who had been there to protect her?

She often wondered what it would have been like to have Ellie around later – when her daughter was born, when she had an exhibition, when she'd nearly given up. Losing her mother had changed so much, it was hard to imagine how it would be if Ellie had been there to make her study, to get her to university, to scream and shout about the marriage to Constantine. Ellie would have dragged her by the hair to get her out of the clutches of Constantine's family. Or perhaps she would just have repeated her old adage, 'Learn your own lessons,' and that would have been enough to open Daphne's eyes. Ellie might not have been the mother waiting at home each day after school, but she was unwaveringly loving. She was also an example of a powerful woman pursuing what she believed was important. Daphne hoped she had passed on these priorities to Libby: make your own way, never rely on a man, go out and see the world.

After Ellie died, Daphne took her jewellery from the leather box in her bedroom. 'She'd want you to have it,' said Ed, but she saw he was miserable when she wore almost everything at once, piling necklaces until they hung heavy on her neck and adding the bangles and bracelets to her own, so she clanked like a prisoner. Most of it wasn't valuable – lots of Indian beads and turquoise earrings – but there were a few precious items, including a diamond ring from Ellie's grandmother and a gold bracelet Ed had bought in an extravagant mood. Within a few years, Daphne had lost the lot. Several of the necklaces broke at a party and there were too many drunk people dancing to scoop up all the beads. She didn't even know what happened to the ornate, Byzantine-style bracelet her father had given her mother; one day she merely couldn't find it.

The end of Ellie's jewels had been like another, more minor bereavement – a reminder that there was nothing left of her mother. Nothing tangible or solid. Not even a gravestone. The only comfort was the idea of Ellie's cells continuing – she often saw reminders of her mother when she caught her reflection by surprise. And of course, Ellie was also there in Libby.

Ellie's diamond ring fell off when Daphne was swimming in Greece with Constantine. She'd met him two years after her mother's death. They were on an Olympic Airlines flight from London to Athens and she spotted him before they boarded, interested in the unusual mix in his handsome face of potential for danger and lazy indulgence – a panther resting. Later, she thought of him more like a snake that would devour you whole and then rest quietly for days while the digesting took place. When they were airborne he came to find her, having arranged that she could sit next to him in the business section. She changed her plans, spending the summer on the Cycladic island of Andros, where his family had a magnificent villa, surrounded by flowering gardens and groves of lemon trees and olives.

Their decision to marry in the autumn was a continuation of the absurd, drugged-up fantasy that should have remained a misjudged holiday romance. He was thirty and she was twenty. Later, she wondered if it was a longing to connect with Greece after the trauma of losing her mother. There was an undeniable pleasure in lying in bed with someone and speaking Greek, as she had done as a child with Ellie. It was so hard to make sense of the murky motives of youth. Constantine had the physical daring and shapely limbs of the bull-leapers on the Minoan frescoes at Knossos. Danger, beauty and youth, backed up by a family whose wealth was intimidatingly vast and assumed by them to be a solution to everything.

If moving to Greece had initially felt like embracing her mother's country, it wasn't long before she'd lost it. And lost a baby. She blamed herself for that. A summer of such concentrated partying that she forgot to take the pill – up all night at clubs, taking whatever looked good, staying awake with coke, sleeping all day. She didn't notice she was pregnant for ages, by which time it was probably already doomed. The implausible marriage had already disintegrated. She returned like a soldier traumatised by war to her father's England. Except that Ed had gone by then – moved to France. If she bought *The Times*, she was able to read his numerous book reviews, but she hardly ever saw him. Theo was already doing something in nanotechnology, and earning fabulous money in Boston. So there was no family left. During that terrible time, Daphne felt orphaned, emptied, robbed.

Skimming through her teenage diaries in search of ideas for *Putney*, she was shocked by how unhappy she'd been, especially when Ralph went to America for a year. She had regularly got drunk on her parents' brandy and bottles of wine, convinced that all meaning had been snatched away from her life. Of course, she dissembled about why she was in such a bad way. Her parents may have been thinking about other things, but they loved her and noticed her misery. Once, they'd been playing a record of Ralph's music on the kitchen gramophone as the family gathered for supper. This was not unusual. Indeed, his music had been a sort of soundtrack to her life – cropping up by chance on the radio or at friends' houses, actively sought out in occasional concerts, and sometimes chosen by her to listen to at home. But this time, hearing *Into the Woods*, the woodwind piece he said represented their first kisses in the green glade, it was too much to bear. She fled from the room and refused to come down to eat. Later, Ellie brought her a plate of spaghetti bolognese and sat on her bed, stroking her, telling her it was never easy being a teenager, that she could always talk to her about anything. Daphne longed to confide in her mother, to be held and comforted, but it was impossible. The pact of secrecy between Ralph and her was their foundation stone. She knew that if she confessed, she would never see him again.

It was all very well, she thought, Ellie acting the part from time to time. She never doubted that her mother was devoted to her. But it was the veering from one extreme to another that was so hard to deal with as a daughter, so that she never knew whether Ellie would be too engrossed with a project to speak to her children or whether she'd come to Daphne's bed and lie there with her for hours singing Greek songs and making up mad stories.

This 'blowing hot and cold', as Ed called it, characterised her mother's approach to many things, including religion. Ostensibly espousing a dogged, left-wing atheism, Ellie periodically dragged her children off to the Orthodox church in Moscow Road. She and Ed had married there in 1958 and they'd baptised both babies there as well. Daphne remembered various occasions standing under the gilded dome, yawning her way through Easter midnight

Mass, standing for an eternity and clutching her decorated candle in a sea of small flames. One year, Ralph had been there with Nina and a baby or two. In the chaos that ensued after midnight struck, when everyone was kissing and greeting friends ('Christ is risen', 'Truly he is risen'), they'd escaped into some sort of vestry and snogged. Outside, firecrackers exploded like warfare.

By the time she picked up Libby and Paige from the party, Daphne felt overheated with anger. It was like an allergic reaction that spiked when she thought of Ralph, of the casual carelessness of her parents and of her own gullible stupidity. The girls stumbled along the pavement, collapsed into the back seat of the car and hardly greeted Daphne. They were evidently drunk.

'Yeah, fine,' answered Libby to her mother's question of how it went. There was a love bite on Paige's neck. Daphne felt helpless and furious. What could she do? What do mothers do? There was certainly no role model.

'You sound as though you've had a drink or two.' It came out sullen and stupid. Should she roar and rant? She couldn't do that to Libby, especially in front of her new friend. She had done far worse at their age.

Back home, her body was rigid with unabated fury and, above all, fear.

'You need to drink lots of water now or you'll be ill.' She made the girls down two large glasses each and, when Paige went to the bathroom, she spoke to Libby. 'I'm not happy about this. You must be careful, my lovely.' She hoped to draw her daughter in close, impart some motherly words of wisdom, show her there was no need to hurry with these new experiences. There was so much time ahead.

'Yeah, Mum. I'll be careful.' It sounded patronising. 'Night, then.' Libby turned to leave, wiping her face and smearing a streak of black mascara across a pale cheek.

After the girls were in bed, Daphne returned to her sewing. She held a small figure of Ralph, wondering how he fitted into the scene this time around. She no longer thought of him as a romantic, floating character in the sky, and she began to wonder about the real, living Ralph. How did he see their story now? Did he harbour any doubts at all or was he as sure as he'd been in 1976, when he'd committed adultery and child abuse simultaneously? She had never formulated that thought before and it had a satisfying cut to it, like a knife. Had it ever crossed his mind? Perhaps she should ask him.

Locating some black rubbery material – scraps of fetish clothing – she snipped out a tiny mask, attaching it so it covered much of the Ralph doll's face. A bit voodoo, she thought with satisfaction.

9

JANE

'Jane! Jane? Aren't you coming?' Michael's voice had a mix of concern and annoyance as he returned to the kitchen. 'Didn't you hear me? I've been calling you for ages. We ought to go now if we're going to miss the traffic.' Having finished the washing-up, she was standing at the sink, staring out of the window at the weak sun that had just broken through the morning mist.

'Sorry, my love. I was a million miles away.' Probably more like two thousand, if she was honest – somewhere in Greece, where Daphne had been, supposedly working, for the last few weeks. This gap in proceedings had been difficult. It had the blank, empty summer feel she had hated as a girl, when she waited in Wimbledon for her friend to return from the Mediterranean.

This summer, it was waiting in Wandsworth, with brief flurries of commotion each time Toby returned from a festival where his university troupe was performing. The previous week, he had arrived home happily exhausted and unwashed, his head shaved and a sparse auburn beard sprouting from his youthful chin. He had four actor friends with him and the two girls took over Josh's old room, while the boys spread out rolls and sleeping bags on Toby's floor. They spent most of the days asleep, emerging in the late afternoon, and Jane had enjoyed coming home from work and cooking suppers for the students, before they went out for the night. Crowding round the kitchen table they put away platefuls of food and quoted lines from their comedy show that had them laughing so much the girls said they would pee themselves and the boys lay cackling on the floor. She was pleased to see Toby happy and doing something he enjoyed, but she had to admit that even having her youngest son home didn't prevent her thoughts being dominated by Daphne and Ralph.

'OK, time to go,' Michael said. 'Car's all packed. Got the coffee?' She held up a basket with a Thermos, some sandwiches and a few apples. Was she turning into her mother, she wondered, remembering the family's long drives down to Cornwall, the sodden beaches, her summer-holiday impatience to see Daphne again. She and Michael were heading in the opposite direction: a few days in the Lake District and then on to Edinburgh to see Toby's troupe perform at the Fringe.

It rained every day in the Lakes and, while Michael insisted on swathing himself in waterproofs and heading for the highest points, Jane mostly stayed indoors. Whenever he returned triumphant and soaked, she pretended she'd been reading. In fact, she'd spent most of the time on the Internet, churning up the bottomless pit of information about children whose lives had been trashed by sexual predators. Uncles with cameras, stepfathers with friends who paid, neighbours watching and waiting, deep-web promises of overwhelming horrors ... an apparently endless supply of marauders looting and plundering youth.

Toby's Edinburgh show was on at an inauspicious 11 a.m. in a tent that smelled of damp and the previous evening's beer spills, but the space was filled with cheering young people Jane presumed were university friends. The play was a satire about transgender aliens and, by the end of it, she felt old and crabbed from not understanding all the jokes and straining to smile as the audience roared and guffawed around her. Afterwards, she and Michael hugged Toby and congratulated him and his friends but, in truth, the best part of her day was getting an email from Daphne that afternoon. It contained a photograph of a vast, ancient-looking olive tree, golden-leafed in low sunlight, and a brief message:

Leaving poor old Hellas tomorrow. Can't wait to see you. Can you come over on Saturday? Lots of love, D.

* * *

Daphne welcomed her into the flat like a long-lost friend. At first, Jane suspected her of overstating the affection – exaggeration had always been a Greenslay trait – but it became clear she was genuine.

'Here, I brought you something from Greece.' Daphne handed over a small box tied with a bow. 'I've been thinking about you. I missed you.'

Jane removed the lid to reveal a pair of earrings made from two small pebbles, their matt-grey surfaces crossed with slivers of gold.

'They're beautiful. So unusual.'

'A friend of mine makes them. Finds little stones on the beach and treats them like jewels. It's like walking around with a bit of Aegean seaside hanging from your ears.'

Jane walked over to a mirror and tried them on.

'I love them. Thank you so much. That's far too generous.'

'They look perfect.'

They did look perfect, but they reminded Jane of the treasure she had once stolen from Daphne. The smooth oval lozenge of amber had been a present from Ralph, and it contained a leggy caddis fly suspended within its golden interior. As an eleven- or twelve-year-old, Daphne had been fascinated by the translucent fossil, which she kept on her bedside table. She showed Jane how to hold it up to the light to examine the perfectly preserved veins on the fly's fifty-million-year-old wings. The miracle of the prehistoric insect had made Jane jealous. It symbolised the unusual, enviable bond between her friend and this adoring man. *She* wanted to be given strange and precious gifts that hinted at unknowable places and infinite love. One day, on a visit to Barnabas Road, Jane had noticed that the walnut-sized piece of amber was missing from its usual place and, when she spotted it underneath Daphne's bed, she said nothing. On her subsequent visit, it was still there, collecting dust, and Jane pocketed it. Daphne only mentioned its absence once and Jane feigned ignorance. The weighty burden of guilt was balanced by the rapture inspired by the creature trapped for eternity in its petrified resin.

'So how've you been?' Jane was itching to continue her campaign but knew she must go gently.

'Oh really well, but there's such a lot I want to talk to you about. Actually, since before I went. I've been waiting almost a month!'

'Sounds a great gig, though, working in the Greek islands!'

'Yeah, it's a nice perk. I was basically just checking on a few clients and villa owners on Zante, Cephalonia and

Paxos. So the rest was holidays. And who'd want to be in London in August when it's like this? It's like living in a swamp.'

'And Libby? I was hoping to finally meet her this time.'

'Yes, you will! She's here, in her room. I can't believe it's taken so long. She went out to stay with Sam before I left, and then we met up just before coming home. I've hardly seen her for six weeks!'

Her smile was not quite convincing, thought Jane. It must be especially hard to let go of your baby as a single mother. She didn't know whether she could have brought up the boys without Michael. And it would have been unbearable when they left. Still, Daphne looked marvellous. Her feet were bare and she'd twisted her hair up on her head with a pencil. It appeared effortless – beauty as natural as a bird's plumage.

'Like a cuppa now or shall we go for a walk first?' Daphne examined the greyness outside. It had been raining all morning and now the afternoon was oppressively humid. 'The charms of an English summer ... Or we could go and see a film. I love a weekend matinee. What do you feel like, Janey?'

Jane was unable to pinpoint what she felt like. She wanted to talk, to persuade and guide Daphne, but she didn't want to be confronted by the hanging with its brutal ability to go straight to her gut. The living room was still in a horrible state, and littered with piles of rags, ribbons and what looked like actual rubbish. In fact the whole flat was verging on somewhere social services might get called to if the owner wasn't a middle-class, well-spoken person. And yet she still felt at a disadvantage with her old friend – a direct line to emotions she should have left behind with her teens. Too big, too pale, her feet pig-pink and cold in their practical open sandals. Her short, blonde hair seemed dull and conventional and the rectangular glasses that had felt like a good decision, a relief after all the fuss of contact lenses over the last thirty years, now made her feel like the dowdy, bespectacled girl of thirteen. How odd that you could go through so much in a life and be transported back to youth in a flash.

'Maybe a walk? Then we could see how we feel after that?'

'Perfect. We could walk across the bridge. Revisit our old haunts, maybe go to Wandsworth Park. I'll just go and get Liberty so you can meet her.'

Daphne returned with a willowy, delicate-featured girl who had evidently inherited the Californian gene more than the Greek. Like her mother, though, she was lovely, her skin glowing and golden. Perhaps there was something of both Ellie and Ed in her, Jane thought.

'Hi, Liberty. I'm Jane. Finally! I'm so pleased to meet you.' She stood somewhat awkwardly, not knowing if she should shake her hand or kiss her, but Liberty came over and gave a dispassionate, one-armed hug.

'Hi. Mum said you were friends when you were my age.'

'Yes, we go back a very long way.' Jane laughed.

'Yes,' agreed Daphne. 'And, Libby, you'll be lucky if you have a wonderful friend from school after so long. Imagine if you still know Paige when you're fifty!'

'So, did you have fun in Greece?' Jane sensed it was an irritating question as it emerged.

'Yes.' Liberty hesitated. 'But it was intense. I was helping my dad with the refugees a lot of the time. It was so hot in Athens. And there are so many people crossing over from Turkey. Thousands arriving off the boats in Athens. It feels biblical.' Jane guessed Libby was quoting someone else. She felt put in her place for asking about fun.

'Good for you. That's amazing. The world needs young people who are looking outwards, doing something, following their principles.'

'Thanks.' The girl looked solemn. 'If I was older, I'd go and stay there and work full-time. Everything else looks a bit pointless in comparison.'

'Libby's so different to me – how I was,' said Daphne. 'I don't mean physically, though that's pretty obvious. She's so clever and organised and knows what she's doing. I don't think I'll ever be that disciplined.'

'Oh you were pretty clever,' said Jane. 'About lots of things.' She laughed, wondering whether Daphne would interpret this as a dig at her patchy academic abilities or as a reference to her judgement in other matters.

'So, Libby, are you artistic like your mum?'

'No, I'm hopeless at art.' The girl smiled, tolerating the adult questioning the child in this manner. 'At school I like biology best. And sports. Especially running.'

'Snap!' said Jane. 'That's exactly like me. Did you know I work in a lab? I do medical research. *And* I love running.'

'Wow, I didn't know.'

'Yes, if you ever wanted to come and see my lab, you'd be more than welcome. I'd love to show you around.'

'Cool. Thank you. That'd be great.'

Libby turned to her mother. 'OK, I'm going round to Paige's now. See you later.'

'Like what time?' Jane noticed an infinitesimal stiffening in Daphne's face.

'Dunno. I'll text you, OK?'

'Rough idea?'

'Like nine thirty and you can meet me at the Tube?'

'OK, deal. Keep me posted.'

The walk took them over the train-bridge and Daphne laughed as they climbed the steps. 'Returning to the scene of the crime,' she puffed. As girls, they'd run up and down two at a time, and Daphne's movements were still more expansive than her size suggested – a kind of bodily largesse. 'We'd never have believed that we could be this old, or that we'd be back here again after so long.'

'I used to come across this bridge from the Tube station and hear opera blaring out from your house. And do you remember when Edmund got the peacock? I'd try to spot it down in the garden when I was approaching. What was it called?'

'Nietzsche.' Daphne giggled. 'Nietzsche the Screecher. Ed could never resist something shiny and colourful.'

'I loved that about your place. It was like a fairground, with the strings of coloured lights and flags in the trees, and then the different animals that came and went. Didn't he buy a collection of oriental ducks at one point?'

'Yes, and they all got ill and died. It was horrible. Chaos, our household, wasn't it?'

The two women reached the ornate cast-iron gate to Daphne's old house and paused, peering in like time travellers. Number 7 had altered – not merely shrunken like most locations remembered from childhood and revisited. The overgrown privet hedge and scruffy patch of grass were gone and the facade was now painted expensive grey, and fronted by neatly planted herb beds and antique brick paths. Jane said, 'So if we came out of the front door aged fourteen or fifteen, would we be wearing flowery Laura

Ashley dresses, punk trousers full of zips, or Victorian knickerbockers with Oxfam leopard skin?' Daphne's outfits had often looked as though she had been playing with a dressing-up chest. You couldn't predict who she'd be.

'I wish we had more photographs,' said Daphne. 'Nobody took them much in those days, did they?'

'No. Not like now, where the photograph becomes the event. We have to take a selfie to know we actually exist.' She wished *she* had taken more photographs. Perhaps she could have captured evidence about what Ralph did – that steady grooming that was heading so inevitably towards his goal.

'I didn't go to your house that much, did I?' Daphne looked wistful. 'It was so calm and peaceful there. Everyone behaving themselves. Your mum so kind. Now I think I probably should have spent more time there with you.'

* * *

Jane's parents did not try to prevent her visiting Daphne, but gave the impression they were not entirely happy about it either. They were warily intrigued by the cautiously modified details Jane relayed: foreign mother, rather famous writer father, peculiar food, lots of visitors. For Jane, the Greenslay household was her escape and refuge – almost an obsession. At Barnabas Road she was able to forget the rules. There was a long list of all the things she did there for the first time. First midnight feast. First fag – up in the tree house. First wine. First sight of a fox. First sneaking out of the house at night. Even her first kiss.

That kiss happened when she was fourteen – too late to admit that she hadn't done it before.

It was a Friday in September, and she'd gone to stay the night with Daphne. 'A school project', she told her parents. There was already a whiff of damp autumn in the air, but the house was warm and alive with bustle. Unusually, all the Greenslays were at home. Ellie was cooking some strange-looking but delicious Greek pasta shaped like rice, baking it in tomato sauce with pieces of garlicky chicken. 'She tries to make us seem like a great big happy Greek family,' Daphne complained. 'But we're not and she knows it. It's like she's playing a game. Tomorrow she'll probably go away and leave us stranded.'

The excitement of the day was Ed's latest acquisition – a hot tub that had just been installed and was due to be tested that evening. As Daphne and Jane laid the table, he gushed about his new toy. 'I tried them for the first time in San Francisco. Utterly beguiling. And extremely beneficial as well as pleasurable.' As he spoke, he waved his arms around, his harlequin sleeves flapping, his long face animated.

'Edmund, my love,' interrupted Ellie from the sofa where she was resting after her efforts at the stove. She was wearing a long, draped dress gathered under the breast and was smoking a cigarette. 'Do give me a glass of wine.' Ed opened a bottle of Chianti – the sort wrapped in raffia – and poured a glass for his wife and himself. 'It's all the joys of a hot bath, but under the stars,' he continued. 'You feel rejuvenated, almost reborn – part of nature, but held in the safe, warm water.'

'I expect Professor Freud would have had something to say about amniotic fluid and a return to the womb,' said Ellie, rather sharply.

'And would you deny me that, my angel?' Ed countered.

A record of Greek music was playing – a deep, female voice singing tragic songs of rebellion – and Ellie joined in with the march-like chorus. The air was thickened with scents from the rich sauces, Ellie's perfume, and the plumes of smoke she blew up towards the ceiling from a tiny cigarette made from a rolled leaf tied with red thread. 'They're from India,' explained Daphne, enjoying her expertise and showing Jane the little paper package of bidis.

When they sat down to eat, Jane discreetly engineered herself next to Liam, Theo's old friend. Both boys were nineteen and considered brilliantly clever. About to return to St Andrews for their second year studying physics, they were already planning postgraduate work. Jane had not admitted to Daphne how much she liked Liam, though it had gnawed at her for ages. She appreciated his delicate, pale hands and the way he exploded into high-pitched laughter. He was mysterious, with fishy green eyes swimming behind black-rimmed glasses and half his face hidden by hair. Sitting beside him at the table, she felt the heat from his thigh. When Edmund toasted 'the scholars' return to the Northern wilds', she clinked her glass against his, looked straight into his eyes and felt her heart flip. Ellie always served a drop of wine for the children at family suppers and they usually said, '*Yeia mas.*' Theo managed to refill everyone's glass, including the girls', while his parents' attention was elsewhere. He smiled wine-red lips when Edmund opened another bottle.

'It's real Californian redwood – the hot tub,' Daphne said proudly, perhaps to boost her father's morale; neither Ellie nor Theo was impressed by Ed's purchase. 'It cost $995! I saw the bill.'

'Yes, well, there's lots of pumps and pipes and so on,' said Ed with a mildly shifty air. 'It looks simpler than it is. And then there's all the bubbling business – you get a hydromassage at the same time.' Jane felt shocked to hear of so much money being spent on a glorified bath in the garden. 'It's the nearest you can get to being out in the wilderness at a volcanic hot spring, gazing up into the universe. And that's not to be sniffed at – even in a back garden in Putney.'

The teenagers did the clearing up – grumbling, but it was agreed that Ed and Ellie would have first go in the tub. Jane spotted them from the kitchen doors, moving shadows as they got undressed, and then, once they were in the water, she saw the glowing tip of whatever they were smoking.

'Definitely hash,' said Theo, eyeing his parents. 'Old hippies. I suspect Ed's preparing for one of his "nocturnal perambulations". He always likes to be "in the mood".'

'A bit Jack-the-Ripperish,' laughed Daphne. 'Not sure I'd want to come across him stoned out of his head down a dark alley.'

'Claims it nourishes the muse,' mocked Theo. 'I don't know how he or Ellie get anything done. I find the stuff makes my mass-times-the-acceleration-of-gravity go berserk and I can't get up.' He smiled at Liam, who looked knowing.

'OK, Theo, stop trying to impress,' said Daphne. 'We've heard that witticism before.' She rolled her eyes at Jane. 'He just means it makes him feel heavy.'

Jane didn't care about the explanation; she was looking at Liam's full lips and the evidence of minor shaving activity around them. Daphne continued to needle her brother. 'And if you can't handle it, poor little poppet, maybe you'd better go and work out some more theories. There's a good boy.' Theo didn't react, merely taking a cloth and wiping the table with excessive care, as though he had more serious things to think about. The five-year gap between him and Daphne gave him the edge in ignoring her provocations.

The parents came back indoors wrapped in towels and carrying their clothes. Their eyes were glassy pink. Ed said it was even better than he remembered. 'A revelation.' Ellie looked quite pleased too and they both left the room to go upstairs.

'So, it's our turn!' said Daphne. She fetched some towels and the two girls went out into the cold, uninviting garden. The hot tub had been positioned near to the plane tree, as far as possible from the house but without being exposed to the river. 'It *feels* like going into the wilderness,' said Jane. They left their clothes on the tree-house ladder, then tiptoed gingerly across the damp, slightly muddy grass, and ascended the wooden steps. The water was astonishingly hot. 'Mega death bath,' said Daphne, groaning as she lowered herself into the frothing bubbles. Jane followed her, submitting to the pain and then letting out a similar moan as her body relaxed into the heat. They leaned back against the edge, their arms along the redwood rim, peacefully paddling their feet and gazing at the mandarin-tinged clouds above the city.

They had been there long enough to stop talking and sink into a silent but companionable reverie, when Jane spotted a figure making its way through the dark garden. Without her glasses she couldn't tell who it was, but it soon became clear. Ralph wasn't as jovial and pretentious as usual. 'Oh, I'm so glad you're here.' He was evidently speaking in the singular and addressing Daphne. 'Hello, Jane. How are you?' His voice lost its urgency and interest as he acknowledged her presence and Jane raised a wet hand in greeting, not replying. He was leaving for New York in a few days and, privately, Jane believed it was a great idea. It was horrible to see Daphne like his pet dog, his toy.

'I'm getting pretty hot,' Jane said, wiping her face. 'I'll go in now. What about you?'

'I'll stay a bit more.' Daphne was so predictable sometimes, but Jane couldn't face hanging around watching them play agonised lovebirds.

'Bring a towel over for Jane, could you?' Daphne pointed to the towels and Ralph obligingly brought one, holding it for Jane and looking politely to one side – the hypocrite. She covered herself as much as possible – not like subsequent hot-tub evenings, when she and Daphne ran naked around the night garden, bodies pink as boiled prawns, feet dirty from the grass, arms stretched up to the moon like pagans dancing. Daphne could do that for her; lull or lure her into forgetting about her size and her awkwardness, into feeling free and wild. This time, though, Ralph had ruined it. Buoyancy gave way to gravity, as she put on her glasses and picked up her clothes, making sure the white pants she'd folded and hidden under her trousers didn't show or fall to the ground.

In the bathroom on the first floor, she locked herself in, dropping the towel and examining herself in the mirror: skin flushed, eyes bright as coloured glass, breasts full, legs long. Not so horrible. She cupped her breasts, squeezing them together to create a cleavage. On a shelf above the basin were various bottles she supposed belonged to Ellie. She opened a cream and smoothed it on to her face, then took some perfume and anointed her wrists and earlobes as she'd seen her mother do before an evening out. When she emerged, dressed and wreathed in musk, Liam was coming up the stairs.

'Was that fun?'

'What? Oh, yeah, yes the hot tub's amazing. Are you going to try it?'

'No, it's not really Theo's thing.' He paused and she could tell he was observing her differently to other times – as if she'd moved up a level by way of a sacred water ritual.

'I was just going up to Daphne's room for a bit. Want to come?' She felt daring. If Daphne could play games, so could she.

'OK.' He made it sound casual, his voice high and non-committal, but he was looking intently, sizing her up.

They went up to the top floor, where Daphne's north-facing room overlooked the garden and the river. Jane resisted the temptation to go to the window and peer past the orange curtains to the shadowy figures at the hot tub. Before she had a chance to change her mind, Liam said, 'Can I kiss you?' He took a piece of chewing gum from his mouth and threw it accurately into the waste-paper bin.

'OK.'

He started gently, his lips to hers, his mouth minty from the gum. Then his tongue met hers and it was like electricity – a circuit of wires connected and creating new energy. He stroked her breasts and pulled her closer, leaning back next to the door that was hung with clothes. She spotted the dress Daphne had stolen from Biba, its broad, horizontal stripes blurring as she removed her glasses. Liam took off his too and flicked the light switch so they were left in darkness. Everything disappeared as they kissed harder and deeper in a hanging jumble of dresses and shirts, which smelled of Daphne. It was almost as though Daphne was there, or as if she had melded with Jane to become one girl. Time evaporated. Trains rumbled past like thunder, making the door tremble and transferring the vibrations to her spine.

Unbearably soon, she heard the thumps of someone pounding up the stairs. Liam pulled back just as the door opened. He turned on the overhead light and Jane spun away, replacing her glasses. So that was it. The moment was gone, crushed by rude light and by Daphne.

'Oh? Hello.' Daphne appeared to hardly take in that they were there, let alone that they'd been in the dark. She sounded wretched. Nobody spoke again until Jane went to the record player, wiping her mouth with the back of her hand and blinking with bewildered disappointment.

'We were just going to put on some music,' she said dumbly. How was it possible to move from one state to another, like extricating oneself from a car crash, and pretending nothing had happened?

Daphne didn't say anything. She didn't ask, 'Where's Theo?' Nor did she appear to spot the glaring evidence of an intrigue, or she would have started teasing with talk of snogging or tonsil hockey. Maybe she didn't give a shit, thought Jane as she put on Pink Floyd's *The Dark Side of the Moon*. Liam smiled at her appreciatively.

'Did Ralph leave?' Jane couldn't think what else to say.

'Mm,' answered Daphne, with a low tremor in her voice as if she might cry.

'OK, I'm going to find Theo.' Liam was awkward now, as if he'd been caught hanging around with kids. 'See you.'

'OK, see you later,' Jane said, bereft as someone waving her sweetheart off to war. She didn't see him after that. The two boys went out for a drink and then Liam went home. Within a day or so they'd left for university.

The girls lay on the floor in Daphne's room, listening to records and not talking much. Jane thought about Liam, her abdomen still tight with the thrill of what had happened, her skin warm with the secret. When she turned to look, Daphne was crying silently, viscous tears sliding slowly down her cheeks, each drop pausing briefly on her chin before falling to the floor. She wasn't making a noise or sniffing. A weeping statue.

'Hey?' She reached over and gripped her friend's shoulder. 'What happened?'

'I want to die,' came the reply.

'Why? What happened?' Jane repeated, more urgently.

'There's no point in anything, in being alive. Ralph's leaving for America. I hate him.'

'Then forget about him.' Her mother used to sing 'I'm Gonna Wash That Man Right Outa My Hair' around the house.

'But I also don't hate him.' She looked distraught.

It was years before Jane told Daphne about Liam, and even then she didn't admit it was her first kiss. Hard to disclose that yet another of Plain Jane's initiations had been enacted on the stage of Barnabas Road.

* * *

They stood before the old house waiting for something to happen. There was an unfamiliar sterility to the place.

'Probably belongs to a banker now,' said Daphne. 'Such a different atmosphere.' She peered over into the corner of the front garden. 'Do you remember the sculpture we all made?'

Jane nodded. 'It was so mysterious and beautiful. I'd never seen anything like it. I couldn't believe it all came from rubbish out of the river. It was like a heathen god standing in the corner of the garden. Your family was so unusual – such an inspiration.'

'Maybe our family looked exotic, but it didn't feel like that on the inside. If you think about it, we were a mess. Even then, before Ellie ...' She didn't finish the sentence. 'That's how I see it now. I always used to think all that freedom was a privilege. That image of us running free, flinging off our clothes, walking barefoot around the streets – like urban Mowgli girls finding our own tracks through the jungle. But now I think of that jungle as dangerous. I didn't really know what I was doing.'

Jane understood that the other side to the fascinating teenager was the skinny girl who was half-foreign, whose mother was unreliable and often absent and whose father was living out fantasies of the literary life with his pretentious clothes, posh car and young girlfriends. As they looked up at the house, a shadow moved behind the gauze curtains on the first floor. Daphne turned away decisively, as though shaking off the memories, and they set off down the road.

They were inside the park before either of them spoke again, walking along a line of elephantine plane trees by the river. Daphne stopped and leaned against the railings, looking across the water at the luxurious green of the Hurlingham Club on the northern side. Nearer to them, a cormorant balanced on a wooden post, sunning itself, wings splayed like a scrawny eagle atop a totem pole.

'Janey, there's something I wanted to ask you.'

'Fire away.'

'It's something to do with Libby. Or no, actually I think it's more to do with Ralph.'

Jane stiffened. 'Has Ralph done something with Libby?'

'No, no. God. No.' Her wide-eyed shock relaxed into a faint smile at the absurdity. 'No, I haven't even seen Ralph for ages – years. No, it's more something inside me that changed. As if I suddenly saw all the same experiences differently. Like when you walk up a hill and understand the shape of a landscape you've been lost in. I realised I'd been remembering my thing with Ralph from a child's point of view. I mean, I know he wasn't a paedophile or anything. He wasn't chasing around molesting little kids. But the truth is, it looks different from a parent's perspective.'

It was tempting to yell, 'Finally! Why did it take you so bloody long?' but Jane gathered her composure. 'Do you know what changed that?' she asked neutrally.

'Yeah, it's funny really, or maybe it's obvious.' Daphne's brow contracted. 'It might sound silly but it all started with Libby and her friend Paige dancing.' She smiled at the incongruity. 'Just before she went away to Greece.' She flicked a glance at Jane and then away again across the water that was pushing its way upriver with the incoming tide. 'They were all done-up, with heels and tarty make-up, and then they started dancing – lots of thrusting and pouting. I suppose it might have been funny if it wasn't grotesque.

They seemed to understand what they were doing while not really understanding. Does that make sense?'

'Completely.' Jane remembered the ugly mess of teenage years, when none of them really knew what they were doing.

'And then I saw the peculiar disconnect that happens when young girls play with sexiness. I do realise it's normal – what they all do – what we all did. But it's like a game, like practising before the real thing. And I thought about me at eleven or twelve and about Ralph. And sleeping with him when I was only thirteen. And it was like being punched in the stomach. I mean, Libby's going to be thirteen soon.' She shook her head and the clip holding her hair fell on to the ground, provoking a spill of Medusa-wild locks. Gathering up her curls and fixing them in place once more, she continued, 'It was such a strange sort of shock – the sort you've known about all along but haven't understood.'

Jane remained silent.

'I thought that if an older man did to Libby what Ralph did to me, I'd ...' Daphne stopped and then said very simply, 'I'd kill him.'

The flood of relief was like bathing in warm water. Warm, scented water that relaxed and invigorated. Like a hot tub! After all these years, all the recent waiting and hating and hopes for justice, and finally Daphne could see things as they really were. Randy Ralph, the old perv, the self-righteous, rapist arsehole was going to pay for his crimes.

A shot of milky sunshine penetrated the clouds before a startlingly loud clap of thunder sounded and the sky turned graphite grey. It felt appropriate.

'I think it often takes a long time for people to realise they've been abused,' said Jane carefully. She'd been reading up and knew the terminology now. 'It's a process. And when you've been in denial, then it's a different sort of trauma.'

Daphne's eyes went distant with the vacancy of someone who'd witnessed a fatal accident and couldn't accept what they'd seen. 'You know that, for me, the time with Ralph was always like a romantic secret. Roses and moonlight stuff. It felt like love – first love. And now it's something else. Something horrible, even though nothing has changed. So bizarre. Do you remember that Oscar Wilde thing Ed always said? "We are all in the gutter, but some of us are looking at the stars." I think I've turned face down in the gutter.'

'You're not, Daphne. It was him in the gutter all the time, never you.'

'Oh fuck it, Jane. When I think of all that emotion spilled out over him.' It started raining. Large, isolated drops to begin with, but increasing so their clothes were quickly mottled with dark spots. There was no obvious cover in sight and they moved over to the nearest plane tree as lightning streaked across the sky.

'We shouldn't stop here,' said Jane. 'It's dangerous.'

'Yeah, what the hell. Let's get soaked. I don't care. We can change at home.' They set off towards the park gate, grinning at the drama of the drenching, as rain coursed down their faces, half blinding them. When they got to the train-bridge, it was too tempting to resist the shelter offered underneath it on the road.

'You know, it was hard for me then. All that emotion, and he was bloody married.' Daphne wiped her wet face with her hands. There were beads of water on her eyelashes.

'I got so worried about you when he went to America and you got terribly skinny and anaemic and had to have vitamin injections.'

'Yes, that was really crap. I was heartbroken. After he left, I burned myself with matches. Look, I've still got the marks.' Daphne pulled up her soaking sleeve and Jane saw a cluster of small white scars below the elbow.

'He was ruthless,' said Jane. 'Ruthless about leaving you, and about being with you. You know, I think you should talk to someone – a specialist, a counsellor. It's the right time now.'

Daphne shook her head and more drips fell from her hair. 'But if I talked to a counsellor, won't it get taken out of my hands? Wouldn't they report him to the police? I think maybe I'll write to Ralph and see how he responds. I'd like some answers. I don't want him arrested.'

It mystified her that Daphne could be so short-sighted when it came to the man who trampled all over her child-hood, but she replied cautiously, wringing out the lower sections of her jacket. 'It's your choice, but you know what I think. There are laws and what he did is illegal. You were a child.'

'But he didn't force me to do anything. Ever. I did love him.'

Jane couldn't bear to hear Daphne mention love again. 'That's completely irrelevant.' She didn't want to sound severe, but it needed to be said. 'I think you're missing something, Daphne. What he did is called grooming. That's illegal – you can go to prison for it. You can't ever say an adult having sex with a child is OK. So it's pointless to talk about the emotions. "Love" makes no difference.'

The rain stopped and a raw, burning sun lit up the wet pavements of Barnabas Road. They walked slowly back across the bridge, not saying much, their damp clothes almost steaming. At her flat, Daphne lent Jane a dry top and skirt.

'I'm there with you, Daphne. Anything you need. I know of someone you can talk to. Can I put you in touch?'

She nodded and held on to Jane's arm. 'Thank you, Janey. You're such a darling. I don't know what I'd do if you weren't helping me through this. I'd be so alone.'

10

RALPH

He enjoyed arriving home in a taxi with the chuckling luxury of the diesel engine singing a song of comfort, abundance and tradition. The driver rushed them up the side of Primrose Hill and then stopped before his house – brightly painted like its neighbours and sporting window boxes planted with red geraniums. The warm summer morning made him feel that the entire street was smiling and he tipped the driver generously. The magnolia he and Nina had planted on moving there over twenty years earlier now reached the first-floor windows.

He was relieved to be back after the five days in Berlin, though the trip had gone far better than anticipated. The invitation was to conduct a performance of *Songs of Innocence and Experience* and he was worried he wouldn't be strong enough after his gruelling treatments. In the event, he amazed himself with a surge of strength. He was feted as never before in Germany. Parties were held in his honour, he gave television and press interviews, and they put him up in a magnificent suite at the Ritz Carlton in Potsdamer Platz. Fearing his vigour might not last, and with the air of a condemned man, he ordered outrageous breakfasts in bed. When tiring of eggs, ham and sausages after the first few days, he progressed to fish, cheeses, waffles and pastries. Best of all, he received a standing ovation at the concert and was laden with bouquets. Nothing like a bit of straightforward adulation for raising the spirits.

Nina had evidently heard the taxi stop, and opened the front door as he came up the steps. 'The hero returns.' Ralph wasn't always sure when she meant things entirely genuinely and without guile and when there was a note of irony. Sometimes he wondered whether she herself was clear – English was still, after all these years, a foreign language.

'Hello, my darling. How are you?' He kissed her and again felt the satisfaction of when things came together in the right way – the warming sunshine, elegant home, devoted wife. Her hands were charmingly smudged with paint, her hair held up with a fetching headscarf, and she was wearing a turquoise linen kaftan of the sort she'd favoured when he first knew her.

On the hall table lay a modest pile of post, evidently already sorted by Nina, who dealt with bills, banks and anything boring. He picked up the letters and walked through into the kitchen – sunny marigolds on the table, something smelling of celery and herbs simmering on the stove. The first letter was in a shabby recycled envelope, and the writing on the label was familiar. Briefly, his breath jagged, somewhere between lung and windpipe. The messy cursive had changed since the days when it was a regular part of his life, when he'd smiled at the experiments with styles, the italic phase, the purple ink. But there was no doubt.

'I'll just take my bag up. There's a little thing I got for you in Berlin.' It was easy to saunter out of the kitchen, casually holding on to the mail, but he saw Nina understand what he was doing. She would have recognised the handwriting too. Upstairs, he dropped his bags in the bedroom and shut the door.

Dear Ralph,

I don't think I ever had the words to describe or understand what happened between us all those years ago. It's almost like another life. There's been such a lot since then. But recently I've begun to see things differently. Libby is now around the age I was when we — you and me — became close. I see her vulnerability very clearly. She's growing up, developing physically, but inside she is so young — a child. Then I started thinking, what if she was involved with a man of thirty. I'd go crazy. I'd know it was wrong.

Can you understand this? I suppose this is the thing. However willing and happy I was at the time, our relationship now looks <u>wrong</u>. *I'm bewildered. I need answers. I wonder if you have any.*

We've never had a conversation about this and I think we should. I'm curious about what you think after all these years.

Daphne

'Fuck!' Ralph whispered. 'Fuck, shit, bugger, cunt!' There was no mistaking this mild-mannered missive for anything but an attack. He'd wondered whether this might happen — dreaded it. He wasn't stupid. But he had hoped the general fixation with children and sex would not poison Daphne's memories and turn her against him. Nobody was in favour of children being abused — of course not. But there was madness in the pseudo-psycho-babble world where people got post-traumatic stress syndrome after stubbing their toes and where students needed 'safe places' to discuss their syllabus. This letter was certainly worrying, but it was asking for something. He needed to find out what that was and give it to her. I must talk to her, he thought. Persuade her that what we had was something marvellous and unique. A beautiful secret.

'I'm going for a little stroll. I think I need some air after all the travelling.' Ralph had slipped the incriminating letter in his pocket and smiled blandly at Nina. He handed her a slim, shop-wrapped package. 'Here, I bought you a scarf.'

'Thank you.' She looked at it as if with sympathy but did not open the present. 'Shall I come with you?'

'No need, my darling. Thanks, but I'd like to clear my mind. There's something bubbling away that I want to get on with this afternoon. A string quartet plus voices – I think I breathed in some Beethoven in Berlin. A walk will help me get it flowing. I'll see you in an hour. Or less.' He didn't feel like walking. Travelling was tiring at the best of times, and with a body bombarded with poisons it was debilitating. The letter was a punch that had nearly winded him and all the contentment of returning home had vanished. A physical, paper letter was such a rare thing these days, where so much communication was read on a small, private screen and retained an abstract quality, vulnerable to a quick tap of a delete button. It was almost as though she'd chosen to make her statement by using a goose quill on ancient papyrus. A proper letter had heft – an objective life of its own that you could only destroy by burning or ripping.

He made his way to the open space of Primrose Hill and, avoiding the sightseers and lovers gathered at the highest point of the park, settled on a bench at a quiet spot in the north-west corner. For years, he was proud of not having a mobile phone, though eventually it became unacceptable, due to all the travel for work. A written response to Daphne would not be a good idea in the circumstances and she had given a number in her letter. He held the phone away as if it smelled bad and thumbed the numbers grudgingly.

'Ralph!' She sounded more surprised than upset. He could hear voices in the background.

'I got your letter. It was waiting when I arrived home today.'

'Ah. I thought maybe you couldn't think how to answer.' There wasn't anger in her voice, and though he hoped there was a tinge of teasing, there was definitely a reserve that he didn't associate with the volatile Miss Greenslay he'd known and adored.

'No, not at all. I've just been away. In Berlin. But listen, we must talk. Can you meet?' He was trying to sound relaxed, to suppress the urgency he felt.

'Well I'm at work.'

He knew he shouldn't broach the subject, but he couldn't resist. 'Listen, Daff, I … This is such a … It's awful that you are having these doubts. I mean, you do know … You understand, well … that I loved you? I always thought it was reciprocated. I mean, I wasn't some sort of pervert in a raincoat lurking under the bridge and flashing at school-girls.' He stopped. This wasn't the right conversation to be having on the telephone. 'So can we meet? What about lunch? Tomorrow?'

There was a pause. 'Um, tomorrow's no good. I'm a bit busy most weekday lunchtimes. I usually just grab a sandwich near the office.' He forgot that she was tied to an office – how tedious her life must have become.

'Working girl! So dedicated.' He tried to put a smile into his voice. 'Saturday then?'

She paused again. 'All right, yes, that'd be OK.'

'Don Luigi's?' He could almost hear Daphne weighing up the appropriateness of this choice.

'God, that's a tumble down memory lane. But yeah, OK. One o'clock.'

* * *

He hadn't been to Don Luigi's for maybe ten years. Somewhat hidden away in a side street off the King's Road, the Italian restaurant had been one of Edmund and Ellie's haunts in the '70s. Ralph had often joined them there, sometimes with Nina. It was the Greenslays' first choice when they wanted an easy dinner with friends or Sunday lunches with children. Luigi would kiss Ellie's hand, bring sweet treats for the children, and pour an extra grappa for the men.

Ed usually paid for these meals as if money was a preposterous game, and afterwards they would often all cram into his green Bentley, which was increasingly bashed and rusting, but drew attention wherever they went. They would speed off somewhere and explore the abandoned docks at the Isle of Dogs or remnants of Roman wall in the City, before returning home tired but exhilarated. The Greenslays had shown him so much about the way to live and he tried to emulate their relaxed grace and risky adventurousness, their wild excesses in the context of a tender, domestic environment. As free agents who successfully managed the confines and burdens of a family, they were his mentors.

It was just as he remembered it: white linen tablecloths, wafts of cooking garlic and earthy prosciutto, a trolley of desserts – that dated it. And there in the back, Luigi, still in a dark suit and shiny shoes, but surely in his late eighties now, collapsed in a comfortable chair like a speckled toad. Ralph greeted him but wasn't sure the old man remembered him, even though he made a good show of clasping his hand and making pleasantries in Italian. Choosing a corner table that was some distance from the few other customers, Ralph asked for a bottle of sparkling water and decided against an aperitif. He could have done with one but was thinking about the picture of solicitous sobriety he wanted to present. He needed a clear head to get out of this.

Through the window he saw her arrive on a yellow bike that was wrapped with plastic flowers, ribbons and rosettes – transport for a brash May Queen. As she chained it up on the far side of the road, he noted she had retained the quick movements of her youth and was dressed in jeans that showed her ankles, a gypsyish blouse and a long rope of green beads. There was no denying, however, that she was middle-aged. Long gone was the creature he'd worshipped. He stood up to greet her and pulled her into a tight hug. A conspiratorial one, he hoped, wanting to convince her through his body that something still belonged to them and that some vestigial vibrations remained. She didn't push him away, and though he felt no erotic spark, there was a private familiarity, the animal smell he recognised beneath the perfume. Intimacy such as theirs remained a memory in the body as much as in the mind.

They sat down and he took charge, asking what she'd like to drink and encouraging the handsome Italian waiter to make a fuss over the Signora. The young man looked ready for anything, Ralph speculated, as he noted the almost blue-black hair and sharp features. Daphne said she'd like a glass of Soave, which he remembered her parents drinking when she was a child. He ordered a bottle and, when it arrived and he took a first sip, the pale, almost green wine brought a sensory rush of time past combined with the buzz of alcohol hitting an empty stomach.

'How are you, Daphne?' he asked. 'How is your daughter?' She answered and enquired politely about his children. It was clear he shouldn't prevaricate for long.

'Are you tired?' she said, examining his face inquisitively and evidently noticing the ravages of his recent trials. He didn't want to mention the dreaded business going on in his body or the hospital humiliations.

'I'm just back from Berlin. Bloody exhausting. We were doing *Songs of Innocence*. We had to change the child soloist, the one doing *your* part, after the first one got tonsillitis two days before the concert. Of course, none of them have been nearly as good or as original as you.' This last statement wasn't strictly accurate but he wanted to please her. 'Little Dagna would squeak on the high notes. Not like your clear, pure voice.' He gulped his wine and grinned. 'And now, very exciting, they're organising a special event for my birthday next year, my big seven-O – at the Barbican. We're gathering ten youth choirs from around England – I'll be travelling about rehearsing and choosing the soloists. It should be pretty impressive. But, Christ, seventy.' She smiled politely.

'Of course *you* still look as though you're thirty,' he said gallantly.

She ignored the compliment. 'So, I think it's really important we ...' She stopped abruptly as the waiter stepped between them, bearing pen and pad and smirking as if he knew something. She chose *spaghetti alle vongole*.

'And for me, *fegato alla Veneziana*,' he said, enjoying rolling some Italian around his mouth. '*Grazie!*' He hoped the liver would give him strength. Red blood cells, iron, prop himself up.

She started again. 'I really want to know how you see it. What it was like for you. You've never told me how it all began or what it meant in your life. Do you remember meeting me as a child? Shit, Ralph! It's as if I don't know this story that had me at the centre.'

'I've been thinking about it a lot since your letter.' He didn't often get flustered but she was already giving him a headache. His plan was to prise open several of his carefully sealed secrets as a way of presenting her with something — at least an inkling of his motives and desires. He had to make an offering.

'You know, I was very unconfident around women when I was young. You didn't meet any at a boys' boarding school. I felt unsure of them.'

Daphne's laugh exploded as a snort of disbelief. 'That's not the reputation you had!'

'No, really, I always felt very shy of women. You didn't board. You can't imagine what it's like. Very extreme. All those years with no females around. And I was only eight when I left home. But right from the first day at prep school, there were deeply intense encounters. It's what we all did. Of course it all got much more serious when I went to Stowe. We had real love affairs.'

He could see this was not what Daphne was expecting. 'But what's that got to do with me? I was a girl. And when you knew me, you'd left all that far behind, hadn't you? I mean, you were in your late twenties. You never mentioned fancying boys.'

'No, there were always boys.' Ralph realised this didn't sound right. 'Young men,' he corrected. Be careful, he thought. 'It remained like a closed world I could dip into.' Daphne laughed another snort before he noticed his unfortunate choice of words.

'Still?'

'Well, maybe not so much.' He didn't want to admit his sorry slide away from sex since the illness took hold. In any case, this was taking the wrong direction. But how to back out? 'It's secret, though. Nobody must know, OK, Daff?'

Perhaps this confession wasn't such a good idea, he thought. Too risky. Probably just more ammunition for her to turn on him. He recalled two boys in Tallinn a few years ago, before his prostate turned traitor. They were both brass players with lips red and swollen from their instruments. And wicked eyes. The naughty ones in a youth orchestra of Europeans aged sixteen to twenty-one. Ras and ... he'd forgotten the other one's name. In their hotel room they had a plastic bag filled with small metal vials. 'For making whipped cream,' Ras, the taller one, explained. There was a device for cracking them open and a packet of party balloons. 'Breathe from this!' He handed Ralph a green one and they all three lay on the floor, sucking gas from the rubbery necks until they cried from laughter. Then they were kissing. It was blurred – lips, head floating, giggling, opening of more vials. In the end he couldn't tell whether the giddiness came from laughing gas or their frantic race to finish each other off. He'd felt like a boy again with them: young and free and swept along by torrents and rapids of hilarity. They'd practically jumped on him; it was like being back at school. Christ! He pulled at his shirt collar as though he needed more air.

The food arrived and the young Italian wielded an osten-
tatiously outsize pepper mill high over Daphne's food.
She appeared mesmerised by his absurd performance and
forgot to tell him to stop until her plate was littered with
an unnerving layer of black shrapnel. Ralph had to say
something and she laughed like a woman you might end
up locking away in the attic. The man's shirt was open and
Ralph noticed the dark stipple of shaved chest hair. The
young were merciless shavers these days; not just the girls
but boys too were often almost as severely depilated. All
a legacy from porn films, apparently, where hair mustn't
get in the way of a good camera angle. But pornography
had never been his preferred vice. He speared the strips
of liver, bolting them down with the thought of loading
a gun with ammunition. She picked out a few minuscule
clams from their shells and hardly touched the spaghetti.
He didn't like her lowered eyes and mistrusted the lack of
interest in her food.

'Does Nina know? Would she mind?' Her questions
were unwelcome and somehow familiar.

'She doesn't ask. I'm careful. And she's careful. We've
learned how to preserve what we have. That's important.'

'This is so strange – about the boys.' She appeared
perplexed. 'And what's it got to do with me, with our
story? Apart from all this messing around, did you actually *love* other girls? Other boys?' She was turning cold and
interrogative. Already, he didn't trust her to understand
him.

'No! No, it was only you.' He realised he had taken the
wrong path and should have focused all his attention on
her. 'You were something delicate and rare.'

'So could I have been a boy?'

He paused, trying to be honest. 'You were something else. A sprite. Like Puck – mischievous and fleeting. Your youth, your energy – even the way you were so dismissive of adults. I felt privileged to enter your world. There was a connection between the child part of me and you as a child. It allowed an unguarded love – non-judgemental, uncomplicated by knowledge of the world. I suppose it was partly that I didn't want to grow up. You gave me freedom. Even more so after I got married and had babies.'

'So it's youth, purity and freedom. An appealing little bundle for the older man.' He hated sarcasm. Her face had a harsh quality he didn't like, and up close she looked old; crows' feet creased her temples when she talked.

'It was like fate,' he persevered. 'You came running down the stairs and something happened. It was extraordinarily powerful. You were nine when I met you. And I was twenty-seven.' He smiled at her with warmth. 'Eighteen years apart. I suppose we still are.' He hoped the implied closing of the age gap was apparent to her. 'Oh shit ...' He tipped the glass to his mouth with too much energy and wine streamed down his chin on to his clothes. Scrubbing the wet patch on my crotch with a napkin doesn't look good, he thought. Shirt dabbing, sweat beading. Shit.

'You weren't a sex object,' he said. 'That's very important. I didn't crave sex.' The waiter reappeared by their side and clearly heard the last words as his eyes darted to Daphne. Ralph wondered if he imagined they were married – they certainly weren't acting like lovers. The young man cleared the plates, and asked Daphne if everything was OK, as she had eaten so little. They both ordered espressos and Ralph suggested sharing an almond tart. She shrugged but he went ahead with the order.

Doggedly, he continued, though he feared it would not help. 'I think what I was seeking was ecstasy. I mean, I know there are other ways ... but there was an enormous excitement being with you. It was almost like being drunk. Something about you made me feel ecstatic.'

'I never doubted that you loved me, Ralph. And you know I loved you. But I was a child. You could do what you liked, come or go. I was always just there. You had power over me.'

'I would never have pressurised you. I always left it to you to choose. When I brought you things, presents or books or flowers, it was like placing offerings on the altar to see if the goddess would respond.'

She was messing with her hair, twisting it and fixing it up with a chopstick-like device that wouldn't stay in place. Neurotic, he thought. Her familiar eyes were still dark as olives, but a delicate mauve colour tinted the lids. He wasn't sure she understood him. Perhaps her lack of education counted against her and she didn't have the imagination. After all, she had never studied anything, never acquired discipline or intellectual rigour. Her working life was a shambles, as far as he knew. Even her recent foray into the art world sounded dubious. He'd seen a magazine article featuring an exhibition she was in, and the photographs made her work look creepy and brazenly female. Sewing, embroidery and appliqué always seemed too floppy and feminine, too steeped in oestrogen to count as real art.

'You can't expect a child to behave like a goddess. It's too much pressure. If I imagine this happening to Libby ... I think it'd be horrific.'

'Oh Christ, Daphne. She wouldn't do it if she didn't want to. And it's all culturally relative, don't you think?

There are no absolutes. Read a bit of anthropology and you see there are a thousand ways and ages to discover sex. Girls get *married* at twelve in some countries. Even in Europe, the age of consent is so varied it's almost arbitrary.'

She shrugged and he tried another tack. 'Or look at it like a fairy tale. Like going into the forest. There's a gingerbread house. The child doesn't say, "I don't want to go into this sweet shop."' He stopped to see if she would respond, then continued. 'It's how the child finds out about the world. In our case … I mean, your life's gone on. You're fine – you look fantastic. Things have to happen to you, don't they?'

'But what if those things are too much for a child to take on? It was so painful for me. First you made me love you, then you abandoned me, then you picked me up again. You offered the sweet shop and took it away. What was that about? When you went off to live in America I was so fucking miserable I thought about killing myself.'

'Christ, Daff. You never said.'

'I didn't want to upset you. There was nothing you could do.'

'I always hoped going away was the right thing – it was meant to protect you.'

'But as soon as you got back we continued.' Her voice was whiny as a teenager's. 'You ran off as if I didn't matter and then just took up with me again.'

He shook his head slowly. 'Oh God. You know how much I missed you. I was desperate too.'

He devoured his half of the almond tart, barely noticing the taste but enjoying the sensation of sweetness in the mouth. Daphne didn't even try it. She was pushing breadcrumbs around the smooth surface of the tablecloth, creating small piles and then breaking them up. He couldn't catch her eye. All he wanted was to lie down and be quiet.

'Do you remember telling me about your sexual conquests?' She flashed a mean, dark eye at him and then continued messing about with the breadcrumbs. 'You thought I could handle it, understand everything – like a confidante. You even told me you slept with Ellie.'

Fuck! he thought. She's coming at me from every angle. 'Oh, Daff. It was like that then. Everyone did that sort of thing. It didn't mean anything. Not to either of us. It had nothing to do with what *we* had – you and I.'

'I don't know. Screwing my mother?'

'You have to put it in context, Daphne. You know what it was like. Never after we … after *us*. The thing with Ellie was soon after we met. And only once. You were still a child. It was how we all went on. There was a dinner for lots of people at Barnabas Road, and she was extremely flirtatious – she could be, you know. We just went upstairs. God knows how we managed.' He remembered lifting Ellie up against the bathroom wall and how she came incredibly quickly, and then several more times – like a magic trick. Taking a gulp of wine he said, 'It wasn't anything more than … you know, a flying fuck.'

Daphne observed him with a baleful expression. 'The thing about Ellie is I never got enough of her. Even when she was alive. She was always away, or busy fighting the colonels. She gave so much to everyone else and not enough to me. And then she died.' She didn't have to say it, but he knew what was on her mind, what this conversation was circling around.

* * *

In the disturbing way the Fates arrange things, they'd been together on the day of Ellie's accident. Daff must have been eighteen. Still at school, though she didn't act like it. She should have been at school that day. He still adored her – he assumed he always would – but if he was strictly honest, their occasional meetings were no longer something that kept him awake at night with anticipation or with a savage ache of remembered bliss. *Panta rhei*, as usual. Desire, pain, the body … everything moves on. The river is never the same water again. She had other boyfriends (none particularly impressive, he reflected), and he was madly busy with his music, the father of three growing children and happy with chancy encounters where they cropped up.

He was using a houseboat on Chelsea Embankment that belonged to a friend who was working abroad for a few years. It provided the perfect space. Removed from the chaos of home life, it was ideal for composing and, with its rugs, cushions and cabin bedrooms, irresistible for trysts. He loved the cradle-like rocking movement and the tides that left the boat stranded in soft mud and then picked it up again, making it creak and judder slightly as it re-floated. That May morning was like the announcement of summer – vivid blue skies, shimmering waters, seagulls playing. Daphne arrived in an outrageous, if fetching get-up of shorts worn over fishnet tights and a shocking-pink mohair sweater.

'So today we have a circus artiste!' he remarked and she spun into a cartwheel along the pontoon, then danced up the gangway.

Her easy athleticism always thrilled him. It was delightful to feel enslaved again, at least for a few hours. Slavery with velvet ribbons, not chains. He'd tried to encourage her to take up dance. She had the body for it and the supple elasticity that enabled her to leap high and do the splits as though she barely noticed. And she was musical enough. But she ignored his entreaties to take lessons and her parents never believed in pushing their daughter. 'Let her find her own way,' was a useful and much-uttered phrase in the Greenslay household. Ed liked quoting Khalil Gibran about children being living arrows sent forth from the parents' bow – a poetic excuse for negligence. Ralph had always believed in a bit of parental discipline (how else do you get them to practise their instruments?), but he admitted that with his own offspring, Nina was the one to implement it.

Sunshine warmed the wooden deck and their flesh and he led her down to the cabin.

They were lying on a deep banquette, entangled in blankets, dazzling light streaming through the window, creating patterns on bare skin. It was still morning, maybe midday, and he was smoking. Barges grumbled by, sending pulsations through the water and into their bones. There was something particularly enchanting about embracing decadence in the morning, amplifying the sense of escape from work, obligation, family. The phone rang. 'Leave it,' he said. 'I don't answer when I'm working. People know that.' They waited for the ringing to end but it didn't. He got up, happy in his nakedness, if irritated by the disturbance.

'Edmundo, *amigo*,' he said, all affability, winking at Daphne. Then he heard the news and his legs buckled. He held on to a polished wooden rail like a passenger in a storm. Ellie was dead. A car crash on the Paris Périphérique. Near Clichy. Yes, with Jean-Luc. He was dead too.

His first reaction was to reach for a blanket to cover his body from sudden shame. 'No, I haven't seen her.' The lie was one of the worst he ever told. Edmund said the school couldn't find Daphne – she was missing. He didn't know what to do. Theo had been informed and was on his way down from Oxford.

'I'll come over.' So as well as having to give Daphne the news about her mother, he had to invent a plausible plot and 'find' her for her father. Christ, it was awful. He managed it all perfectly efficiently, duping the widower, delivering his daughter home as if by magic. Poor little Daff. Struck dumb, initially. Unable to cry or speak. Looking back, he saw it had been the end of their era in one blow. He'd expected it to happen gradually, but this was extremely sudden. She didn't go back to school. They met a few times before the final break but she was like a wounded animal that lashes out and he felt unable to cope, unable to understand what she wanted from him. And it wasn't long before she went off and married that Greek shit.

* * *

Daphne got up from the table and headed off for the lavatory. She had done that sort of thing as a child – not announcing or explaining what she was doing, leaving others to catch up with her actions. The coffee arrived. He drank his. He turned periodically to peer across the other diners towards the back of the restaurant in the hope of spotting her. She was taking a long time. Finally, he got up, made his way down the narrow steps and called for her outside the Ladies, quietly at first, then louder. Pushing the door open, he found the two cubicles empty. The Gents too. He went back to the table and asked their waiter.

'I think she go out back door,' he said, looking with increased interest at Ralph. 'She gone. While ago.'

11

DAPHNE

Daphne waited inside the ladies' lavatory, hoping in vain that the choking feeling would pass. The combination of anger and fear was like a physical malady. Heavy head, queasy gut, eyes hot and dry. She ran cold water and splashed her face and neck. She had imagined this conversation with Ralph might bring relief: he would be repentant, she would be magnanimous, he would be grateful. A resolution would be found. Instead, they had stirred up a storm of poisons and she couldn't face going back for more. The idea of sitting down at the table again and listening to his self-absorbed excuses sickened her.

Emerging into the corridor next to the kitchens, she noticed an emergency fire door, which looked like an opportunity. She pushed it and walked out into the restaurant's back yard. The relief of fresh air and of getting away was immense. The right decision. I don't need to explain myself, she thought. I'll pick up the bike later, so he doesn't spot me. Sidestepping Don Luigi's dustbins and the piled-up crates of empty bottles, she opened a gate and found herself in an alleyway. There was birdsong. Small clouds hung high in the sky. It was like escaping from prison.

She strode the warm pavements, allowing herself to be carried along as if her legs were choosing the way. It didn't matter where. After a few minutes her phone buzzed in her jeans pocket: Ralph. She switched it to silent and only then saw that the voice recorder was still on. One hour forty-one minutes, much of which was Ralph's confessions. She'd only decided to do that at the last minute, remembering Jane's recommendation: 'If you do talk to him about all this, you could record it, you know. If you ever wanted proof or even if you just wanted to go over it yourself, it would be useful.' The tip of the phone had been sticking out of her back pocket throughout the lunch, picking up Ralph's secrets and turning them into evidence.

She stopped the voice memo and saved it. Seeing Ralph made her remember herself as a child – how she was swept into things she didn't understand, how the world appeared out of control. The recording was like taking action for the young Daphne. Stupidly perhaps, she had expected to find some version of mutual understanding or a truce with Ralph. Instead, he presented a vision of her as an object of his fantasies and desires, as though he had created and defined her. There had been no recognition of what it meant for her. She hated that he called her Daff. He was the only person who shortened her name like that and his affectionate soubriquet transported her straight back to those days.

He had infuriated her. Why did she even need to know about the boys? How did they explain what had happened to her? At this stage, a lustful Peter Pan about to hit seventy was ludicrous. It was true that his light-boned physique and wily charm were still there, though the degradations of ageing were clear. The expensive-looking indigo linen and the Japanese-y scarf couldn't disguise the haggard eyes and the hint of something hurting when he stood up.

She scarcely noticed the hordes of Saturday shoppers as she hurried across the King's Road. A black-cab driver shouted, 'Trying to get killed, are we?' after she ran between him and a bus to get to the other side. She kept going. Only when she got to the river did she realise she had arrived at the houseboats. A return to the scene of the crime. There was an unsettling synchronicity: the place where she'd learned of Ellie's crash, one of the last times with Ralph; back at the monstrous river again, with its colour of canteen coffee and its dangerous, muddy pull. Hauling herself up on to the wall in the shade of a plane tree, she sat, legs dangling, facing the moored boats.

She hoped she wouldn't cry, having always mistrusted the weakness of women's weeping. But there was nothing delicate or feminine about the violent gush of salty blubbering that engulfed her as her body convulsed with sobs.

She hadn't cried like that when Ellie died. The shock of being motherless stunned her into stony silence. Ed caved in on himself, unable to share the tragedy with his children, and Theo, always the practical, unflappable member of the family, threw himself even deeper into his PhD. Though only five years older, her brother seemed a distant adult, who could not engage emotionally or offer comfort. The three of them had gone to Paris to identify the body, but Daphne refused to go into the morgue. There were days of suffocating bureaucracy, organising the 'repatriation of the deceased'. And then the quarrel with Ellie's mother, who wanted her daughter buried in Greece, though Ed was organising a cremation in London. *Yiayia*'s fury scorched down the phone. 'You can't burn a person. It's the deliberate desecration of God's creation.' The Greek family threatened to boycott the funeral. 'In Greece it's illegal,'

Aunt Athena told Daphne over the phone. On the day, Ellie's three sisters and mother appeared at Putney Vale Crematorium, dressed in black, as imposing in their anger as a masked, tragic chorus.

Ralph came to the funeral – obviously. Thin-lipped and grim-faced, he was there with Nina, who wept openly, her eyes puffed and red. But after that, he edged back from the quagmire of grief surrounding the Greenslays. Nina tried to be helpful. She had loved Ellie, looking up to her like an older sister, she told Daphne. 'It's impossible to believe her powerful energy is gone.' Arriving at Barnabas Road with pans of soup and oven dishes filled with stuffed vegetables, Nina sat in the kitchen and tried to encourage Ed and Daphne to eat. 'You need your strength,' she said. 'Ellie would want you to keep going, to eat good, nour-ishing, Greek food.' The cross-cutting contradictions of death and betrayal made it almost unbearable to see Nina. Daphne wouldn't touch her meals and left the room as soon as she could, preferring instead to drink herself into nothingness.

Ralph was far warier than his wife of wading through the sad swamp towards Daphne, though she longed to find comfort with him. The first time she visited him at the houseboat after the funeral, she got drunk and they lay together on a bed. He didn't make a move and she hardly knew what she was doing. The second time they met, she was angry with him. 'It's easy for you to pick me up and put me down when it suits you. What am I supposed to do when you go home to perfect Nina and your adorable children?' He tried to placate her but she became even more infuriated. Their relationship had been poisoned by Ellie's death, as though their secret was petty, pitiful even, and meaningless in the face of this destruction. 'What's the point?' she raged.

There was no point in anything. School seemed absurd, even though her A levels were only weeks later. Mr Gray, the headmaster, came to visit her at Barnabas Road and explained about losing her future and 'throwing everything away'. But that looked irrelevant when life could be extinguished so suddenly. Vodka became her preferred medication, making her dazed and relaxed, loose-mouthed like a baby sated on mother's milk, and even the hangover took her mind off the misery.

Whatever it had been between her and Ralph ceased to exist. They didn't make love again. She sensed he was relieved to retreat, though he did write a requiem dedicated to Ellie. 'It's all about female strength and anger,' he said. 'More *Dies Irae* and not much *Lux Aeterna*,' he pontificated, waiting for her to ask what that meant, which she didn't. Both sounded stupid. There was a women's choir and no musical instruments except percussion, also played by women. 'Terrifying and raw,' wrote one critic. Ed was deeply touched by their old friend's gesture. Daphne didn't care.

She didn't go to the first performance of Ralph's *Requiem*, instead getting smashed at a party held by friends who were leaving the next day for university, Jane included.

'It's fine. Have a gap year, then you can take your A levels and go to university.' Jane's own bags were neatly packed, her exam results ludicrously good, her future sitting on a plate and smiling. Later, Daphne used to say she was on a permanent gap year. 'Mind the gap.'

Eventually, Daphne stopped sniffing and the tears and snot on her sleeves dried in the sun. It was like the times she'd sat on the wall at the end of the garden as a teenager, legs swinging over the water, a surreptitious cigarette smoked, secrets wept and whispered into the wet air. Or sobbing inconsolably, drunk on her parents' booze, contemplating the river's drifting cargo of rotting planks, plastic toys and dead dogs. When she rolled her legs back towards the pavement and jumped off the wall it was unclear how much time had passed since she'd got there. Thirty-three years perhaps?

Her limbs were heavy but her head lighter, as though the storm of emotions had left new, clean air. She walked home slowly along the back streets. Ralph's attempt at an 'explanation' had turned out even more damning than his previous silence. Why would he think that his surreptitious love of boys made sense of his relationship with her as a young girl? And why the gingerbread house as a metaphor? He must realise, she thought, that it's a tale of two abused children. Hansel and Gretel are abandoned in the woods by their parents, and tricked into the witch's clutches through the temptations of sweets and cakes. The gingerbread house is a child trap – an alluring candy construction that is actually a prison containing a cannibalistic witch and an oven for cooking children. Ralph had kept on with the sweetmeats and sweet-talking with such skill that Daphne didn't even notice when he had her trapped in a cage and slowly began 'eating' her. She even thought she liked it.

She always believed that Ralph had been gentle and kind with her. Now it was clear his actions were inherently brutal towards the spirit and body of a child. He had abetted her in lying to her parents and in taking her away from Ellie, as if he could offer something better than mother-love. The lunch at Don Luigi's inverted the Ralph she remembered as an essentially good, if mischievous, adult boy into a scheming, grooming paedophile. Grandmother into wolf, prince into frog, god into swan, girl into bush; she knew transformations were part of many stories.

The flat felt hot and airless on her return and the hall mirror offered a pitiful picture of swollen, red eyes and frizzed hair. Fortunately, Libby was staying with Paige for the weekend, so she wouldn't have to explain. She opened as many doors and windows as possible and, replacing her clothes with a long, baggy T-shirt, drank two glasses of water and collapsed into an armchair.

There were three messages on the house answerphone and seven on her mobile – all from Ralph. 'Daphne, are you OK? What happened? I'm worried. Please let me know what happened.' Exhausted as if she'd climbed a mountain, she admitted a sweet sliver of satisfaction in not returning his calls.

She was woken by the ping of a text message. Jane. How did it go? Daphne rang her and described the meeting.

'I can't believe the gingerbread house!' Jane was almost gleeful with outrage.

'Yeah, that's apparently how he sees it.' Daphne felt even more tired than before and closed her eyes. 'Oh God, what a mess. Shit, bugger, fuck … as we used to say.' She didn't want to continue with this fairy-tale analysis, even if it was true, but Jane wasn't giving up so easily.

'Of course, you remember how Hansel and Gretel ends?' Her voice was calm and sly.

'Uh, yes. They kill the witch and escape back home?'

'Exactly. It's Gretel, the little girl, who outwits the witch and shoves her into the oven, saves her fattened-up brother from the cage, and finds a way out of the dark forest. It's never too late to kill the witch, Daphne. Think about it. There's a natural balance in getting justice, even if it's much later. The witch shouldn't get away with it. I know you think your case was unique, but you can bet there were other children tempted by the candies ...'

* * *

'It's not an emergency,' Daphne replied when Jane said a friend could organise an emergency appointment on Monday.

'Maybe not, but it's important you go.'

Daphne lied to Jelly ('a gynae thing') and left during her lunch break, making her way by Tube to Embankment and walking to a road off the Strand. National Society for Survivors of Child Sexual Abuse. It was on the sign in bold lettering. At least they offered the more optimistic version of surviving rather than being a victim, like in news reports. But while she had never seen herself as either victim or survivor, she was now plagued by the image of Gretel tempted by walls of cake before the witch closed in.

'What would you like to discuss with me today?' Vivien was around sixty, with chic grey hair and a tailored white shirt. Her beaky nose and discerning eyes lent a hawkish aspect, though her manner was efficiently compassionate.

'It's hard to know where to begin – like trying to sum up a whole lifetime of ideas that have turned back-to-front and upside down.' To Daphne's dismay, tears pricked her eyes. She coughed to disguise it. Then out poured the whole bloody shebang: her crazy parents, Ralph's devotion, their subsequent relationship, Ellie's death, Constantine, and on until she reached Libby's dancing. 'I never believed Ralph harmed me – it was as though the mutual affection guaranteed that everything was OK. But it doesn't look like that any more. I don't know what to do.'

'It's very common for people to feel close to the person who abused them – to get something from the relationship.' Vivien's voice was low and measured. 'But what's significant is that a child cannot give consent. That's the law. A person under sixteen can never consent to sex under any circumstances.'

'They do, though,' said Daphne.

'Yes.' Vivien half-smiled, patiently. 'And it's different when it's with someone of their own age. It's not about saying yes, it's having the capacity to understand what that consent means – the full consequences. A child doesn't have that.' Vivien held her questioning air until Daphne nodded. 'The same thing holds if someone is very drunk: they're not considered capable of agreeing to have sex. So when an adult has sex with a child, the power imbalance means it's not OK in any circumstances, however caring anyone was. Even if the child believes it is OK. Does that make sense?'

Daphne nodded again, childlike. She wanted to go and curl up beside Vivien and be protected, as though this stranger could take on the role that Ellie should have played by pointing out right and wrong and then providing comfort and love.

'If you don't mind I've got a quick checklist that helps with assessment?'

'Sure. Fine.'

'So how's your sleep?'

'Dreadful, always.' Daphne smiled. 'You name it and I've tried it. Sleeping pills, herbal sedatives, acupuncture, homeopathy, breathing exercises ... even mindlessness.'

'Mindfulness?'

'Yes, anything and everything.'

'What about substance abuse?'

'Yes.'

Vivien waited for an explanation, pen poised.

'Oh all sorts.' Daphne laughed as though the list would be too long to enumerate, then regretted her levity. 'I've been through AA and NA years ago. I'm pretty good now. I drink a bit, but mostly just wine.'

'Eating disorders?'

'Yes, but ages ago, when I was young.' She recalled starving herself after she and Constantine broke up. It provoked a strange satisfaction. You could obtain a giddy high from extreme hunger. She only got over it when her skin became furry and her periods stopped.

'OCD?'

'No.' That was a relief. She didn't want Vivien to tick every bloody box on her page.

'Promiscuity?'

'Not really. Depends on the definition. Maybe, occasionally.'

Vivien didn't ask her any more about that and she was glad not to have to dredge up the faces of men who weren't worth remembering.

'Depression or suicidal thoughts?'

'At one point, yes. Long gone.' She looked at Vivien's thoughtful expression. 'So, do you think this stuff is linked to what happened with Ralph?'

Vivien took a while to reply, like a kind teacher waiting for a slow child to grasp an elementary lesson. 'What do you think, Daphne?'

She didn't answer.

'I'd say his behaviour was likely to be a factor. At the very least.'

'It's confusing. Like I'd got it all wrong.' Hot tears forced their way out. She hated to be seen crying.

Vivien handed her a box of tissues. 'Perhaps your body is giving you the answer?'

Daphne nodded and blew her nose. 'So much makes sense when I think of it from the perspective of being an abused child.' All the bad decisions I've made, she thought. All that destruction I believed came from within – it forms a pattern that started on the outside. And it's starting to be clear where it all began.

'I feel so angry,' she said. 'I want to punish him, to make him pay for what he did.' She let out a dry, one-syllable laugh like a dog bark that brought no responding smile from Vivien. 'After a lifetime of thinking everything was fine, it's sort of freaking me out. I don't know what to do.'

'Have you thought about prosecuting?' Vivien paused, head cocked. 'It's your choice. But it can be a very empowering experience, even if it is a long time later. A relief.' Vivien rubbed her hands, dry and papery. 'Of course, it's entirely your decision. But the police are well trained these days in handling historical child sexual abuse.' Daphne didn't say anything. 'You need to know that the whole process is challenging. The outcome is never guaranteed. The abuser can still be acquitted if the evidence is limited or if the Crown Prosecution Service say it's not viable. But from what you say, there's evidence. I think there's a good chance of success.'

* * *

Returning on the Tube to Shepherd's Bush, Daphne felt buoyant, almost elated. Vivien's weighty diagnosis was that she had been raped as a child, but at least it brought clarity.

'Don't answer his messages,' Vivien recommended. 'It's better you don't have any more contact with him.'

Back at 'Hell', she received an email from Ralph ('At least let me know that you're OK') and another voice message ('I'm very sorry if I said something to upset you'). While she was speaking on the office phone to an old client requesting a villa on Paxos, her mobile rang and Ralph's name appeared on the screen. Distracted, she forgot what she was talking about.

'Daphne? Hello? Are you there?' Mrs Wheeler's voice went from concerned to irritated. She was a demanding client who always required much handholding throughout the booking and the holiday itself. 'If you're busy with something else, you can call me back.'

'No. Sorry, Mrs Wheeler.' Quick, find an excuse. 'It's just that three of the most enormous dogs stopped outside our office. Wolfhounds, I think. Bizarre.' Daphne had always been speedy with a surprising alibi – early training perhaps. Jelly was staring at her, jolting her back to the job in hand. 'So, I have the most beautiful house for you. It's perfect, with olive trees, a pool. Only ten minutes' walk to the beach. I know you'll love it.'

When Daphne got home, Libby was back from a dance day camp for the last week of the summer holidays.

'How did it go?'

'Sick!' came the verdict. 'The teacher was amazing.' She made a leap across the kitchen, limbs extended and impressively coordinated. A gazelle in black Lycra. 'But it seems stupid when I think of what's going on in Greece.

Why should I be doing dance lessons when kids there are drowning and homeless? Did I tell you Dad's going to put two Syrian families in the house on Hydra over the winter? But there are so many more with nowhere to go.'

Daphne nodded, partly diminished by Sam's new super-hero status, but relieved that Libby had her mind on other things. She had no idea how to tell her about Ralph, and while she liked them being open with one another, she was clear that a certain amount of information needed to be lost between the generations. There were things that shouldn't have to be understood or elucidated. No girl wants to know details of her mother's sex life.

She deleted another message from Ralph without listen-ing to it and lay on the sofa sketching a new piece of work called *Gingerbread House*. She envisaged it covered with laminated, old-fashioned biscuits (chocolate bourbons, custard creams, squashed flies), sweets (liquorice allsorts, jelly babies), and shreds of wrappers from her favour-ite chocolates (Cadbury's Flake, Fry's Chocolate Cream, Milky Way). The candy-covered doors and windows would open to reveal a terrifying man-witch lurking inside next to a cage and an oven. Odd, she thought, how the term wizard held none of the same menace as witch. In any case, this hanging would be a far more appropriate testimony to Ralph's legacy than *Putney*, which now distressed her.

The door buzzer sounded, raucously intrusive on her thoughts. She went to answer and saw Ralph's face flicker-ing in and out of focus on the screen. 'Daphne? Please. Can I talk to you?'

'No, not now. I can't. Sorry, but you need to go.'

'But I've been so worried. What happened? Please just put my mind at—'

'Goodbye,' Daphne cut in, wiping him off the screen and silencing him. The buzzer went again and though she saw him leaning towards the camera she didn't answer.

'Who was that?' Libby asked from the open doorway of the kitchen, eating an apple and lifting one leg high against the doorframe in an elegant stretch.

'It's Ralph. A friend of my parents. I had an argument with him and I can't face seeing him. Don't open the door, OK?'

'How do you mean, an argument?'

'Oh, you know? Old stuff. I'll tell you another time. OK, my curious little Liberty darling?'

Libby groaned resignedly. 'OK, my Daphne darling. Secrets, secrets.'

The buzzer sounded once more, mother and daughter caught each other's eye, and then the flat went quiet except for the bass thump and tinny hiss of something playing on a portable speaker in Libby's room.

Nearly an hour later, Daphne was sketching the witch – a raven-feathered, pockmarked, hunchbacked, claw-footed man – when she heard the entrance buzzer again.

'That's Paige,' shouted Libby. 'She just texted that she was arriving.'

Daphne heard the sounds of the girls greeting each other – more subdued than the normal squeals, she noticed.

'Hi,' said Paige, peering into the room and giving a restrained wave.

'Uh, Mum …' Libby was hovering too. 'There's a … there's someone to see you.'

Daphne jumped up to see Ralph slinking, hangdog, through her front door. 'Daphne, just let me sit down for five minutes. I need to tell you something.'

Libby and Paige watched, frozen, sensing the tension.

'So you must be Liberty?' said Ralph. He was trying every trick, thought Daphne, her anger rising.

'Ralph, right? How's it going?' Libby's eyes were narrow with curiosity and flicked over to her mother to assess the situation.

'Oh not too bad, thanks. How are *you*? You look as though you're a dancer. I always thought your mother should have danced when she was young.'

Daphne burned with fury. Was he now going to start eyeing up her daughter? He mustn't be allowed to continue.

'OK, guys. Listen, Ralph and I need to discuss something. I'm going to take him out for a quick drink. Right! Ralph, let's go.' She mustn't sound out of control. Don't panic. Not in front of the children!

'Could I just have a glass of water first?' He steadied himself on a chair – a ham actor playing ill to gain time, she thought.

'I'll get some water.' Libby twisted on one foot and skipped dancer-like in the direction of the kitchen.

The cunning old sod, thought Daphne. 'No, Ralph.' She tried to keep her voice firm. 'Come on. We can get some water outside.' She set off towards the front door, grabbing a jacket on the way, ignoring the astonishment on the girls' faces. As she held the door open and sternly ushered Ralph out, she heard Libby's stage whisper: 'What the hell?'

'Daphne, what's going on?' Ralph looked distraught as he dragged behind her brisk steps in the muffled calm of the carpeted corridor. She pressed the lift button without looking at him.

'I can't do this now, OK? You shouldn't have come. It's harassment.'

'But what happened? Daff? Why did you abandon our lunch? Why aren't you answering my calls? I can't just leave it – it's agony.'

A new, detached purity of anger liberated her. 'If you can't understand, then——' She broke off as the door to the lift opened and a man emerged and walked in the opposite direction from them.

'Are you trying to destroy me?' whispered Ralph. 'What can I do? Should I jump in the river?'

'You can do what you like, but leave me alone.'

They entered the lift and Daphne felt like a trapped animal. It reminded her of how he would sneak into her room at Barnabas Road without anyone knowing he was in the house – the front door was rarely locked and family and friends came and went as they liked. They only once had a burglary and even that didn't change her parents' approach. One spring evening, when Ed and Ellie were having dinner with friends down in the kitchen, Ralph entered the house, crept upstairs and appeared in Daphne's bedroom. She was lying on the floor in her pyjamas, listening to records, when she heard a scratching noise at the door. At the time it was thrilling. She couldn't remember how old she'd been, just the urgency of their kisses, the excitement generated by risk, the fear when they thought they heard someone coming – he leaped up and hid behind the door. And then they laughed so hard her nose tingled like Coca-Cola and her stomach hurt.

Ralph caught up with her at the railings by the edge of the communal gardens. She was looking at a plump, black coot mooching about in the low-tide sludge.

'Daphne, please. Just tell me. I'll do anything. I can see you're upset. You can't just freeze me out.' She didn't reply.

Three white geese were braying like donkeys, their heads raised to the heavens.

'Let me take you for a drink, Daphne? We could go to the King's Head. It's still there. We've been through too much not to be friends.'

His pathetic pleading made her furious. He couldn't make a straightforward apology – something even the Pope had managed to do on account of his child-molesting priests. If they were going to talk it could be on her terms. She cast about for what those terms might be and spotted some fenced-off steps leading to the riverbed. A prominent sign read NO ENTRY. 'OK, we can talk if we go down there.' Pretending not to see his disconcerted expression, she climbed over the railings to a flight of stone steps that was covered in slimy weed and strewn with washed-up debris. She heard him struggling behind her, and then saw him follow her cautiously down the steps, one hand on the damp wall.

The silt gave way satisfactorily under her feet and olive-coloured sludge squelched up around her white canvas shoes. She checked Ralph's progress: treading gingerly, his arms were outstretched for fear of losing his balance.

'Where are you going?' he said, whingeing like a tired child. 'It's horrible down here.' His objections made her more reckless. It was enjoyable having the upper hand. Trailing the geese, she waded into the murky river up to her calves, feeling both the pull of the water emptying towards the sea and the delight of shocking him.

'You've shown you can't understand,' she called, as if she was now about to leave him and swim into the distance. 'And I don't feel like trying to explain again.'

He came to where the opaque water was slapping gently against the mud and she took another step away. 'Daphne, you're mad. Get back – it's dangerous.'

Some men passing on a small cruiser stared at them and one called, 'Nice evening for a dip!' Laughter sounded above the engine and the men waved their beer bottles.

Daphne ignored them. The cold wet was up to her thighs. 'Come on,' she called. 'Let's go for a swim. Don't you dare?'

There was liberation in accepting a dare. He'd taught her that. Truth or dare had been her favourite game as a teenager and she and Ralph had pushed and coaxed each other into countless thrills by following its rules.

He reached out an arm towards her and slipped, falling forwards into the water. For a brief moment he became completely submerged, then rose on all fours, gasping and spitting. He tried to get up, water streaming from his soaked clothes. 'Shit.' She watched him make several attempts and fail. 'I can't.' Slowly, pondering the alternatives, she moved over to give him a hand, pulled him upright and left him to shuffle out of the water. He fell again, toppling backwards this time, so he sat, legs outstretched, body deflated, hair flattened, face a grimace like the masked Guy Fawkes effigies Daphne constructed as a child.

Smeared with mud and shocked by his dowsing, Ralph appeared to have lost the will to talk. That, at least, was a relief. And the scene was funny – she could see that, though she didn't laugh. She observed him from a distance as he unlaced his shoes, emptied them of water, then remained there as though unable to move. He was wheezing slightly. He didn't catch her eye, afraid perhaps of mockery. 'Shit,' he repeated, examining his father's old

Swiss watch, presumably damaged by the plunge. She knew its bold-numbered face well – once familiar as the back of his hand.

The sun disappeared, turning the sky drab, and a cold wind picked up. She walked back towards the steps, water-logged shoes gurgling. A rat, the same colour as the river deposits, sped along the base of the wall and slithered into a drainage hole.

'Time to go home. Are you going to get out of the mud?' she shouted, but Ralph didn't answer. Let him sulk, she thought, sitting down out of sight at the top of the steps to see if he would budge. She was tempted to leave him to sort out his own mess, but a couple of minutes later she heard him grunt irritably as he got up and made his way across the sludge in her direction. 'Goodbye, Ralph,' she yelled, cheered by the strange interlude that she had engin-eered. 'Don't call me.' It couldn't be classified as revenge, nor exactly *folie à deux*, but it had stopped her feeling like a victim.

She tried to let herself into the flat quietly so she wouldn't be noticed, but Libby and Paige were in the kitchen.

'Mum?' Libby observed the wet trousers and dirty shoes. 'Mum, what's going on? What the hell?'

'You OK?' asked Paige.

'Yes, fine,' Daphne smiled. This was not something she could explain simply to anyone, let alone two teenage girls. It would be risky even to begin describing her anger, her desire to humiliate Ralph, his ridiculous attempt to win her around again, his pathetic inability to pick himself up from the mud. 'I went for a little walk after leaving Ralph – down by the river. I slipped. I'm an idiot, I know.' She looked at the two girls' puzzled faces. 'I'll just go and change.'

JANE

Daphne was late, but Jane was content to stand outside the police station in the September sunshine. Daphne had postponed the interview until Libby was back at school, but in the end Jane hadn't needed to put much pressure on her friend, merely offering to accompany her on this daunting mission. A small tap and everything fell into place. Taking time off work reminded her of occasional days away from school, where the world looked brighter and unexpected. The air was fresh and energising, despite the city cranking up for the day: bus exhaust, fry-ups and passing gusts of pungent aftershave.

She sipped a takeaway coffee and managed with one hand to send a text to Josh. Her firstborn son was not more beloved than the second, but he was closer to her in his interests. She appreciated his scientific approach to life. 'Are you still coming for lunch on Saturday? Hope so!' She relied on Josh, though she hoped he didn't see it like that. Even sending him a message made her feel more balanced and contented. When her phone pinged with a reply, she was momentarily chastened to find it was Toby.

Hey Mum – best one in the world. Any chance of you driving me up to B'ham at the weekend? Have too much stuff for the new house to take by train. Your truly grateful son, T.

Sure she texted back. Sunday's fine for me. See you later. Daphne swept up on her clanking yellow bike in a flurry of hair, bags, plastic flowers and a long scarf that was dangling dangerously. She apologised for being late, and then held Jane in a hug. 'I can't believe I'm actually doing this. Where would I be without you, Janey?'

'My pleasure,' she said, with honesty.

'I feel like shit, though. Didn't sleep all night.'

'I remember you were always a night bird, weren't you? It's tough, I know. But it'd be tougher if you didn't do it.'

Daphne nodded obediently and allowed Jane to take her arm and lead her up the steps.

They waited at reception for a long-winded old man reporting something about vandals and rubbish bins and then Daphne spoke clearly, as if reciting something she'd practised.

'Good morning. I'm Daphne Greenslay. I've been in touch with Detective Constable Medlar and I have a meeting with him at nine thirty.' She signed her name in a book, was given a visitor's pass and told to take a seat. Jane put her hand on Daphne's light cotton sleeve, feeling the warm flesh below. 'I'm sure it'll go well. Apparently the police have improved so much – for this sort of thing.'

Daphne winced. 'Oh God.'

'No, really. They've had to become experts. I think they all have specialist Child Abuse Investigation Units now.'

A bulky man strode over. 'DC Medlar.' He held out a hand. 'Thanks for coming in. Now, which of you is Daphne?' He looked nice enough – fortyish, with biscuit-coloured hair that must have been naturally curly before it was shorn. 'Call me Gareth,' he said, explaining that Jane should wait where she was while the interview took place. Daphne looked small, almost childlike, next to the tall policeman as he led her away.

She turned to give a discreet wave. As if she is being led to the cells for life imprisonment, thought Jane. With any luck, it'll be Ralph who is locked up. Rape of a child should mean years. It may have taken decades, but here we go. His smug superiority and seedy wiles won't be any use to him in prison. Let him try charming his cellmates or enchanting his guards! She almost smiled at the image.

She waited, listening to voices at reception, phones ringing, sirens sounding as police cars set off. Waiting. More waiting. There'd been a lot of that in her relationship with Daphne – not the recent experiences of her friend's lateness, but an underlying inequality that Jane used to believe was linked to Daphne's beauty, or to the way that people loved her. Maybe it was even reflected in the way Ralph worshipped her – a grown man bowing down before a girl queen. Both Ralph and Jane had been waiting for Daphne's approval, her affections. Jane may have been an intellectual step ahead, but she was always a large step behind in terms of glory, like a puffy young lady-in-waiting. Even later, when she was with Michael, when they were in love, when she was soon to take his name and become Dr Butterfield, as though they were running into a meadow full of golden flowers. Even then, there was a part of her that believed this good fortune was a mirage, an aberration that couldn't last. Inside the capable, professional, loving adult skulked a hormone-ravaged, sebum-soaked teenager, defined in relation to Daphne.

Of all the occasions she'd spent hanging around for Daphne, waiting for her in the reception area of the police station was the one to be cherished. A personal victory. Almost absent-mindedly, she dashed off some work emails, half an eye remaining on the people parading their quotidian dramas before her. Eventually, DC Medlar escorted Daphne back. He addressed Jane as though she was her minder. 'I've said I'll be her Family Liaison Officer, so she can ask me anything. I'm usually at the end of a phone. I've given her my mobile for emergencies.' He had a slight Yorkshire accent she found reassuring. 'We'll make this as smooth as possible.' They all shook hands and he walked off, big-boned and affable.

'How did it go?'

'Oh, fine.' Daphne spoke breezily. 'Let's get out of here and I'll tell you.' She looked blank – probably her old way of displacing the issue. They went into the first café they came across on the North End Road – a greasy spoon, serving all-day, fry-up breakfasts and smelling of fatty bacon. Both agreed tea would be a better bet than coffee, and were served large mugs of a muddy, brown brew.

'It's strange but good,' said Daphne, finally, grimacing slightly from the tea. 'As though I can start letting go of something I was carrying alone. It's become external and public. Out of my hands.'

'Well yes and no.' Jane was cautious. 'You have to want this to go ahead.'

'He asked me if there were any children in Ralph's life, and I mentioned grandchildren and his youth choirs. I could see that that changed things. They see him as still being a potential threat.'

'Did he say if they'll arrest him?'

'He's going to come and see what I have as "evidence" – the diaries and letters and my phone recording. They need to know exactly what happened and when. Then they'll investigate everything and let me know.' She looked pleased, buoyant. 'He said that the time I travelled to Greece with Ralph was abduction! It's so peculiar to understand it like that. This story was a secret for so long, I almost doubted it was real. And now it's been given labels, a file, a number, and off it runs with a life of its own.'

'It's a huge relief,' said Jane. 'There's a reason we talk about justice. It recalibrates, brings back a balance, even if it's much later. Like having a body to bury.'

'You're so right,' Daphne said. 'I remember that feeling of balance when we scattered Ellie's ashes into the river. It took us ages, well over a year, before we could face doing it. All that time they were just sitting there in a box in the kitchen. Horrible. You remember what it was like then. Purgatory. In the end, we had a ceremony at the river wall. Just me, Ed and Theo. And a bottle of champagne. It must have been windy because when we threw the ash up into the air it floated like a cloud before falling into the water. What I remember is the relief, as though she wasn't in our hands any more. There was nothing more I could do.'

Jane refrained from remarking that it was right after this that Daphne entered the worst phase of all.

'I know I wasn't exactly a model for what to do when you're bereaved,' said Daphne, possibly anticipating Jane's objections. 'I don't mean that the scattering got rid of the sadness or anything. I know I struggled. But it marked a change. A weight shifted.' Jane tried to remember any sign of this shift, but she had never felt further from her old friend than then, when Daphne went off to Greece and came back married. Jane was a student, while Daphne was living the high life with Constantine. A natural rebel and child of the '60s, she seemed to have easily embraced the world of private yachts and helicopters.

Once, during that unappealing millionaire phase, Daphne was over from Greece and invited Jane to Barnabas Road. Edmund was giving a Last Lunch before selling the place. The walls of the staircase leading down to the kitchen were still papered with faded revolutionary posters and curling newspaper cuttings. That would all be gone before long. No doubt the whole house would be stripped. They sat at the massive kitchen table marked by the cuts and burns of thousands of gatherings and Ed made an effort to provide a nice meal, with plates of charcuterie, cheeses and salads and some good red wine. He had aged – his tall frame more hunched, his face tired and hair greyer and shorter. The limp that had always been there was more pronounced and even his hippy glad rags had been replaced by a dark, sober shirt and jeans.

Jane was filled with nostalgic pleasure to see her and to attend this last meeting in Barnabas Road, where every painting and piece of furniture provoked a chain of memories. She hoped they would walk around, sit in Daphne's old room and watch the boats go by, remember things that had seemed important at the time. But it hadn't been like that at all. Daphne was skeletally thin with an absent expression – she'd probably taken something – though her suntan gave her a superficial radiance. She was wearing an astonishing gold necklace that glittered and distracted.

'Looted from an ancient tomb?' enquired Edmund tartly.

Her pale silky dress hung in complex, asymmetrical layers and, when Jane complimented her on it, Daphne admitted it was couture. 'Constantine had it made for me in Milan,' she laughed, part apologetic, part charmed by this unlikely turn of events. 'I had to go for a fitting.' Jane thought Ellie would be turning in her grave – if she'd had one. That flimsy piece of fabric probably cost as much as her term's living expenses in Norwich.

She had hoped Daphne would notice *her* metamorphosis – she was no longer a plain, bespectacled heifer; there'd been several boyfriends. Later, though, she realised her own alterations were modest in comparison with the personality-altering, fashion-twisting transformations that Daphne sped through without a backward glance. It sometimes seemed she was pretending, so often had she shed her skin and changed her story. Pretending to be someone else, or, perhaps more worryingly, pretending to be herself. It wasn't just the jumps from barefoot wood-sprite to punk-romantic to designer-brand, jet-set wife, it was the chameleon ability to make the alterations seem substantial and part of her character.

Now, with her denunciation of Ralph, Daphne had changed yet again. She had become a moral crusader, model mother and righteous survivor confronting the wrongs of the past. Of course I'm pleased, Jane thought. Ralph deserves everything he gets. I was there. I know what he did. Roll on the chains. Nevertheless, Daphne's capacity for changing her mind sometimes made it look as if nothing in the world was fixed or true, as if there were no hard certainties of the sort that fired Jane's work and steeled her opinions.

Daphne paid for the tea and held out her arms ceremoniously, as her father used to do. 'I'd never have got this far without you.'

Jane stooped slightly into the smaller woman's embrace. 'You've done it! I'm so pleased for you.' Then she said something she suspected was untrue. 'That was the hard part. Now you can wait for the system to step into action.'

1 3

RALPH

He was deep inside an intricate dream of early morning, making love in a hidden garden to a boy who might have been Daphne. The noise of knocking and voices were far enough away to be irrelevant. It was only when Nina repeated his name and gripped his shoulder that he woke. It is surprising how much you can think in the seconds before reality sets in – the stage when you've fallen over the edge of the cliff but haven't hit the ground is long enough to recall a lifetime. His mind flashed to a holiday in 1975, when the entire Greenslay family came to stay at Nina's parents' house in Pelion. His almost permanent state of arousal for Daphne worked as an aphrodisiac for him with Nina. Although Jason was only five months old and Nina was often exhausted, she was swept along by his fervour. They made love like teenagers, grasping moments while the baby was asleep, when he woke in the night or during siesta time after lunch. Although Nina never demonstrated a great interest in sex, she allowed herself to be taken, as though offering him a gift. His urgency puzzled and pleased her. The intrinsic betrayal – Daphne was in the same house – only made it more thrilling. He was perfectly aware of attempting to slake his unquenchable thirst for the dark-eyed, hard-limbed animal-child by cleaving to soft, milky-breasted Nina.

'There are two policemen downstairs. They need to talk to you.' Nina looked afraid. 'They won't say what it's about.' Her long, grey hair hung loose over her purple robe so she resembled a benign witch.

'What time is it?' The curtains were shut and it felt like the middle of the night. He still had one foot in the green dream-garden.

'Seven. What's going on, Ralph? Do you know what it's about?'

He didn't reply, but sat on the edge of the bed, blinking himself into the day, beginning to suspect what had happened. 'No. No idea.'

'They need you to come down quickly.'

'OK. I'll just go for a pee.' It took a long time to arrive then dribbled sadly, mocking the randy night visions of youthful potency and transmuting lovers. He washed his hands, splashed water on his face, drew the belt tight on a dressing gown, put on some espadrilles and descended the stairs as sturdily as possible.

The policemen looked ludicrously young. The one with porcine features was surely too plump for this line of work, the other a skinny boy with a weasel face and a bad case of acne. He would have pitied them if the cold dread had not been so overwhelming.

'Mr Boyd?' Piggy said. 'I am arresting you on suspicion of child sexual abuse.' Ralph didn't take in many of the following words that had been heard too often to ring true – incantations or Bible quotes, seen in a thousand films. 'You do not have to say anything, but it may harm your defence if you do not mention ...'

Shit, bugger, fuck. 'Anything you do say can be given in evidence.'

Nina's face caved in as though she were disintegrating from shock.

'It's a mistake. I haven't done anything.' He turned to Nina. 'It's all right.' So this is how I end up, he thought. Strung up and vilified.

'But what happened?'

Ralph shook his head. 'I have an idea — I think it's revenge.'

'He's ill,' Nina said to the policemen. 'Can't he be questioned here? It's not right. He should not be put under a strain.' Her Greek accent increased from tension.

'It's fine,' Ralph said. 'Don't worry. Nina, please.' He gave her a look that was meant to mean, 'Stay quiet, don't fuss,' but she kept talking to the young men, louder this time.

Piggy Boy interrupted her, lips wet. 'Madam, let us do our job. Your husband needs to come with us. Now, sir, if you'd like to get dressed as quickly as possible, we'll take you down to the station. We've got a car outside.' He was evidently enjoying the alarm he could induce in two people old enough to be his grandparents, thought Ralph.

He put on a jacket for dignity, but then they handcuffed him. The metal bracelets surprised him — weighty and uncomfortable, preventing him from walking tall. Nina watched, holding the front door as the uniformed Laurel and Hardy led him down the steps. He stared ahead, hoping nobody would see him, but Justin, their awful neighbour, was setting off for work at exactly the same time. Ralph saw him start to raise his plump hand for a jovial wave and then do a double take, nod in recognition and continue his merry little jog down to the pavement like a president descending from his jet.

As Ralph got into the back seat, the boyish policeman held his arm and, sure as a priest giving his blessing, placed a hand on his head so it wouldn't bang. Leaning his forehead against the cool window, he stared as the familiar streets of Primrose Hill passed like a film.

He surrendered to the processes in the police station, retreating inside himself. Another example of how boarding school can help you in later life, he thought. Let them do what they like. They took away his phone, wallet and watch and removed his shoelaces, leaving him to shuffle. It wasn't unlike the hospital. He relaxed his hands while fingerprints were taken on an electronic machine, obediently opened his mouth for the DNA swab and sat still when he was photographed; these procedures were less stressful than many of the medical scans he'd undergone recently. He was in a system; it was better not to fight. A kindly, pink-cheeked policewoman who reminded him of his school matron asked whether he would like to make a call before she took him to a cell. He almost said no, then remembered why he was there.

Jeb Rosenberry had been his lawyer for such a long time, he knew the number by heart from the quaint days of pocket address books and coin-operated, public telephones. From the start, a shared appetite for success had fuelled their friendship and professional collaboration. Maybe it had not been exactly friendship, thought Ralph. Jeb called him Boydie, but they'd never been drunk and confessed things or been on an adventure together. Nevertheless, they knew each other's wives and children and, in the end, all those years counted for something.

'OK. I see.' Jeb sounded grave, but when he heard who was bringing charges, his voice rose an octave. 'Daphne Greenslay?' Jeb had known the family. He'd been to Sunday lunches at Barnabas Road, for goodness' sake. 'It's an epidemic, this historical-child-abuse business. Hideous. Any middle-aged woman – or man – with nothing better to do remembers someone who stroked their bum back in the last century and the taxpayers have to cough up for endless police investigations and court hearings. And for what?' Ralph didn't answer. 'All right, don't say any more now, Ralph. It'll be OK. We'll sort this. Kentish Town, you said? An hour at the most and I'll be there.'

Matron took him to a cell. 'I'll bring you a cup of tea. I expect you'd like something to eat too?'

'Thank you so much,' he said, polite as a prep-school new boy and looking into her eyes to make the point. 'I'd really appreciate that.' She smiled and he felt a tiny victory.

The cell resembled a large, tiled shower room. A narrow bench topped with a plastic-covered foam mat served as a bed and there was nothing else but a minimalist, stainless-steel lavatory and basin. It reeked of cleaning chemicals with an underlying hint of more organic matter. The window offered dull light through blurry glass tiles but no view. Ralph had never been locked up before, but he refused to panic. Instead, he tried to think of it as a secret hiding place. At least he was alone. The tea, when it came, was comfortingly hot and strong and, after wolfing the plastic-wrapped cheese sandwich, he felt better. The evil, blood-and-eggs, metallic taste in his mouth was gone. He lay down on the bench, fighting off squeamishness at the foam mat's sticky surface. Various names and messages were scratched on the tiles:

Wankers
Dave ♥ Linda
Fuck

A lone tear pressed its way out of one eye and ambled down his cheek.

The round window in the cell door opened with a metallic scrape, an eye and nose appeared and then the cover closed again. This happened about three times before Jeb arrived, incongruous in the hose-down lock-up with his snappy suit and groomed, gun-grey hair. He shook Ralph's hand and attempted a tentative Englishman's hug that was more a pat on the shoulder. 'Don't worry, Boydie. We'll get you out of here.' They sat down on the bench and Jeb leaned forward, hands on thighs, glancing down as though checking his handmade shoes. 'Nina called,' he said. 'She told me about your health issues. I'm sorry you've been having a hard time. Of course, the good thing is it should help with getting bail.'

Ralph looked at him with disbelief. 'You mean otherwise they might keep me locked up?'

'I'm afraid the system's bonkers. They go into overdrive with this abuse business. If they know you work with children's choirs they might consider you a risk. But I'm confident we can get you out.' His smile provoked a rush of renewed fear in Ralph.

'Now listen, I've seen the charges and I don't want to hear your version. Yet. OK?' Jeb looked straight at Ralph who nodded. 'You need to think hard about this before you give me your instructions. She says she was thirteen. And younger when other … acts took place. Now, if a man has unlawful sexual intercourse with a thirteen-year-old girl, that's rape. Your only way out is, "It didn't happen." There's no other excuse. Zilch. It can't be a "reasonable mistake". And if you admit it or try to excuse it to me, I'll be buggered in running a defence for you. You can't change your defence to me later. And I can't misrepresent your case to the court. Understand?'

This was a relief. He had never spoken to anybody about Daphne and the prospect of revealing his precious secret to a man of the world like Jeb was atrocious. Only worse was the prospect of public scrutiny – about as welcome as having his bowels pulled out on a busy pavement.

Jeb stood up and stretched as naturally as a cat changing its position by the fireplace. 'I'm afraid there might be a bit of publicity. The excuse is that it can bring other "victims" out of the woodwork. But don't fret. That'll blow over.'

'Christ, I just remembered you've done this before. The guy from that pop group. What was his name?'

'Tony Teller, from The Lost.' Jeb used a neutral voice, though the sorry story came back to Ralph now. The lead singer from a famous 1980s boy band. In his fifties, with cheeks turning flabby and several young children by a second wife, he'd been hauled through the system, the poor sod, accused of raping numerous underage girls. 'The tabloids called it the groupies' revolt,' said Jeb. 'Nothing like your case, of course,' he added – unnecessarily, thought Ralph. 'You can't imagine what it was like for pop groups with all those girls hanging around. They threw themselves at bands. Not a subtle form of seduction. More like raping the boys than the other way round. For the band it was just a question of choosing – like picking out the lobster from the restaurant tank.' Neither man mentioned that Teller had gone to prison. 'Jailbait time bombs – that's what they were. Though nobody knew it then, least of all the girls.

'Anyway,' continued Jeb, 'the good thing about your problem is that it's all so long ago and if it's a one-off case then it's basically her word against yours. From what I remember, didn't she go off the rails? Drugs, that sort of thing? Dodgy boyfriends? If she's revealed as an unreliable witness, that's a good start. False memory syndrome and so on. And if we show her character's a mess, it could all go your way.'

'And the bad thing?'

'The bad thing is the police seem to think the CPS will go for this – that they have enough evidence. But we have to wait and see. It'll probably take weeks for them to assess everything.'

'And then what?'

'Let's cross one bridge at a time.'

'Give me an idea, Jeb. I need to know.'

'So, the accusation refers to 1976.' Jeb stared at the wall, calculating. 'That's "vaginal penetration by the accused's penis" under the 1956 Sexual Offences Act.' The phrase echoed in the empty space. I could turn that into a piece of music, thought Ralph. Bitter, authoritarian words describing something so beautiful – using a machine gun on a butterfly. He gripped the blue plastic mattress and winced at its tacky surface.

'I don't want to scaremonger, Boydie. But if you're found guilty, it's prison. Couldn't say for how long, but the watchword at this stage is caution.'

Jeb looked down to admire his shoes again, then turned to Ralph. 'So remember, "No comment" when they interview you. Don't give them anything they can twist and use against you. The most important thing is to get you home.

Then we work out how to proceed.' He slapped Ralph on the back, said 'Good luck!' and knocked to be let out, his face steeled with a show of optimism. A guard unlocked the heavy cell door and Jeb fled without a backward glance.

Matron brought some lunch: chicken tikka and a slimy, strawberry dessert in a plastic pot. He ate both mechanically, putting the disgusting rations into his body as fuel, hardly noticing. I need to retract and curl up so I can face the barrage, he thought. How has it come to this, where my life is about to collapse? Everything I built up will crash down because one stone has been pulled out. And that particular stone isn't just some brick in a wall, it's a rare gem of a stone. How could she do this?

He stretched out on the bench and shut his eyes. What could have brought about this horrific change in Daphne? In all the years he'd known her, he only remembered loveliness. They'd been friends and allies, and even after they were no longer intimate, there was the whiff of collusion and affection that remain after a love that was not shattered or ripped apart, but that merely ran its course. It was true that they had not seen a great deal of one another in the thirty or so intervening years. As a rule serendipitously rather than by design, but she never appeared hurt or angry. He knew she'd been through grim times, but that was nothing to do with him. She had emerged on the other side and he was glad. No, there was nothing he could identify to hint that Daphne would turn on him and rip him apart.

He thought back over the occasions he'd seen her since Ellie died. There weren't many. Once, they'd run into one another at a party when she was still in her early twenties. He supposed it must have been when she'd separated from the Greek fucker, but they didn't discuss it. Nina wasn't at the party – probably at home with children, too tired, or getting on with her painting. He and Daphne drank vodka shots and went into a bathroom where she produced a tiny paper package. He watched her familiar, monkey hands chopping the powder, fast and efficient with a razor blade, the way Nina cut garlic on a board.

'Have you got a fiver?' He gave her a ten-pound note and she rolled it up, placed a finger over one nostril, sniffed up one of the four tidy, white lines and then briskly did the same on the other side. He copied her and then put down the money, which she pocketed. Staring at their reflections in the bathroom mirror, he liked what he saw of himself – energetic and tousle-haired. He felt unassailable as an emperor. Daphne was skinny and fragile with dark patches around her eyes. A lost waif, he thought, but marvellous. He put his arms around her and they kissed hard and without tenderness until someone banged on the door. Afterwards, they danced and it seemed as if they had an unspoken pact that would always keep them close.

He heard about her downfall, mainly via Nina, whose Greek friends and family passed on doom-laden stories about drink, drugs, divorce and disasters of all sorts that she apparently brought upon herself. He had not seen her then, or at least not in a context where he could ask. There had been a few meetings in the intervening years, but always in a crowd. There was a rerun of *Oedipus Blues* and she had shown up at the opening night looking like a tramp. He had seen Ed's discomfort at being confronted by a daughter with matted hair and a face as pale and grimy as if she was sleeping under a bridge. She had greeted him and Nina as though she only just remembered who they were. It was disconcerting and he kept his distance, ignoring her for the rest of the evening. At the end, the audience cheered and he and Ed went up on stage and then there were several fantastic reviews: 'Astounding,' he remembered.

The next time he encountered Daphne was when Edmund returned from France for his seventieth-birthday dinner. By then, she had undergone a remarkable transformation and, though she must have been forty, she looked more like thirty – untamed, dark hair piled on her head, glinting gold earrings like a Persian princess and a contented relaxation to her slim body.

As Ed's guests gathered in a private room at the Garrick Club, Ralph felt an almost embarrassing nostalgia for the old days. By the time they were on to the port, he had to wipe away a tear of joy. He noted but didn't care that Nina was sitting next to Margaret, Ed's Canadian wife, and that they both looked stolidly bored, unable to keep a conversation going. Across the table from him, Daphne was exquisite – a worthy inheritor to the wild thing he had venerated. He gave her no wink and, needless to say, there was no kiss, but he felt their old secret was safely concealed – wrapped in precious silks and stored in a carved, wooden trunk for private contemplation.

* * *

In the end, the police kept him in overnight. He suspected it was revenge for his stubborn repetition of 'No comment' to their dogged questioning. They took him to an interview room twice, playing the 'good cop, bad cop' game. The first detective had a breezy air of someone who'd seen it all before and wasn't particularly bothered. He was tall, with the unremarkable features of a man who might advertise DIY tools. 'So how about you help me out here and just confirm a few things. And then we can all go home?' He was less cheery by the time Ralph was led back to his cell, having given his retort of 'No comment' over and again so that it came to seem like a poem. I could turn this into a song, he thought, along with 'the accused's penis' and those haunting legal phrases uttered by Jeb. I'll call it *Habeas Corpus* and there'll be a chorus of policemen chanting, 'And then we can all go home.'

The second interrogator was a thin-lipped, dried-up lizard of a woman, who called him back to the interview room as it was getting dark. 'Mr Boyd, is it true that on Tuesday, 20th July 1976, you had sexual intercourse with Daphne Greenslay? She claims that you inserted your penis in her vagina on that day and on various other occasions.'

They brought him a blanket and he curled up on the repulsive bench, but it was impossible to sleep. The shock and misery hardened into anger about what Daphne had done to him. What happened to the free spirit of my sparkling Ariel, he thought. What transformed her into an embittered, narrow-minded *hausfrau* out to destroy me? All these decades later? Why did she turn sour and vengeful? Even their lunch, only weeks earlier, was mysterious. Everything had seemed fine until she abandoned him without a word, and blocked his calls. He was still unable to comprehend the terrible scene at her flat when she'd treated him like vermin. Then the madness of her wading into the river like a melodramatic Virginia Woolf figure about to end it all, the grotesque indignity of his fall into the mud, his failure even to stand up, the jeering men on the boat. What did she want? It was a nightmare.

He pulled himself up and shuffled the few steps between the door and the bed and repeated it until he felt ridiculous. When he lay down again, he was aching all over and furious. It took a long time before daylight turned the glass window tiles a mustard-gas, yellowish grey and at 7 a.m., Matron (less rosy-cheeked today) passed him coffee and a plastic tray of watery scrambled egg, bacon and sausage through the hatch in the door. He couldn't eat, but drank the weak coffee that reminded him of American diners, where you could put away pints of the stuff without noticing any effect.

Nina was waiting at the front desk and he could tell she hadn't slept either. She had aged since yesterday – an old woman. And I'm an old man, he thought. She opened her mouth to speak as she saw him and then stopped as though words would make things worse.

'Thank you,' whispered Ralph and she nodded. A wise old woman, he thought. 'Speech is silver, silence is golden' was a preferred saying. If much of his time was involved in the noises of music, many achievements in his life had been attained with silence.

Numerous forms had to be completed before he was released on conditional bail. No contact was to be made with Daphne Greenslay and the terms of his release included a ban on unsupervised meeting with children, including his granddaughter Bee. He was not allowed to work with children until further notice and the names of several youth choirs and musical organisations he was associated with were listed. They'd done their homework. He was given a plastic bag containing his confiscated belongings and he sat down to thread his shoelaces, grunting with the effort as he bent forward. I should be put down like a dog, he thought.

In the car, Nina said, 'They came again, those two policemen, and took away your computer and my laptop. And all the papers from your desk. They spent hours going through the books and DVDs. It felt like rape. You have to tell me what's going on, Ralph. What happened?' When he didn't reply, she continued, 'Jeb said it's Daphne.' He coughed then groaned, attempting to find appropriate words that still hadn't arrived when Nina's phone rang and transferred through to the car's loudspeaker. 'Jason – Spain' was displayed on the screen in front of them both.

'*Agapi mou*,' said Nina carefully, her driving becoming even more erratic; she hated cars and brought to England a Greek disrespect for road signs and rules. 'Are you OK, my love?'

'What's going on?' Jason's voice broke up as it left Madrid and arrived in England. 'I just read that Dad's been arrested. It was on the BBC website. It says he's accused of child sexual abuse. What the hell's happening? Are you there?'

'Yes, Jason, I'm here. And your father is here, so maybe it's better if he tells you.' Nina used the exaggeratedly calm tone that denoted fear. She was splendid in a crisis, holding herself and everyone together, but he knew it would come out later.

'Hello, Jason.' Ralph waited.

'Dad, what happened? Is it true?' He was shouting and there was a rumble of street noise in the background. Ralph pictured his son walking along in the sunshine of a Spanish morning, about to face his colleagues in the sleek design company. Son of a paedophile. Disgrace. It was the first point he realised that there was much more to ruin than just his own miserable life. What about Lucia?

How would she deal with having a pervert for a father? And little Bee ... not allowed alone in a room with him! Shit!

'What did they say?'

'Dad, what did you *do*? That's what's important.'

'I didn't do it. It's Daphne ...' He stopped, wondering if Jason even remembered her. 'You know, Daphne Greenslay. I don't know why she's doing this, but it's like a fixation here, this child-abuse business. They've all gone mad. Listen, don't worry. It'll be all right. I can't talk now. We'll speak later, OK?'

Jason didn't sound reassured. 'I'll call again. I can't believe this.' He hung up without saying goodbye.

Three men were waiting outside the house, bulky cameras slung over their shoulders like threatening weapons. As Nina parked, they ran up to the car aiming and pulling triggers. 'Walk in quickly and don't say anything.' Ralph got out and moved past the photographers, who circled him as easily as wolves outmanoeuvring a sheep. 'Ralph! Over here, Ralph! Do you deny the charges?' shouted one. The others snapped and clicked. Ralph fumbled with the house key, his hand shaking, and then hid behind the front door, slamming it as soon as Nina got in.

In the kitchen, Nina emitted a low, agonised sound that reminded him of a horse he'd once seen with a broken back, which had to be shot. She's tried the dignified approach of silence, thought Ralph, and that wasn't much use. As if in reply, she picked up the ceramic bowl of fruit from the table and flung it on the floor where it shattered with rich, splintering cracks, the apples and pears rolling with comic energy across the room. 'You have to explain,' she shouted, operatic now. 'You can't pretend it will all go away if you don't speak. That won't work this time. Tell me, Ralph. Tell me what you did. Enough of the silence, the hiding.'

He was opening his mouth to say something to appease her – anything that would soothe, so he could establish the version he would have to present – when they heard the sound of a key in the front door. They both froze with the vigilance of the hunted. Could the photographers be forcing their way in? A female voice called out, 'Hello. It's me.' They'd forgotten it was one of Anka's cleaning days. Unable to cope with the situation, Nina rushed out of the room and hurried upstairs.

He didn't find it hard to deal with the young Polish woman. I've lived a whole life dissembling, he thought. It's easy. 'How are you, Anka?'

'Why there men taking photos?' she asked, unsettled, breathing gently through her mouth, grey eyes rounded from surprise. Her plump, freckled hands flapped vaguely as though they were autonomous creatures.

'They're from the newspapers. I'm afraid there's been a misunderstanding. I'm in a bit of trouble. I can't say more at the moment. But make sure you don't speak with any of them, OK?' He could see she wasn't satisfied with this answer, but she obediently nodded her head of scraped-back, mouse-brown hair.

'Sorry, Anka, the fruit bowl got knocked over. Great if you could clear this up. Thanks.' He gestured towards the shard-littered, slate floor and gave her a grateful, busy look. 'I'm afraid I need to get on.'

Without going to find Nina, he went straight to the bathroom and locked himself in, running a bath as deep as it would go. Through the venetian blinds, he spotted two more men with cameras on the opposite pavement. All five were drinking coffee and smoking. They chatted companionably, waiting with the patient good humour of soldiers beginning a siege. He dropped his clothes on the floor, kicking them into a pile. They were contaminated by captivity and interrogation, soiled with adrenaline sweats, night fears and urine leaks. Standing naked for a moment, he caught sight of his reflection as if it were someone else's, before he could straighten or rearrange to give his best. He saw a man as crumpled and wilted as his clothes: the pitifully lax belly on a slim but undeniably sagging body, the nest of grey hairs above his cock, the pallid skin. Without clothes, he could never claim to be a *puer aeternus*. No, he thought, whatever eternal boy there was has now been destroyed. What remains is an old, cancerous paedophile destined for jail.

He lowered himself into the bath and plunged as far underwater as possible, holding his breath. When he emerged he sobbed as he hadn't done since his mother's sudden death from heart failure, almost twenty years before. Like a baby without inhibition or reason, his eyes flooded, his nose blocked, his throat choked and his limbs clenched. Afterwards he lay quietly, exhausted, emitting small gulps that ruffled the surface of the water.

By the time he entered the bedroom in his dressing gown, Nina had calmed down too. She had clearly wept her own storm.

'I took a Stedon. Would you like one?' That was something he appreciated about his wife: people assumed she was a purist, earth-mother type from her clothes that looked homespun, the organic food and the willingness to drop everything for children or grandchildren, whereas she was actually a highly pragmatic consumer of modern comforts and conveniences. He took the proffered pill and knocked back his head to swallow it without water.

They lay on their respective sides of the bed, still and separate as the tombs of a medieval knight and his lady. When the diazepam turned his limbs into liquid lead, he gave her a version of the story that was close enough to the truth to be plausible and far enough to avoid pain. No, he corrected himself, pain is unavoidable, but no need to say it was years, or that it was a grand passion: a judicious version.

'Did you love her?' The question was horribly simple.

'It's so long ago.' He corrected himself. 'Yes, in a way. But different to you, to the children. It was something completely separate. I'm not sure if you can understand that?'

'How many years have I known you?' She waited but he didn't reply. 'It's forty. This year. We were meant to be having a party, *gamo to*.' Nina always swore in Greek. 'That's a lifetime, Ralph. We've brought up three children. We're grandparents. I'm not stupid. We didn't need to spell everything out and sign a document. Don't think you are the only one with secrets.'

He remained motionless and didn't react to this slap. Perhaps he was the credulous one, having never suspected he might be wearing the cuckold's horns.

After a minute, she placed a hand on his arm. 'You need my help. So you must be clear with me. But now let's rest. See if you can sleep.'

He heard Anka's phone ringing a pop-song jingle, and her voice through the floorboards, speaking hurried Polish. High-pitched astonishment gave way to urgent questions and a sudden lowering of her voice. So she knows, he thought, and fell asleep.

14

DAPHNE

Gareth rang her early in the morning to say that Ralph had been arrested. 'Are you OK? Ready?'

'Really well. I'm happy. Happy it's going ahead.' The energising quality of righteous anger impressed her. There is a razor-sharp purity to knowing I am right and he is wrong, she thought. Libby moved ghost-like around the flat, earphones throbbing a distant beat, transporting her to another realm as she ate breakfast and gathered up school stuff. Daphne had not been able to face telling her about Ralph's arrest, even though Gareth said it was important to keep her informed as things moved along. But how on earth did you open up a subject like this to a twelve-year-old? She would see her mother as a victim, as a brutalised child victim of abuse and abduction, grooming and rape. Daphne couldn't bear that. These things could never be unsaid. They would change their relationship for ever and at a point where Lib needed to get her own life into gear and would be thinking about her own sexuality. She knew she could not continue to hide the matter. There would probably be a court case. Libby would need to know. But, for the moment, it was too formidable a test to take her daughter to the edge of this cesspit and make her peer down inside.

Late for work, she cycled so hard that small petals from the plastic flowers wound around the handlebars flew off in the wind. Once inside Hell, however, the day dragged even more slowly than usual. There was a soul-destroying to-do list of calls to Greek utility companies, a series of unreliable island plumbers and electricians, and the director of a yachting company who kept leaving her pervy messages. Fortunately, Jelly had several morning meetings outside the office and Daphne used the time to felt pieces of wool and stitch features on a tiny figurine made from satin that would finish a birthday present for her father.

In the arid wastelands of mid-afternoon, when Jelly was back, sewing was out of the question, and she was jittery from the dullness. An email arrived from Jane containing a link to the BBC website with a brief statement saying that the composer Ralph Boyd had been arrested on charges of historical child abuse in the 1970s. Daphne had already told Jelly, but hadn't mentioned any details.

'Wow!' said Jelly, when Daphne couldn't resist showing her. 'He's famous, isn't he?' Now that this was in the news and Daphne's rapist was worthy of media attention, a macabre glamour attached itself to the ensuing scandal. 'So ... the shit hits the fan.'

Daphne didn't reply. It struck her that maybe this was an opportunity.

'Are you OK?'

'Actually, not that great.' She tried to strike the right balance between plucky courage and the need for compassionate leave.

'Want to go home early?'

'Would that be OK?' She knew she must receive this little bonus with gratitude.

That night, she was so tightly wound she couldn't sleep. After Libby went to bed she spent hours cutting up fragments of fabric. When that got tiring, she stretched out on Connie's frayed sofa with its landslide of material creating a colourful nest. At about 3.30 a.m. she jumped up and pulled down *Putney* from its dominating position covering a whole wall. What had been an act of homage to a riverside utopia in the 1970s had become a perverse endorsement of the way Ralph came along and shat all over them. Recalling how she'd carefully sewed sweet little figurines of Ralph and herself in affectionate poses was so alarming that she wanted to stamp on it, spit at it, burn it, or fling it into the river. Or perhaps she should stick spikes and pins through the male figures. Then she stopped, afraid of her ferocity and, at some level, protective of her work. Perhaps Vivien would have a suggestion at their next session.

She bundled *Putney* up in a black rubbish sack and tossed it to the back of the hall cupboard, the same place where she'd kept a bag with childhood diaries, letters and the carefully-retained objects that stood as physical markers of her youth and of Ralph's role in it. In order to assist Gareth, she had placed yellow stickers in the notebooks to indicate where crimes were chronicled. Several pressed petals had fallen out like evidence of guilty secrets.

She felt so bad in the morning that she rang Jelly and said she was ill. 'Must've caught a gastro thing,' she lied. 'Running to the loo all night.'

'Oh, don't worry,' said Jelly, evidently enjoying her magnanimity. 'Rest up and keep me posted.' In any case, late September was always a quiet time at Hell. Few were planning a trip to Greece and the Greeks themselves were drawing breath after the great summer onslaught.

'Thanks, darl. You're my guardian angel. Promise I'll be back tomorrow.'

After Libby went to school, Daphne dozed fitfully for a couple of hours. She *did* feel unwell, as if she was bruised and damaged, as if her muscles and internal organs had been hurt. My body has been holding on to this pain since then, she thought. It's part of my fibre. Those experiences created me. And I continued the abuse on myself. I cut my skin, starved myself and filled my mind with chemical dreams. And worst of all, I blamed myself for everything.

When she woke, there was an email from Jane with an online article from the *Daily Mail*. 'Successful "wild child" composer Ralph Boyd arrested for preying on underage girl.' There were several photographs, including one where Ralph stood grinning, surrounded by a large group of children from his Youth Music Festival in Hackney. Some had their arms around him. A picture from the '70s showed him as a young man holding an African lute. Grainy, faded colours, unkempt hair, a sheepskin jerkin and ludicrous bellbottoms conspired to create a mood of creepiness. Apparently, he had been released on bail.

When her father rang, her first thought was that he'd heard the news, but he was merely confirming that he and Margaret had arrived the previous evening and were now ensconced in a friend's empty mews house in Holland Park. They'd be there for the next couple of weeks, with various celebrations planned around his eightieth birthday. There was to be a dinner at the Garrick Club, just like his seventieth. 'Feels like it was last year. I can't believe it's been a decade,' he mused. He told her which family and friends he'd invited: 'Those that haven't died.' His sadness was undercut by the burgeoning pride of someone who had made it this far. 'They're dropping like flies.' Theo was flying over from Boston specially, he said. His first trip back to Blighty for several years.

'With chilly Lindsay?' she asked, and his wicked, falsetto cackle confirmed the eternal pleasure of blood-based collusion against an incomer.

'She's just mistrustful,' he said. 'The beady-eyed disapproval of a broody hen. Don't know what she's scared of.'

'Us, probably.' They both laughed.

The more they spoke the more Daphne was daunted by the prospect of telling him about Ralph. She didn't have the words to inform her father that his old friend was a paedophile and, even worse perhaps, that she had denounced him to the police. She had already tried versions in her head, but she couldn't get them out. Even before he rang it was like the dreaded brown envelope that lies about unopened. The longer you leave it, the worse the consequences. So you keep it closed, holding its unpleasantness out of sight. She'd had her share of those envelopes in the past, when ignoring bills was often the only possible approach. Once, she avoided her rent demands for so long that bailiffs showed up; two big men with fighting-dog faces, who removed her pathetically meagre possessions and left her holding a couple of plastic bags on the pavement outside her studio flat near Ladbroke Grove. In hindsight, that was probably the famous rock bottom from which she could only go up.

'So, we'll bring the wine,' said Ed. 'Margaret's very proud of her little vineyard. Actually, it's an excellent Merlot.'

'Perfect. And so you know, I'm not going to cook. There's a small Turkish place near here with delicious food, so I'll order from them.'

'Much better,' said Ed with tactless relief.

'Oh life's too short to go stuffing tomatoes and whipping up sauces.' She pictured her mother nonchalantly throwing together vast pies filled with spinach and feta, while entertaining friends, drinking wine, bringing up children and plotting against dictatorships.

'Too true. So long as someone else will.' He laughed. Apart from the brief wilderness immediately after Ellie's death, there'd always been someone else doing all that for him.

She understood that holing up in the Dordogne with Margaret had been her father's method of running away from his wife's death, but it still provoked a childish sense of abandonment. Without Ellie, the house at Barnabas Road quickly became a dried husk, emptied of the vitality that made it a home. Even the building reflected their psychological state, as cracks appeared across walls and there was talk of subsidence and dry rot. Daphne hadn't been willing or able to take on the role of housekeeper to Ed, and when he flung himself back into writing, she slithered down the silver-lined rabbit run of mind-altering substances. After her Athenian marriage was over and she returned to London, there was nobody to care for her – a phantom from the underworld. Ed occasionally wrote a well-phrased letter in his elegantly flowing script and, very rarely, they spoke on the phone, but in those days before emails, mobiles and Skype, the cut was sharp and the scar was still tender.

She must have drifted off to sleep again because she woke to the sound of her phone. It was Nina. She didn't say hello or introduce herself. 'I don't understand,' she shouted in Greek. 'I don't understand what you are doing.'

Her voice trembled. Daphne replied in English, 'Can I try to explain?' However, Nina was not ready to listen and continued in her mother tongue. 'I hope you are happy to destroy a family, destroy a man. This will kill him.' Trust a Greek to exaggerate, thought Daphne.

'I suppose you know he's very ill?'

'No.' This was unexpected. 'No, what's wrong with him?'

'The unspeakable sickness.' Nina used the outmoded term and waited briefly for a response, but what could Daphne possibly answer? 'Yes, cancer. So you say you were abused as a child. But it seems to me, Daphnoula, that you weren't a child. You were a teenager – a young woman. You were chasing Ralph, testing him. Don't think I didn't notice your pathetic little games, even if I chose to ignore them. So what is this now? Perhaps it's all hormones again and you are going through the climacteric? Surely you can see it's beside the point – who slept with whom back in the 1970s.' Daphne had only ever seen Nina calm. Ralph gave the impression she was a sexless mother figure to him as well as their children, an introverted painter of obscure abstracts – someone who wouldn't mind about his naughty predilections for tree houses and sleeper trains. This knife-wielding ferocity was a new side to the woman who must have always detested her and whose suspicions were now vindicated.

'I never believed you were very intelligent, Daphne. I know your life has been a mess. But I thought you had a good heart. Now I can't believe this hatred. What do you want?'

'What I want—' she began.

'Daphne, listen,' Nina butted in. 'Ralph and I have grandchildren. We are old. He is sick. We don't know how long he'll last. What will you achieve by this?' The rage was dying down into exhaustion. 'Tell me that.' And finally, she stopped, waiting for a reply that could never be satisfactory.

At another point in her life, Daphne might have backed down. 'I'm sorry if your husband's behaviour is hard for you. But that's not my problem. That's something he should have thought of. I'm sorry, but I have to go now. Goodbye.' She hung up with an internal thwack of adrenaline that was like a shot of neat alcohol. As if in confirmation of Nina's jibes about her hormonal state, a hot flush took hold with shocking intensity. Her face burned with a furnace-fired blush and her hairs prickled like spines. She felt as though she might suffocate.

* * *

She began to prepare for the evening, and made a brief foray to buy flowers, olives and candles. She struggled to find the will to tidy up. Ellie had always managed to play it both ways over matters of domestic hygiene. 'Only as much as the mother-in-law will see,' she used to say in Greek when straightening up a room for guests. Definitely a believer in dust-under-the-rug as a solution, her mother would occasionally plunge into manic 'spring cleaning' – more warfare than housework.

Unpredictability was the only reliable rule with Ellie; her belief in Freedom (her name, after all) was the perfect get-out clause. Out of nowhere, the force that generations of her family's women had brought to this role would erupt with volcanic impulsiveness and she would transform into a version of her female predecessors, engulfing her offspring with maternal concern. With her worn dungarees and free-flowing hair, she didn't look like most Mediterranean mamas, but she could turn her hand to it if she desired. For a few days, there would be mad mountains of food, loud concerns expressed about children catching cold, and dedicated bursts of checking schoolwork. So on any particular day, Daphne could never predict whether her mother would be an absent, ideology-driven protestor or a smothering mother. What did she imagine went on when she was out or away? wondered Daphne. When I was little, I never knew where she was or what to expect and then she'd swoop in like an avenging angel.

In the afternoon she worked on Ed's present. There was still about a week before her father's birthday and she'd almost finished the large cushion sewn with appliqué pictures for each decade of his life. First, a child in a leg brace, standing under a Kentish apple tree – a German war plane flying overhead. Then a lanky teenager by a ruined Mediterranean temple, to illustrate his youthful travels. His student years had him surrounded by flying books, while as paterfamilias she depicted him in colourful robes with wife and children. In his forties he was lying on an analyst's couch – for several years he had retreated down the complex coils of his psyche, at a time when Ellie was forging outwards and embracing political activism. Inevitably, his fifties was France and Margaret – she had them at a café table drinking pastis. The last two decades were tricky, but she showed him receiving an honorary degree from his alma mater, King's College London, and then writing in his Dordogne garden.

She'd constructed the cushion with an uncharacteristically gentle sweetness, avoiding irony or the dark rawness, with explosions of kitsch, that often entered her work. Standing back from the cushion and examining it, she wondered how Ed had failed to see what was happening with Ralph. Why didn't he save her? What did her parents imagine was going on when their friend went to their daughter's bedroom or whisked her off in his car? It was hard to conceive that she would ever let a man visit Libby or take her on picnics and theatre trips. Had Ellie and Ed ever discussed it? she wondered. Ever worried about her?

When Libby got back from school she set to work with the Hoover.

'God you're a marvel.' Daphne gazed in admiration as tumbleweed fluff balls were sucked up, rugs lost their crust of hairs and grit and the flat took on a new sparkle. 'You've saved us.' Libby had demonstrated her precocious affinity with order and cleanliness from around the time she said her first words, preferring games that involved folding cloths or sweeping to those with dolls or building blocks. Sometimes she would take out all of Daphne's tangled clothes from their drawers and, just for fun, place them all back in perfectly arranged sequence of colour or type. While her daughter's neatness was undeniably useful, there were times when it was almost scary.

She changed into a velvet dress – still ruby red even if it was so old as to be balding – lit candles and poured a glass of wine from an open bottle in the fridge. Gulping some down in a medicinal manner, she hoped to get rid of the knot of worry taking hold. This was not an ideal time for a reunion with her father.

The buzzer always made her jump, even when she was expecting it. 'Hello. Welcome,' she shouted into the intercom, observing her father's looming nose as he stared into the camera. 'Fourth floor,' she added before remembering that, while it was his first visit to their new home, he knew the place from his sister's day. 'They've arrived,' she called to Libby, feeling the tension spike.

They watched Ed and Margaret emerge from the lift at the other end of the corridor, waving and calling, encumbered by bags and clanking bottles. Ed was using a stick and moved slowly, so Daphne walked towards them, followed by Libby.

'Look at my marvellous girls!' He dumped his bags and stood, arms spread in theatrical wonder, then turning to Margaret for affirmation. She smiled dutifully.

'Daphne, darling.' He was bonier than before, the sharp angles more evident as she put her arms around him and breathed in a scent she didn't recognise and assumed was French. Still, he looked well. His formerly pale, English skin had a healthy suntan and, with his silk scarf and maroon homburg hat, he was still acting the dandy at the end of his eighth decade.

'Liberty! An angel of loveliness. Margaret, have you seen? She's become a young lady.'

Libby squirmed awkwardly as she went to kiss her grandfather and Daphne moved to greet Margaret, kissing her on both cheeks and asking her how she was. 'Lovely to see you, Daphne,' she said calmly.

Ed held court as though he was the host. Daphne opened the first bottle of three they'd brought from Margaret's small vineyard. It was one of her many projects that included helping at a local orphanage and editing all of Ed's collected essays and reviews for an upcoming bumper edition. Approaching seventy, she was apparently tireless. Margaret and Ed sniffed and swilled and slurped the wine and Daphne had to suppress her irritation as they both made French-sounding noises of approval while she and Libby exchanged glances.

'Like time travel,' said Ed. 'Being back in Connie's place after so long. Even after her funeral, we didn't come here, did we, Margaret?' He looked around the walls where Daphne's work was hanging. 'And now I can feel her presence along with yours, Daphne. It was genius to leave you her flat.' He turned to Libby: 'What do you think, Liberty? Are you happy here in your ...' He paused to work out the relationship between his granddaughter and his sister. 'In your great-aunt's place?'

Libby nodded obediently. 'Yeah, it's nice.'

Ed stood up, a restless old stork, peering down his long beak into the darkness beyond the window. He'd grown a beard — trimmed and white and rather fashionable, Daphne thought. But his voice was old-fashioned — like a BBC announcer from the '60s, the antiquated intonation set firmer by the preservative of expat existence.

'You know, Daphne, in the old days, when we were over there,' he gestured across the river towards the back gardens of Barnabas Road, some of which were lit up, 'I often nipped across the bridge to see Connie for a drink. Stiff gin and tonics were her speciality. Such a wise bird, my sister, even back in the days when most people were so giddy they didn't know if they were coming or going. She gave sage advice. I'd always leave here understanding the world slightly more, always in a better state.' Libby handed round olives — guests first, and topped up the wine glasses. Daphne's was already empty.

It was true, thought Daphne, that Ed had a tendency to disappear in those Putney days. She rarely knew whether either parent would be at home and, if they weren't, where they'd gone. There was an assumption that each person, adult or child, was free to come and go as they liked. No explanation necessary. When she returned from school, the house was often bleakly silent. It was even worse when she ran around, calling out, checking whether anyone was home. And you could never tell whether it would remain miserably empty until way past suppertime or whether there would suddenly be a dinner party and her parents were merely out buying provisions.

It was infuriating to hear Ed witter on about boozy, pseudo-intellectual chats with his sister, when he never stopped to wonder what his daughter had been doing at the same time. Why hadn't he looked after her?

'I'm just going to sort out the food,' she said, standing up too quickly, almost missing her footing, and realising she was already well through her third glass of wine.

'Can I help?' said Margaret, a shade too brightly, as though casting doubt on what might make its way to the table. Though she was the modest foil to Edmund's showy exterior, dressing herself down in loose-fitting beiges and greys, Margaret had once been the owner of a successful little restaurant in Ottawa, and a jobbing journalist before that. There was no doubting her capabilities.

'No need.' She knew it sounded ungrateful and followed up with, 'I'm fine. Thanks.'

She advanced carefully to the kitchen, sparks of anger firing in different directions. The Turkish food had already been delivered and she had transferred the spinach and cheese pies, aubergine stew, rice-stuffed vegetables and parsley-filled salad into her own dishes. She reheated the ones that needed it. It was only as she stirred the yogurt with garlic and dill that she realised they were all versions of the Greek food her mother used to make. Now she felt angry with Ellie as well as Ed, and the knowledge that this was forty years too late only made it worse. Nothing could turn them into steady, reliable parents at this stage, but she could still dive deep into the chaotic emotions of an eleven-year-old.

'Daphne,' Ed leaned against the doorway to the kitchen, 'I wanted to ask you something.' The public bonhomie was replaced by something more sober.

'Of course.' She continued gathering a mismatched assortment of plates – the 1970s collection was already irritating her with its cloying colour palette of caramel, avocado green and tomato red. I'd like to ask you some-thing too, she thought. Do you have any idea what I went through?

'Just before we left to come here, I rang Ralph.' Daphne gripped a plate and looked at him. How would Ralph have phrased it? she wondered.

'I was checking that he and Nina were coming to my birthday,' he continued. 'And it was very mysterious. He said he wasn't able to talk, that something had happened, and that I should ask you.' He looked at her anxiously, as if hoping this was a misunderstanding. 'What on earth is he on about?'

It wasn't easy. When she used the word rape, Ed's whole body flinched as though he'd had an electric shock.

'Did he force you?'

And then she had to explain that it wasn't necessarily like that in the case of children.

'Did you love him?'

She parroted that love didn't count in this sort of thing. 'They call that grooming, when an adult makes a child love them. I've been imagining what I'd think if something like that happened to Libby.'

'But, darling girl, why didn't you tell us?' He stooped, looking at the floor, picking at the doorframe with long, oval fingernails and shaking his head. It was as if he couldn't fit this rewritten history into his brain. 'So you went to the police,' he said, as though telling himself the story from another angle.

Daphne wasn't sure what she'd expected from her father – a comforting embrace and practical advice, or even a word of encouragement would have been good. But Ed acted as he usually did in the face of setbacks, attacks or disasters: he recoiled. 'Pulling up the drawbridge' was what he called it. No entry or exit, just the castle's thick walls with slits for assessing the lie of the land or shooting the enemy. You could see his features turning stony, his eyes glassy. He'd always been like that, his moods and communications exaggerated one way or the other. In good humour, he'd be booming from the castle walls to the crowds below, welcoming them all inside. Daphne made no attempt to continue the conversation. Despite having drunk enough wine to make her less restrained, she knew nothing she could say would make the drawbridge come down again this evening.

Dinner was subdued; no mention of the revelations. The four of them gathered at Connie's old pine table and Margaret made soothing comments about the dinner, even though Daphne had singed the Turkish pies. There were more than enough distractions, she reasoned, though it didn't help to be viewed as someone who couldn't even warm up a takeaway. Margaret sat next to Ed and fussed when he only picked at his food.

Ed refused the syrupy pastries and pistachio ice cream and, as soon as the others finished theirs, he said, 'I'm still very tired. The journey, you know. I'm an old man now.' He laughed, as though the idea was ludicrous. The older Daphne got, the more she comprehended how the treachery of age was baffling when it caught you. As a younger woman, she had seen the elderly as a different species, cut off from smooth-skinned, swift-limbed youth. It was only before her fiftieth birthday that she began to realise the old were just people like her who had lived longer — a shaming revelation. When she noticed the first white strand nestling amongst her black pubic hair, she thought it must be a mistake. Until there was another one. That was how it went, she supposed, until it was dodgy hips, swollen joints and all the rest. It was only those like her mother who, by dying young, got away without these mortifications.

'I think, Margaret, that perhaps we should wend our way.' Ed held out a tapering hand, speckled, but still graceful.

'London is *so* exhausting,' said Margaret to Daphne, precluding any misunderstanding about them rushing off. Ed looked grateful at his wife's attempt to lubricate the situation.

'We saw Ed's agent for lunch and hoped to drop into the Royal Academy for an exhibition after that but, wherever you go, it seems to take an hour to get there. We gave up and went home. I'm afraid we've become timid country mice.' She laughed apologetically, satisfied with the excuses.

After the grandparents left, Libby helped clear up while listening to music on headphones. Daphne was relieved not to talk and, after her daughter went to bed, she sat by the window looking out into the night, locating the dark shadow of her old house across the water and watching as the lights were switched off.

JANE

She waited until late morning to call Daphne, and managed to fit in a run and a few errands first. It was important to stay close, keep her on track, maintain the momentum of hunting the monster. She admitted that it had become an obsession. The previous evening was not the first time she had spent hours at her computer scrutinising sex-abuse cases. It brought on a satisfying pain, like picking at a scab that was not ready, the raw, pink wound visible below. It wasn't just the historical cases, it was big business: children drugged and raped on camera then watched by thousands on the deep web; or silicone child sex dolls weighted to feel like real children when you carried them to bed.

'Oh God, I think I'm hung-over,' Daphne said. 'And I'm just generally feeling crap, like I hate everyone.' She sounded like a teenager, Jane thought; like Toby the morning after a party. Daphne added, 'Not you,' and made a poor attempt at a laugh.

'Did something happen?'

'Not really. Seeing Ed wasn't the easiest thing. And it's definitely unsettling knowing that Ralph was arrested and I'm the mysterious, unnamed thirteen-year-old in the media.'

'Yes, I can imagine that's strange.'

'Oh, by the way, when I told Ed I'd become friends with you again, he said I should invite you to his party. His eightieth. On the 17th. I don't know if you're interested?'

'Great. I'd love to. Thank you. Hey, do you feel like company? I could come over.' Jane asked tentatively, unsure of her ground, wary of pressing too hard, but she was surprised by Daphne's reaction.

'Ah! That would be so nice. I don't think there's anyone else that I can talk to about this whole thing. It's such a muddle. I still haven't managed to tell Libby.'

They walked over the river and had lunch at the Star and Garter opposite Putney Pier. Extravagant quantities of artisan cheeses arrived on a large board from a special cheese room and Daphne chose a nice burgundy ('my treat') as though she knew something about wines. 'Yes, at least my time with Constantine gave me a crash course in fine dining! Not much else, though. More of a car crash, otherwise.' She smiled and scowled simultaneously.

Jane didn't usually drink in the middle of the day, and the wine went to her head with a rush, summoning memories of when she and Daphne sneaked drinks from the Greenslays' large supply – it was never missed.

Once, when they were thirteen, Daphne came over to Wimbledon with half a bottle of whisky and an already opened bottle of red wine.

'Oh God,' she puffed as if she'd been sprinting. 'It was so funny. I sat next to this man on the bus. Said I was running away from home. And he believed me. Then I said I was adopted, that my evil parents practised black magic ...' She crowed with laughter and Jane presumed she'd already had a drink. 'Hilarious. He was getting really worried and offered to help me. Then I got creeped out and went downstairs to escape.'

'I wish I'd been there.' They had sometimes played this game on trains, cobbling together alarming stories and trying them out on unsuspecting passengers, but Jane would never have done it alone.

'Then he came down and wanted to talk some more, so I said, "Please leave me alone, sir!" very loudly.' Daphne flopped over with laughter and gripped Jane's arm. 'The conductor asked him to go upstairs or get off the bus!'

They took alternate swigs from the bottle of wine until it was nearly finished. An unfamiliar heat spread across Jane's middle and her head couldn't keep up with her movements. Her mother had cooked shepherd's pie and didn't realise that both girls were tipsy. 'Giddy goats!' she commented, not unkindly, when they gave a raucous rendition of songs from *Joseph and the Amazing Technicolor Dreamcoat*, shrieking and almost falling off their chairs. They were rehearsing it at school and considered it stupid and babyish.

'Spastics, more like,' said David, who was no longer afraid to insult his sister. Her father hardly spoke at the meal, which was normal. He frequently returned home from the office in a state of numbed quiet, though his appearance was always buffed and shined, from his hair to his own father's leather briefcase that he carried to and fro each day.

'Only fruit salad for dessert,' said her mother – tinned fruit with pieces of apple and banana added. Daphne left the cough-syrup-red cherries and then broke a plate while drying up. Afterwards, the girls went back to Jane's room and got to work on the whisky. Jane disliked the earthy, dangerous hit of the Johnnie Walker that Daphne passed between the two of them, but she took a few sips, watching in admiration as her friend gulped it down, gasping and shuddering each time.

They played Lou Reed's 'Walk on the Wild Side', over and over until they were word perfect. The lyrics sounded devastatingly sexy and wicked despite their obscurity. They didn't understand much but intuited the decadent allure of Manhattan's underbelly and the dark thrill of siren songs. From the chest of drawers, her old dolls sat staring at them below the posters of David Bowie in skin-tight trousers and zany make-up. On the other wall was a photograph of Donny Osmond, only kept there because Daphne had desecrated his puppyish face by adding warts, horns and vampire fangs, blood dripping down his wholesome chin.

Clumsily, Daphne flicked through a library book. It explained the biology of puberty – Jane was desperate for information that might explain more about this disconcerting and overwhelming phase, in which the ground was constantly shifting, along with one's body. Daphne squawked at the sensible instructions on self-examination. *Wash your hands and sit on the floor ... Take a hand mirror ... knees apart ... inner fleshy lips ... discharge ...* They both laughed until it hurt and there was no way of stopping. Jane later supposed their reaction was mostly due to being drunk, but it was also their awkwardness. Even in that age of supposed liberation and openness, neither of them had an easy word to describe their vulva, caught between the formality of 'vagina' and the rudeness of 'cunt'. Linda, the most 'experienced' girl at school, mentioned 'beef curtains', and boys' 'pork swords'. Jane hated these ugly expressions, but almost worse was 'front bottom', as her mother called it. This mysterious 'down there' was a place without a name – too scary to be referred to, or denied an existence. Dark, desired, disgusting.

As the light faded, they headed outside. 'Just going for a walk, Mum.' Jane felt unsteady, and Daphne was stumbling and acting so abnormally it was getting worrying. They climbed through a hole in the fence of Cannizaro Park, propping each other up and attempting to stifle their high-pitched hilarity. The gardens were locked for the night, quiet and illicit, and filled with beds of tulips – an army of flowers, formal and proud, their brash colours becoming dimmed by the darkening sky.

'Ridiculous,' Daphne yelled. 'They're so stupid. What do they think they're doing, just standing there?' She picked up a stick and began swiping at the tulip heads. The flowers snapped off with horrifying ease, spinning through the air before landing on the ground – toy-coloured, dead things. 'I'm the executioner,' she shouted, leaping across the path to another bed and addressing the flowers. 'And you're all Anne Boleyn.'

Jane loved tulips – she'd put them on a list of favourite things. 'Hey, Daphne. Maybe ...' Daphne took a running jump to mow through a circular display of yellow tulips with her improvised sword and slipped on the grass, cackling as she landed on her bum like a slapstick clown. VANDALS WILL BE PROSECUTED, read a sign.

'I hate them,' slurred Daphne, staying where she was on the grass and patting it. 'Give us a drink.' Jane moved reluctantly and sat down, opening her army-surplus shoulder bag with the remaining whisky. They'd already drunk about a third of it. Daphne took a slug. 'I just hate them – hate those flowers, all stiff and snooty. What's the point? In their stupid lines.' She looked genuinely upset at the tulips. 'I want to kill them. They deserve to die.'

'D'you think, maybe we ...' Jane tried to take back the bottle. Exhaustion had struck, but she saw that Daphne was heading towards something more extreme.

'D'you think? D'you think? Jou fink? Jou Fink Janey. A new name!' Daphne collapsed back on to the grass laughing uncontrollably. 'Jou-Fink-Jane, don't complain.' Pleased with her rhyme, she repeated it over and over.

'I think we need to go now. Otherwise we'll never get home.' Jane's eyes welled and she dug her fingernails into the palm of her hand to stop the tears. Daphne didn't notice. She was rolling on the grass, crushing the decapitated tulip flowers in her wake and laughing to herself like a lunatic.

'I'm not sure I'll find that bit of the fence where we got in. It's really dark now.' Fear concentrated her mind and she held on to both of Daphne's wrists, giving all her strength to pulling her up.

The two girls swayed along for a few yards before Daphne fell over. She didn't crumple on to the ground but plummeted headlong as though she'd been shot.

'Oh come on, Daphne. Get up! Please!' Jane yanked at her, but there was no response. She patted her cheeks. 'Come on, we need to go home. We can't stay here.' The park was spinning and Jane was overcome with leaden exhaustion and sat down on the damp grass. She could smell dog shit. 'I'll have to leave you! Get up, Daphne. We can't stay.'

Daphne let out a groan, a gush of vomit shot from her mouth, her body was convulsed by spasms and then she lay immobile, her hair and clothes covered with sick.

Jane couldn't stand sick. It made her feel like throwing up too. 'Daphne? Hey, get up now.' No answer. She was completely motionless and Jane wondered if she might be dead. You could die from alcohol, couldn't you? 'Oh, for God's sake. Don't do this. Please.' She was begging, nudging her friend's shoulder to make her move, to bring her back to life. What would happen now? she wondered. Imagine the phone call to Daphne's parents. What would it be like at school? An icy panic set in. She put her hand on her friend's chest and a slow breath raised the ribcage. Alive, then, but she looked awful. Jane tried to roll her into the recovery position as they'd been taught in life-saving, touching her gingerly so as not to get too much sick on her.

Afterwards, retching, she wiped her hands on the grass, hoping to miss the dog shit. Then she threw up herself. She sat for a few minutes, feeling slightly better. Deciding to go for help, she lurched about in the dark, trying to locate the hole in the fence, crawling through bushes to no avail. The point of entry had been so obvious from the street. It was odd to find herself muttering small prayers. 'Please, God. Please don't let her die.' Eventually, she located the right place, scraping her cheek on a piece of wire as she scrambled out on to the pavement. She ran heavy-footed and groaning through the street-lamped, suburban hush to her house. Her parents were watching telly and she couldn't get the words out properly. She saw in the mirror that her face was bloodied and her long hair tangled with twigs and leaves like a lost child.

It all took ages. Her father marched her back to the park. When she lagged, he muttered in muted fury, 'Come on! Hurry.' Daphne was still out cold and he tried to wake her by slapping her cheeks rather hard. She'd become a disgusting Sleeping Beauty, who stank of sick. A bad girl who sliced through flowers and stole whisky. When Daphne remained unconscious, Jane's father attempted to lift her and, with difficulty, grunting and coughing, carried her some way. Jane tried to assist in hauling her through the hole in the fence but it was impossible; she was far too crumpled and, despite her small frame, seemed absurdly heavy.

Jane stayed with her while her dad went to call an ambulance. 'She could die from alcohol poisoning,' he snapped as he left. Jane felt like dying too. The night was cold and she shivered with fear. A siren, flashing blue lights, men with uniforms and torches. It had turned into something official. The police came too, so that the park could be opened. Daphne didn't wake up, even when she was bundled on to a stretcher and carried away.

Her parents took Jane with them to Putney Hospital, scolding her as they drove. 'You need to see how serious this is,' her father said. 'How could you be so stupid?' Naturally, they rang Daphne's home and Ellie arrived soon after them. Jane cried even more when Ellie tried to question her about what happened because she was so kind, even though she looked terrified. By the time they were allowed to see Daphne, it was nearly 3 a.m. She was tucked inside white sheets, hooked up to a drip, her stomach pumped, and her face and hair wiped clean. She was still unconscious, but the doctor said she was out of danger and should be left to sleep it off. 'Are you able to tell me exactly what she drank?' he asked Jane, who replied so quietly she had to repeat three times that it was probably almost half a bottle of whisky in addition to several glasses of wine.

The next day, Jane's head was jagged with pain, her stomach roiling with bilious nausea. People made a hangover sound like a joke, but this was like hanging over the abyss, hanging from a rope, hangdog, hang it all. She took some of her parents' Alka-Seltzer from the bathroom without asking, but it didn't help. Surprisingly, they gave her permission to visit Daphne, but they had already set the punishment: after the hospital, no going out or seeing friends outside school for a month. 'And you can wash up every evening,' added her mother.

Daphne was sitting up in bed in a children's ward. She looked like a child in an old-fashioned storybook, gently convalescing after a long illness. Gone was the wicked, Lou Reed-listening, liquor-guzzling, teenage vomit queen. She wore a white nightie, her hair was brushed and Ellie was feeding her rice from a plastic spoon and making small noises of stern satisfaction each time she swallowed. They exchanged grim-mouthed smiles as a greeting.

'Sorry,' Daphne frowned. 'What a mess.'

Ellie spoke to them in a low, restrained voice that did not hide an impressive, incandescent anger, as though she was burning inside. 'You will never, never do something like this again. Daphne? Jane? Do you understand? This isn't about fun or independence. You could be dead, Daphne. Jane, she could be gone. Does that mean something to you both?' Jane noticed the young boy staring at them from the next bed. He had hollow, lethargic eyes and a bulky bandage wrapped around his head.

'Have you seen these children?' asked Ellie, gesturing at the other beds and to a mother slowly leading her bald daughter and drip stand along the ward. 'Think about it.'

Ellie went home to rest; she hadn't slept all night. Ed was due back from a trip and she needed to tell him what had happened. Almost as soon as Ellie left, Ralph appeared with a bounce in his step and a bumptious smile on his face. He was clutching a potted strawberry plant covered in pretty flowers and a bottle of Lucozade. Jane cringed with irritation. He was like an actor wanting to make an impact — scheming for maximum effect, calculating his charm. She noted how quickly several smiling nurses came to help — a plate for the plant, a plastic beaker for the drink. He is so fake, she thought, and the nurses' reactions so obvious.

'Naughty girls. Very naughty.' Ralph chuckled indulgently. 'What a fright you've given your parents. Crikey, a hangover is one thing, but hospitals … not a good idea.' Bending over, he kissed Daphne very gently on the forehead, closing his eyes and taking a deep breath — like Dracula. Then he opened the sweet, fizzy drink and poured some for Daphne, who took a few sips.

'Mm, it really helps,' she said and smiled at Ralph as if she was a brave veteran of war saying, 'It was nothing really.'

'I rang your house this morning and Ellie told me. What a fandango. But, you know, the greenish tinge to your pallor is quite appealing. And, Lady Jane, you don't have your usual rosy colouring either.'

Jane longed for some Lucozade, but didn't ask and it wasn't offered. She felt ill and fed up. She'd wanted to talk with Daphne and saw how unimportant she became to her friend when Ralph was around. *She* wanted a handsome man bringing love and bearing gifts. A man to stroke her, a man with a penis to press against her.

'I have to go,' she said. 'See you.'

As she walked past Maurice in the hospital car park, she kicked its side as hard as she could. At home, she told her mother she was going to do her homework and lay on her bed, pulled down her jeans and masturbated. She pictured Ralph naked, shocked by the crushing surge of furious lust that swept her quickly to a shuddering orgasm.

16

RALPH

When Nina woke him at eight with green tea, he felt like a drowning man being pulled from the sea. Painful limbs, bitter-tasting mouth. Sleep had hovered just out of reach that night, and at three he'd raided her Greek supply of Stilnox for a few hours of oblivion. Now she made him toast and honey with the crusts cut off, knowing how to tempt, as she'd done when the children were ill. These days she forbade coffee and he was too tired to argue.

He insisted on taking a cab to the hospital, fearing Nina would crowd him out with kindness. From habit he packed his worn leather bag with the usual comforters, including tattered cashmere wrap, book and salted crackers, though they were more like superstitious charms, as his appointment was only to see his surgeon. Unsurprisingly, Mr Goodlove was running late. Plenty of time for thought, slumped in a waiting-room chair, eyes closed. His previous hospital-displacing technique was out of the question. The landscape he usually summoned had transformed from garden of paradise into treacherous hellhole. Where images of the flinty-eyed, wild-haired girl up a tree had been part of his healing, they were now like poison. Yet he couldn't prevent himself returning, addict-like, to the thoughts that had kept him going through his therapies.

His mobile rang. 'Jeb' showed on the screen. He answered, if only for the distraction. Jeb sounded wired, as though he'd drunk five espressos. 'Not guilty is the way forward. Riskier but cleaner. We'll focus on Daphne as a bit "complicated". Loopy, in other words. A difficult life with addictions, rehab, evictions and so on. Yes, you were friends when she was a kid friends with her parents and brother too. You took her *and her friends* out to the cinema or the occasional theatre. *Not* swimming. Meals with your family. Wholesome stuff. You were a happily married man with young children, a blossoming career. We'll go over all this. The trip to Greece was a chore – a favour to her parents. You can't understand why she'd make this up after all this time. Envy perhaps?' Ralph let Jeb witter on with his comforting clichés. 'There's at least another week or two for the CPS to get back, but I can't imagine … Anyway, we cross each bridge. OK, Boydie? Chin up. Got to go.'

It was almost two hours before he went into Mr Goodlove's office and the doctor apologised for the delay, gesturing for him to sit down. If he did know about Ralph's disgrace, he gave no sign. Unlike all the nursing staff who used his Christian name, Ralph appreciated that his surgeon called him Mr Boyd. On the desk was a black and white photograph of an intelligent-looking young man. 'Your son?' Ralph attempted a social nicety, hoping it would act like a fire blanket to his smouldering fear.

'Yes. Christopher.' He smiled. 'He died five years ago.' Impressively, the medic kept eye contact. We are all walking around with invisible weights and chains, thought Ralph.

Mr Goodlove was straightforward, but not ruthless, respecting a patient's terror while not pandering to it. The scan showed the chemotherapy wasn't working, he said. There was no point in continuing; the chemicals were only weakening his whole system. The disease was in the lymph nodes. And perhaps it had spread to the bones, but that would need a different scan. As things stood, there was little the NHS could do any more. A couple of trials using hormone treatment were going ahead soon. If he was interested, he could certainly join one. *If* he fulfilled the requirements. Of course, he wouldn't know if he was taking the drugs or a placebo, but exciting work was being done. At the very least, it was a way of offering something back. 'What would *you* like to do?'

'I fear I have very little choice.' He tried to emulate Mr Goodlove's dignity, though his brain was cloudy with dread. They spoke about pain relief. Morphine patches and syrup. Palliative care. A Macmillan nurse. And that was that.

Ralph went home and didn't tell Nina. He didn't want panicked sons flying in from abroad wanting death-bed speeches before it was time. He wasn't dead yet. Pretending his exhaustion resulted from a treatment, he went straight to bed. Nina had changed the sheets and he lay in their cool cleanness, watching the drawn curtains billowing gently from the half-open window. She brought him some plain rice and stewed apple on a tray with a rose-bud from the garden in a glass. He ate all the food before falling into opaque, dreamless sleep.

He slept for several hours and woke feeling incongruously invigorated. Perhaps a death sentence is like that, he thought. It brings you back to life. He shut the window on the darkening skies and the smells of incipient autumn – leaf mould and what he imagined were musky squirrel nests.

It was now afternoon, but he decided to treat it like a second morning. Cup of tea, shower, painkillers for the twinges and clothes for action: jeans (belted two holes tighter now), Chelsea boots, a canvas jacket. Nina was at a table in the sitting room painting one of her minuscule abstracts – so small he could hardly make it out. She jumped up, quickly washing the paintbrush in a tin cup. Yes, he *was* hungry. She started to prepare an omelette – *aux fines herbes*, as he liked, with tarragon and chives. Slightly runny in the middle. Nina didn't eat, but sat companionably at the kitchen table, reproaching him mildly when he drank a glass of red wine.

'I've spoken with all the children again today,' she said. 'I explained that it's a misunderstanding. But Jason wants to hear from you, to understand exactly what happened. He asked if you can call him back later. Alexander sent you lots of love. He said, "Of course Dad's innocent."' She shot an enquiring glance and he offered back a small smile of confirmation. 'And Lucia is actually coming over. Quite soon,' she said. 'She and Bee are in London for the day. You need to explain a little bit to her. She's been upset. You know ...' She left it hanging and then talked of minor family things: Alexander was moving house in Seattle (she suspected a girlfriend was involved but he wasn't saying); little Sydney's new nursery school in Madrid. He admired her delicacy for not quizzing him on the hospital. Nor did she mention that this evening was Ed's birthday and that they weren't going. He knew she had cancelled their anniversary party in a few weeks' time, putting it down to hospital schedules rather than possible court sessions. She understood that you don't always have to hit things head-on. He liked this quality, though a tremor of guilt and dread passed through him like vibrations from a distant earthquake.

The wine had brought an agreeable, warm blur to his brain and dulled the aches better than the hospital analgesics. But as Nina cleared the table and there was a knock at the front door, the fear made his heart thud as though he'd been running. Christ, he thought, how will I face my daughter now? My lovely little granddaughter? Even terminal illness cannot absolve the sins of which he was accused. He was trapped on all sides. Remaining in the kitchen, stalling, while Nina went to greet their girls, he heard the familiar sounds of female voices – three generations of them. Nina and Lucia spoke in Greek, and Bee complained she didn't understand, bags were dropped, coats removed. He winced at the thought that Bee must not remain alone in a room with him. The sensation of unjust accusation was overwhelming; he would never, ever do anything that would harm his daughter or granddaughter. It was outrageous even to think of it.

'Hi, Dad.' Lucia came into the kitchen with a diffident expression, as though wondering whether they would greet each other in the normal way, and her eyes glittered slightly as if fighting tears. He stood up and pulled her into a hug. 'My darling girl.' She was wearing a voluminous dress made from what looked like green potato sacks, rough under his hands, and, below that, blue tights and red ankle boots. Spotting little Bee in the doorway, he released his daughter and called, 'And how's my sweetest honey bee?' The girl came over and, as he kissed her on both cheeks, a surge of shame heated his face. Nina and Lucia were watching him. Judging, wondering, recalibrating the family structure. Through the open window, a blackbird was trilling its beautiful song in the garden and, hoping to please Bee, he whistled and warbled a decent reply. A delicate duet ensued, back and forth. Nobody spoke, but Nina looked so sad, he wondered whether she might cry. Instead, she laughed drily. 'You can still lure the birds from the tree, Ralph.'

'So, Bee, come with me upstairs, I have something to show you.' Nina held out a hand and Bee grasped it, trotting out of the kitchen with her. This had evidently been prearranged.

'Dad …' Lucia began, then stopped. 'I need to know. I need you to tell me the truth. What happened, what's going on.' He recognised her fear and the desperate need for reassurance. It was vital to convince her he was not a criminal, not a paedophile rapist, but the adoring father he'd always been.

'I'm innocent,' he began. 'I don't know what's going on with Daphne, but it must be a sort of breakdown — another one. She's had lots, I believe. And it's true that she had a tricky childhood. Bohemian family — you know the sort of thing, with feral children left to their own devices.' He glanced at Lucia, but she stared blankly, waiting for him to continue. 'You probably don't really remember Ed — he's still a good friend, but lives abroad. A marvellous man, a writer. I don't know about his fathering skills.' Ralph hardly felt the icicle of disloyalty. 'Your mother and I were very good friends with him and Ellie, his wife. But after Ellie was killed in a car crash, I suppose Daphne went pretty bonkers. She got into all sorts of drugs and stuff. A grotesque marriage to a billionaire Greek — private jets and priceless jewels and things. Then penniless for ages. Now she's a single mother. And, all of a sudden, after all these years, she's making things up about me. I don't have a clue.'

'Really?' said Lucia, trying to understand. 'But why would she do that? Why now?'

'I just don't know,' he said, believing his own story, caught up in self-righteousness. 'It's appalling. I've never experienced something like this. Maybe it's that thing, what's it called, false memory syndrome or whatever.'

'That's terrible.' Lucia's face softened with pity and Ralph risked stretching his hand across the kitchen table and placing it on hers.

'I'd never harm a child. I hope you know that.'

'That's what I'd like to believe, Dad. But I needed to hear it from you. They're such awful accusations.'

'Jeb thinks it'll probably all just go away when they realise what —' he almost said 'that woman' '— what she's like.'

They sat in silence for a moment and when Lucia asked him about his health, he sensed she was bringing the other topic of conversation to a conclusion.

'Oh, not too bad, you know, just trying to get on with it all.' He couldn't face dragging her into that mess as well. The relief of his daughter appearing to believe him gave him strength and he almost forgot Goodlove's death sentence.

They didn't stay long. There was a train to catch. Bee's bedtime, obligations he didn't take in. But their departure was far better than the arrival.

'It'll all be fine,' whispered Ralph as he embraced Lucia in the hall. 'Believe me.' He stooped, hoping to squat down to kiss Bee, but a stabbing pain prevented him. He straightened, took a deep breath and, instead, ruffled her hair, took her hands and sang, '"Every honey bee …"'

After they'd left, he said, 'I think I'll go to my workroom for a bit.' When Nina turned her back, he poured another glass from the bottle and scurried out with it before she noticed. This second glass of wine made him angry. He pictured Ed's party, presumably getting under way: the yeasty tingle of champagne, flickering candlelight, the rumble of conversation in counterpoint with shrieks of laughter and exclamations of joy. Why should he be barred from his old friend's celebrations? At this stage in the life cycle, just before the deluge, it was more important that they all call it quits and have a final embrace. Surely they would understand that it had become irrelevant for Daphne to continue with her spiteful scheming? When death is dancing outside your door, you must do what the hell you want.

He told Nina he wasn't hungry for supper and lied that he was going to meet Jeb.

'So late? It's almost nine.' He saw her notice the jacket he had just put on and was glad he'd placed the tie in his pocket.

'Just a friendly drink in a pub. Won't be long.' Funny how often lies were so much easier than the truth.

* * *

By the time he stepped out of the taxi in front of the Garrick Club, he was tempted to abort the mission and go home. He knew it was folly. Merely breaking the conditions of his bail and coming into contact with his accuser was risking arrest and worse. They'd warned him. Shooting pains were knifing his back and he felt shrivelled and malevolent, an inebriated Rumpelstiltskin. As he shuffled inside he was met by the familiar hit of lavish air – distant creamy sauces, expensive perfumes, polished wood. The porter was all obliging smiles and showed him upstairs. They both ignored the noticeable if muffled ripple of reaction when a small group of members recognised him on the way. This muted excitement was something Ralph associated with celebrations, like the polite audiences at his concerts or lectures. He knew it was for a different reason now but chose to pay no attention. They had not yet locked him in the stocks or pelted him with rotten fruit.

The porter motioned to Ralph to stand aside as two waitresses hurried up behind them with a large chocolate cake covered in raspberries and blazing with candles. They opened a door on to a private room and the party guests began a dirge-like rendition of 'Happy Birthday'. What a dismal, droning, little song, he thought, watching phantom-like through the open door to where about twenty-five people were sitting around a long, white-clothed table laden with flowers and twinkling tealights. They were all turned away from him towards Edmund and the cake. Edmund had the dignified charisma of a medieval king with his towering height and his extravagant but elegant gestures, which threatened to spill a glass of red wine held precariously in one hand. However, there was also a frail list to his lanky frame – an old, white-haired king dressed in a burgundy velvet jacket. The guests were like courtiers, murmuring encouragement, laughing easily. They were at the point in a dinner where a good deal of drinking has happened and their faces looked pink and happy. When Edmund blew out the candles (could there really be eighty? Ralph wondered) everyone applauded excessively, as though he'd done something much more remarkable.

'Speech! Speech!' someone called and Edmund stood up, one hand on the table steadying himself, his glass held out towards the gathering.

'My friends. Friends and family. Margaret. Thank you for making me feel such a phenomenally lucky bugger and turning this into such a marvellous day for me. I never imagined I'd reach fourscore years, and I can't say I feel any different from how I did at twenty – leaving aside a few unmentionables.' There were some polite titters. 'As a young man, I thought old age would be like going to a different country and changing nationality, but actually it's only the way other people see you that changes. And the awful thing is, you only discover that once it's too late. Trotsky was on to something when he said, "Old age is the most unexpected of all things that happen to a man."' Several people grunted in agreement. 'There's that terrible first time when you smile at a pretty girl and she looks through you as if you were a ghost – as if you already didn't exist.'

Looking around the table from his place in the shadows, Ralph tried to identify the diners. He spotted Daphne – the terrible, *old* Daphne, a middle-aged harridan who wanted him in prison, who wouldn't open her door to him, who led him down to the stinking riverbed and left him for dead. Nearby was her pale-haired daughter. And on the other side, a woman, who after all these years was clearly recognisable as Jane. She was like a sinewy witch disguised with a severe haircut and ugly librarian's specs. Perhaps she was the hateful inspiration behind the plot for his downfall.

Edmund finished his speech to yet more clapping and whistling and, during the moment of quiet immediately afterwards, Ralph walked into the room and approached the head of the table. Edmund was holding a large knife, ready to cut the cake, and the quiet became like the pause after an explosion, when air has been sucked away.

'Many happy returns of the day, Edmund.' Ralph's voice came out as a crow's croak and he noted Edmund's double take of shock and pleasure. The stretched out arm became an ambiguous gesture, somewhere between a consecration and an order to halt. The knife remained in the other hand. 'Happy birthday!' Ralph added, bowing slightly as if addressing royalty. The ominous buzz of bees swarming was the muttering and whispering around the table.

Edmund overcame his hesitation and held out his free hand and Ralph pulled himself into an embrace he then realised hadn't been on offer. There was a physical reluctance in Edmund's sinewy arms, one of which was holding the knife away from Ralph's back.

'Oh Ralph. What on earth is going on? The world is going mad. I'm too old for all this.' Edmund's voice was still the whinny of an anxious horse. As he moved to sit back in his chair, he stumbled slightly and thrust out a hand, which landed in the centre of the candle-covered cake. 'Bugger!' He let out a yelp of laughter that released some of the room's tension and there was a sympathetic echo amongst the guests.

A waiter brought some large napkins with which Edmund cleaned his hands, and he licked off the chocolate fondant with the expression of a naughty child. The cake was taken away for repairs and another waiter fetched a chair for Ralph and placed it next to Ed. 'Edmund. I merely came to …' His words emerged skewed, as if someone else was speaking, reminding him of being stoned in the ancient days of smoking joints together. He wasn't even clear what he wanted to say. 'To wish you many happy returns of the day. Marvellous! Eighty!'

'Thank you, Ralph. I can't believe ... all this time.'

Ralph interrupted. 'I also came to say I'm dying. I wanted to tell you myself.'

'Come now, dear boy. I realise that you're in a difficult ... But as to dying, well we all are.'

'No, really dying. Dust and ashes. I'll soon be dead.' Ralph raised his voice to emphasise the point, as if reminding himself, and noticed that everyone was turned towards him. 'Cancer.' He wanted to use the word riddled, to say that the tumours were swelling and creeping through his blood and bones, that his body had become his enemy. Instead, he said, 'They've stopped the treatment. There's nothing left. I came to say goodbye.' He glanced over towards Daphne, hoping to see a change of expression – some softening in her face, perhaps, after hearing his terrible news – but her eyes were turned away from him towards her daughter and her tight-lipped silence was not encouraging.

He caught the eye of a man who looked familiar. 'Hello, Ralph.' It was the voice that enabled Ralph to recognise him – the tone of detached calm that had been there even as a teenager. This grey-haired, professorial type was Daphne's brother, not seen for half a lifetime, since he was scrawny young Theo, with his electrical devices and genius for numbers. A professor now. Ralph had occasionally heard the updates.

'A surprise to see you here,' old Theo continued. He had the hunched and watchful look of a raptor, while the angular, mouse-faced woman by his side must be his American wife.

'Hello, Theo. How are you?' He's still got a beady, suspicious eye, Ralph thought.

Theo never liked Ralph, and regularly made that apparent in the old days. Ralph once drove halfway across Greece for a few hours alone with Daphne. It was August, hot as hell. He and Nina were staying in Pelion with the children, while Daphne was with her aunt on Poros. He fabricated a whole story for Nina involving a prospective concert, then borrowed his father-in-law's car and drove the four or five hours down to Athens. Daphne told her aunt she wanted to visit a friend in Athens for the day and took the ferry to Piraeus. At the last minute, Theo insisted on going with her – he wanted to buy something in the city – and, by the time Ralph spotted the gawky nineteen-year-old walking down the boat's gangplank alongside Daphne, it was too late to hide. The disapproving, lopsided smile on the boy's face said, 'I know.' Ralph improvised a tangled tale about having dropped a friend at a nearby ferry, but it was less than convincing.

'OK, have a nice time,' Theo called, setting off towards the electric train, shoulders stooped, skinny legs protruding from baggy shorts.

They sat on the same bench as a year earlier, before their trip to Aegina. It must have been soon before he left for New York – he remembered feeling frantic, out of control. There was a sordid little hotel in a stinking back street where they took a room for a few hours, both so miserable about the prospect of his American future that even the moments of bliss were soured. They lunched in a canteen-style place filled with port workers and old men and then she caught her boat and he drove all the way back to Pelion in tears, arriving in the night like a ghost.

Ralph didn't catch ageing Professor Theo's reply as it was cut off by a sharp bark. 'You shouldn't be here.' Jane, the arch bitch, was standing right behind his chair so he had to twist awkwardly to see her. She wore a hideous dress and her pale eyes were like something frozen behind the black-rimmed glasses. 'It would be better if you left quietly,' she said with the air of an outraged headmistress. It sounded like a threat of violence and he wouldn't put anything past her, the brute. 'I don't want to call the police, but I will if you stay.'

From behind her came another female voice. 'She's right, Ed. He should go.' A Canadian twang: Margaret — desiccated as a dried fig.

Hags unite, he thought. Kick me while I'm down. 'I won't stay long. Don't worry.' He tried to laugh at them, hoping this would be the best form of punishment for these Furies that looked ready to tear him apart. 'Perhaps you've forgotten, but a man is innocent until proved otherwise. I've done nothing wrong.'

He felt Daphne's eyes on him. Her daughter stared as though watching a horror film.

'I've been caught up in a witch-hunt, Ed.' Ralph turned away from everyone else and addressed his old friend. '*You* know what I'm like – I'm no dirty old man or child abuser. It's all mistaken. I'm dying, but I don't want to die in prison.' His plan to announce his death didn't have a second phase and, now the declaration had been made, he wasn't sure what to do. Perhaps they could lynch him and that'd be an end of it. He picked up a glass of white wine that stood available before him and took a large gulp as though staking a claim to being part of this feast.

Daphne was whispering in her daughter's ear, planning their escape perhaps. Or maybe they really were about to call the police and he'd be back in that cell on the sticky plastic mattress within the hour. He grasped his opportunity in the continuing quiet. 'There are murderers out there, boatloads of refugees drowning, bankers destroying the global economy. The whole planet is burning up and all anyone in England cares about is child abuse. It's upside down. It's mad.'

'OK, we're off.' Daphne jumped up, holding out a hand to her daughter and they hurried over to Edmund, who observed the scene with the detached interest of King Solomon. Ralph wondered whether he'd take notes later. 'Happy birthday, Ed.' Daphne kissed her father briskly, waved goodbye to the nonplussed guests and left without looking at Ralph, her daughter in tow like a foal following the mare. Jane stomped out in their wake, huffing noisily as if to say, 'I'll get you yet,' though Ralph gave no indication of noticing.

Breaking into the awkward hush, a woman said, 'Would someone be able to give just a tiny explanation?' Ralph recognised her face from the old Putney days. She must have been a colleague or a student of Ed's, though he couldn't recall exactly which. One of his former 'pretty girls', no doubt, though now she must be around sixty – grey hair cut in one of those 'pixie' crops and great jangling earrings that rattled when she spoke. She looked across at Ralph with a glinting eye of someone who'd read the *Daily Mail*.

'Perhaps we should let Ralph say his piece?' said Edmund, examining the chocolate icing that still dirtied his fingernails. Ralph sensed a small collective group sigh, like an audience settling down in the theatre as a play begins. Every face was focused on him, full of expectation. His legs hurt; most of his body hurt. But he stayed upright so as to properly address everyone at the table. It was an opportunity.

'I'm guilty,' he announced, consciously aiming for drama. 'If guilty is love between two people who need to be together. For those of you who don't know, I was arrested on charges of child abuse. I admit I haven't always done the right thing. I've fallen in love when I shouldn't have. But I've been true to myself. We don't approve of adultery, but in this country, at least, we don't lock people up or stone them or execute them for being married and having an affair.'

The pixie-haired woman was shaking her head and butted in. 'It's not called an affair when it's with a child. That's called abuse.'

'Naturally,' said Ralph, who had just recognised her: it was Dizzy, Ed's old squeeze. 'But who do you call a child? Girls who are now classified as children in England are *required* to get married and have babies in other countries. For Christ's sake, we're talking about grand passion and love, not legal systems. What about Romeo and bloody Juliet?' He felt drunk and bizarrely liberated by knowing death lurked at such close quarters. He wanted to address the room as though he was singing an aria. 'These are matters of the soul. They're untidy. You can't bundle a spirit into little, legal packages.' Nobody spoke. 'I'm no paedophile. I didn't lurk in kindergartens or abduct anyone. It's as though everyone is a pervert and all anyone thinks about is having sex with children.'

Grey-haired Dizzy stood up, muttering, 'I can't take this.' She said goodbye to Edmund and the remaining guests and stalked out, followed by a man Ralph assumed was her husband and who called in mock cheeriness, 'Happy birthday, Edmund! Thank you!' Edmund waved back like the courageous captain of a sinking ship as the passengers are evacuated.

'Thank you, dear, wise Ed,' Ralph said, realising he should go too. Turning around, he saw Nina in the doorway. She was evidently in high dudgeon, as Edmund might have said. Shit. Who told her? Before Ralph could summon up the correct reaction, she swept over, placed her hands on his shoulders as though arresting him and, ignoring the audience, she said, 'Come on, Ralph. We're going home. You're not well.' She didn't even greet Edmund.

It would have been a rather tidy solution, he thought later. She'd have spirited him away as if his entire appearance had been a mass hallucination. In fact, the blood drained from his face and a curtain of darkness descended. He didn't realise he was falling. When he opened his eyes, he was lying down and had no idea of his whereabouts. An unknown man was holding his wrist.

'You fainted,' announced the man. 'I'm a doctor – I was in the bar when they called me.'

'It's nothing,' said Nina, as she usually did when someone injured themselves or was ill, especially if she was worried. Ralph looked up to the curious faces of Edmund's friends peering down. He almost smiled. It was an odd perspective – looking up people's noses. The floor smelled of carpet cleaner.

He refused to go to hospital. 'No need. I'm fine now. It was just a swoon.' They took a taxi back to Primrose Hill and Nina did not speak all the way, staring out of the window away from him at the rain-smudged, scowling city. She opened the front door, struggling with the key, which often stuck, and he pictured her as an old widow, bent and arthritic but fiercely capable. It managed to be both a desolate and somehow cheering image – the familiar world continuing after he was no longer there.

Before they took off their coats she turned to face him. 'I won't say this again, Ralph, so listen to me. Tomorrow morning, I am going to leave and I won't come back. That is my plan.' She looked grave and fierce as an Aztec Boadicea, her grey hair curled by the damp night air. 'It's not because I don't love you, but I can't take this any more. You can't go on being false, making me guess, lying about where you go. So … You have a choice. You tell me everything. Not just some stupid little excuse like last time. And you keep telling me everything. Then I'll stay.' She removed her green woolly coat and hung it up. 'Or continue as you are and you won't find me here tomorrow. We're too old. It's too late for this.'

She left him in the hall and, with bewildering calm, boiled the kettle, made two cups of camomile tea and then, seeing him watching her from the kitchen doorway, said, 'You decide.'

Without speaking, they got into bed, propped themselves up on pillows, and sipped the yellow tea tasting of old meadows. He started with his treatment. 'I'm now officially dying.' She didn't say anything, just nodded, and he told her about Mr Goodlove. 'I'm frightened of …' He stopped, unaccustomed to revelations. 'I'm frightened.' For the first time in his life, his sexual secrets appeared petty, and he realised what he'd done to her by lying, by thinking he could divide up the world to suit his requirements. He tried to be as truthful as he could; her expression implied that she knew much of it anyway, or was not surprised. Sometimes she wiped away a tear but nothing more. She remained silent when he admitted how obsessed he had been with Daphne.

He even told her about the boys, or rather, the young men. 'Not for years now,' he said, arguing inwardly that even two years counts as years. 'Ages.' Then he remembered Luke, the music student who was assigned to him as an assistant when he conducted in Edinburgh the previous year. Determined not to lie, he said, 'Nothing for at least a year.' She didn't say anything, just nodded some more.

A grey light was diluting the darkness outside when he ran out of words and noticed she was already sleeping. His confession had drained him of poison and he felt sapped and weak but clean. He stroked her hand with its familiar broad palm, the muscular thumb, the small rough spots of oil paint, the two swollen finger joints. Then he nestled against her back, one arm round her waist as he'd done when they were first together forty years earlier, and slept.

17

DAPHNE

'God, what a drama. It's a relief to be out of there. Who'd have thought your grandpa's party would turn into such a hullabaloo?' She was trying to make light of it; Libby hadn't spoken since they got into the Uber. It had been horrendous to see Ralph gatecrashing her father's birthday. He was manic, almost demoniacal, and, rather than take charge of the situation, she had become frozen. It felt like being a witness to an avalanche, where there is a ghastly fascination at the horror and you are helpless to do anything. She wondered whether she should have called the police as Jane threatened. Or confronted him directly, perhaps. After their hurried departure, Jane had sat with them in the entrance hall of the club for a few minutes, but they hadn't felt free to discuss Ralph with Libby staring at them both.

'I'll call you first thing in the morning, OK?' said Jane. 'Get a good night's sleep.'

It was soothing being driven home along the Embankment, with its succession of glittering, lit-up bridges and the easy flow of night traffic heading west. Then Libby spoke. 'It was you, Mum, wasn't it? The girl?'

'What do you mean?' said Daphne, understanding exactly.

'Paige saw him on telly after that day when he came round. Ralph Boyd. She recognised him. And then … well we remembered you being so annoyed. You know, when you made him leave.' She waited for a response. 'Weren't you going to tell me?'

Daphne edged up closer to her daughter, whose face was tinted a pallid orange from the street lights. 'I'm so sorry I didn't tell you.' She took Libby's hand and spoke very quietly near her ear so the driver would not hear. 'I didn't have the words. I couldn't bear the idea of dragging you into that bloody mess.' Daphne had tried to avoid mentioning her past, the shambolic childhood, the havoc of her marriage, the mad years and even her recovery. That was all put away, unmentionable. And so was Ralph.

'Look, I'll try to explain it to you.'

'OK.'

'It started off that Ralph was a family friend, a friend of your grandparents. And my friend too, when I was a child.'

Libby nodded, concentrating, looking down and glancing occasionally at her mother.

'And then, at a certain point, we … no, he … he got close to me. Then he abused me. You know, sexual abuse.' She whispered the last sentence, glancing towards the driver's head and wondering if his dogged forward gaze implied he was trying to listen.

'That's so gross,' said Libby, picking at her fingernails and not looking up.

'I know, but it's complicated. The thing is, I didn't properly realise it was abuse at the time. He persuaded me it was OK.' She didn't want to say too much.

'Like Internet grooming?'

'I suppose so, yes. Grooming, anyway.'

'But it's never right, is it? Not with a child.' Libby stared at Daphne through a fog of disbelief. 'I mean, "Your body belongs to you." You've even told me that.' Libby's tone was slightly accusing. 'How old were you?'

Daphne didn't say, 'Around your age.' It was hard enough to meet the outraged, grey-blue eyes. 'I suppose I was about thirteen when it started.'

'Gross,' Libby repeated. 'That's so horrible, Mum. And what about him? How old was he?'

'About thirty.'

Libby was like the scolding parent and Daphne felt she was losing control of the conversation. 'But, Mum, that's so wrong. Why didn't you tell anyone? Your mum? What about Childline?' It was almost impossible to answer.

'You're right, Libby. It's wrong and bad, but I didn't understand.' She held Libby's hand tighter. 'I don't know why it took me so long. Maybe it was almost like brainwashing. But when I did finally get it, I went to the police. That's why it was in the news. So now there'll probably be a court case.'

'So when were you going to tell me? What was I meant to think? And what ...' Libby couldn't finish the sentence, her voice constricted. Tears plopped on to her legs.

'Oh, come here, darling.' Daphne drew her close and into a hug. 'I've made a mess of this,' she said over the top of Libby's head. 'A regular dog's dinner,' she added, trying to provoke a smile with one of their pet expressions. 'I was trying to keep you out of my problems. I didn't want to upset you or worry you. But I suppose I only made it worse. Of course you have to know.'

Libby extracted herself from her mother's arms.

'Do you promise you'll explain everything from now on?' Libby was regaining control over herself and the situation – a dynamic that was more familiar to Daphne. 'It's unfair, otherwise.'

'I do. I'll keep you posted each step of the way. And I'll tell you whatever you want to know. I promise. I'm so sorry.'

Ed rang early the next morning, when Libby was still sleeping and Daphne was pottering about the quiet flat in her dressing gown.

'Well that was quite a party for an old man!' He sounded rather gratified, she thought, at the scandalous events. 'I suppose I won't see you before we head back to France, and I wanted to touch base.' She could tell he had something on his mind and was leading up to it.

'I can't believe what Ralph did,' she said. 'Turning up like that. It's as if he feels no remorse. He's still trying to justify himself.'

'Oh, I'm not sure about that, Dafflings.' Ed paused slightly. 'Did you know that he was so seriously ill?'

She began to suspect where he was heading. 'Um, well Nina told me.'

'You missed the commotion at the end, when she arrived at the Garrick and he collapsed on the floor. Ghastly. We thought he'd died. But it turned out he'd only fainted. Still, it brought it home. Apparently, he doesn't have much time left. Months or even weeks. I thought perhaps you didn't know, what with the police and the court case and everything.'

Daphne didn't reply.

'I'm not trying to justify what he did. You know that?'

She made a small noise, signifying only that she'd heard him.

'But what will you gain by prosecuting him at this point in his life? I'm not defending his behaviour, which was awful – obviously. I've been discussing it with Margaret and she's appalled.'

'Well that's all right then,' said Daphne.

'Oh, Dafflings, don't be cross. Life is so complicated. So much happens. Sometimes we just have to let it go.'

'But didn't you ever wonder about what was going on? Didn't it ever seem strange that your friend was always taking me off when I was a child? And what about Ellie? Did she never suspect something? It's all very well to be relaxed, but ...' She stopped, feeling the futility of railing against her father.

'Of course we didn't imagine something like that.' Ed sounded indignant. 'That's unfair, darling. All I'm saying is that a court case won't stop it having happened.'

She couldn't be bothered to discuss justice with him. It was evidently a waste of time to explain her rationale to someone who had lived out the same 'liberated' times with such indulgence. After saying goodbye to her father and wishing him bon voyage back to France, she smoked a soothing cigarette perched on the window ledge, carefully blowing the smoke outside so Libby wouldn't smell anything – she had such a finely-tuned nose that Daphne's ploys to hide her bad habit were often in vain.

Almost immediately, her mobile rang again. Jane this time, still outraged.

'He's completely shameless!' she said. 'How could he just barge in there like that? I should've called the police. I regretted that later. They'd have locked him up again. He's just revolting, trying to justify himself in front of everyone, ruining the party. I must say, it was a shock to see him again after all these years.'

'You sound more annoyed than me,' said Daphne, realising suddenly that this was true. It was Jane who had demonstrated the way to loathing Ralph, who hated and resented him as much as she did.

'Oh, I doubt it.' Jane laughed without mirth. 'You're the child he raped.' It sounded horrible, almost accusatory. 'I just don't want him to knock you off track with his games. He's so cunning. And you never know with someone who is utterly lacking a moral compass. I only want to support you. You know I'm there for you all the way. I'm so proud of how well you're doing.'

* * *

The following weekend, Libby went to stay with Sam. He was over from Greece for a week and took her to some friends in Dorset.

The prospect of being alone was the perfect antidote to the mayhem in Daphne's life. All week she had felt tightly wound, pressed on every side by people who had become part of her private story – or what she'd believed was her private story. Now, in twisted, awkward ways she hadn't imagined, it involved her daughter, her father and her friend. Gareth Medlar had also become an instrument of pressure, pushing her towards the successful case he wanted to win. Anybody who read the papers or saw the news was now privy to something that had lain concealed and undisturbed since she was a girl.

She only had a couple of days before she needed to deliver her latest work to Adrian for an exhibition. The finished pieces were hung on the walls of the sitting room – she'd taken down two of Connie's paintings and an African mask to make space. *Putney* would not be submitted for the show – it skulked out of sight in its plastic sack – but she had completed *Gingerbread House* and a full-length, life-size portrait of Connie. Her aunt had been nearly six foot tall, so the result was imposing. Like Ed, Connie had an elongated, El Greco physique with pale colouring and a saintly aspect but, in both siblings, the physical hints of gentleness were misleading. Connie was steely, not just in the steadfast dedication to her work, but in rejecting marriage and children. Daphne had admired her spirited, self-sufficient approach to life, her refusal to follow convention. 'Oh, there were plenty of lovers,' she once said proudly to her niece. 'But why would I want to cook them dinner every day or darn their socks?'

Daphne had used the clothes she'd found in Connie's wardrobe to dress the collage figure. Even in the days when her contemporaries chose orange miniskirts and white patent-leather boots, she wore pencil skirts and cashmere jerseys in moss green, heather mauve and mouse grey. Over the next decades, she stuck to the same outfits and, although her brown hair went white, she always wound it into the same French plait. Daphne found the perfect wig and was so pleased with the result it was almost like having her aunt return to life. There was still lots to be done, attaching all the book covers and pages, which she'd printed on to fabric. Her aunt had spent an entire professional life in publishing and handled books with the same knowledgeable affection and confidence that a midwife shows to babies.

She worked almost all day, apart from a short walk before it got dark. Then she continued through the night, drinking coffee to stay awake. It was enjoyable to be alone and she concentrated so deeply that she hardly noticed the sounds punctuating the low-level city grumble – distant sirens, shouting from some drunks walking home from a party and, at about 5 a.m., the first Tube trains reverberating with the familiar rumble and rattle that had lulled her to sleep as a child. As the sky showed its first hints of light, she went to bed and slipped straight into a dreamless sleep.

It was around midday when she woke refreshed and happy. She showered, ate two fried eggs, drank coffee and went back to work. Inspired by putting the finishing touches to Connie's portrait, she played some of her aunt's old records, laying them carefully on the elderly but functioning turntable. There was a wonderfully varied collection of jazz, masses of Mozart and an overload of Wagner. Flicking through them, she paused briefly on noticing Ralph's *Songs of Innocence and Experience*. The sleeve had the deep familiarity of objects known when young. She'd spent so many hours as a girl staring at the William Blake watercolour and listening to the recording, checking her name amongst the credited singers. She had listened to the disc so much, it often felt as though the music ran through her and was embedded physically. But this was not the moment to replay these songs. Instead, she pulled out a Miles Davis LP and gently lowered the needle on to the vinyl, enjoying the slight crackle of anticipatory scratches. Then, standing by the open window, she lit a cigarette, exhaling carelessly into the glistening autumn day and watching small waves ripple prettily across the river.

She worked for the rest of the day, finishing *Aunt Connie* and turning her attention to tidying the unsatisfactory or straggly areas that remained on the other piece. In the early evening, she ordered some Indian food from a local restaurant and ate from the foil containers, pacing around the room with the unsettling, if exhilarating feeling of straddling the ground between madness and inspiration. When she continued with her work, the needle sped its way through material as though her fingers were mechanised, scissors snipping and cutting with precision.

Coffee kept her going through that night too and she listened to more of the old records, the volume turned down low. She found one she remembered Connie playing by a French singer called Barbara, whose dark eyes stared out from the sleeve. Daphne still didn't understand most of the words, but felt the sadness in the voice that she had recognised as a child, when it made her imagine Paris and her mother's trips there. As she stitched details on to the largest of her works, she was overcome by something like time vertigo. It had been only six months ago that she'd conceived of *Putney*, with its affectionate images of herself as a child and Ralph as her benevolently amorous friend, flying and dancing, sitting and talking – depictions of harmony and happiness in the landscape of her youth. The question of why she had made such a turnaround to seeing Ralph as an abuser was difficult to answer, but she doubted she could ever go back to seeing it the other way. On the other hand, she felt weary of the process, of the public dimension to something so private. What was she going to gain from these revelations, from crushing Ralph as he died?

Sunday's sunrise turned the sky into stripes of candy pink and powder blue and the river slid from darkness to gilded mauve. The grandeur of the sight increased the unaccustomed high she already felt from being awake all night for two days in a row. It reminded her of the times when she didn't need to distinguish between night and day – before Libby, before she started her steady work at Hell. She realised she was not her normal self, but she also felt an unusual clarity.

At just after seven, she sent a text to Ralph.

Can we meet?

He texted back almost immediately.

Why?

I want to show you something I made. Can you come to my place?

There was no reply for ages.

I don't know. I'm not allowed to see you, am I?

Afterwards, she pictured him talking to Nina, dismissing her as a malicious lunatic. He must hate her. Of course he wouldn't come. The high drained quickly into numb exhaustion and she lay down on the sofa, covering herself with a worn, tartan rug that smelled of picnics. The Tube trains crossed the bridge like intermittent lullabies and she was carried off by sleep.

The harsh entrance buzzer woke her and she jumped up, disoriented and unclear what time it was. Bright sunshine was streaming through the window. As she hurried to the intercom she saw on her phone that it was still only 8.30 a.m. Ralph was staring into the camera.

'Hello.' She pressed the button to let him in the main door and hurried to the bathroom to wash her face in cold water. Twisting her hair up with a clip, she opened the front door just as Ralph was emerging from the lift. He limped slowly along the carpeted corridor towards her and she saw him for the first time as a small, old person. Gone was the man who was always larger than her, larger than life. It was pitiful. Neither said a word. They didn't kiss each other either and he stared at her with a tired, puzzled expression.

'I'll get some coffee. Would you like some?' It was almost impossible to make sense of her contradictory thoughts: how this man had harmed her and loved her; how she had taken her revenge; and now, how it looked meaningless.

'OK.' Instead of following her into the kitchen, he walked into the sitting room to wait. She spotted him through the open door, looking out at the river, and they didn't speak until she joined him bearing a tray laden with toast, butter and marmalade, from which she'd hastily scraped the mould. Hunger and lack of sleep were making her weak and she needed sustenance even if he didn't. He was standing before her portrait of Connie.

'What do you think?'

'So like her. Quite creepy, what she's wearing.' He appeared repelled rather than impressed.

'Yes, I kept her clothes after she died. I think I found the perfect use for them. But wait a sec, there's something else I need to show you.' She went to the hall cupboard, pulled out the rubbish bag and returned with *Putney*. 'I wanted you to see this one.' She spread it out over the sofa so the edges draped down to the floor and he examined it.

'Hmm,' he grunted. 'And?' The impatience in his voice made it clear he was waiting for an explanation as to why she'd dragged him over there early in the morning, after everything that had happened.

'It's meant to be about you and me. My childhood, Barnabas Road. These are our figures floating about in different places.'

'I think we look rather happy.' He sounded annoyed, but he looked scared. Perhaps he believed she was toying with him, a cat luxuriating in pawing a wounded bird before it delivers the *coup de grâce*.

'I think we are,' she said, wondering immediately what she was doing, what the implications were of admitting this. They stood in silence, the room streaked with lemony sunshine and filled with the comforting smells of toast and coffee.

He lowered himself into an armchair and she saw he was weeping. There was an awful noise like a whimper covered up with a grunt and he rubbed his hands hard against his eyes, as if to expunge the weakness. She kneeled down on the floor and put her hand on his. He looked genuinely shocked, groaned and leaned forward, gripping her arms and pressing his face on her shoulder. 'Oh Christ.' His body felt slight and angular against hers. Sobs erupted from deep within his belly, making him shudder violently, while his tears seeped through her shirt and wet her skin. When the gasping dwindled to hiccoughs and raucous sniffs, he spoke.

'I know it's not enough that I loved you.' He looked up, his face a swamp of misery. 'It was wrong. I'm a weak man. I was out of control and couldn't stop myself. That's not an excuse – it's an admission of guilt. I deserve to be punished.'

She stood up and went to sit opposite him so she could see his face.

'Daff, it's the end for me, and I'm seeing things differently. I realise that you're right. Nina shouldn't have said you were responsible. Shit! You were a child. Oh Christ. But there's nothing I can do to make it not have happened. What should I do?'

Ralph levered himself upright and staggered to the window like a lost person.

'Here, let's have some breakfast.' Daphne guided him as she might a child, leading him to the sofa, removing *Putney* and helping him sit down. Pity had replaced anger and she saw before her an aged, dying man who had made mistakes and repented. She noticed his familiar smell, though it was altered, whether merely from growing old or from all the chemicals he'd been dosed with, she didn't know.

Sitting next to him, she poured out the lukewarm coffee, buttered two slices of cold toast and dolloped on some marmalade. They chewed and sipped, their silent commensality broken only by Ralph's intense, apparently involuntary sniffs. What would anyone gain by dragging this into a courtroom? She agreed with him, she couldn't stop it having happened.

I 8

JANE

It should not really have been a surprise when Daphne called and announced she was dropping all charges against Ralph. Shape shifting, scene swivelling, mood altering and clothes swapping had always been her prerogative. Mind changing came naturally to her. Once, she even became a Buddhist. For about a week. Nevertheless, Jane had dreaded this, and when she heard the familiar, gravelly voice, she knew what was coming before the words were said. Her initial reaction was quiet, compressed anger – after all they'd been through this was a betrayal. She allowed Daphne to blurt out her cobbled-together reasoning, and didn't argue back. There was no point.

'It's such a weight lifted,' said Daphne. 'It's not that I think what happened was OK or justified. I'm just leaving it behind. Maybe the Christians are on to something with their talk of forgiveness!' She laughed. 'I already feel liberated.' Changing tone, she said, 'So! I'm going a bit mad and taking some days off work. Libby's half-term starts this weekend and I found some crazy-cheap tickets to Athens. We're leaving tomorrow. We'll stay with my aunties in Maroussi. Maybe nip over to Aegina. And Libs will have her birthday out there.'

She hardly slept that night. It seemed bitterly unfair that Daphne had wriggled out of everything and was walking off into some Greek sunset, while Jane had been abandoned as though she was irrelevant. The duvet smothered her, the pillows jammed hard against her head and Michael snuffled and snored his way through her distress. Even their relationship had changed. For the first time in their marriage, she didn't want him to touch her. Certainly not sexually, but even his affectionate embraces as they sat on the sofa or when he returned from a day away were unwelcome. She experienced a strange revulsion that she knew was not his fault, was nothing to do with him, but that engulfed her.

At 4.30 a.m., when the first aeroplanes could be heard following the Thames on their flight path into Heathrow, she got up. Putting a fleece over her pyjamas, she pulled down the extension loft ladder and climbed up into the roof space. The small suitcase had a padlock, but she twisted in the digits of her birth year – 1963 – and rifled through the contents until she found an item of clothing folded inside an old, brown-paper greengrocer's bag. Good. She picked up the case and carefully made her way back down the ladder.

She spent a couple of hours sorting through the relics of her youth, sustaining herself with cups of tea. Some of the memorabilia was so familiar, handled and examined so many times that the objects were like extensions of her physical self. Daphne's prized piece of amber was there with its lifelike fly suspended within – the stolen insect now aged fifty million and thirty-eight years. Amongst the theatre programmes, birthday cards and bleached-out Polaroid snaps, she located a couple of notebooks and pocket diaries and placed them on the kitchen table along with the bulging paper bag. At six thirty she ate a bowl of muesli, reading through the diaries with attention and taking notes. She showered, dried her hair with care and greeted Michael with a smile, unwilling to drag him into her plan yet. Even after so little sleep, she felt like a soldier before battle – afraid, but ready to face the fire.

DC Medlar had not come in when she called the police station at eight, so she left her mobile number and asked that he ring her as soon as possible. This spoilt her plan of going straight there – her first work meeting was not till eleven. She tried ringing him again from the bus to no avail. 'Please tell him it's important.' At lunchtime, there was a message from the policeman on her mobile: 'Hi, Jane, sorry to miss you.' He left his number, but it went straight to voicemail. By the time they eventually spoke it was mid-afternoon and the exhaustion of the previous night was kicking in. She explained she needed to talk with him urgently about Ralph Boyd's case, even though it had been shelved. She had evidence that Daphne was not the only child he abused. 'Please-call-me-Gareth' was caught up for the rest of the day and away all weekend on work, but could she come and make a statement on Monday morning?

On the way home, the bus took so long she fell asleep, waking to find her cheek pressed against the cold condensation on the window. The roads were choked with the Friday evening rush hour and she considered getting off and walking, but was too tired. Daphne and Libby would be in Greece by now, she thought. Excited, relieved, happy to be doing something spontaneous. It was bewildering that Daphne could forgive Ralph's crimes as simply and unquestioningly as turning off a light. Could she not see that she was actually harming other young people with this behaviour? One can only protect the vulnerable and the underage from sex attacks and rape by exposing wrongdoing and making it clear that actions have consequences. If men can't keep their penises in their pants around a child, they must know there'll be trouble. Why the hell should future Ralphs get away with crimes against children?

* * *

She had never told anyone what happened with Ralph – how could she? The memories were nauseating but clear, like meat in aspic. She had now written down the exact timeline for Gareth. It had become external and real. It was a document. *On Saturday 1st July 1978, Mr Boyd sexually assaulted me and we had unlawful sexual intercourse. I was fifteen at the time and a virgin.* She knew how the questioning would go. It was a relief to face it squarely, cutting slices of the disgusting aspic dish and placing them in a line for analysis. There had long been two versions of the story – the one she told herself as a girl and the one she understood as a woman – but, unlike Daphne, she knew which version was correct. Children cannot always judge what is best for them and they certainly don't always do the right thing. That is why they need care and protection.

It was a grey summer's day, that Saturday in 1978. She had the date written down. The skies threatened rain but never delivered. She had arranged to go over to Barnabas Road but they hadn't specified exactly when. It was like that then – you could just show up at someone's home and no one thought it strange. By the time she knocked at Daphne's house it was after lunch. There was no answer. The front door was usually left unlocked and she pushed it open and went inside, calling out 'Hello?' Theo came mooching barefoot down the stairs.

'Oh, hello. Everyone's out. Are you looking for my sister?' He seemed bored, or maybe stoned. She could hear distant music playing, presumably from up in his room: Kraftwerk – electronic and geeky like him.

'Do you know when she'll be back? We were meant to be meeting up.'

'Haven't a clue. She might've gone shopping or something on the High Street. Want to wait in her room?'

She made herself at home in the top-floor bedroom, fidgeting pleasurably in the leatherette beanbag and listening to Elton John – comforting as a bar of chocolate. When that got boring, she looked through the clothes in the wardrobe and tried on a few things that didn't look too tiny. Her first choice was the racoon-tailed Davy Crockett hat, which made Daphne look raffish and funny as well as pretty. Jane longed to be that sort of girl. Then, despite it being summer, she put on the short Afghan coat with embroidered flowers across the back. Finally, the most irresistible item: a pair of purple, needlecord shorts. Having squeezed herself into them, she lay down on the floor and squirmed as they did with new jeans. The zip edged its way up and, though the tiny shorts barely covered her pants, she felt triumphant. Several minutes were spent posing in front of the mirror, admiring her corseted tummy, and turning this way and that as the racoon tail swung back and forth. She inhabited Daphne through her clothes, taking on her aura of boldness. It was so liberating, she felt inebriated and transformed.

There was a small scratching noise at the door, but before she could say anything or move, Ralph was standing there, a cartoon of disappointment: expectant eyebrows plummeted, the smile drooped, and his gaze flickered around the room as if he might spot Daphne concealed beneath the bedcovers. He managed, 'Hello, Lady Jane!'

'Hello.' Though she was desperately embarrassed to be found crammed inside Daphne's clothes, she also felt protected by them, as though she might be able to behave more as her friend would. She stared back at him, before casually removing the hat and coat and dropping them on the floor. There was nothing she could do about the shorts.

Ralph had only been back from America a few weeks and she hadn't seen him for almost a year. He looked tired. She knew Daphne was playing games since his return, as if punishing him for going away. She missed appointments and told him about parties with boys of her age. Appearing to gather his wits, Ralph strode over and kissed Jane on each cheek. 'How lovely! You do look well. And where's our friend? Hiding?'

She felt a blush rising and, to conceal it, she went to the record player, where *Goodbye Yellow Brick Road* had finished, and returned the disc to its sleeve. 'No,' she replied. 'I haven't seen her. Theo says she might be on Putney High Street. I was just waiting.'

Ralph spoke with his back to her, staring out of the window at the river. 'Shall we make a search party? I've got Maurice here – we could drive around and see if we spot her.' She saw him notice her bare legs and felt a flash of the power of youth that usually eluded her. This was the realm of desire in which Daphne existed and which she longed to taste. She hurried down the stairs ahead of Ralph, imagining his eyes on her, hoping, treacherously, that Daphne would not return before they left.

For a long time, Jane felt guilty about her eagerness on that day and certainly hadn't held anything against Ralph. Indeed, she remembered being rather pleased when, at Daphne's summer-solstice party the following year, Ralph appeared to resurrect his interest in her and pulled her into a clinching dance on the unmown grass. It was only in recent years that she had finally been able to view these events through the correct lens: adolescents want to experiment and push boundaries, they are obsessed with their bodies and it's up to adults to help them do the right thing. But, even now, she could summon up the tightly knotted fear and sexual craving that overwhelmed her.

Maurice stank of mould and was hardly glamorous, but she enjoyed getting in next to Ralph and watching him coax the old crock into action, pulling out the choke then letting it in again until the engine stayed fired. She wound down the window for fresh air and leaned out as they progressed up Putney High Street and then turned along some of the side roads. It quickly became clear that they were unlikely to find Daphne like this.

'She's probably in a shop or something.'

'Yes, fuck it,' said Ralph. She thought he was going to ask her to get out of the car, but he continued. 'Shall we go for a little drive? Get some air?'

They chugged their way to the top of Putney Hill and along the side of Wimbledon Common, until they got stuck behind an ice-cream van playing a jingle from *Popeye the Sailor Man*. Ralph sang the words in an embarrassing tenor voice and, when the van turned into a road leading to the common, he followed, stopping behind it in a car park. 'Fancy an ice cream?' he said. He bought two Cornish strawberry Mivvies and they sat in silence in the car, biting through the icy pink shell to reveal the creamy inside. She was intensely aware of her naked legs — freshly shaved the night before, she was glad to remember. Her tummy was squashed so tightly by the shorts she noticed every breath, but, bewilderingly, the constriction was not disagreeable.

She longed for something to happen. The wave of yearning that filled her was almost overwhelming and beyond reason. When Ralph touched her thigh she almost screamed. Very softly, he drew his finger across her skin and she closed her eyes, turning herself invisible, holding her breath. Then, without warning, he cupped his hand against her crotch, squeezed a finger under the leg of the shorts and thrust it inside her. It was utterly shocking. He did not kiss her, but she smelled wine on his breath, and he pulled her hand and placed it on his trousers — on the hard bulge she didn't dare look at. This was what Daphne did, she thought. This was how men behaved. It was raw and outside regular, rational time and space.

The episode ended as abruptly as it began. Ralph jerked away his hand and she opened her eyes to see a couple with a toddler walking towards the car. They passed by without even looking inside, but whatever had happened was over. The whole episode lasted maybe a minute. But that is long enough, she thought, when writing down the estimated time for Gareth. After all, you can kill a person in a second; why should it take much longer to complete a sexual assault?

Ralph's expression was as unreadable as a cliff face when he started up Maurice's sputtering engine and drove off. She was not clear what had happened and neither of them spoke. Were they getting involved? she wondered.

Is this what happens? The combination of the corset-like shorts, the ice cream and the sexual riddle were giving her a tummy ache. She discreetly undid the shorts' button under her shirt.

They parked back in Barnabas Road and walked wordlessly through the front garden with its unmown grass and straggly privet hedge that the Greenslays hated but never got around to trimming or removing. The eccentric, home-made sculpture was gradually disintegrating into a pile of rubbish.

'No need to knock,' said Ralph, pushing open the door. She followed him in, imitating his easy, buoyant steps. They paused to listen at the top of the stairs leading down to the kitchen, but there was no sound of human activity so they went upstairs to see if Daphne was there. Her deserted bedroom was airless and flies hammered against the windowpanes. Ralph imitated their whining thrum and the abrupt impact against glass. 'Can you hear? They're a chorus of buzzing.' His smile was like a miraculous gift. He continued, getting faster and madder, and they both laughed, which was a relief after so much strangeness.

Theo and Liam were lolling in languid poses on the river wall at the end of the garden. They were smoking – probably dope. There had not been any sign from Liam after the previous year's kiss. Ralph followed her gaze and nipped out of the line of vision so he couldn't be spotted.

'Ask them where she's gone,' he hissed. 'Don't say I'm here.'

She pushed up the sash window and, at the grinding sound, both boys turned.

'Hi!' she shouted, waving so they'd see her. 'Did Daphne come back?'

Liam raised a lazy hand in greeting and Theo called out, making his diction like a railway announcer, 'Gone to Portobello Road with Billy and Martin. Back about six.' Liam said something inaudible and Theo sniggered then pulled himself together. 'She said ...' there was more laughter '... you can wait if you like.'

Pulling down the window, Jane wondered how to get changed out of the purple shorts. She suspected Ralph would be in a bad mood after being stood up by Daphne again, and was caught off-guard when he grabbed her shoulders. He was not rough, but his movements left no room for discussion and he didn't speak. Decisions were taken out of her hands, like being swept into a river with a powerful current. Perfect. It just happened.

He was no taller than her and his build was light, but he was wiry and strong. In an almost acrobatic move, he tipped her on to the floor and rolled on top, looking into her eyes without smiling. In other circumstances this might have been unpleasant and she might have protested, but so strong was her feeling that she had become Daphne that she played along with the imagined role. In Daphne's room, dressed in her clothes, and getting off with her secret lover. The carpet rubbed static against her hair and Ralph pressed down, kissing as if he was eating her face. There was nothing tender or affectionate. His urgency reminded her of those nature documentaries where a lion mauls its prey, its muzzle covered in blood, eyes half-closed as it gnaws.

He grunted from the effort of tugging at her shorts that refused to roll down, despite being unzipped. It was a point where they might have stopped; embarrassment was an efficient killer of passion. But she lifted her buttocks off the ground to help him undress her, going through the squirming process in reverse. The sight of her ugly blue knickers was mortifying.

'I think we should stop,' she said, hesitantly. She had changed her mind. This all looked like a dreadful idea. Out of the corner of her eye she could see the racoon hat lying on the floor like roadkill.

He didn't reply. It was almost as though she wasn't there. After that, there was no delay and she felt a knifing pain as he penetrated her, and pinned her down, thrusting quickly and arching his back. He pulled out in a precarious coitus interruptus that left semen smeared across her thigh and a globule on her pubic hair, which hung, trembling like a dewdrop.

Ralph grasped the purple shorts and scrubbed at her leg, trying to tidy up. He attempted a smile. Zipping his fly, he flicked a watchful eye at the boys in the garden and then down at Jane, who was trying to put her trousers back on without revealing too much.

It wasn't how she'd imagined losing her virginity. She'd been seduced, she thought, enjoying the word, with its aroma of boudoirs, lace and mustachioed scoundrels. In films, after a couple had done it, they lay back in bed and smoked an affectionate cigarette, but there was nothing like that. This was strange and awkward, but she was also pleased. It was a relief. She'd done it, like having a vaccination.

Once she was dressed, she sat on the floor, leaning back against Daphne's bed. 'Just going for a pee,' he said and disappeared. That was when her feelings of guilt began. There was no doubting that this was betrayal. On his return, he looked businesslike and crouched down to sit by her, not quite touching.

'What will happen now?' Her voice emerged squeaky with anxiety. The act of putting his body inside hers surely tied them in some way or had repercussions. There were unfamiliar, corporeal smells and the room was hot and stuffy.

'Nothing!' came his cheery baritone. 'We're friends, aren't we? Friends can do nice things together if they like.' He paused. 'And that was very nice.' He was trying to disguise his worry but it was so clear, it was almost written in letters across his face. 'Nobody needs to know. If Daphne ...' The sentence wasn't finished. 'We'll keep this as our secret, eh Janey?' He shot her a radiant smile and locked his eyes on to hers – his golden bullet for a difficult situation that she'd seen used on other people. It worked perfectly. Before getting up, he rested his hand on her arm like a kindly vicar offering condolences.

She went home on the 93. From the top floor, she looked out at the places she'd been to with Ralph only hours earlier, but the excitement and intrigue were evaporating, leaving her sore and miserably guilty. It would be hard to see Daphne ever again, she thought. There was blood on her pants and, walking home through the dull streets, the wodge of toilet paper she'd placed there chafed. She banged her bag against dusty hedges in frustrated anger and scuffed her shoes. Wrong. Bad. Disloyal. Ugly. The words in her head were so strong she almost spoke them.

Her mother was in the kitchen like an advert for cleaning products – hair sprayed, a pretty apron and the floor shining with germlessness.

'Hello, poppet! I thought you were staying with Daphne tonight.'

Jane tried to answer and knew tears would betray her.

'Everything all right? Is something the matter?'

'No, nothing.' She started crying. 'I felt unwell. That's why I came home.'

Her mother came over and felt Jane's forehead with a hand that was damp and cool and smelled of raw potatoes. 'Yes, you are a bit warm. Why don't you go and lie down and I'll make you some tea?'

Upstairs in her room, Jane removed the purple shorts from her bag, sniffed the dry, translucent snail trails, and flung them into the darkness of her wardrobe. She changed into pyjamas and got into bed and, when Daphne rang later that evening, she told her mum to say she was feverish and could not come down to the phone. The next day, when her mother returned from shopping, Jane took a green-grocer's paper bag, recently emptied of apples, and placed the stolen shorts inside it. She locked the package in a tatty ladies' suitcase her parents had given her when it was no longer fit for travel and that was now filled with secrets and souvenirs. By the afternoon, she actually was ill with a throat infection that kept her off school all the following week. Old Dr Wittingham came to see her and prescribed antibiotics and bed rest.

Unable to face seeing Daphne, she spun out her conva-lescence for the last few days of term and stayed at home, claiming dizziness. By this time, she was also terrified. Her periods always came with precise regularity, usually falling on the same days as her mother's. They didn't discuss the matter, but her mother bought the 'STs' and it was quite clear when the large packet in the bathroom was being used. By the time she was a week late, she was beside herself with worry. She gripped her belly, squeezing the pale flesh, panicked that her body might betray her. Punishment for *her* betrayal. Her pinching got more violent, leaving weals and scratches from her nails – the pain a welcome distraction. It seemed fair.

For a few days, she removed some sanitary towels from the bathroom and threw them in a litterbin in some public toilets. She could not face being questioned by her mother. After another two weeks, there was still no blood and she went to the doctor. Horrified by the prospect of this disaster being discovered, she begged him not to tell her parents and he agreed that he would keep her secret unless she was pregnant. 'In that case, they would have to be informed,' he said. She longed to laugh and shriek with Daphne about the awfulness of being poked and prodded up the vagina by Dr Wittingham's hairy old fingers. 'Palpated,' he said. But she couldn't tell anyone. He demanded a sample of her urine for a pregnancy test and said the results would take up to two weeks. He would send a letter or she could phone.

Theo had once told her and Daphne that pregnancy tests were done by injecting a woman's pee into a frog. If she was up the duff, the frog started laying eggs. It sounded like a surreal nightmare. Jane pictured an enormous toad oozing quantities of spawn, slimy as the vats of tapioca at school lunches that were eaten with a spoonful of red jam.

The long-planned family holiday in Newquay was an ideal excuse not to see Daphne, but ten days imprisoned in a small hotel with her parents and brother was almost unbearable. She infuriated them by staying in bed till midday, picking fussily at her food and giving monosyllabic answers to their questions. The beach was lacerated by wind and she lay on the damp, grey sand, covered in goosebumps and feeling nauseous. For a change of scenery, she took solitary walks by the port and ate ice lollies sitting on a wall. Once, she bought a strawberry Mivvi, but it made her feel sick and she threw it away. Almost paralysed by fear, she had no one to confide in – Daphne least of all. Her parents? Ralph? None of the options were appealing. Abortion sounded like sharp surgical instruments, blood on metal, masked doctors, sleeping gas. She'd heard of hot baths with gin and clothes hangers in back streets, but she couldn't imagine how you did any of these things. Adoption? She pictured a chubby, pink-cheeked baby being carried off by a nurse in starched headgear.

On the return drive to London, her period started – a wonderful red oval on her pants. At home, a letter was waiting for her from Dr Wittingham and she snatched it from the pile of mail on the doormat before anyone noticed. Negative, it said. The frog was not laying human-fuelled eggs this time.

Daphne went to Greece and the rest of the summer holidays dragged by in a depressing desert of emptiness. Jane got a part-time job waitressing in a café near Wimbledon station, but mostly she hung about in her bedroom, listening to records and ranting in her diary about boredom and misery. She didn't consider getting in touch with Ralph. Nor did she blame him for what occurred. Their hurried coupling was something that just happened, like getting caught in a storm. That it had been a mistake was clear, but she had no sense that he had done anything worse than she had. Disgust with herself and her body eclipsed even the germ of anger, which took many years to grow. Much more powerful were her feelings of guilt towards Daphne. They hurt like a physical injury, as if she'd sliced off her toes and could hardly walk.

As an adult, Jane admitted the guilt of the innocent; she had wanted Ralph. She could confess to that. Not that she had engineered it, but she had been complicit. She was equally clear that she had been raped.

* * *

On Monday, she went to see Gareth at Fulham police station as arranged. A plastic food bag tied with a twist contained the purple shorts. DNA could be extracted from samples that were decades old and she was optimistic. She also had her diary, with its long and detailed description of Ralph's crimes and her subsequent summer of misery. Tucked inside it was the letter from Dr Wittingham like the perfect cross-check. Even if Daphne had dropped charges, they still had this new collection of evidence.

Gareth was rather overexcited, she thought. Almost breathless. He had been furious about Daphne's withdrawal, but now there were 'developments'. Two men had been to see him, he announced. They claimed Ralph had sexually abused them as teenagers. They had been playing in an orchestra he was conducting. 'This case is looking good again,' Gareth said.

At the lab, she texted Josh asking if he'd like a drink after she finished work. She knew she must tell her family and, though Michael should have been first, there was something about their oldest son's cool rationality that made her want to confide in him. Perhaps it was their shared belief in science and clear-cut lines of demonstrable truth, where right and wrong are laid out with proof. Josh suggested a pub near his department and when she got there he hugged her warmly. She wondered whether he'd sensed she was upset, but when she returned to their table with two glasses of Guinness, his grin told another story.

'You look very happy,' she said and it didn't take much for him to reveal he had a new girlfriend. 'Jessica,' he said. 'She's a medic. Still two years to go till she qualifies.' His eyes shone with the same sharp blue as his father's. 'I really want you to meet her.'

After that, she couldn't launch into her sordid story of violation. It would be like desecrating Josh's happiness and transforming herself into someone damaged – a victim. Before she arrived at the pub, she had even wondered whether she could discuss the forensic science involved in her case; she loved it when they talked shop. But now, the idea of telling her son about semen-stained shorts was out of the question. She knew it was cowardly, but it felt more important to keep his image of her as a strong and capable mother intact.

'Bring Jessica over at the weekend,' she said. 'If you can. She sounds wonderful.'

She waited to talk to Michael until they were sitting at supper, hoping this would lend an atmosphere of order and civilisation to muffle and contain the explosive device she had already activated on a timer. It was her week for cooking and, overwhelmed by everything else, she had resorted to heating up a ready-made, supermarket vegetable bake in the oven. It was on the poor side of mediocre but Michael didn't mention it. He had never been fussy.

Foolishly, perhaps, she hadn't expected him to be so upset.

'I can't believe you've been holding on to this since you were fifteen. Why didn't you tell me before? Oh God, Jane. Even recently – all this time you told me about

Daphne ... And you'd been raped.' He looked devastated, his eyes pink around the rims and then spilling over. 'Is that why you wanted to help Daphne report him? But then ...' Michael stopped, unable to speak for a moment, and then cleared his throat. 'Was there never a time you could have explained it to me? How could you shut me out?' His bewilderment was as great as his shock. 'That bastard should have been locked up years ago ...'

'I was ashamed,' she said simply. 'I couldn't face telling you. It was unbearable to admit I was such a poor friend to Daphne, that I had such bad judgement, that I betrayed her. I always disliked Ralph, but I ...' She couldn't go on and wept too. It felt impossible to explain to Michael that she had wanted to become Daphne, and that she longed to be her. And the closest she came to this inhabiting of her friend was the day when she donned Daphne's clothes, lay on her bedroom floor and had sex with her secret lover. Even now, she felt mortified – how much easier it had been to let Daphne be the victim of historical child sexual abuse.

Michael stood up and walked over, crouched down before her chair and put his arms around her. They breathed in unison without speaking until they were both calmer.

'Does Daphne know?'

'No. Not yet. She's away in Greece.'

'And what about the boys? Oh my God.' He was just starting to realise what the extent of the explosion would be. 'This is really big for all of us.'

She nodded. 'I know I need to tell Josh and Toby as soon as I can see them in person. I just couldn't do it with Josh today.'

Later in bed, she let him hold her, sensing that he was deeply shaken. Now, the trauma was not only hers. He was injured too, and it was clear that, even if only subconsciously, he felt she was partially responsible. She had shut him out of the story for their entire marriage, and then ignored him until the whole thing was official and registered with the police. It was as though their family field of golden buttercups, nurtured for so long, had something dark and stinking seeping up through the ground.

RALPH

Take-off was his favourite point in a flight – the weight-defying moment when a vast metal container gently lifted upwards and you left behind whatever your existence had been. Despite decades of travelling for work, he still thrilled as the plane roared its way into the heavens. This time, he knew it was beyond ordinary good luck to be escaping the toytown landscape of boxy houses and fenced-off fields and cutting through the clouds into unblinkered sunshine.

He caught Nina's anxious glances out of the corner of his eye and gave her a smile he hoped was not too obviously false. They had both been through a lot that week and he hated the idea of making her suffer more than was necessary. That they were on this aeroplane, pointing south towards the Mediterranean, was almost entirely down to her. He drew his mother's cashmere wrap around his head, hoping it was not this that emitted the mild odour of vomit. His body was dealing with an impressive number of pains and he had already thrown up at the airport. It was hard to prevent the occasional groan, but he hoped the engine's roar drowned them out.

When Daphne dropped her charges and the poisonous terror started to drain away, it was Nina who suggested they go to Greece. She did not say, 'for the last time'. Mr Goodlove was against the idea. 'Risky,' he said. 'You can't predict what might go wrong. I'd recommend a holiday closer to home – and to the hospital.' There was a certain pleasure in defying the urbane doctor; it reminded him of disobeying the headmaster at school. If I'm dying, he thought, why not do it in Greece? Why expire in London, wired up to machines and perforated by needles?

Nina's village was a pretty good place to end up. Their three children had spent most summers there when they were young, just as Nina always had. Milies ('Apple Trees') was tucked on the steep slopes of Mount Pelion amongst leafy chestnut trees, bubbling streams and marble fountains. It was reputed to be the home of centaurs, and there was always a sense of mystery, as though a mythical creature might indeed dart out from the shadows.

In the past, he had not usually remained there for weeks and months, like his family, but Milies had a comfortable familiarity that allowed him to work well and to relax. The village offered the purity of timelessness – a place to sidestep the grinding cycles of clocks, calendars and centuries. He liked sitting in the coffee house with the unintelligible old men, all bristling moustaches and clacking *komboloi* beads, who would treat him to a 'heavy sweet' coffee or a Metaxa Five Star. Once, he recorded them for a composition and they chuckled sceptically, humouring him. *Centaurs* used Byzantine hymns as themes and, if you knew what to listen for, there were worry beads and backgammon pieces clicking, the burble of masculine chatter, and the metallic rhythm of Greek coffee being stirred over the charcoal. It had not been a huge success, but the Greek side of the family appreciated the connections.

He pushed a button to summon an air hostess. No, they're called something else now, he thought. Something irritating and gender neutral, but what? In any case, it was a man (an air host?) who came, crouching down in the aisle beside him and smiling briskly. 'I'm sorry but I'm feeling nauseous,' said Ralph. 'Could I possibly have a brandy and ginger ale?' This had been a lifetime's therapy for travel sickness, nerves and much more. In bars, he asked for a Horse's Neck, and in America they flung in a twist of lemon. A trusty, old-fashioned medicine that usually did the trick.

'We'll be along with the drinks trolley in a little while, sir.'

Ralph looked at the young man's soft lips and the roll of flab around his middle. 'I'm not very well – I'd be so grateful,' he said, noting an expression of intransigence from this chubby pup in his tight uniform.

'He's suffering from cancer,' whispered Nina, leaning across Ralph towards the flight attendant. 'You look like a kind man. Please help him.'

Within minutes, he was sipping his Horse's Neck from a plastic cup. 'Thank you,' he said to Nina, realising how dependent upon her he was, had always been, even if it had taken him forty years to admit it. She had prepared a whole bag with his medicines, including morphine capsules. 'Will they give me marvellous visions?' he'd asked the nurse. 'Will it be like an opium den?' The male nurse hadn't laughed, but replied, deadpan, 'It may make you a bit drowsy.' He was a West African with a beautiful face and musical voice and he managed the delicate business of helping Ralph fill out the forms for whether or not to be resuscitated if he had a cardiac episode or worse.

'It's a better way to go, isn't it?' he asked the nurse. 'A heart attack, I mean?'

The man placed his hand on Ralph's. 'You will find your way, Ralph.' It felt like a benediction from the Pope.

The brandy was doing the trick and, as his muscles relaxed, he sank deeper into the seat. The rattling from the drinks trolley and slamming of metallic drawers reminded him of the hospital and he looked away towards the perfectly puffed clouds below in the expanse of unblighted blue. It was like a version of heaven – as if there should be chubby putti perched there, strumming harps, and, somewhere in the distance, the great old bearded man himself. He didn't believe in an afterlife, and refused to admit that the concept held more attraction now than he'd ever imagined it might. However, it was hard not to dwell on the end; he was dreadfully afraid of extreme pain. The prospect of revealing his vulnerability in an uncontrolled manner was particularly appalling.

There had not yet been any talk of funerals with Nina, but he couldn't help pondering over those he'd been to and creating a mental list for his own. A female choir singing a section from his *Requiem* was appealing, he thought, as tears welled at the image of himself inside a coffin, his children white-faced and weeping. Would Daphne be there? he wondered. After all that had happened in recent times, how would she feel? It was impossible to predict whether she would be sobbing in sackcloth and ashes or blithely untouched by his demise. Quite possibly veering between the two, he thought.

Once, when he'd gone to Barnabas Road, there'd been a Greenslay family drama. Daphne must have been about eleven – that evanescent tipping point at the cliff edge of adolescence. It turned out that the monkey, whatever its name was, had died. According to Ed, it had got a cough and, before they could even take it to the vet, dropped dead. They were preparing for the animal's burial when Ralph arrived. He ascertained that his presence at the proceedings was welcome – a weight to balance the family's instability, perhaps. Hugo (that was his name!) was curled stiff and pathetically small in a cardboard box, partially covered by his favourite, blue, baby blanket. Ed and Theo were digging a hole in the garden, which looked dank and unappealing, Ellie was assembling a little funerary wreath of ivy pulled from an outside wall, and Daphne was creating a large commemorative picture. Around Hugo's name, she was sticking Victorian style cut-outs as you might see on old screens: flowers, hearts, cats with bows, feminine hands holding sentimental messages. Then she stuck feathers and leaves on to the collage, turning it suddenly strange and unsettling. He saw now that it was an early precursor to her current work with textiles.

He joined the sad ceremony and took his turn shovelling clumpy earth on to the makeshift coffin. Each person made a brief farewell. He said, 'Rest in peace, dear Hugo, beloved monkey of the Greenslays, provocateur of the first order and devourer of grapes.' The two adults smiled indulgently, but he recalled Daphne's flash of fury at his light tone. She had adored the animal. They plodded back towards the kitchen door, the prospect of warmth welcome after the chilling damp of the riverside garden, but Daphne didn't move. He watched her from the long kitchen table, where he sat drinking a glass of red wine given to him by Ed, despite it being only late morning. First, she placed her strange memorial card on the grave and sat down beside it on a muddy patch of wet grass. Ellie called once or twice to her daughter, but Daphne ignored her. Ralph saw her take a box of matches from her trousers and set light to the card. In an improvised mourning ritual, she rubbed her hands in the mix of earth and ashes and smeared them across her face. It was deeply shocking to see his feather-light sprite racked by raw grief.

After twenty minutes, she got up and walked inside, ignoring the adults and passing them erect and dignified, even if her face was pinched with cold and streaked in dirty grey. He was impressed by her poise. Now, he realised how young she was — a child. He preferred not to dwell on how he had gone to her room, after asking Ellie and Ed if he could 'try to cheer her up'. They accepted the offer with gratitude, and he found Daphne prostrate on the floor, raging and sobbing, one eye on the flames that were flickering up the sides of her waste bin and threatening to set fire to the curtains.

'Shit! Daff! What's going on?' He saw the desperation on her face and the danger that a child's gesture could transform the situation into a grand tragedy. By the time he had ripped the blankets from her bed and thrown them over the bin, one curtain was alight. He pulled so hard at it that the pole and both curtains fell to the floor and then he stamped all over them until the fire was out. Acrid smoke filled the room and pieces of paper ash floated like black snow. Daphne watched as he opened the window and waited for the air to clear.

Neither of them spoke. What could he say in the face of this pain? He lay down beside her, put an arm across her back and, with his other hand, stroked her hair. The dark strands were still cool from being outside so long, with droplets of mist clinging to them. There was something about the magnificent passion of her reaction that he found entrancing. She was not crying any longer and he picked her up and placed her in his lap, rocking her like a baby. He felt elated, as though they had some mystical communion. If he was brutally honest, there was something mildly erotic about it too, but he didn't act on it. How could he have allowed himself to do that? he wondered. He pictured his own darling Lucia at that age and shivered with revulsion. What was he thinking?

It was about half an hour before they both went downstairs and told Ed and Ellie what had happened. 'A little accident,' he explained bluffly. 'Daff lit a candle for poor old Hugo and it fell into some paper in the bin. I'm afraid one curtain is a bit singed.' They hadn't overreacted. In fact, Daphne said they hadn't even been to see the damage until the evening, and the next day Ellie and she had gone to Brick Lane and bought another orange sari to replace the burnt one.

Ralph knew that he'd enjoyed – no, exploited – the girl's reckless tendency. Her aptitude for leaping from on high into unknown waters was part of what initially attracted him. As she grew older, she went too far. Diving into unfamiliar seas was careless and irresponsible if one didn't take into account the possibility of rocks and monsters below the surface. He had kept away from her after she appeared to self-destruct, with the poisonous marriage to the Greek oligarch, the drugs, the undernourished limbs and nightmare eyes. She had become toxic – entirely different from the girl he had worshipped.

Unlike Daphne, he always made calculations before any move, careful as a chess player. It was not that he eschewed risk, far from it. After all, his relationship with Daphne always threatened a daunting array of penalties. But, from his schooldays, he had learned to hold things in and bide his time, so that even the madness of love was efficiently delayed or disguised. There was no escape from that perspective now – no way of arguing that she had not been a child, or that he had not understood at some level. The prosecution was no longer a threat, but he knew he had been far more toxic to her than she could ever have been to him. I was one of those marine monsters, he thought. And she just leaped into my jaws.

He pulled his mother's soft old wrap around his head and tried to sleep.

* * *

They took a taxi from the airport to the apartment in Pangrati, the busy, central neighbourhood where Nina had grown up and which her mother preferred to the village for winters. The driver revved and slammed on the brakes in a series of unsuccessful shortcuts, which Nina believed increased the journey time. When they finally arrived, a dusty wind whipped their faces and the pavement was piled with stinking bags of rubbish – presumably another strike. He'd always found Athens impossible, with its chaos and the intensity of stimulants for the senses that took one to both extremes, often simultaneously – if you came across sweet-scented flowers, there was sure to be a sewer nearby.

His mother-in-law called the formulaic greeting of welcome in Greek through the intercom and Nina answered with the 'Well found!' response that he never quite got the hang of. He had once hoped to learn Greek, but failed to master more than a few basic phrases. Nina's mother spoke French but barely any English, and his French was almost as rusty as he pretended to her, so they had got through decades with minimal verbal communication. Probably just as well. Even at nearly ninety, his mother-in-law was a daunting woman – nothing playful in her old eagle eyes. He sensed she didn't quite trust him.

The flat was on the third floor of a 1930s building and, with its mahogany wardrobes and formal dining room, it seemed stuck in the era of Nina's childhood, when Pangrati had been more sedate and middle class. Now, the neighbourhood was crowded, complicated and much poorer.

'She asks if we're hungry,' translated Nina. 'There's chickpea soup and *spanakopita*.'

'I think I'll lie down for a bit,' he said, unable to contemplate eating anything as robust as these classic Greek dishes. His mother-in-law's spinach pies were legendary in the family and, packed with feta and dripping golden olive oil, they lay heavy on the stomach.

Nina hadn't told her mother about Ralph's cancer. It was customary in their family to believe they were protecting each other by lying about bad news. Nina's father had died after almost two years with pulmonary fibrosis and they did not tell their only daughter until he was actually expiring in hospital. With the same logic, his mother-in-law knew only that Ralph had had some sort of flu and was under the weather. She offered to make him some mountain tea as she followed the couple into the room that had always been Nina's. A small oil lamp was burning below the icon in the corner. Rather beautiful, he thought, enjoying the aesthetic of Orthodoxy from a safe distance. He sat down on the double bed. It was covered with a pink satin bedcover, which had been there from when they were first married and generated recollections of making love with Nina across its slippery surface during the 'public quiet hours' on sunny afternoons.

The room reeked of a portable gas heater. Apparently the building's central heating was no longer turned on, as the occupants could not afford the fuel bills. 'She saw her neighbours hacking branches off the bitter orange trees in the street so they could light a fire at home,' translated Nina, as her mother rattled on from the doorway. 'The whole city gets covered in a cloud of smoke when it's cold and soon we won't have any trees left.' During the last years of the crisis, her briskly unsentimental mother had volunteered at a soup kitchen in the area, helping feed hundreds of the dispossessed, the elderly and, more recently, the refugees, who were otherwise going hungry. 'It's not so different from when Nina was born after the war,' she said. 'Everybody needs to do what they can until we get through it.'

When Nina returned with the tea, he was nearly asleep, but raised himself to drink some. It was boiled dark, but soothed him nevertheless. He slept fitfully, listening to Nina's steady breath next to him and the raucous noises of an Athenian night.

In the morning, he was determined to get up despite feeling frightful. Nina made him breakfast, and he sat in his mother-in-law's kitchen, basking in the astonishing sunshine that filled the room with a limpid, Attic glow.

'My mother says we can keep her car as long as we like,' said Nina. 'She doesn't need it in the city.' She lowered her voice to a whisper, 'And she's better off not being able to drive. A threat to public safety.' She chuckled so sweetly that Ralph glimpsed her as she'd been in her twenties.

'Thank you, darling.' He meant it as an acknowledgement of what she had been to him over a lifetime, but she took it as gratitude for the breakfast she'd served him: still-warm bread her old mother had been out to buy that morning and home made quince preserve. She asked, 'More coffee?'

He thought about explaining but it seemed absurd. You can't just say: 'Thank you for being married to me since 1974.' And what then? 'Thank you for suffering my infidelities. Thank you for ignoring my egotism and for bringing up the children while I kept travelling and working and putting so much else before you. Thank you for being here at the end when I've been revealed as one of the disgraced – a social leper of the worst sort, who raped a child. Repeatedly. And never even realised it till now.' The crimes were far too many and too severe for mere thanks to be enough.

Nina prepared everything, loaded their cases into the boot and they set off in her mother's old car, which spluttered and struggled on the hills.

'Worse than Maurice,' she said and they both smiled at the memory of the Morris Traveller, which had eventually refused to budge and was towed ignominiously to the scrapyard. The late October sun was surprisingly hot as they sat in traffic, waiting to get out of the centre. He opened the passenger window to be confronted with gusts of exhaust, Greek pop songs going full blast from a nearby car radio and several motorbikes that surged past so close that he felt their breeze. The familiar landmarks were like beacons of dignity in the urban chaos: the marble curves of the old

Olympic Stadium; Lycabettus Hill with its glistening white church; and of course the Parthenon, perched pluckily above the sprawl as if nothing could ever make it crumble. He was fond of Athens, even if it appalled him, but he knew it was a superficial opinion. They never spent long enough there for him to understand it better, and with her preference for nature – her wooded mountains and the sea – Nina never tried to convince him that Greece's capital was worthy of respect or love.

They did not talk as they moved steadily away from the city along the main northbound highway, until Nina said it felt like time for a coffee and maybe a little cheese pie, and she'd fill up with petrol. As she parked outside a small roadside service station, Ralph's phone rang. Jeb Rosenberry.

'Hang on a sec,' he said to Jeb, making a gesture to Nina that indicated he was going for a short stroll with his phone, though he could tell she didn't understand.

'Everything OK over there?' asked Jeb.

'Fine, yes.' Of course it's not fine, he thought, as he hobbled gingerly around to the back of the building in search of privacy.

'So, it's not great news, I'm afraid, but don't worry. Nothing we can't deal with.'

'What happened?' A couple of scabrous dogs were nosing through piles of rubbish and an exhausted-looking woman in a waitress's tunic was leaning against the back door of the cafeteria, smoking. She avoided his eye.

'So first of all, Jane Butterfield has gone to the police with a new accusation against you.'

Ralph did not reply, but edged over to the rusting fence, where an outcrop of rock offered a place to sit. Lowering himself on to the sun-warmed stone, he crushed some pink, autumnal cyclamen growing directly out of the grey surface as if by a miracle.

'I wouldn't have worried so much about this,' continued Jeb. 'After all, we know Jane dislikes you. It's supposedly referring to a one-off occasion when she was fifteen. Says she lost her virginity with you. But still, one might argue for a "reasonable mistake". Also, the police are so annoyed with Daphne for letting them down that they're wary of having anything to do with her or her friends. She's on their blacklist since she made her evidence unusable – wasting police time and all that. Apparently, she just took off on holiday to Greece.'

Ralph shuddered. A curse on mobile phones. He was tempted to cut off the call and throw the device away. 'I don't think we have to take this seriously, do we?' As he spoke, Ralph pictured the pink-skinned girl and their perfunctory business on Daphne's bedroom floor. Surely she'd been sixteen? Not that those details mattered so much then. A great giraffe of a girl. So long ago, he'd almost forgotten the whole incident. It was not something that had ever preoccupied him; filed away in a distant backroom of his mind. Now, however, the memory caught him as though someone had grabbed his throat. What the hell had he been thinking? He didn't even like 'Big Fish', who at best was a useful co-conspirator and excuse for Daphne's absences from home. He had not considered her feelings or even been kind to her. They had both betrayed Daphne, but his actions now provoked revulsion. Perhaps this is what makes a monster, he thought. Someone who has no idea of the damage they are wreaking. It was perplexing and horrifying that he had managed to avoid seeing this for so long. Nearby, a couple of greasy-feathered crows hopped about with tentative watchfulness, jabbing at something on the ground.

'The thing is,' said Jeb, 'there's more. Do the names Ber Schneider and Rasmus Lepik mean anything to you?'

'No,' Ralph answered without giving it much thought. 'Who the hell are they?'

'They're two teenagers – a German and an Estonian. They came forward after the press stories, saying something about an "episode" with you in Tallinn. A concert you were conducting in 2012. They were in the orchestra – a ...' He paused as if checking something. 'A French horn player and a trumpeter. They allege they were fifteen and sixteen. They're now eighteen and nineteen. I've checked the dates. Annoyingly, you were there.'

The image clicked into Ralph's mind like a picture on a screen – Ras and Ber. Of course. The raging, almost painful laughter as they lay on the floor in the boys' shared hotel room. How they'd pulled off his trousers so efficiently, one leg each. The silver ampoules and coloured balloons. They'd all been so happy – boys together. Pure fun. Why on earth would they do this? His chest hurt and sweat trickled down his face like liquefied fear.

'They're saying it was abuse of your position of authority as their teacher and conductor. There was some mention of drugs too – nitrous oxide? But, Ralph, remember, don't tell me anything I shouldn't know, OK? You need to think before you answer. We probably shouldn't discuss any details at this point.'

Ralph gave a wretched grunt of acknowledgement.

'The police haven't asked to see you yet and they certainly haven't decided whether to press charges. The Daphne debacle has burned them. But if they do want a little chat, it'll be better to come back willingly for a day or so. Otherwise, you'll force them to charge you. And then you'll be nicked by the Greek police and extradited straight back to Blighty. And we don't need that at this stage in the game.'

'OK. Thanks, Jeb,' he croaked. His heart was hammering, the pain had become excruciating, and he did not wait for an answer before flinging his phone on to the scrubby grass. It was unbearable to see himself as Jeb must – someone who abused young people, who raped and groped and lied. At the time, he had loved it that the Tallinn boys were naughtier than him. It had been so simple to think of these episodes as fun. *They* were the ones feeding him laughing gas and ripping off his clothes. But it now looked abysmally different: seedy, dirty, illegal and wrong. He was responsible for them and they were only boys.

His arms ached and throbbed and the burning weight on his chest was like a gorilla sitting on him. Perhaps this is it, he thought. We rarely choose the place we end up in. So mine is alone on a rock in some anonymous, arse-end roadside in Greece, surrounded by rubbish, scavengers and black-feathered auguries of death. It became like a loud noise – an overwhelming wave of agony that swept everything else away, its majesty almost cleansing. Even the scale of his crimes was diminished. The prospect of death was no longer horrifying. He was ready.

DAPHNE

The half-term trip started out very promisingly. When they landed at Athens airport and stepped out into the lilac light of late afternoon, Daphne's body was buoyant as if she had set down a heavy load. Ralph's apology allowed her anger to subside almost as mysteriously as it had arrived.

The train sped past giant billboards that had once been garish with adverts but were now blank spaces splattered with graffiti. *Vasanizomai*, declared one persistent person with a spray can, over and over. 'I'm suffering.'

They got out at Maroussi and wheeled their cases up the suburban hill as the skies turned to indigo ink. The evening air was so sweetly warm, Daphne felt she could taste it. Her mother's three sisters all lived in a small apartment block built on the site where their old family house had been. There was still a bit of garden that she remembered playing in as a child, and the same stone-pillared gateway through which *Pappou*'s coffin was carried out to the hearse. Now in their early eighties, both Georgia and Katy had middle-aged children who had moved back in with them, along with their own offspring, after losing jobs or being unable to afford their rent. Only Aunt Athena had space for Daphne and Libby, living alone on the top floor since her husband had died some years earlier.

It had taken a long time to re-establish trust with her three aunts and numerous cousins after the years when everything she touched went wrong. They had seen the reality of her life with Constantine – they visited the absurdly swanky villa in Kifissia and were dragged into the mess when it all ended. She had used them, lied to them and borrowed money she never paid back. Not that anyone would have guessed that from the way the clan gathered at Athena's place almost immediately after their arrival. Each familial group brought a new flurry of kissing, exclamations about Libby's charms, and a rush to exchange news and comment on physical changes. They gave no sign that they were wary of Daphne. Aunt Athena brought out cakes and cherry brandy and toasts of welcome were made. There was constant movement as people wandered into the kitchen to make coffee, or went back down the stairs to their own apartments to fetch something. Libby looked thrilled to be taken out for a walk with her slightly older cousins, Pavlos and Alexis, and they trooped off with expressions of innocent mischief. At least that's what Daphne hoped she witnessed.

Exploiting her daughter's absence, Daphne joined the boys' mother out on the balcony where she was smoking. Evgenia had become a middle-aged matron with thickened midriff and hair stiff with spray. We're getting old now, Daphne thought, remembering the glamorously sexy teenager she'd admired as a girl. Evgenia gave her a Marlboro Light from a packet with a health-warning picture of a corpse lying on a morgue table.

'We would all leave if we could,' she said, putting an arm round Daphne's waist. 'There's nothing for Pavlos and Alexis here. We can't even afford to send them to university abroad. I always believed that we would keep getting better, richer, more European. And now it's all turned upside down. We're in our fifties and moving back into our parents' homes.'

'Yes, but look at this.' Daphne gestured at the city's expanse of sparkling lights spilling all the way down to the sea, and the surrounding mountains making dark shadows against a sky still tinged with stripes of the long-departed sunset. 'You don't get this in London.'

'Yes, well that's not going to pay the bills. You're lucky to be here on holidays – that's all Greece is good for.'

They spent two days in Athens so Libby could see Sam and, on the third morning, Daphne woke early in anticipation of the trip to Aegina. The aunts had agreed that, with her knowledge of tourism and mother-tongue English, Daphne was the ideal person to organise holiday lets at the old island house. It was either that or sell it. And nobody was buying property these days – you could hardly give it away.

'People are refusing their inheritances,' said Aunt Athena. 'They reject their parents' homes because they can't pay the taxes and there's no way to sell them.' All three aunts were adamant that it would be terrible to lose their beloved *patriko*, their father's home.

Aunt Athena plied them with a resplendent breakfast, including boiled eggs, cheese, soft *tzoureki* bread and an orange cake. Dainty, cut-glass dishes contained samples of her preserves.

'This feast reminds me of when Ellie made me name-day breakfasts,' said Daphne, remembering the infinite bounty of her mother's feverish nurturing sessions that were simultaneously opportunities for expressing love and female domination. It was like getting an extra birthday each year on April 9th – a bonus of having a Greek parent. Athena looked tearful, then wiped the slate of her face clear again and smiled.

'I still miss her so much,' said Daphne, shocked by the knife of grief that stabbed, as though her mother's death had been quite recent.

Daphne and Libby wheeled their cases back down the bumpy streets to Maroussi's station and took the electric train down to Piraeus. The carriage was packed with people heading in to work and it wasn't until Omonia, where crowds got out, that they found seats. An unshaven old man swayed about playing 'Cloudy Sunday' on his accordion. Most of the travellers paid little attention and very few gave him small change when he proffered his hat. The journey only took half an hour, though it cut through an entire cross-section of Athenian neighbourhoods, starting in the privileged, northern high ground, traversing the anguished plain of an overcrowded inner city and terminating down in the anarchic bustle of the port.

They had just left the train terminus at Piraeus when Daphne stopped to answer her phone. It was Ralph.

'I can't hear you very well,' she shouted, holding one hand to her ear against the rumbling cacophony of passing lorries and a café blaring dance music. 'What did you say?' She heard the word 'hospital' and her chest felt heavy in anticipation. 'I'm in Greece,' she yelled. 'I can't really talk.' She didn't want Libby to think she was chummy and chatting with her old abuser.

'I know,' came the reply, much clearer now. 'I am too. At the Metropolitan Hospital, in Neo Faliro. I almost died yesterday. It seems heart failure is another charming side effect of my disease. I don't think I have much longer. Nina's gone. Will you come to say ... so that I can say goodbye?'

'I'm in Piraeus with Libby,' said Daphne. 'We're catching a ferry.' She didn't want to be pulled into Ralph's drama, but she could not help feeling sorry for him. 'I suppose ... well maybe we could get a later one.' He didn't reply. 'OK, I'll come,' she continued, noting Libby's concerned air and holding up a hand in a pacifying motion. 'We'll take a taxi and be there in ten minutes. I'll see you soon.'

'I can't say no,' Daphne said, hoping to get in her point before Libby began complaining.

'He doesn't deserve it.'

'No, you're right. But when someone's about to die you can't refuse to see them.'

'You *can*. He should be in prison. Just let him die.'

'You're right, my Libs. But I'd prefer to say goodbye in peace. It'll make it easier for me. And actually, the hospital is very close to here.'

Libby made a grumbling sound indicating her realisation that she had no chance of success, but that she hadn't forgotten the accusations against Ralph or her revulsion about them. 'But no way am I going to see him, OK? I hate hospitals.'

'Thanks, my gorgeous girl. It won't take long, I promise.' She held her daughter's head and kissed it.

The hospital was a modern block, opposite a tangle of bridges and underpasses. Libby managed — bewilderingly — to look both forlorn and angry when Daphne left her in a café on the ground floor, though she agreed to call Sam to make birthday plans and arrangements for staying with him on their return from the island. Daphne took the lift to the fourth floor as instructed and asked for *kyrios* Boyd at the nurses' reception desk.

'*Kyrios* Boont,' replied the nurse, correcting Daphne with the Greek interpretation of the spelling, 'is in room 11.' She pointed casually along the corridor.

Daphne opened the door gently and saw him before he noticed her. He was facing away and appeared shrunken, hair lying flattened against his skull. Tubes and wires connected him to winking machines. Here was the man who had loomed so large in her life. Here was the person who had introduced her to love. And, of course, he had been meaningful enough to make her hate him and want revenge, even as a grown woman with a child of her own. Yet before her was a frail body on the verge of leaving the world, drained of strength and power.

'Hello?' She couldn't see if he was asleep, but he turned quickly to face her.

'Christ! You came.' He sat up, his face feverish or mad, his skin tinged a dispiriting yellow. 'I didn't know if you would. Jeb said you were in Greece.'

'Yes, I'm with Libby. We're taking the boat to Aegina.' How strange that Libby was about to have her thirteenth birthday, she thought. She'll be the same age I was when Ralph and I took the Magic Bus.

'Ah.' It was more of an outbreath than a word. 'Aegina.' He continued in a more practical manner. 'You know, I thought I'd died. I was sitting on this rock in the middle of nowhere ... The pain was astonishing. It's peculiar, but I was fine with the idea of leaving.'

'What happened? How did you get here?'

'Someone must have spotted me keeling over. They got an ambulance and by that time Nina found me. I was taken to the nearest town, which was Thebes.' He made a noise that was meant to be a chuckle but sounded like a dog coughing. 'That would have been rather a good place to have died. Oedipus and all that jazz. You know, King of Thebes ...' His voice trailed off.

'Anyway, Nina sorted out everything. I was brought here. Doing rather well in the circumstances. Quite perky, really.' He coughed and winced in pain. 'I'm a bit bruised from the fall, that's all.'

'Did you want to tell me something?' She felt pity for the wreck before her, but it was unclear why she had been summoned.

'Yes. Could you close the blinds, please?' he said, as though that was the reason for requesting her presence. He squinted at the intense sunshine flooding in through the window and she lowered the grey venetian blinds, throwing the room into stripes of shade.

'And what did you mean, Nina's gone?'

'She's gone. Or at least, gone to her mother's house. I think she spoke to Jeb. Anyway, she finally understood I'm a fiend. Should have gone years ago.' He sounded resigned and Daphne assumed he was exaggerating.

When she returned from the window to his bedside, there was a change in his manner. 'So you're going to Aegina?'

'Yes.'

'On the boat?'

'Yes?' She wondered briefly whether he was all there or whether he might have sustained some brain damage after his heart failed.

'So I need your help with something. Please don't refuse me right off. Listen and see if you can grant me a final wish, even if it doesn't make sense.' He had apparently come back to life and was definitely not brain damaged. 'You know I'm dying? Nothing can keep the cancer at bay. The next thing is probably organ failure. There's not long left, whatever happens now.'

'Mm.' Daphne felt anxious.

'Daff, I've realised things, I ...' He couldn't finish the sentence. 'Look. Look at me here, wired up like an experimental monkey in a lab. It's humiliating. I don't want to bloody die like this. I can't do it, splayed out on a fucking hospital bed. I must get out. I'm desperate. And you're the only person.'

She couldn't understand what he was asking her to do. 'Are you saying I should take you away from the hospital so you can die somewhere else? I can't help you do that. That's impossible.'

'No. No. Of course not.' He calmed his voice so it was soothing. 'No, that's not what I meant. I just need to get some different air, to see that the real world is still out there. That's all. You could do this last thing for me – grant a dying man his final wish.' He smiled coaxingly. 'Just let me get to the sea. Give me the smell of freedom. Take me with you and Libby on the boat so I can breathe in the salt air of the Aegean. I don't want anything more. Let me have a last trip and I'll be content. Then I'll be a good boy and do whatever the doctors order. Scout's honour.'

'I don't know, Ralph.'

'The thing is, at this stage in the game, I have a new perspective on so much. Maybe you can't imagine, but it looks different when you know you'll soon be gone. You start to think about eternity, how to bid farewell to the world.'

She shook her head. Ralph said, 'You can't understand, darling Daphne. It's all much worse than you think.' She assumed he was talking about his health and didn't ask him to explain. 'You know, I always think about you when times get rough. You give me strength.' He reached out hesitantly and touched her hair, then quickly retracted, as if wary of what physical contact might imply. His hand was slack-skinned and almost grey in colour, with a purple bruise. 'When I was in the hospital in London, when I was having treatments, I felt you were there with me.'

She didn't want to hear all this. He was overloading her with weights she'd thrown away.

'All right,' he said, evidently noticing her unease. 'So how about this? You take me with you to the boat. I come over to the island and I don't even get off. What is it? An hour or so? Nothing! Afterwards, I'll come straight back to Piraeus.' Daphne opened her mouth to speak but he raised a hand and continued. 'We've been through so much together, Daff – terrible things as well as all the wonderful stuff. But you probably have no idea of what you've meant to me, how you've kept me going through my treatments – like a guardian angel, smiling and laughing close by.' He looked straight into her eyes. 'You're the only person in the world who is free-spirited enough to understand why I need to feel liberated once more, to be part of the elements, sprayed with sea salt for the last time. Do you remember that John Ireland song?' In a low, husky voice that cracked, he sang a couple of lines of 'I Must Go Down to the Seas Again'.

She stared at him, fascinated by the power of a dying man's desires and torn between the attraction of abetting the grand gesture, the daunting practicalities of transporting a terminally ill patient on to a ferry, and the knowledge that she should have nothing more to do with him. There was something seductive about the idea of a last time; last meals prepared for the condemned prisoner or words of wisdom whispered on the deathbed.

'Let me leave behind this bone-tinted, white city and see your island, with its warm, beautiful colours – those ochre walls and terracotta tiles,' he said. 'You see, I've never forgotten.' She shook her head, trying not to reveal how tempted she felt. Without formulating it in her mind, this plot recreated an after-echo of the clandestine excitements of her youth. It was wrong and it was almost irresistible.

'No, Ralph. I'm sorry. I can't do it. I mean, how would we even get you there? What about all this?' She gestured at the medical paraphernalia connecting him to machines and drips. Ralph didn't reply. Instead, with incongruous vigour, he swung himself up and sat on the edge of the bed, legs dangling pallid and spindly from his hospital gown, as he tore the tape from his hand and pulled out the cannula. He ripped off the patches stuck to his chest and a shrill bleeping made them both start, but he flicked at various switches, quickly solving the problem by yanking a plug from the mains.

'You can't do this,' she said more urgently. 'I'm not getting dragged into this madness. Sorry, but I'm going to go now.' She put a hand on his arm, said, 'Goodbye, Ralph,' and left the room.

She and Libby sped back towards the port in another taxi, past crumbling, pre-war stone buildings, shiny glass business blocks and the roadside flea market where vendors had laid out pitifully meagre offerings on blankets – a few mismatched cups or some crumpled clothes.

'I always think of your grandpa Ed in Piraeus,' said Daphne, trying not to think about Ralph. 'You know it's where he met your grandmother Ellie. He was so good at describing the vibrancy mixed in with poverty. *Oedipus Blues* was an extraordinary book. I hope you'll read it soon. And really, the place hasn't changed that much.' That wasn't quite true, thought Daphne, when they arrived at the embarkation gate and saw several groups of Middle Eastern people, probably Syrians.

'I came down here with Dad in the summer,' said Libby. 'We were handing out baby carriers and nappies and stuff when people got off the boat with nothing.'

The refugees were sitting in family groups that included both the elderly and the very young. They looked nice, Daphne thought, if dazed. And they were dressed with remarkable respectability given what they had been through.

The boat to Aegina was due to leave in twenty minutes and she sat on a bench and sent Libby to buy tickets from the kiosk. Gulls wheeled in the blue expanse above, their yelps recreating the soundtrack to so many previous sea journeys: childhood holidays with her parents; yacht trips with Constantine; the work expeditions with Libby. And of course, there was the time she and Ralph had sat on just such a bench as this, almost forty years before.

A distracted crewman took their tickets and they clattered up the metal steps to the main deck of the *Agios Nektarios*, occupying several orange plastic seats and tipping their faces towards a benevolent, autumnal sun. It was only a few minutes before the ferry was due to leave, when Libby said, 'Oh my God!' Daphne followed Libby's horrified stare. Ralph was staggering up the last few steps towards their deck, helped by a young man, who held his arm. He was grimacing with effort and pain.

'No!' Her exclamation came before thought. This was like a new violation. How on earth had he managed to follow them, she wondered, immediately picturing his lurch to the taxis waiting outside the hospital, the bountiful tip to the youthful driver, Ralph's persuasive powers getting him through right to the end – evidence, even as he was dying, of his weaselling ability to wriggle out of a problem.

'Mum, he's chasing you. It's creepy.'

'Quick, let's go,' Daphne hissed. She grabbed their cases and led Libby away from the spectre that was trying to haunt them. She wouldn't speak to him, she decided. She'd had enough. Let him have his own dramas.

The boat advanced slowly out of the harbour, past the disused warehouses painted with giant murals, and the cluttered, hillside neighbourhood of Kastella. As it took up speed in the open waters, a chill wind blustered around them and waves slapped against the hull, sending showers of seaspray on to the deck. After about ten minutes, Libby said, 'It's freezing. Let's go inside.' They edged along the narrow passage of deck to the side of the boat, looking for a way in, and Daphne kept an eye out for Ralph, not wanting to encounter him. She spotted him standing upright, if hunched, at the stern, gripping the rail and looking back at the frothed, white trail in the sea.

As they settled themselves inside near the cosy clattering of the cafeteria, she became more worried. He'll die out there in the cold, she thought. Shit. He's impossible. It was unnerving to be the person responsible for Ralph's welfare.

'Libs, I think I need to tell someone official that he's on board,' she said. 'I can't just leave him out there like that. They need to make sure he doesn't get off the boat, that he goes straight back to Athens.'

'Yeah, well don't go and talk to him, OK? He's probably trying to make you feel sorry for him.'

Later, Daphne raked over these moments until her brain ached. She tried to identify a clue that might have enabled her to act differently. It took almost fifteen minutes until she returned with a crewmember the captain had grudgingly appointed to accompany her. Ralph was no longer standing where he had been. Mild irritation became unease after they made a tour of the entire deck on that level and did not find him. The crewman went into the men's toilets but they were empty.

'Are you sure this friend was on board?' the sailor asked suspiciously. 'Maybe he got off before we left the port?' They made a rapid sweep of the other decks, inside and out, to no avail. Unease became heart-thumping dread. Evidently annoyed by the inconvenience, the captain turned the boat around and went back in case he could spot Ralph in the sea. Nothing. The ferry circled again and headed on towards Aegina.

As they approached the harbour, she could see the ancient temple on the promontory, its one remaining column poking up and sheered off at an angle. Police were waiting at the port and, when they walked over to speak to her, there was the strange sense that she was now the one in trouble. The officers agreed she and Libby could put their luggage in the back of the car and drove them the short distance to the island's main police station – a colourful old villa with lemon trees outside it and a surrounding wall painted custard-yellow and blue.

'A coastguard boat has already been sent out,' confirmed *kyrios* Kranidis, the chief of police. He spoke slowly with a lack of urgency, as though people disappeared every day, which maybe they did. There was no sign she was a suspect, but it was shocking to be officially thrust into the centre of what was probably Ralph's last performance.

Libby was given a bottle of lemonade and a straw and made to wait in the reception area, while *kyrios* Kranidis set up the paperwork to open the case. It all took ages. He also rang Nina, and Daphne overheard his side of the conversation as he gave the bald, brutal facts, extrapolating from the notes he had just taken.

Nina caught the Flying Dolphin hydrofoil and arrived only a couple of hours later. She made it clear she did not wish to see Daphne and the police tactfully arranged that they should not encounter one another. Daphne was requested to stay on the island till the next day, but she and Libby were permitted to go to the family house. Old *kyria* Lemonia's daughter, Eleni, came to check up on them. She had taken over as caretaker now that her mother was too frail to work; though, as she explained, she didn't actually do much – there wasn't the money to pay her. The shuttered-up building looked fine to Daphne, and the sun-filled courtyard was occupied by a family of cats. Libby set about finding food and water for them and coaxing them with Greek 'Pss, pss' sounds.

'Tragic,' said Eleni, plump, gimlet-eyed and failing to hide the enjoyable excitement so easily felt at someone else's calamity. 'So terrible, to fall overboard. And you say he was very ill anyway?'

'It may have been a heart attack. We don't know anything yet,' said Daphne. Dread and panic were subsiding into bewilderment and anger. Fuck, shit, bugger, wanker … As they used to say. And bloody, bastard, bollocks, pools of poxy piss, as Ralph would have added.

They returned to Athens the next day on the *Agios Nektarios* — she couldn't face staying on Aegina in the circumstances. Sam stepped into the breach, meeting them off the boat, taking Libby to stay with him and Xenia in Kalithea and promising to arrange the entire business of her birthday celebrations. He struck her as being more solid, as though he'd finally stopped being a boy. He hugged Daphne and said, 'What a fricking mess. I'm really sorry.'

In the end, Libby's party was held at To Spiti — 'The House' — one of the places where Sam volunteered with young refugees.

'It's what she wanted,' he said to Daphne on the phone, when she questioned it as an unlikely choice. 'It'll be fun.' And it was. There was food cooked by the kitchen staff, a gigantic cake, and although Daphne couldn't face dancing, there was much merrymaking, despite the foundation of suffering and uncertainty that showed on many of the guests' faces.

It did not take long for the Greek and foreign media to identify several ingredients for a juicy story: a mysterious, unsolved death, a famous composer, and the recent accusations of child sex abuse. Somehow, Daphne's name was revealed as the plaintiff as well as being the last person to see Ralph alive. The Greek press unearthed an old picture of her at a party wearing a skimpy summer dress, taken soon after her marriage to Constantine.

A few days later, fishermen found Ralph's body near the small island of Angistri, close to Aegina. He was caught in their nets.

* * *

It was horrible back in London. She did not attend Ralph's funeral. In all the chaos, nobody thought to fill her in about Jane's revelations or the Swedish boys or whatever they were. For about a month, Jane made what sounded like excuses not to meet, but eventually she asked to see her, arriving one wet, weekday evening in early December.

'How are you doing?' Jane hardly smiled, as though she did not care. Daphne wondered why she had come. What had happened to their resurrected friendship that seemed so sincere?

'Oh, you know, pretty low really. It wasn't the ending to the saga that I'd have chosen.'

In the kitchen, Jane took a sip of wine from the glass Daphne handed her and laid down her gauntlet. 'Well that was certainly a major fuck-up, concocting a death-bed elopement with Ralph.' Daphne's initial reaction was puzzlement at the sarcastic tone. It was so unlike her – the supportive friend who had helped her through so much over this strange, discomforting year. 'I didn't take him to the boat, you know. He followed me. Crap knows how.'

'Well, whatever happened, in the end he got away with it. He never had to pay for any of his crimes. I hope you're pleased.'

'How could I possibly be pleased?' Daphne felt the hot injustice of the wrongly accused, while still floundering with bewilderment at Jane's transformation from someone who had always appeared solidly reliable and kind into an acid-tongued cynic. 'It wasn't my fault. It was a nightmare. Just when I thought I'd broken free of the whole story … I'd made my peace with it. With him. And then I was sucked back into the middle of a shit storm that was even worse.'

Jane ignored these attempts to explain or justify and went on as though Daphne had not spoken. 'I couldn't believe the obituaries. Did you see them? The way they hardly mentioned his arrest. All that gushing about his brilliance. A complete whitewash! And you probably know they were even continuing with the idea of his seventieth-birthday-concert thing, only turning it into a memorial instead. Still at the Barbican! I contacted the organisers. They said it was all going ahead with bloody children's choirs. Unbelievable. So I told them everything. Said they couldn't do it — that it was grossly inappropriate. I sent them details.' Daphne nodded miserably.

And then, Jane's secret. It spewed out with sudden violence. Daphne felt such shock she feared she might faint. Jane saw her turn white and made her put her head between her knees and take deep breaths. Once she recovered enough to speak, Daphne absorbed the gravity of betrayal by both Ralph and Jane. So Ralph *was* a rapist. You couldn't dress it up any other way. And although he appeared to have repented, he never told her the truth. She was not so special after all. Jane's hideous cover-up made every aspect of it worse.

'Why didn't you tell me? And not just back then, but more recently? All that endless talking about Ralph. Shit, it was you telling me the rules about abuse, about confronting it. What the hell was that? What was your plan? To pull it out of the bag like a magic trick? It's such a big lie. Too big.'

Jane didn't try to defend herself; her face was a mask of blank acceptance. She did murmur, 'I hoped you'd be the one to slay the dragon. I wanted to do that for you.'

'Why couldn't we have done that together? It would have been so different, so much better. You left me alone and you didn't even allow me to see the real dragon.'

Before she went, Jane let drop the other accusations against Ralph from the young musicians in Tallinn. Displaying a cruelly detached calm, it was as though she was quoting facts from a story in the news that had nothing to do with her or Daphne. She mentioned their names, something about drugs.

'I don't want to hear any more.' Daphne's voice was quiet because otherwise she would shout. It was clear they could no longer be friends.

'Go now!' she said.

* * *

It was months before the inquest took place and she returned to Athens as a witness. Ralph's oldest son Jason flew in from Madrid. She had not seen him since he was a child and he looked at her as if she was dangerous, responsible for his father's death – almost a murderer. He nodded at her outside the courtroom but they did not speak. Nina was there too, but her gaze had turned inwards and away from the world. She did not appear to talk to anyone, certainly not Daphne.

Given that she should have been dragging him through the legal system in London, it was surreal to find herself ordered into an Athenian court on his behalf. It was so awful as to be almost funny when it looked as though she might be in trouble for her part in Ralph's death. The investigators were not initially convinced that Ralph had the strength to climb over the ship's rails and jump into the sea. By any standards, it was deemed negligent to leave a critically ill man alone on deck.

Whatever the method and reason for his tumble from the *Agios Nektarios*, Ralph was still alive when he entered the water. According to the autopsy, he died from drowning. It was possible that he leaned over the rail and fainted or had a heart attack, slipping forward unconscious into the sea. Nobody could be sure. 'Death by misadventure' was the final verdict. A good enough interpretation, thought Daphne. The end to a great series of misadventures, some of which might have resembled adventures but were not.

After the inquest, she no longer felt so furious. Ralph was gone and she had decided to leave London and begin something completely new. It was impossible to go on looking out of the window at her childhood across the stodgy blur of the winter river. The rumble of trains on the railway bridge had become the beat to a rhyme of deceit, betrayal and people she hoped to forget.

The best thing about the new plan was Libby's eagerness. Daphne had imagined she would need persuading to approve yet another change in a life that had already required so much adjusting. She presented the idea as a year's escapade – some time out, during which Libby would go to school in Athens, acquire perfect Greek and then, if they wanted, they'd return to London. Or not, if life there suited them. She laid out the joys of Greece as though she was tempting a client: the warm weather, swimming trips and relaxed social life, not to mention Sam and the crowd of cousins who would take her under their wings. But Libby had said, 'Yeah, I told you I'd like to spend more time there. And that way I'd get to hang out with Dad more and help him and ...' She ran out of breath, but it was clear she was more than willing to embark on a new life. Perhaps the apple did fall closer to the apple tree than I imagined, thought Daphne.

Discovering surprising reserves of patience and perseverance, she arranged for Libby to finish her school year, gave Jelly plenty of notice so she could find a replacement, and obtained ideal tenants for the flat – a friendly, professional couple taking early retirement. Nothing flimsy this time. By renting out Aunt Connie's place, they'd have more than enough money to pay for somewhere in Athens and Daphne was confident of finding jobs here and there; Jelly said there could be part-time work for Hell.

The day after summer term ended, she and Libby flew out to Athens, their belongings arriving a week later in a van. Cousin Evgenia had found them an apartment and had given a modest down payment. Ano Petralona was a noisy inner-city area but it was only a short walk from the cafés and art galleries of Gazi and close enough to Philopappos Hill to smell the pine trees. The landlords were an elderly couple returning to their Peloponnesian village after a working lifetime in the city. They were both there to welcome Daphne and Libby and explain the quirks of the temperamental water heater and how to read the meter. The woman admitted the rooms hadn't been revamped since the 1970s, but the atmosphere was hardly reminiscent of Aunt Connie's place. It was more like something from the '30s, with its marble basins, mosaic concrete floors and sliding, wood-framed doors. There were two small bedrooms, a sitting room overlooking the street and a kitchen at the back that faced another block of flats.

Over the next days, the intimate view of their neighbours reminded her of Hitchcock's *Rear Window* and she and Libby became well acquainted with their habits: the hirsute man who wandered about in his underpants, television booming; the woman with two young children, whose high-pitched threats were often audible from out in the street; and the old widow directly across from them who called and waved from her kitchen's open window and invited Daphne to collect a jar of her home-made grape 'spoon sweet'.

During the September elections, Daphne discovered that Constantine had been voted in as a Conservative Member of Parliament. All she could do was laugh when she saw him on television. He was still handsome but had softened around the edges – plumper and gentler, as if time had rubbed away the sharpness; less lone wolf and more Labrador. Her short marriage with him had been underpinned by danger and filled with speed and risk. What a relief to laugh, to see Constantine's hackneyed political statement about 'Making a difference', and 'Love for my homeland', and to feel only mild irritation, even pity. She realised now that her husband had only ever been a spoilt boy. He had certainly been mixed up and troubled, and he took far too many drugs, but he was not the villain she had built him up to be. It no longer felt plausible that he had been the malign presence which caused nightmares and cold sweats. From this perspective, she could see that the villain had always been Ralph. Constantine had taken the blame over all these years for crimes committed before she even met him.

With the perspective of time and distance, Jane also appeared less deserving of blame. She, too, had suffered abuse. In fact, she had been so traumatised by her experiences that she could not even confide in her old friend. From the safety of Athens, Daphne wondered whether she might write to Jane — not to reopen their friendship, but to close it on a gentler note.

* * *

The early-morning sun warmed her face as she sat on the balcony sipping a 'first coffee', as Ellie always called it. She could smell the sweet tang of the small-leafed basil and spearmint plants she'd placed in a row beside a small, round café table and two folding chairs. Noises echoed from the nearby Saturday market where one man's fervent call made selling sweet oranges sound like a war cry: '*Portokalia, glyka portokalia.*' She lit a cigarette, enjoying every illicit breath.

She was still on the balcony, typing emails on her laptop, when Libby appeared.

'Hello, early bird. Did you sleep OK?' She had a lurking fear of passing on her insomnia, not to mention any number of other undesirable traits.

'Yeah, all good. Caught you smoking, though.' She looked pointedly at the cigarettes Daphne had forgotten to hide. 'Bad example, Mum. "Smoking causes fatal lung cancer,"' she read slowly in Greek from the packet. Even with a tangle of unbrushed hair and bobbly, mismatched pyjamas, Libby gave the impression of streamlined efficiency. She had grown so much in the last year that now, at almost fourteen, she was taller than her mother and had bouts of womanly maturity that Daphne felt she herself would never achieve.

'So you'll spend the whole day at The House? Will Sam be there?'

'Yes, the usual deal. I need to be there by ten thirty.'

Daphne saw that Libby was flourishing with not only a father and a wider family of cousins, aunts and uncles, but also the young refugees she volunteered with every weekend. It made her realise what a tiny, tight nucleus they had been in London. She had always seen the positive aspects of their exclusive bond, but now it was clear that Libby was happier to have all these other people around her. Daphne's old fears of losing control were gradually evaporating, as if from exposure to sunshine.

'But I'm a bit worried about today,' Libby said. 'I'm meant to be starting a project with these three sisters who arrived a few weeks ago. They're from Iraq. And they don't talk. Or hardly. The oldest one's sixteen. They're still really upset from what they've been through. Their parents died – drowned when they were crossing from Turkey. And now they're completely alone.'

'God, how awful.' The stories that Libby brought home were often upsetting, but she appeared to take them on with a practical attitude.

'I know. And Dad and Xenia had this idea of some sort of art project or something, to get them to express themselves another way. But it's not really my thing. We've got paints and paper there, but I don't know. How do you inspire them after something like that? They look so sad. And when I talk they just look at me and I feel stupid.'

Daphne paused before speaking, weighing up the potential pitfalls of getting involved. The House was Sam's thing, after all. She was busy enough with a bit of private English tuition and some part-time work for Jelly – it turned out that much of what she'd done in Shepherd's Bush could be achieved just as well if not better in Ano Petralona. She even had the offer of exhibiting some work in a small gallery in Psyrri, with new subjects based on the city life she saw around her. (In the end, *Putney* had gone into the Shoreditch exhibition and sold on the opening night; she assumed nobody would ever guess the real story behind the images.) In Athens, however, it was impossible to ignore the wave of pain that was flooding across Greece with the constant arrival of refugees. Each time she accompanied Libby to The House for her weekend volunteering, they passed through Victoria Square – an ad hoc camp for people who had lost everything. There was something absurdly cheerful about the garden square in the warm, October weather, with its air of former gentility and rows of pollarded mulberry trees. Colourful clothes were hung out to dry, young children played clapping games in the sunshine and men stood around the sculpture of Theseus rescuing Hippodamia from a drunken centaur, discussing the next, northerly leg of their journey. Daphne knew there was also a terrible darker side to life on the square. Some unaccompanied children and teenagers survived by selling themselves, often for a few euros or just a cheese pie. Athenian men arrived in the evening, strolling around until they located a boy they could take along the road to the Field of Mars park.

'Have you thought of doing a sewing project or a collage with fabrics? You know, something like the pieces I do. Figures in a landscape telling a story?'

'I don't know if I could.' Libby's face spread into a pleading smile. 'But maybe you could help?'

'Well I don't want to step on Sam's toes.' Daphne was already envisaging the three wordless girls as figurines in a tableau – a long strip with a narrative, like the Bayeux Tapestry. They could create the sisters' home in Iraq, the fearful sea journey, Athens as a chaotic sanctuary, and maybe even the future. They wouldn't need speech in order to tell their story. 'Why don't you call Sam and talk to him about it? I'm going to nip out to the market now anyway, so let's discuss it again when I'm back.'

She took their landlady's abandoned shopping trolley and returned home with a harvest festival of autumnal produce. On the top was a Dionysian wealth of grapes and thin-skinned, purple figs, some of which they ate for breakfast with yogurt.

'Dad's really keen. He said, "Go for it!" So please do come with me today.'

Daphne gathered up some sewing gear. 'Here we are! A roll of canvas for the backing. And two big bags stuffed with beautiful rags!'

* * *

The next day was Sunday and she and Libby had planned to go swimming before another sewing session at The House in the afternoon. They caught the tram down to Kalamaki.

'Maybe we could take the sisters to the beach one weekend?' said Daphne. The three silent, solemn girls had immediately pulled her into their orbit and she couldn't stop thinking about them. They turned out to be accomplished at sewing and, with Daphne's help, had soon created a rough cut of the collage's first scene. It depicted their old home – a two-storey, stone house in Nineveh, with cherry trees, several striped cats and their parents standing by the front door. When Daphne produced three identifiable figurines of the sisters, all with dark, almond eyes and prettily wrapped head-scarves, they smiled – for the first time since their arrival, according to Libby. At the end of the afternoon, they said goodbye and still did not speak, but they held Daphne's arm with such tenderness, it was all she could do not to cry. She promised to return with Libby the next day and to help them until they finished the project. It was clearly the beginning of something significant – the wind had changed direction for them as well as for her.

Daphne knew an Italian *gelateria* not far from the tram stop and she and Libby chose two scoops each, then ambled back towards the beach, slowly eating the ice cream. Her favourite flavour had always been pistachio, the green-scented, nutty taste summoning memories of her grandmother's home-made version. The family had their own pistachio grove on Aegina and *Yiayia* concocted the irresistible ambrosia every summer, using honey and local sheep's milk.

The sun was burning hot now – one of those late-October weekends before the first rains change the atmosphere, when people grasp the last chance for a day at the seaside. Several families were already ensconced with umbrellas and picnics, and little groups of elderly, white-hatted swimmers were treading water, chatting cheerfully. The slap and crack of backgammon pieces resonated across the beach from the shack housing the Winter Swimmers' Club, where tawny-skinned players sat outside at tables.

Daphne laid out two towels beneath a tree and they made themselves comfortable, the tiny, smooth pebbles crunching beneath their bodies.

'I'm going straight in.' Ready with her bikini under her clothes, Libby plunged into the sea and swam strongly away from the shore.

Daphne looked out to the horizon and the blurry outline of Aegina's pointed Mount Ellanion. It was only a year since Ralph's death. And yet she was calm – happy, even. Seeing that small, beloved island across the Saronic Gulf and thinking of her visits, she realised that only a few of the recollections were associated with Ralph.

Some of her earliest memories of Aegina were family holidays with Ellie, Ed and Theo. *Yiayia* always insisted on long siestas after lunch, before a swim was allowed, and, as a child, she loved the shady peace of hot afternoons indoors. She remembered being so young that when they all went out to dinner at a taverna, she fell asleep, leaning over from her chair to rest on her mother's lap, feeling Ellie stroke her hair, her perfume drifting in and out of the easy slumber. Later, when it felt like the middle of the night and she was too tired to walk, Ed picked her up and carried her home. His pace was uneven from his limp, but she enjoyed the slow rhythm in his arms, the mumbling of adult voices. He laid her on the brass bed opposite Theo's, and removed her sandals, leaving her to sleep undisturbed in her clothes. The cotton pillowcase was slightly stiff against her cheek. She could hear chirruping cicadas outside. When Ed closed the shutters, a brief breeze of jasmine wafted across the room.

The sun had turned the water a brilliant turquoise and, as a white gull barked its complaining cry, Daphne pulled off her clothes and followed her daughter into the sea.

ACKNOWLEDGEMENTS

Heartfelt thanks to Gillian Stern, first reader and editor, for her boundless support.

I was extremely lucky to have Alexandra Pringle as my wise and wonderful publisher and editor. Thank you. And to Sarah-Jane Forder, copy-editor *extraordinaire*, Angelique Tran Van Sang, Allegra Le Fanu, Philippa Cotton, Janet Aspey and all at Bloomsbury.

Jonathan Burnham and Mary Gaule at HarperCollins US have been amazing. Many thanks.

Alan Hollinghurst was wildly generous with advice and editing. Thanks to him and also to Vesna Goldsworthy for very helpful comments on an early draft.

A number of people assisted with research and support while I was writing. They include Sarah Horrocks, Cressida Connolly, Leo Zinovieff, Katy Barrow-Grint, Tan Lea, Melanie Jones, Stefan Bertram-Lee, Lara Muller, Amalia Zepou, Adam Nicolson, Effie Basdra, Katerina Bakoyianni and Maria Ribeiro. Thank you all.

As ever, I am hugely grateful to my agent Caroline Dawnay, and to Sophie Scard and all at United Agents.

Love and thanks to Vassilis. Our daughters, Anna and Lara, took on this book with zeal and have been brilliant critics and consultants. *Putney* is dedicated to them.